THE LAST LIGHT OF THE SUN

Guy Gavriel Kay was born and raised in Canada. In 1974–5 he spent a year in Oxford assisting Christopher Tolkien in his editorial construction of JRR Tolkien's posthumously published *The Silmarillion*. Widely regarded as one of the pre-eminent fantasy novelists currently writing, he has subsequently published nine books, which have been translated into twenty-two languages and appeared on bestseller lists around the world.

Visit the authorized website for Guy Gavriel Kay: www.brightweavings.com

Also by Guy Gavriel Kay:

The Fionavar Tapestry:
The Summer Tree
The Wandering Fire
The Darkest Road

Tigana
A Song for Arbonne
The Lions of Al-Rassan

The Sarantine Mosaic:
Sailing to Sarantium
Lord of Emperors

The Last Light of the Sun
Ysabel
Under Heaven

Beyond This Dark House (Poetry)

GUY GAVRIEL KAY

The Last Light of the Sun

HARPER
Voyager

HarperVoyager
An Imprint of HarperCollins*Publishers*
77–85 Fulham Palace Road,
Hammersmith, London W6 8JB

www.harpercollins.co.uk

This paperback edition 2011
1

First published in Great Britain by
HarperCollins*Publishers* 2004

A catalogue record for this book is
available from the British Library

ISBN: 978 0 00 734207 5

Printed and bound in Great Britain by
Clays Ltd, St Ives plc

Mixed Sources
Product group from well-managed
forests and other controlled sources
www.fsc.org Cert no. SW-COC-001806
© 1996 Forest Stewardship Council

FSC is a non-profit international organisation established
to promote the responsible management of the world's forests.
Products carrying the FSC label are independently certified
to assure consumers that they come from forests that are managed
to meet the social, economic and ecological needs
of present and future generations.

Find out more about HarperCollins and the environment at
www.harpercollins.co.uk/green

for George Jonas

I have a tale for you: *a stag bells;*
winter pours   *summer has gone.*
    The wind is high, cold;   *the sun is low;*
its course is short   *the sea is strong running.*
    The bracken is very red;   *its shape has been hidden.*
The cry of the barnacle goose   *has become usual.*
    Cold has taken   *the wings of birds.*
Season of ice;   *this is my tale.*

—FROM THE LIBER HYMNORUM MANUSCRIPT

CHARACTERS
(A PARTIAL LISTING)

&

The Anglcyn

Aeldred, son of Gademar, King of the Anglcyn
Elswith, his queen
Athelbert ⎫
Judit ⎬ his children
Kendra ⎪
Gareth ⎭

Osbert, son of Cuthwulf, Aeldred's chamberlain
Burgred, Earl of Denferth

The Erlings

Thorkell Einarson, "Red Thorkell," exiled from Rabady Isle
Frigga, his wife, daughter of Skadi
Bern Thorkellson, his son
Siv, Athira, his daughters

Iord, seer of Rabady, at the women's compound
Anrid, a woman serving at the compound

Halldr Thinshank, once governor of Rabady Isle, deceased
Sturla Ulfarson "Sturla One-hand," governor of Rabady Isle

CHARACTERS

Gurd Thollson
Brand Leofson
Carsten Friddson } Jormsvik mercenaries
Garr Hoddson
Guthrum Skallson

Thira, a prostitute in Jormsvik

Kjarten Vidurson, ruling in Hlegest

Siggur Volganson, "the Volgan," deceased
Mikkel Ragnarson } his grandsons
Ivarr Ragnarson

Ingemar Svidrirson, of Erlond, paying tribute to King
    Aeldred
Hakon Ingemarson, his son

The Cyngael

Ceinion of Llywerth, high cleric of the Cyngael,
    "Cingalus"

Dai ab Owyn, heir to Prince Owyn of Cadyr
Alun ab Owyn, his brother
Gryffeth ap Ludh, their cousin

Brynn ap Hywll, of Brynnfell in Arberth (and other
    residences), "Erling's Bane"
Enid, his wife
Rhiannon mer Brynn, his daughter
Helda, Rania, Eirin, Rhiannon's women

Siawn, leader of Brynn's fighting band

Other

Firaz ibn Bakir, merchant of Fezana, in the Khalifate of
    Al-Rassan

The Last Light
of the Sun

CHAPTER I

A horse, he came to understand, was missing.
Until it was found nothing could proceed. The
island marketplace was crowded on this grey morning in
spring. Large, armed, bearded men were very much
present, but they were not here for trade. Not today. The
market would not open, no matter how appealing the
goods on a ship from the south might be.

He had arrived, clearly, at the wrong time.

Firaz ibn Bakir, merchant of Fezana, deliberately
embodying in his brightly coloured silks (not nearly
warm enough in the cutting wind) the glorious Khalifate
of Al-Rassan, could not help but see this delay as yet
another trial imposed upon him for transgressions in a
less than virtuous life.

It was hard for a merchant to live virtuously. Partners
demanded profit, and profit was difficult to come by if
one piously ignored the needs—and opportunities—of
the world of the flesh. The asceticism of a desert zealot
was not, ibn Bakir had long since decided, for him.

At the same time, it would be entirely unfair to
suggest that he lived a life of idleness and comfort. He
had just endured (with such composure as Ashar and the
holy stars had granted him) three storms on the very long
sea journey north and then east, afflicted, as always at sea,
by a stomach that heaved like the waves, and with the
roundship handled precariously by a continuously
drunken captain. Drinking was a profanation of the laws

of Ashar, of course, but in this matter ibn Bakir was not, lamentably, in a position to take a vigorous moral stand.

Vigour had been quite absent from him on the journey, in any case.

It was said among the Asharites, both in the eastern homelands of Ammuz and Soriyya, and in Al-Rassan, that the world of men could be divided into three groups: those living, those dead, and those at sea.

Ibn Bakir had been awake before dawn this morning, praying to the last stars of the night in thanks for his finally being numbered once more among those in the blessed first group.

Here in the remote, pagan north, at this wind-scoured island market of Rabady, he was anxious to begin trading his leather and cloth and spices and bladed weapons for furs and amber and salt and heavy barrels of dried cod (to sell in Ferrieres on the way home)—and to take immediate leave of these barbarian Erlings, who stank of fish and beer and bear grease, who could kill a man in a bargaining over prices, and who burned their leaders—savages that they were—on ships among their belongings when they died.

This last, it was explained to him, was what the horse was all about. Why the funeral rites of Halldr Thinshank, who had governed Rabady until three nights ago, were currently suspended, to the visible consternation of an assembled multitude of warriors and traders.

The offence to their gods of oak and thunder, and to the lingering shade of Halldr (not a benign man in life, and unlikely to be so as a spirit), was considerable, ibn Bakir was told. Ill omens of the gravest import were to be assumed. No one wanted an angry, unhoused ghost lingering in a trading town. The fur-clad, weapon-bearing men in the windy square were worried, angry, and drunk, pretty much to a man.

The fellow doing the explaining, a bald-headed, ridiculously big Erling named Ofnir, was known to ibn Bakir from two previous journeys. He had been useful before, for a fee: the Erlings were ignorant, tree-worshipping pagans, but they had firm ideas about what their services were worth.

Ofnir had spent some years in the east among the Emperor's Karchite Guard in Sarantium. He had returned home with a little money, a curved sword in a jewelled scabbard, two prominent scars (one on top of his head), and an affliction contracted in a brothel near the Sarantine waterfront. Also, a decent grasp of that difficult eastern tongue. In addition—usefully—he'd mastered sufficient words in ibn Bakir's own Asharite to function as an interpreter for the handful of southern merchants foolhardy enough to sail along rocky coast-lines fighting a lee shore, and then east into the frigid, choppy waters of these northern seas to trade with the barbarians.

The Erlings were raiders and pirates, ravaging in their longships all through these lands and waters and—increasingly—down south. But even pirates could be seduced by the lure of trade, and Firaz ibn Bakir (and his partners) had reaped profit from that truth. Enough so to have him back now for a third time, standing in a knife-like wind on a bitter morning, waiting for them to get on with burning Halldr Thinshank on a boat with his weapons and armour and his best household goods and wooden images of the gods and one of his slave girls . . . and a horse.

A pale grey horse, a beauty, Halldr's favourite, and missing. On a very small island.

Ibn Bakir looked around. A sweeping gaze from the town square could almost encompass Rabady. The harbour, a stony beach, with a score of Erling ships and his own large roundship from the south—the first one in, which *ought* to have been splendid news. This town, sheltering several hundred souls perhaps, was deemed an important market in the northlands, a fact that brought private amusement to the merchant from Fezana, a man who had been received by the khalif in Cartada, who had walked in the gardens and heard the music of the fountains there.

No fountains here. Beyond the stockade walls and the ditch surrounding them, a quilting of stony farmland could be seen, then livestock grazing, then forest. Beyond the pine woods, he knew, the sea swept round again, with the rocky mainland of Vinmark across the strait. More farms there, fisher-villages along the coast, then emptiness: mountains and trees for a very long way, to the places where the reindeer ran (they said) in herds that could not be numbered, and the men who lived among them wore antlers themselves to hunt, and practised magics with blood in the winter nights.

Ibn Bakir had written these stories down during his last long journey home, had told them to the khalif at an audience in Cartada, presented his writings along with gifts of fur and amber. He'd been given gifts in return: a necklace, an ornamental dagger. His name was known in Cartada now.

It occurred to him that it might be useful to observe and chronicle this funeral—if the accursed rites ever began.

He shivered. It was cold in the blustering wind. An untidy clump of men made their way towards him, tacking across the square as if they were on a ship together. One man stumbled and bumped another; the second one swore, pushed back, put a hand to his axe. A third intervened, and took a punch to the shoulder for his pains. He ignored it like an insect bite. Another big man. They were all, ibn Bakir thought sorrowfully, big men.

It came to him, belatedly, that this was not really a good time to be a stranger on Rabady Isle, with the governor (they used an Erling word, but it meant, as best ibn Bakir could tell, something very like a governor) dead and his funeral rites marred by a mysteriously missing animal. Suspicions might fall.

As the group approached, he spread his hands, palms up, and brought them together in front of him. He bowed formally. Someone laughed. Someone stopped directly in front of him, reached out, unsteadily, and fingered the pale yellow silk of ibn Bakir's tunic, leaving a smear of grease. Ofnir, his interpreter, said something in their language and the others laughed again. Ibn Bakir, alert now, believed he detected an easing of tension. He had no idea what he'd do if he was wrong.

The considerable profit you could make from trading with barbarians bore a direct relation to the dangers of the journey—and the risks were not only at sea. He was the youngest partner, investing less than the others, earning his share by being the one who travelled . . . by allowing thick, rancid-smelling barbarian fingers to tug at his clothing while he smiled and bowed and silently counted the hours and days till the roundship might leave, its hold emptied and refilled.

"They say," Ofnir spoke slowly, in the loud voice one used with the simple-minded, "it is now known who take Halldr horse." His breath, very close to ibn Bakir, smelled of herring and beer.

His tidings, however, were entirely sweet. It meant they didn't think the trader from Al-Rassan, the stranger, had anything to do with it. Ibn Bakir had been dubious about his ability, with two dozen words in their tongue and Ofnir's tenuous skills, to make the obvious point that he'd just arrived the afternoon before and had no earthly (or other) reason to impede local rites by stealing a horse.

These were not men currently in a condition to assess cogency of argument.

"Who did it?" Ibn Bakir was only mildly curious.

"Servant to Halldr. Sold to him. Father make wrong killing. Sent away. Son have no right family now."

Lack of family appeared to be an explanation for theft here, ibn Bakir thought wryly. That seemed to be what Ofnir was conveying. He knew someone back home who would find this diverting over a glass of good wine.

"So he took the horse? Where? Into the woods?" Ibn Bakir gestured at the pines beyond the fields.

Ofnir shrugged. He pointed out into the square. Ibn Bakir saw that men were now mounting horses there—not always smoothly—and riding towards the open town gate and the plank bridge across the ditch. Others ran or walked beside them. He heard shouts. Anger, yes, but also something else: zest, liveliness. The promise of sport.

"He will soon found," Ofnir said, in what passed here in the northlands for Asharite.

Ibn Bakir nodded. He watched two men gallop past. One screamed suddenly as he passed and swung his axe in vicious, whistling circles over his head, for no evident reason.

"What will they do to him?" he asked, not caring very much.

Ofnir snorted. Spoke quickly in Erling to the others, evidently repeating the question.

There was a burst of laughter. One of them, in an effusion of good humour, punched ibn Bakir on the shoulder.

The merchant, regaining his balance, rubbing at his numbed arm, realized that he'd asked a naive question.

"Blood-eagle death, maybe," said Ofnir, flashing yellow teeth in a wide grin, making a complex two-handed gesture the southern merchant was abruptly pleased not to understand. "You see? Ever you see?"

Firaz ibn Bakir, a long way from home, shook his head.

He could blame his father, and curse him, even go to the women at the compound outside the walls and pay to have them evoke *seithr*. The *volur* might then send a night-spirit to possess his father, wherever he was. But there was something cowardly about that, and a warrior could not be a coward and still go to the gods when he died. Besides which, he had no money.

Riding in darkness before the first moon rose, Bern Thorkellson thought bitterly about the bonds of family. He could smell his own fear and laid a hand forward on the horse's neck to gentle it. It was too black to go quickly on this rough ground near the woods, and he could not—for obvious reasons—carry a torch.

He was entirely sober, which was useful. A man could die sober as well as drunken, he supposed, but had a better chance of avoiding some kinds of death. Of course it could also be said that no truly sober man would have done what he was doing now unless claimed by a spirit himself, ghost-ridden, god-tormented.

Bern didn't think he was crazed, but he'd have acknowledged freely that what he was doing—without having planned it at all—was not the wisest thing he'd ever done.

He concentrated on riding. There was no good reason for anyone to be abroad in these fields at night—farmers would be asleep behind doors, the shepherds would have their herds farther west—but there was always the chance of someone hoping to find a cup of ale at some hut, or meeting a girl, or looking for something to steal.

He was stealing a dead man's horse, himself.

A warrior's vengeance would have had him kill Halldr Thinshank long ago and face the blood feud after, beside whatever distant kin, if any, might come to his aid. Instead, Halldr had died when the main crossbeam of the new house he was having built (with money that didn't belong to him) fell on his back, breaking it. And Bern had stolen the grey horse that was to be burned with the governor tomorrow.

It would delay the rites, he knew, disquiet the ghost of the man who had exiled Bern's father and taken his mother as a second wife. The man who had also, not incidentally, ordered Bern himself bound for three years as a servant to Arni Kjellson, recompense for his father's crime.

A young man named to servitude, with an exiled father, and so without any supporting family or name, could not readily proclaim himself a warrior among the Erlings unless he went so far from home that his history was unknown. His father had probably done that, raiding overseas again. Red-bearded, fierce-tempered, experienced. A perfect oarsman for some longship, if he didn't kill a benchmate in a fury, Bern thought sourly. He knew his father's capacity for rage. Arni Kjellson's brother Nikar was dead of it.

Halldr might fairly have exiled the murderer and given away half his land to stop a feud, but marrying the exile's wife and claiming land for himself smacked too much of reaping in pleasure what he'd sowed as a judge. Bern Thorkellson, an only son with two sisters married and off the island, had found himself changed—in a blur of time—from the heir of a celebrated raider-turned-farmer to a landless servant without kin to protect him. Could any man wonder if there was bitterness in him, and more than that? He'd loathed Rabady's governor with cold passion. A hatred shared by more than a few, if words whispered in ale were to be believed.

Of course no one else had ever *done* anything about Halldr. Bern was the one now riding Thinshank's favourite stallion amid stones and boulders in cold darkness on the night before the governor's pyre was to be lit on a ship by the rocky beach.

Not the wisest action of his life, agreed.

For one thing, he hadn't anything even vaguely resembling a plan. He'd been lying awake, listening to the snoring and snorting of the other two servants in the shed behind Kjellson's house. Not unusual, that wakefulness: bitterness could suck a man from sleep. But somehow he'd found himself on his feet this time, dressing, pulling on boots and the bearskin vest he'd been able to keep so far, though he'd had to fight for it. He'd gone outside, pissed against the shed wall, and then walked through the silent blackness of the town to Halldr's house (Frigga, his mother, lying somewhere inside, alone now, without a husband for the second time in a year).

He'd slipped around the side, eased open the door to the stable, listened to the boy there, snuffling in the dreams of a straw-covered sleep, and then led the big grey horse called Gyllir quietly out under the watching stars.

The stableboy never stirred. No one appeared in the lane. Only the named shapes of heroes and beasts in the gods' sky overhead. He'd been alone in Rabady with the night-spirits. It had felt like a dream.

The town gate was locked when danger threatened but not otherwise. Rabady was an island. Bern and the grey horse had walked right through the square by the harbour, past the shuttered booths, down the middle of the empty street, through the open gates, across the bridge over the ditch into the night fields.

As simple as that, as life-altering.

Life-ending was probably the better way to describe it, he decided, given that this was not, in fact, a dream. He had no access to a boat that could carry the horse, and come sunrise a goodly number of extremely angry men—appalled at his impiety and their own exposure to an unhoused ghost—would begin looking for the horse. When they found the son of exiled Thorkell also missing, the only challenging decision would be how to kill him.

This did raise a possibility, given that he was sober and capable of thought. He *could* change his mind and go back. Leave the horse out here to be found. A minor, disturbing incident. They might blame it on ghosts or wood spirits. Bern could be back in his shed, asleep behind Arni Kjellson's village house, before anyone was the wiser. Could even join the morning search for the horse, if fat Kjellson let him off wood-splitting to go.

They'd find the grey, bring it back, strangle and burn it on the drifting longship with Halldr Thinshank and whichever girl had won her spirit a place among warriors and gods by drawing the straw that freed her from the slow misery of her life.

Bern guided the horse across a stream. The grey was big, restive, but knew him. Kjellson had been properly grateful to the governor when half of Red Thorkell's farm and his house were settled on him, and he had assigned his servants to labour for Thinshank at regular times. Bern was one of those servants now, by the same judgement that had given his family's lands to Kjellson. He had groomed the grey stallion often, walked him, cleaned out his straw. A magnificent horse, better than Halldr had ever deserved. There was nowhere to run this horse properly on Rabady; he was purely for display, an affirmation of wealth. Another reason, probably, why the thought of taking it away had come to him tonight in the dangerous space between dream and the waking world.

He rode on in the chill night. Winter was over, but it still had its hard fingers in the earth. Their lives were defined by it here in the north. Bern was cold, even with the vest.

At least he knew where he was going now; that much seemed to have come to him. The land his father had bought with looted gold (mostly from the celebrated raid in Ferrieres twenty-five years ago) was on the other side of the village, south and west. He was aiming for the northern fringes of the trees.

He saw the shape of the marker boulder and guided the horse past it. They'd killed and buried a girl there to bless the fields, so long ago the inscription on the marker had faded away. It hadn't done much good. The land near the forest was too stony to be properly tilled. Ploughs broke up behind oxen or horses, metal bending, snapping off. Hard, ungiving soil. Sometimes the harvests were adequate, but most of the food that fed Rabady came from the mainland.

The boulder cast a shadow. He looked up, saw the blue moon had risen from beyond the woods. Spirits' moon. It occurred to him, rather too late, that the ghost of Halldr Thinshank could not be unaware of what was happening to his horse. Halldr's lingering soul would be set free only with the ship-burial and burning tomorrow. Tonight it could be abroad in the dark—which was where Bern was.

He made the hammer sign, invoking both Ingavin and Thünir. He shivered again. A stubborn man he was. Too clever for his own good? His father's son in that? He'd deny it, at a blade's end. This had nothing to do with Thorkell. He was pursuing his own feud with Halldr and the town, not his father's. You exiled a murderer (twice a murderer) if need be. You didn't condemn his freeborn son to years of servitude and a landless fate for the father's crime—and expect him to forgive. A man without land had nothing, could not marry, speak in the *thringmoot,* claim honour or pride. His life and name were marred, broken as a plough by stones.

He ought to have killed Halldr. Or Arni Kjellson. Or someone. He wondered, sometimes, where his own rage lay. He didn't seem to have that fury, like a *berserkir* in battle. Or like his father in drink.

His father had killed people, raiding with Siggur Volganson, and here at home.

Bern hadn't done anything so . . . direct. Instead, he'd stolen a horse secretly in the dark and was now heading, for want of anything close to a better idea, to see if woman's magic—the *volur*'s—could offer him aid in the depths of a night. Not a brilliant plan, but the only one that had come to him. The women would probably scream, raise an alarm, turn him in.

That did make him think of something. A small measure of prudence. He turned east towards the risen moon and the edge of the wood, dismounted, and led the horse a short way in. He looped the rope to a tree trunk. He was not about to walk up to the women's compound leading an obviously stolen horse. This called for some trickery.

It was hard to be devious when you had no idea what you were doing.

He despised the bleak infliction of this life upon him. Was unable, it seemed, to even consider two more years of servitude, with no assurance of a return to any proper status afterwards. So, no, he wasn't going back, leaving the stallion to be found, slipping into his straw in the freezing shed behind Kjellson's house. That was over. The sagas told of moments when the hero's fate changed, when he came to the axle-tree. He wasn't a hero, but he wasn't going back. Not by choice.

He was likely to die tonight or tomorrow. No rites for him when that happened. There would be an excited quarrel over how to kill a defiling horse thief, how slowly, and who most deserved the pleasure of it. They would be drunk and happy. Bern thought of the blood-eagle then; pushed the image from his mind.

Even the heroes died. Usually young. The brave went to Ingavin's halls. He wasn't sure if he was brave.

It was dense and black in the trees. He felt the pine needles underfoot. Wood smells: moss, pine, scent of a fox. Bern listened; heard nothing but his own breathing, and the horse's. Gyllir seemed calm enough. He left him there, turned north again, still in the woods, towards where he thought the *volur*'s compound was. He'd seen it a few times, a clearing carved out a little way into the forest. If someone had magic, Bern thought, they could deal with wolves. Or even make use of them. It was said that the women who lived here had tamed some of the beasts, could speak their language. Bern didn't believe that. He made the hammer sign again, however, with the thought.

He'd have missed the branching path in the blackness if it hadn't been for the distant spill of lantern light. It was late for that, the bottom of a night, but he had no idea what laws or rules women such as these would observe. Perhaps the seer—the *volur*—stayed awake all night, sleeping by day like the owls. The sense of being in a dream returned. He wasn't going to go back, and he didn't want to die.

Those two things together could bring you out alone in night approaching a seer's cabin through black trees. The lights—there were two of them—grew brighter as he came nearer. He could see the path, and then the clearing, and the structures beyond a fence: one large cabin, smaller ones flanking it, evergreens in a circle around, as if held at bay.

An owl cried behind him. A moment later Bern realized that it wasn't an owl. No going back now, even if his feet would carry him. He'd been seen, or heard.

The compound gate was closed and locked. He climbed over the fence. Saw a brewhouse and a locked storeroom with a heavy door. Walked past them into the glow cast by the lamplight in the windows of the largest cabin. The other buildings were dark. He stopped and cleared his throat. It was very quiet.

"Ingavin's peace upon all dwelling here."

He hadn't said a word since rising from his bed. His voice sounded jarring and abrupt. No response from within, no one to be seen.

"I come without weapons, seeking guidance."

The lanterns flickered as before in the windows on either side of the cabin door. He saw smoke rising from the chimney. There was a small garden on the far side of the building, mostly bare this early in the year, with the snow just gone.

He heard a noise behind him, wheeled.

"It is deep in the bowl of night," said the woman, who unlocked and closed the outer gate behind her, entering the yard. She was hooded; in the darkness it was impossible to see her face. Her voice was low. "Our visitors come by daylight . . . bearing gifts."

Bern looked down at his empty hands. Of course. *Seithr* had a price. Everything in the world did, it seemed. He shrugged, tried to appear indifferent. After a moment, he took off his vest. Held it out. The woman stood motionless, then came forward and took it, wordlessly. He saw that she limped, favouring her right leg. When she came near, he realized that she was young, no older than he was.

She walked to the door of the cabin, knocked. It opened, just a little. Bern couldn't see who stood within. The young woman entered; the door closed. He was alone again, in a clearing under stars and the one moon. It was colder now without the vest.

His older sister had made it for him. Siv was in Vinmark, on the mainland, married, two children, maybe another by now . . . they'd had no reply after sending word of Thorkell's exile a year ago. He hoped her husband was kind, had not changed with the news of her father's banishment. He might have: shame could come from a wife's kin, bad blood for his own sons, a check to his ambitions. That could alter a man.

There would be more shame when tidings of his own deeds crossed the water. Both his sisters might pay for what he'd done tonight. He hadn't thought about that. He hadn't thought very much at all. He'd only gotten up from bed and taken a horse before the ghost moon rose, as in a dream.

The cabin door opened.

The woman with the limp came out, standing in the spill of light. She motioned to him and so he walked forward. He felt afraid, didn't want to show it. He came up to her and saw her make a slight gesture and realized she hadn't seen him clearly before, in the darkness. She still had her hood up, hiding her face; he registered yellow hair, quick eyes. She opened her mouth as if to say something but didn't speak. Just motioned for him to enter. Bern went within and she pulled the door shut behind him, from outside. He didn't know where she was going. He didn't know what she'd been doing outside, so late.

He really didn't know much at all. Why else come to ask of women's magic what a man ought to do for himself?

Taking a deep breath he looked around by firelight, and the lamps at both windows, and over against the far wall on a long table. It was warmer than he'd expected. He saw his vest lying on a second table in the middle of the room, among a clutter of objects: conjuring bones, a stone dagger, a small hammer, a carving of Thünir, a tree branch, twigs, soapstone pots of various sizes. There were herbs strewn everywhere, lying on the table, others in pots and bags on the other long surface against the wall. There was a chair on top of that table at the back, and two blocks of wood in front of it, for steps. He had no idea what that meant. He saw a skull on the nearer table. Kept his face impassive.

"Why take a dead man's horse, Bern Thorkellson?"

Bern jumped, no chance of concealing it. His heart hammered. The voice came from the most shadowed corner of the room, near the back, to his right. Smoke drifted from a candle, recently extinguished. A bed there, a woman sitting upon it. They said she drank blood, the *volur*, that her spirit could leave her body and converse with spirits. That her curse killed. That she was past a hundred years old and knew where the Volgan's sword was.

"How . . . how do you know what I . . . ?" he stammered. Foolish question. She even knew his name.

She laughed at him. A cold laughter. He could have been in his straw right now, Bern thought, a little desperately. Sleeping. Not here.

"What power could I claim, Bern Thorkellson, if I didn't know that much of someone come in the night?"

He swallowed.

She said, "You hated him so much? Thinshank?"

Bern nodded. What point denying?

"I had cause," he said.

"Indeed," said the seer. "Many had cause. He married your mother, did he not?"

"That isn't why," Bern said.

She laughed again. "No? Do you hate your father also?"

He swallowed again. He felt himself beginning to sweat.

"A clever man, Thorkell Einarson."

Bern snorted bitterly, couldn't help it. "Oh, very. Exiled himself, ruined his family, lost his land."

"A temper when he drank. But a shrewd man, as I recall. Is his son?"

He still couldn't see her clearly, a shadow on a bed. Had she been asleep? They said she didn't sleep.

"You will be killed for this," she said. Her voice held a dry amusement more than anything else. "They will fear an angry ghost."

"I know that," said Bern. "It is why I have come. I need . . . counsel." He paused. "Is it clever to know that much, at least?"

"Take the horse back," she said, blunt as a hammer.

He shook his head. "I wouldn't need magic to do that. I need counsel for how to live. And not go back."

He saw her shift on the bed then. She stood up. Came forward. The light fell upon her, finally. She wasn't a hundred years old.

She was very tall, thin and bony, his mother's age, perhaps more. Her hair was long and plaited and fell on either side of her head like a maiden's, but grey. Her eyes were a bright, icy blue, her face lined, long, no beauty in it, a hard authority. Cruelty. A raider's face, had she been a man. She wore a heavy robe, dyed the colour of old blood. An expensive colour. He looked at her and was afraid. Her fingers were very long.

"You think a bearskin vest, badly made, buys you access to *seithr*?" she said. Her name was Iord, he suddenly remembered. Forgot who had told him that, long ago. In daylight.

Bern cleared his throat. "It isn't badly made," he protested.

She didn't bother responding, stood waiting.

He said, "I have no other gifts to give. I am a servant to Arni Kjellson now." He looked at her, standing as straight as he could. "You said . . . many had reason to hate Halldr. Was he . . . generous to you and the women here?"

A guess, a gamble, a throw of dice on a tavern table among beakers of ale. He hadn't known he would say that. Had no idea whence the question had come.

She laughed again. A different tone this time. Then she was silent, looking at him with those hard eyes. Bern waited, his heart still pounding.

She came abruptly forward, moved past him to the table in the middle of the room, long-striding for a woman. He caught a scent about her as she went: pine resin, something else, an animal smell. She picked up some of the herbs, threw them in a bowl, took that and crossed to the back table for something beside the raised chair, put that in the bowl, too. He couldn't see what. With the hammer she began pounding and grinding, her back to him.

Still working, her movements decisive, she said suddenly, "You had no thought of what you might do, son of Thorkell, son of Frigga? You just stole a horse. On an island. Is that it?"

Stung, Bern said, "Shouldn't your magic tell you my thoughts—or lack of them?"

She laughed again. Glanced at him briefly then, over her shoulder. The eyes were bright. "If I could read a mind and future just from a man entering my room, I'd not be by the woods on Rabady Isle in a cabin with a leaking roof. I'd be at Kjarten Vidurson's hall in Hlegest, or in Ferrieres, or even with the Emperor in Sarantium."

"Jaddites? They'd burn you for pagan magic."

She was still amused, still crushing herbs in the stone bowl. "Not if I told their future truly," she said. "Sun god or no, kings want to know what will be. Even Aeldred would welcome me, could I look at any man and know all of him."

"Aeldred? No he wouldn't."

She glanced back at him again. "You are wrong. His hunger is for knowledge, as much as for anything. Your father may even know that by now, if he's gone raiding among the Anglcyn."

"Has he? Gone raiding there?" He asked before he could stop himself.

He heard her laughing; she didn't even look back at him this time.

She came again to the near table and took a flask of something. Poured a thick, pasty liquid into the bowl, stirred it, then poured it all back into the flask. Bern felt afraid still, watching her. This was magic. He was entangling himself with it. Witchery. *Seithr*. Dark as the night was, as the way of women in the dark. His own choice, though. He had come for this. And it seemed she was doing something.

There was a movement, from over by the fire. He looked quickly. Took an involuntary step backwards, an oath escaping him. Something slithered across the floor and beneath the far table. It disappeared behind a chest against that wall.

The seer followed his gaze, smiled. "Ah. You see my new friend? They brought me a serpent today, the ship from the south. They said his poison was gone. I had him bite one of the girls, to be sure. I need a serpent. They change worlds when they change skin, did you know that?"

He hadn't known that. Of course he hadn't known that. He kept his gaze on the wooden chest. Nothing moved, but it was there, coiled, behind. He felt much too warm now, smelled his own sweat.

He finally looked back at her. Her eyes were waiting, held his.

"Drink," she said.

No one had made him come here. He took the flask from her hand. She had rings on three fingers. He drank. The herbs were thick in the drink, hard to swallow.

"Half only," she said quickly. He stopped. She took the flask and drained it herself. Put it down on the table. Said something in a low voice he couldn't hear. Turned back to him.

"Undress," she said. He stared at her. "A vest will not buy your future or the spirit world's guidance, but a young man always has another offering to give."

He didn't understand at first, and then he did.

A glitter in her coldness. She had to be older than his mother, lined and seamed, her breasts sunken on her chest beneath the dark red robe. Bern closed his eyes.

"I must have your seed, Bern Thorkellson, if you wish *seithr*'s power. You require more than a seer's vision, and before daybreak, or they will find you and cut you apart before they allow you to die." Her gaze was pitiless. "You know it to be so."

He knew it. His mouth was dry. He looked at her.

"You hated him too?"

"Undress," she said again.

He pulled his tunic over his head.

It ought to have been a dream, all of this. It wasn't. He removed his boots, leaning against the table. She watched, her eyes never leaving him, very bright, very blue. His hand on the table touched the skull. It wasn't human, he saw, belatedly. A wolf, most likely. He wasn't reassured.

She wasn't here to reassure. He was inside another world, or in the doorway to it: women's world, gateway to women's knowing. Shadows and blood. A serpent in the room. On the ship from the south . . . they had traded during the banned time, before the funeral rites. He didn't think, somehow, they would be troubled by that here. *They said his poison was gone.* He felt whatever he had just drunk in his veins now.

"Go on," said the seer. A woman ought not to watch like this, Bern thought, tasting his fear again. He hesitated, then took off his trousers, was naked before her. He squared his shoulders. He saw her smile, the thin mouth. He felt light-headed. What had she given him to drink? She gestured; his feet carried him across the room to her bed.

"Lie down," she said, watching him. "On your back."

He did what she told him. He had left the world where things were as they . . . ought to be. He had left it when he took the dead man's horse. She walked about the room and pinched shut or blew out the candles and lamps, so only the firelight glowed, red on the farthest wall. In the near-dark it was easier. She came back, stood over against her bed where he lay—an outline against the fire, looking down upon him. She reached out, slowly— he saw her hand moving—and touched his manhood.

Bern closed his eyes again. He'd thought her touch would be cold, like age, like death, but it wasn't. She moved her fingers, down and back up, and then slowly down again. He felt himself, even amid fear and a kind of horror, becoming aroused. A roaring in his blood. The drink? This wasn't like a romp with Elli or Anrida in the stubbled fields after harvesting, in the straw of their barn by moonlight.

This wasn't like anything.

"Good," whispered the *volur*, and repeated it, her hand moving. "It needs your seed to be done, you see. You have a gift for me."

Her voice had changed again, deepened. She withdrew her hand. Bern trembled, kept his eyes tightly closed, heard a rustling as she shed her own robe. He wondered suddenly where the serpent was; pushed that thought away. The bed shifted, he felt her hands on his shoulders,

a knee by one hip, and then the other, smelled her scent—
and then she mounted him from above without hesitation
and sheathed him within her, hard.

Bern gasped, heard a sound torn from her. And with
that, he understood—without warning or expectation—
that he had a power here, after all. Even in this place of
magic. She needed what was his to give. And it was that
awareness, a kind of surging, that took him over, more
than any other shape desire might wear, as the woman—
the witch, *volur,* wise woman, seer, whatever she would
be named—began rocking upon him, breathing harder.
Crying a name then (not his), her hips moving as in a
spasm. He made himself open his eyes, saw her head
thrown back, her mouth wide open, her own eyes closed
now upon need as she rode him wildly like a night horse
of her own dark dreaming and claimed for herself—*now,*
with his own harsh, torn spasm—the seed she said she
needed to work magic in the night.

"GET DRESSED."

She swung off his body and up from the bed. No
lingering, no aftermath. The voice brittle and cold again.
She put on her robe and went to the near wall of the
cabin, rapped three times on it, hard. She looked back at
him, her glance bleak as before, as if the woman upon
him moments ago, with her closed eyes and shuddering
breath, had never existed in the world. "Unless you'd
prefer the others see you like this when they come in?"

Bern moved. As he hurried into clothing and boots,
she crossed to the fire, took a taper, and began lighting
the lamps again. Before they were all lit, before he had his
overshirt on, the outside door opened and four women
came in, moving quickly. He had a sense they'd been
trying to catch him before he was dressed. Which meant
they had . . .

He took a breath. He didn't know what it meant. He was lost here, in this cabin, in the night.

One of the women carried a dark blue cloak, he saw. She took this to the *volur* and draped it about her, fastening it at one shoulder with a silver torque. Three of the others, none of them young, took over dealing with the lamps. The last one began preparing another mixture at the table, using a different bowl. No one said a word. Bern didn't see the young girl who'd spoken to him outside.

After their entrance and quick glances at him, none of the women even seemed to acknowledge his presence here. A man, meaningless. He hadn't been, just before, though, had he? A part of him wanted to say that. Bern slipped his head and arms into his shirt and stood near the rumpled bed. He felt oddly awake now, alert—something in the drink she'd given him?

The one making the new mixture poured it into a beaker and carried it to the seer, who drained it at once, making a face. She went over to the blocks of wood before the back table. A woman on each side helped her step up and then seat herself on the elevated chair. There were lights burning now, all through the room. The *volur* nodded.

The four women began to chant in a tongue Bern didn't know. One of the lamps by the bed suddenly went out. Bern felt the hairs on the back of his neck stand up. This was *seithr*, magic, not just foretelling. The seer closed her eyes and gripped the arms of her heavy chair, as if afraid she might be carried off. One of the other women, still chanting, moved with a taper past Bern and relit the extinguished lamp. Returning, she paused by him for a moment. She squeezed his buttocks with one hand, saying nothing, not even looking at him. Then she rejoined the others in front of the elevated chair. Her gesture, casual and controlling, was exactly like a warrior's with a serving girl passing his bench in a tavern.

Bern's face reddened. He clenched his fists. But just then the seer spoke from her seat above them, her eyes still closed, hands clutching the chair arms, her voice high—greatly altered—but saying words he could understand.

THEY'D GIVEN HIM BACK his vest which was a blessing. The night felt even colder after the warmth inside. He walked slowly, eyes not yet adjusted to blackness, moving away from the compound lights through the trees on either side. He was concentrating: on finding his way, and on remembering exactly what the *volur* had told him. The instructions had been precise. Magic involved precision, it seemed. A narrow path to walk, ruin on either side, a single misstep away. He still felt the effects of the drink, a sharpening of perception. A part of him was aware that what he was doing now could be seen as mad, but it didn't feel that way. He felt . . . protected.

He heard the horse before he saw it. Wolves might eat the moons, heralding the end of days and the death of gods, but they hadn't found Halldr's grey horse yet. Bern spoke softly, that the animal might know his voice as he approached. He rubbed Gyllir's mane, untied the rope from the tree, led him back out into the field. The blue moon was high now, waning, the night past its deepest point, turning towards dawn. He would have to move quickly.

"What did she tell you to do?"

Bern wheeled. Sharpened perceptions or not, he hadn't heard anyone approach. If he'd had a sword he'd have drawn it, but he didn't even have a dagger. It was a woman's voice, though, and he recognized it.

"What are you doing here?"

"Saving your life," she said. "Perhaps. It may not be possible."

She limped forward from the trees. He hadn't heard her approach because she'd been waiting for him, he realized.

"What do you mean?"

"Answer my question. What did she tell you to do?"

Bern hesitated. Gyllir snorted, swung his head, restive now. "Do this, tell me that, stand here, go there," Bern said. "Why do all of you enjoy giving orders so much?"

"I can leave," the young woman said mildly. Though she was still hooded, he saw her shrug. "And I certainly haven't ordered you to undress and get into bed for me."

Bern went crimson. He was desperately glad of the darkness, suddenly. She waited. It was true, he thought, she could walk away and he'd be . . . exactly where he'd been a moment ago. He had no idea what she was doing here, but that ignorance was of a piece with everything else tonight. He could almost have found it amusing, if it hadn't been so thickly trammelled in . . . woman things.

"She made a spell," he said, finally, "up on that chair, in the blue cloak. For magic."

"I know about the chair and cloak," the girl said impatiently. "Where is she sending you?"

"Back to town. She's made me invisible to them. I can ride right down the street and no one will see me." He heard the note of triumph enter his voice. Well, why not? It *was* astonishing. "I'm to go onto the southerners' ship—there's a ramp out, by law, it is open for inspection— and go straight down into the hold."

"With a horse?"

He nodded. "They have animals. There's a ramp down, too."

"And then?"

"Stay there till they leave, and get off at their next port of call. Ferrieres, probably."

He could see she was staring straight at him. "Invisible? With a horse? On a ship?"

He nodded again.

She began to laugh. Bern felt himself flushing again. "You find this amusing? Your own *volur*'s power? Women's magic?"

She was trying to collect herself, a hand to her mouth. "Tell me," she asked, finally, "if you can't be seen, how am I looking at you?"

Bern's heart knocked hard against his ribs. He rubbed a hand across his forehead. Found that he couldn't speak for a moment.

"You, ah, are one of them. Part of, ah, the *seithr*?"

She took a step towards him. He saw her shake her head within the hooded robe. She wasn't laughing now. "Bern Thorkellson, I see you because you aren't under any spell. You will be taken as soon as you enter the town. Captured like a child. She lied to you."

He took a deep breath. Looked up at the sky. Ghost moon, early spring stars. His hands were trembling, holding the horse's reins.

"Why would . . . she said she hated Halldr as much as I did!"

"That's true. He was no friend to us. Thinshank's dead, though. She can use the goodwill of whoever becomes governor now. Her capturing you—and they will be told before midday that she put you under a spell and forced you to ride back to them—is a way to achieve that, isn't it?"

He didn't feel guarded any more.

"We need food and labour out here," she went on calmly. "We need the fear and assistance of the town, both. All *volurs* require this, wherever they are. You become her way of starting again after the long quarrel with Halldr. Your coming here tonight was a gift to her."

He thought of the woman above him in the bed, lit only by the fire.

"In more ways than one," the girl added, as if reading his thoughts.

"She has no power, no *seithr*?"

"I didn't say that. Although I don't think she does."

"There's no magic? Nothing to make a man invisible?"

She laughed again. "If one spearman can't hit a target when he throws, do you decide that spears are useless?" It was too dark to make out any expression on her face. He realized something.

"You hate her," he said. "That's why you are here. Because . . . because she had the snake bite you!"

He could see she was surprised, hesitating for the first time. "I don't love her, no," she agreed. "But I wouldn't be here because of that."

"Why then?" Bern asked, a little desperately.

Again a pause. He wished, now, that there were light. He still hadn't seen her face.

She said, "We are kin, Bern Thorkellson. I'm here because of that."

"What?" He was stunned.

"Your sister married my brother, on the mainland."

"Siv married . . . ?"

"No, Athira wedded my brother Gevin."

He felt abruptly angry, couldn't have said why. "That doesn't make us kin, woman."

Even in darkness he could see that he had wounded her.

The horse moved again, whickered, impatient with standing.

The woman said, "I am a long way from home. Your family is the closest I have on this island, I suppose. Forgive me for presuming."

His family was landless, his father exiled. He was a servant, compelled to sleep in a barn on straw for two more years.

"What presumption?" Bern said roughly. "That isn't what I meant." He wasn't sure what he'd meant.

There was a silence. He was thinking hard. "You were sent to the *volur*? They reported you had a gift?"

The hood moved up and down. "Curious, how often unwed youngest daughters have a gift, isn't it?"

"Why did I never hear of you?"

"We are meant to be unattached, to be the more dependent. That's why they bring girls from distant villages and farms. All the seers do that. I've spoken to your mother, though."

"You have? What? Why . . . ?"

The shrug again. "Frigga's a woman. Athira gave me a message for her."

"You all have your tricks, don't you?" He felt bitter, suddenly.

"Swords and axes are so much better, aren't they?" she said sharply. She was staring at him again, though he knew the darkness hid his face, too. "We're all trying to make ourselves a life, Bern Thorkellson. Men and women both. Why else are you out here now?"

Bitterness still. "Because my father is a fool who killed a man."

"And his son is what?"

"A fool about to die before the next moon rises. A good way to . . . make a life, isn't it? Useful kin for you to have."

She said nothing, looked away. He heard the horse again. Felt the wind, a change in it, as though the night had indeed turned, moving now towards dawn.

"The snake," he said awkwardly. "Is it . . . ?"

"I'm not poisoned. It hurts."

"You . . . walked out here a long way."

"There's one of us out all night on watch. We take turns, the younger ones. People come in the dark. That's how I saw you on the horse and told her."

"No, I meant . . . just now. To warn me."

"Oh." She paused. "You believe me, then?"

For the first time, a note of doubt, wistfulness. She was betraying the *volur* for him.

He grinned crookedly. "You are looking right at me, as you said. I can't be that hard to see. Even a piss-drunk raider falling off his horse will spot me when the sun comes up. Yes, I believe you."

She let out a breath.

"What will they do to you?" he asked. It had just occurred to him.

"If they find out I was here? I don't want to think about it." She paused. "Thank you for asking."

He felt suddenly shamed. Cleared his throat. "If I don't ride back into the village, will they know you . . . warned me?"

Her laughter again, unexpected, bright and quick. "They could possibly decide you were clever, by yourself."

He laughed too. Couldn't help it. Was aware that it could be seen as a madness sent by the gods, laughter at the edge of dying one hideous death or another. Not like the mindlessness of the water-disease—a man bitten by a sick fox—but the madness where one has lost hold of the way things are. Laughter here, another kind of strangeness in this dark by the wood among the spirits of the dead, with the blue moon overhead, pursued by a wolf in the sky.

The world would end when that wolf caught the two moons.

He had more immediate problems, actually.

"What will you do?" she asked. The third time she'd seemed to track his thoughts. Perhaps it was more than being a youngest daughter, this matter of having a gift. He wished, again, he could see her clearly.

But, as it happened, he did know, finally, the answer to her question.

Once, years ago, his father had been in a genial mood one evening as they'd walked out together to repair a loose door on their barn. Thorkell wasn't always drunk, or even often so (being honest with his own memories). That summer evening he was sober and easy, and the measure of that mood was that, after finishing the work, the two of them went walking, towards the northern boundary of their land, and Thorkell spoke of his raiding days to his only son, something that rarely happened.

Thorkell Einarson had not been a man given to boasting, or to offering scraps of advice from the table of his recollections. This made him unusual among the Erlings, or those that Bern knew, at any rate. It wasn't always easy having an unusual father, though a boy could take some dark pride in seeing Thorkell feared by others as much as he was. They whispered about him, pointed him out, carefully, to merchants visiting the isle. Bern, a watchful child, had seen it happen.

Other men had told the boy tales; he knew something of what his father had done. Companion and friend to Siggur Volganson himself right to the end. Voyages in storm, raids in the dark. Escaping the Cyngael after Siggur died and his sword was lost. A journey alone across the Cyngael lands, then the width of the Anglcyn kingdom to the eastern coast, and finally home across the sea to Vinmark and this isle.

"I recollect a night like this, a long time ago," his father said, leaning back against the boulder that marked the boundary of their land. "We went too far from the boats and they cut us off—Cuthbert's household guard, his best men—between a wood and a stream."

Cuthbert had been king of the Anglcyn in the years when Thorkell was raiding with the Volgan. Bern knew that much.

He remembered loving moments such as that one had been, the two of them together, the sun setting, the air mild, his father mild, and talking to him.

"Siggur said something to us that night. He said there are times when all you can do to survive is one single thing, however unlikely it may be, and so you act as if it *can* be done. The only chance we had was that the enemy was too sure of victory, and had not posted outliers against a night breakout."

Thorkell looked at his son. "You understand that *everyone* posts outlying guards? It is the most basic thing an army does. It is mad not to. They had to have them, there was no chance they didn't."

Bern nodded.

"So we spoke our prayers to Ingavin and broke out," Thorkell said, matter-of-factly. "Maybe sixty men—two boats' worth of us—against two hundred, at the least. A blind rush in the dark, some of us on stolen horses, some running, no order to it, only speed. The whole thing being to get to their camp, and through it—take some horses on the run if we could—cut back towards the ships two days away."

Thorkell paused then, looking out over summer farm-lands, towards the woods. "They didn't have outliers. They were waiting for morning to smash us, were mostly asleep, a few still singing and drinking. We killed thirty or forty of them, got horses for some of our unmounted, took two thegns hostage, by blind luck—couldn't tell who they were in the dark. And we sold them back to Cuthbert the next day for our freedom to get to the boats and sail away."

He'd actually grinned, Bern remembered, behind the red beard. His father had rarely smiled.

"The Anglcyn in the west rebelled against King Cuthbert after that, which is when Athelbert became king, then Gademar, and Aeldred. Raiding got harder, and then Siggur died in Llywerth. That's when I decided to become a landowner. Spend my days fixing broken doors."

He'd had to escape first, alone and on foot, across the breadth of two different countries.

You act as if it can be done.

"I'm crossing to the mainland," Bern said quietly to the girl in that darkness by the wood.

She stood very still. "Steal a boat?"

He shook his head. "Couldn't take the horse on any boat I could manage alone."

"You won't leave the horse?"

"I won't leave the horse."

"Then?"

"Swim," said Bern. "Clearly." He smiled, but she couldn't see it, he knew.

She was silent a moment. "You can swim?"

He shook his head. "Not that far."

Heroes came to thresholds, to moments that marked them, and they died young, too. Icy water, end of winter, the stony shore of Vinmark a world away across the strait, just visible by daylight if the mist didn't settle, but not now.

What was a hero, if he never had a chance to *do* anything? If he died at the first threshold?

"I think the horse can carry me," he said. "I will . . . act as if it can." He felt his mood changing, a strangeness overtaking him even as he spoke. "Promise me no monsters in the sea?"

"I wish I could," said the girl.

"Well, that's honest," he said. He laughed again. She didn't, this time.

"It will be very cold."

"Of course it will." He hesitated. "Can you . . . see anything?"

She knew what he meant. "No."

"Am I underwater?" He tried to make it a joke.

Shook her head. "I can't tell. I'm sorry. I'm . . . more a youngest daughter than a seer."

Another silence. It struck him that it would be appropriate to begin feeling afraid. The sea at night, straight out into the black . . .

"Shall I . . . any word for your mother?"

It hadn't occurred to him. Nothing had, really. He thought about it now. "Better you never saw me. That I was clever by myself. And died of it, in the sea."

"You may not."

She didn't sound as if she believed that. She would have been rowed across from Vinmark, coming here. She knew the strait, the currents and the cold, even if there were no monsters.

Bern shrugged. "That will be as Ingavin and Thünir decide. Make some magic, if you have any. Pray for me, if you haven't. Perhaps we'll meet again. I thank you for coming out. You saved me from . . . one bad kind of death, at least."

It was past the bottom of the night, and he had a distance to go to the beach nearest the mainland. He said nothing more, and neither did she, though he could see that she was still staring at him in the dark. He mounted up on the horse he wouldn't leave for Halldr Thinshank's funeral rites, and rode away.

Some time before reaching the strand south-east of the forest, he realized he didn't know her name, or have any clear idea what she looked like. Unlikely to matter; if they met again it would probably be in the afterworld of souls.

He came around the looming dark of the pine woods to a stony place by the water: rocky and wild, exposed, no boats here, no fishermen in the night. The pounding of the sea, heavy sound of it, salt in his face, no shelter from the wind. The blue moon west, behind him now, the white one not rising tonight until dawn. It would be dark on the ocean water. Ingavin alone knew what creatures might be waiting to pull him down. He wouldn't leave the horse. He wouldn't go back. You did whatever was left, and acted as if it could be done. Bern cursed his father aloud, then, for murdering another man, doing that to all of them, his sisters and his mother and himself, and then he urged the grey horse into the surf, which was white where it hit the stones, and black beyond, under the stars.

CHAPTER II

"Our trouble," muttered Dai, looking down through green-gold leaves at the farmyard, "is that we make good poems and bad siege weapons."

A siege, in fact, wasn't even remotely at issue. The comment was so inconsequential, and so typical of Dai, that Alun laughed aloud. Not the wisest thing to do, given where they were. Dai slapped a hand to his brother's mouth. After a moment, Alun signalled he was under control and Dai moved his hand away, grunting.

"Anyone in particular you'd like to besiege?" Alun asked, quietly enough. He shifted his elbows carefully. The bushes didn't move.

"One poet I can think of," Dai said, unwisely. He was prone to jests, his younger brother prone to laughing at them; they were both prone under leaves, gazing at penned cattle below. They'd come north to steal cattle. The Cyngael did that to each other, frequently.

Dai moved a hand quickly, but Alun kept still this time. They couldn't afford to be seen. There were just twelve of them—eleven, with Gryffeth now captured—and they were a long way north into Arberth. No more than two or three days from the sea, Dai reckoned, though he wasn't sure exactly where they were, or what this very large farmhouse below them was.

Twelve had been a marginal number for a raiding party, but the brothers were confident in their abilities, not without some cause. Besides, in Cadyr it was said that any one of their own was worth two of the Arberthi, and at least three from Llywerth. They might do the arithmetic differently in the other two provinces, but that was just vanity and bluster.

Or it should have been. It was alarming that Gryffeth had been taken so easily, scouting ahead. The good news was that he'd prudently carried Alun's harp with him, to be taken for a bard on the road. The bad news was that Gryffeth—notoriously—couldn't sing or play to save his life. If they tested him down below, he was unmasked. And saving his life became an issue.

So the brothers had left nine men out of sight off the road and climbed this overlook to devise a rescue plan. If they went home without cattle it was bad but not humiliating. Not every raid succeeded; you could still do a few things to make a story worth telling. But if their royal father or uncle had to pay a ransom for a cousin taken on an unauthorized cattle raid into Arberth during a herald's truce, well, that was . . . going to be quite bad.

And if Owyn of Cadyr's nephew died in Arberth it could mean war.

"How many, do you think?" Dai murmured.

"Twenty, give or take a few? It's a big farmhouse. Who lives here? Where are we?" Alun was still watching the cows, Dai saw.

"Forget the cattle," Dai snapped. "Everything's changed."

"Maybe not. We let them out of the pen tonight, four of us scatter them north up the valley, the rest go in after Gryffeth while they're rounding them up?"

Dai looked thoughtfully at his younger brother. "That's unexpectedly clever," he said, finally.

Alun punched him on the shoulder, fairly hard. "Hump a goat," he added mildly. "This was *your* idea, I'm getting us out of it. Don't be superior. Which room's he in?"

Dai had been trying to sort that out. The farmhouse—whoever owned it was wealthy—was long and sprawling, running east to west. He saw the outline of a large hall beyond the double doors below them, wings bending back north at each end of that main building. A house that had expanded in stages, some parts stone, others wood. They hadn't seen Gryffeth taken in, had only come upon the signs of struggle on the path.

Two cowherds were watching the cattle from the far side of the fenced enclosure east of the house. Boys, their hands moving ceaselessly to wave at flies. None of the armed men had emerged since a cluster of them had gone in through the main doors, talking angrily, just as the brothers had arrived here in the thicket above the farm. Once or twice they'd heard raised, distant voices within, and a girl had come out for well water. Otherwise it was quiet and hot, a sleepy afternoon, late spring, butterflies, the drone of bees, a hawk circling. Dai watched it for a moment.

What neither brother said, though both of them knew it, was that it was extremely unlikely they could get a man out of a guarded room, even at night and with a diversion, without men dying on both sides. During a truce. This raid had gone wrong before it had even begun.

"Are we even certain he's in there?" Dai said.

"I am," said Alun. "Nowhere else likely. Could he be a guest? Um, could they have . . . ?"

Dai looked at him. Gryffeth couldn't play the harp he carried, was wearing a sword and leather armour, had a helmet in his saddle gear, looked exactly the sort of young man—with a Cadyri accent, too—who'd be up to mischief, which he was.

The younger brother nodded, without Dai saying anything. It was too miserably obvious. Alun swore briefly, then murmured, "All right, he's a prisoner. We'll need to move fast, know exactly where we're going. Come on, Dai, figure it out. In Jad's name, where have they got him?"

"In Jad's holy name, Brynn ap Hywll tends to use the room at the eastern end of the main building for prisoners, when he has them here. If I remember rightly."

They whipped around. Dai's knife was already out, Alun saw.

The world was a complex place sometimes, saturated with the unexpected. Especially when you left home and the trappings of the known. Even so, there were reasonable explanations for why someone might be up here now, right behind them. One of their own men might have followed with news; one of the guards from below could have intuited the presence of other Cadyri besides the captured one and come looking; they might even have been observed on their way up.

What was implausible in the extreme was what they actually saw. The man who'd answered Alun's question was smallish, grey-haired, cheeks and chin smooth-shaven, smiling at the two of them. He was alone, hands out and open, weaponless . . . and he was wearing a faded, telltale yellow robe with a golden disk of Jad about his neck.

"I might not actually be remembering rightly," he went on affably. "It has been some time since I've been here, and memory slips as you get older, you know."

Dai blinked, and shook his head as if to clear it after a blow. They'd been completely surprised by an aging cleric.

Alun cleared his throat. One particular thing had registered, powerfully. "Did you, er, say . . . Brynn ap Hywll?"

Dai was still speechless.

The cleric nodded benignly. "Ah. You know of him, do you?"

Alun swore again. He was fighting a rising panic.

The cleric made a reproving face, then chuckled. "You *do* know him."

Of course they did. "We don't know you," Dai said, finally recovering the capacity for speech. He'd lowered the knife. "How did you get up here?"

"Same way you did, I imagine."

"We didn't hear you."

"Evidently. I do apologize. I was quiet. I've learned how to be. Not quite sure what I'd find, you know."

The long yellow robes of a cleric were ill suited to silent climbing, and this man was not young. Whoever he was, he was no ordinary religious.

"Brynn!" Alun muttered grimly to his brother. The name—and what it meant—reverberated inside him. His heart was pounding.

"I heard."

"What evil, Jad-cursed luck!"

"Yes, well," said Dai. He was concentrating on the stranger for the moment. "I did ask who you were. I'd count it a great courtesy if you favoured us with your name."

The cleric smiled, pleased. "Good manners," he said, "were always a mark of your father's family, whatever their other sins might have been. How *is* Owyn? And your lady mother? Both well, I dare hope? It has been many years."

Dai blinked again. *You are a prince of Cadyr,* he reminded himself. *Your royal father's heir. Born to lead men, to control situations.* It became a necessary reminder, suddenly.

"You have entirely the advantage of us," said his brother, "in all ways I can imagine." Alun's mouth quirked. He found too many things amusing, Dai thought. A younger brother's trait. Less responsibility.

"All ways? Well, one of you does have a knife," said the cleric, but he was smiling as he said it. He lowered his hands. "I'm Ceinion of Llywerth, servant of Jad."

Alun dropped to his knees.

Dai's jaw seemed to be hanging open. He snapped it shut, felt himself going red as a boy caught idling by his tutor. He sheathed the knife hurriedly and sank down beside his brother, head lowered, hands together in submission. He felt overwhelmed. A saturation of the unexpected. The unprepossessing yellow-robed man on this wooded slope was the high cleric of the three fractious provinces of the Cyngael.

He calmly made the sign of Jad's disk in blessing over both of them.

"Come down with me," he said, "the way we came. Unless you have an objection, you are now my personal escorts. We're stopping here at Brynnfell on our way north to Amren's court at Beda." He paused. "Or did you really want to try attacking Brynn's own house? I shouldn't advise it, you know."

I shouldn't advise it. Alun didn't know whether to laugh or curse again. Brynn ap Hywll was only the subject of twenty-five years' worth of songs and stories. Erling's Bane they'd named him, here in the west. He'd spent his youth battling the raiders from overseas with his cousin Amren, now ruling in Arberth, of whom there were stories too. With them in those days had been Dai and Alun's own father and uncle—and this man, Ceinion of Llywerth. The generation that had beaten back Siggur Volganson—the Volgan—and his longships. And Brynn was the one who'd killed him.

Alun drew a steadying breath. Their father, who liked to hold forth with a flask at his elbow, had told tales of all of these men. Had fought with—and then sometimes against—them. He and Dai and their friends were, Alun thought, as they walked down and out of the wood behind the anointed high cleric of the Cyngael, in waters far over their heads. Brynnfell. This was *Brynnfell* below them.

They had been about to attack it. With eleven men.

"This is his stronghold?" he heard Dai asking. "I thought—"

"Edrys was? His castle? It is, of course, north-east by Rheden and the Wall. And there are other farms. This is the largest one. He's here now, as it happens."

"What? Here? Himself? Brynn?"

Alun worked to breathe normally. Dai sounded stunned. His brother, who was always so composed. This, too, could almost be funny, Alun thought. Almost.

Ceinion of Llywerth was nodding his head, still leading the way downwards. "He's here to receive me, actually. Good of him, I must say. I sent word that I would be passing through." He glanced back. "How many men do you have? I saw you two climbing, but not the others."

The cleric's tone was precise, suddenly. Dai answered him.

"And how many were taken?"

"Just the one," Dai said. Alun kept quiet. Younger brother.

"His name is Gryffeth? That's Ludh's son?"

Dai nodded.

He'd simply overheard them, Alun told himself. This wasn't Jad's gift of sight, or anything frightening.

"Very well," said the cleric crisply, turning to them as they came out of the trees and onto the path. "I'd account it a waste to have good men killed today. I will do penance for a deception in the name of Jad's peace. Hear me. You and your fellows joined me by arrangement at a ford of the Llyfarch River three days ago. You are escorting me north as a courtesy, and so that you might visit Amren's court at

Beda and offer prayers with him in his new-built sanctuary during this time of truce. Do you understand all that?"

They nodded, two heads bobbing up and down.

"Tell me, is your cousin Gryffeth ap Ludh a clever man?"

"No," said Dai, truthfully.

The cleric made a face. "What will he have told them?"

"I have no idea," Dai said.

"Nothing," Alun said. "He isn't quick, but he can keep silent."

The cleric shook his head. "But why would he keep silent when all he had to say was that he was riding in advance to tell them I had arrived?"

Dai thought a moment, then he grinned. "If the Arberthi took him harshly, he'll have been quiet just to embarrass them when you do show up, my lord."

The cleric thought it through, then smiled back. "Owyn's sons *would* be clever," he murmured. He seemed pleased. "One of you will explain this to Ludh's boy when we are inside. Where are your other men?"

"South of here, hidden off the road," Dai said. "And yours, my lord?"

"Have none," said the high cleric of the Cyngael. "Or I didn't until now. You are my men, remember."

"You rode alone from Llywerth?"

"Walked. But yes, alone. Some things to think about, and there's a truce in the land, after all."

"With outlaws in half the forests."

"Outlaws who know a cleric has nothing worth the taking. I've said the dawn prayers with many of them." He started walking.

Dai blinked again, and followed.

Alun wasn't sure how he felt. Curiously elated, in part. For one thing, this was the figure of whom so many stories were told, some of them by his father and uncle, though he knew there had been a falling-out, and a little part of why. For another, the high cleric had just saved them from trying a mad attack on another legend in his own house.

A man of Cadyr might be worth two Arberthi, but that did not—harp-boasting and ale-born songs aside— apply to the warband of Brynn ap Hywll.

These were the men who had been fighting the Erlings before Dai and Alun were born, when the Cyngael lived in terror of slavery and savage death three seasons of every year, taking flight into the hills at the least rumour of the dragon-prows. It was clear now why Gryffeth had been captured so easily. They'd have had no chance trying to attack this farm tonight. They'd have been humiliated, or dead. A truth to run back and forth through the mind like the shuttling of a loom.

Alun ab Owyn was very young that day, a prince of Cadyr, and it was greenest springtime in the provinces of the Cyngael, in the world. He'd no wish to die. Something occurred to him.

"My cousin was only carrying the harp for me, by the way. If anyone asks, my lord."

The cleric glanced back over his shoulder.

"Gryffeth can't sing," Dai explained. "Not that Alun's much good."

A joke, Alun thought. Good. Dai was feeling himself again, or starting to.

"There will be a feast, I expect," Ceinion of Llywerth said. "We'll find out soon enough."

"I'm actually better with siege weapons," Alun said, not helpfully. He was rewarded by hearing his older brother laugh, and quickly smother it.

"YOUR ROYAL FATHER I knew very well. Fought against him, and beside him. A disgraceful youth, if I may be blunt, and a brave man."

"It would be too much to hope that we might one day receive such a judgement from you, my lord, but to that we will aspire." Dai bowed after he spoke.

They were in the great hall of Brynnfell, beyond the central doors. A long corridor behind them ran east and west towards the wings. It was a very large house. Gryffeth had already been released—from a room at the end of the eastern corridor, as the cleric had guessed. Alun had had a whispered word with him, and reclaimed his harp.

Dai straightened and smiled. "You will permit me to add, my lord, that disgrace among the Arberthi is sometimes honour in Cadyr. We have not always been favoured with the truce that brings us here, as you know."

Alun smiled inwardly, kept his expression sincere. Dai had had a lifetime shaping this sort of speech, he thought. Words mattered among the Cyngael, nuance and subtlety. So did cattle-raiding, mind you, but the day's game had changed.

The scarred older warrior—a head taller than the two brothers—beamed happily down on them. Brynn ap Hywll was big in every way—hands, face, shoulders, girth. Even his greying moustache was thick and full. He was red and fleshy and balding. He wore no weapon in his own home, had rings on several thick fingers and a massive golden torc around his throat. Erling work: the hammer of the thunder god replaced by a suspended sun disk. Something he'd captured or been offered as ransom, Alun guessed.

If Ceinion of Llywerth felt displeasure at seeing something made to hold pagan symbols of Ingavin, he didn't show it. The high cleric was not at all what Alun had expected him to be, though he couldn't have said what he *had* expected. Certainly not the man who had been kissed so enthusiastically by the Lady Enid, as her husband smiled approval.

Alun had a recollection that the cleric's own wife had died long ago, but he was murky about the details. You couldn't remember everything a tutor dictated, or a tale-spinning father by the fireside.

"Well spoken, young prince," Brynn boomed, bringing Alun back to the present. Their host looked genuinely pleased with Dai's answer. He'd a voice for the battlefield, Brynn, one that would carry.

Their arrival at Brynnfell had gone easily, after all. Alun had a sense that things tended to go that way when Ceinion of Llywerth was involved. If there had been something odd about the cleric arriving with a Cadyri escort when he usually walked alone to his destinations, and was widely known not to have spoken to Prince Owyn for a decade and more . . . well, sometimes odd things happened, and this *was* the high cleric.

Brynn was prepared to play along, it seemed, whatever he might privately think. Alun saw the big man's gaze slide to where Ceinion stood, smooth face benign and attentive, slender hands folded in the sleeves of his robe. "Indeed, it would seem you have set your feet on the path of virtue already, serving as escorts to our beloved cleric, avoiding the scandalous conduct of your sire in his own youth."

Dai kept a level expression. "His lordship the high cleric is persuasive in his holiness. We are honoured and grateful to be with him."

"I've no doubt," said Brynn ap Hywll, just a little too dryly.

Dai was afraid Alun would laugh, but he didn't. Dai was fighting to control exhilaration himself . . . this was the dance, the thrust and twist of words, of meanings half-shown and then hidden, that underlay all the great songs and deeds of courts.

The Erlings might choose to loot and burn their way to some glorious afterlife of . . . more looting and burning, but the Cyngael saw the glory of the world—Jad's holy gift of it—as embodied in more than just swords and raiding.

Though that, perhaps, might explain why they were so often raided and looted—from Vinmark overseas, and under pressure from the Anglcyn now, across the Rheden Wall. He'd said it himself today: poems over siege engines. Words above weapons, too often.

He wasn't dwelling upon that now. He was exulting in the presence of two of the very great men of the west, as a springtime raid conjured out of boredom and their father's absence, hunting without them (Owyn was meeting a mistress), had turned into something quite otherwise.

Young Dai ab Owyn was, in other words, in that elevated state of mind and spirit where what occurred that evening could almost have been anticipated. He was alert, receptive, highly attuned . . . vulnerable. At such times, one can be hammered hard by a variety of things, and the effect can last forever—though it should be said that this did happen more often in tales, bard-spun in meadhalls, than on an impulsive cattle raid gone strange.

Just before the meal began Alun had taken the musician's stool at the Lady Enid's request. Brynn's wife was tall, dark-haired, dark-eyed, younger than her husband. A handsome woman with no shyness among the men in the hall. None of the women here seemed shy, come to think of it.

He was tuning his harp (his favourite *crwth*, made for him), trying not to be distracted. They were playing the triad game in the hall, drinking the cup of welcome after the invocation by Brynn's own cleric, before the food was brought. Ceinion had predicted a feast and had been proven right. They were drinking wine, not ale. Brynn ap Hywll was a wealthy man.

Some of the company were still standing, others had taken their seats; it was a relaxed gathering, this was a farmhouse not a castle, large and handsome as it might be. The room smelled of new rushes, freshly strewn herbs and flowers—and hunting dogs. There were at least ten wolfhounds, grey, black, brindled. Brynn's warband, those with him here, were not men to put great weight on ceremony, it seemed.

"Cold as . . . ?" called out a woman near the head of the table. Alun hadn't sorted the names yet. She was a family cousin, he guessed. Round-faced, light brown hair.

"Cold as a winter lake," answered a man leaning against the wall halfway down the room.

Cold was an easy start. They all knew the jokes: women's hearts, or the space between the legs of some of them. Those phrases wouldn't be offered now, before the drinking had properly begun, and with the ladies present.

"Cold as a loveless hearth," said another. Worn phrases, too often heard. One more to complete the triad. Alun kept silent, listening to his strings as he tuned. There was always one song before the meal; he was being honoured with it, wasn't sure what he wanted to sing.

"Cold as a world without Jad," said Gryffeth suddenly, which wasn't brilliant but wasn't bad either, with the high cleric at the head table. It got him a murmur of approval and a smile from Ceinion. Alun saw his brother, next to the cleric, wink at their cousin. Mark one for Cadyr.

"Sorrowful as . . . ?" said another of the ladies, an older one.

Trust the Cyngael, Alun thought wryly, to conjure with sorrow at a spring banquet's beginning. *We are a strange, wonderful people,* he thought.

"Sorrowful as a swan alone." A thin, satisfied-looking man sitting close to the high table. The ap Hywll bard, his own *crwth* beside him. An important figure. Accredited harpists always were. There was a rustle of approbation. Alun smiled at the man, received no response. Bards could be prickly, jealous of privilege, dangerous to offend. More than one prince had been humiliated by satires written against him. And Alun had been asked to take the stool first tonight. A guest indeed, but not a formally trained or licensed bard. Best to be cautious, he thought. He wished he knew a song about siege engines. Dai would have laughed.

"Sorrowful as a sword unused," said Brynn himself, leaning back in his chair, the big voice. Predictable pounding of tables as the lord of the manor spoke.

"Sorrowful," said Alun, surprising himself, since he'd just decided to be discreet, "as a singer without a song."

A small silence as they considered it, then Brynn ap Hywll banged a meaty hand down on the board in front of him, and the Lady Enid clapped her palms in pleasure and then—of course—so did everyone else. Dai winked again quickly, and then contrived to look indifferent, leaning back as well, fingering his wine cup, as if they were always offering such original phrasings in the triad game back home. Alun felt like laughing: in truth, the phrase had come to him because he *had* no song yet and would be called upon in a moment.

"Needful as . . . ?" suggested the Lady Enid, looking along the table.

A new phrase this time. Alun looked at Brynn's wife. More than handsome, he corrected himself: there was beauty there still, glittering with the jewellery of rank upon her arms and about her throat. More people were seated now. Servants stood by, awaiting a signal to bring the food.

"Needful as warmed wine in winter," someone Alun couldn't see offered from down the room. Approval for that, a nicely phrased offering. Winter memory in midsummer, the phrase near to poetry. Their hostess turned to Dai, politely, beyond her husband and the cleric, to let the other Cadyri prince have a turn.

"Needful as night's end," Dai said gravely, without a pause, which was *very* good, actually. An image of darkness, the fear of it, a dream of dawn, when the god returned from his journey under the world.

As the real applause for this faded, as they waited for someone to throw the third leg of the triad, a young woman entered the room.

She moved quietly, clad in green, belted in gold, with gold in the brooch at her shoulder and on her fingers, to the empty place beside Enid at the high table—which would have told Alun who this was, if the look and manner of her hadn't immediately done so. He stared, knew he was doing so, didn't stop.

As she seated herself, aware—very obviously aware—that all eyes were upon her, including those of an indulgent father, she looked down the table, taking in the company, and Alun was made intensely conscious of dark eyes (like her mother's), very black hair under the soft green cap, and skin whiter than . . . any easy phrase that came to mind.

And then he heard her murmur, voice rich, husky for one so young, unsettling: "Needful as night, I think many women would rather say."

And because this was Rhiannon mer Brynn, through that crowded hall men felt that they knew exactly what she was saying, and wished that the words had been for their ears alone, whispered close at candle-time, not in company at table. And they thought that they could kill or do great deeds that it might be made so.

Alun could see his brother's face as this green-gold woman-girl turned to Dai, whose phrase she had just echoed and challenged. And because he knew his brother better than he knew anyone on the god's earth, Alun saw the world change for Dai in that crossing of glances. A moment with a name to it, as the bards said.

He had an instant to feel sorrow, the awareness of something ending as something else began, and then they asked him for a song, that the night might begin with music, which was the way of the Cyngael.

∽

Brynnfell was a spacious property, well run by a competent steward, showing the touch of a mistress with taste, access to artisans, and a good deal of money. Still, it was only a farm, and there were a dozen young men from Cadyr now staying with them, over and above the thirty warriors and four women who'd accompanied ap Hywll and his wife and oldest daughter here.

Space was at a premium.

The Lady Enid had worked with efficiency informed by experience, meeting with the steward before the meal to arrange for the disposition of bodies at night. The hall would hold fighting men on pallets and rushes; it had done so before. The main barn was pressed into use, along with two outbuildings and the bakehouse. The brewhouse remained locked. Best not to put such temptation in men's way. And there was another reason.

The two Cadyri princes and their cousin shared a room in the main house with a good bed for the three of them—honour demanded the host offer as much to royal guests.

The steward surrendered his own chamber to the high cleric. He himself would join the cook and kitchen hands in the kitchen for the night. He was grimly prepared to be as stoic as an eastern zealot on his crag, if not as serenely alone. The cook was notorious for the magnificence of his snoring, and had once been found walking about the kitchen, waving a blade and talking to himself, entirely asleep. He'd ended up chopping vegetables in the middle of the night without ever waking, as his helpers and a number of gathered household members watched in rapt silence, peering through the darkness.

The steward had already determined to place all the knives out of reach before closing his eyes.

In the pleasant chamber thus yielded to him, Ceinion of Llywerth finished the last words of the day's office, offering at the end his customary silent prayer for the sheltering in light of those he had lost, some of them long ago, and also his gratitude, intensely felt, to holy Jad for all blessings given. The god had purposes not to be clearly seen. What had happened today—the lives he had likely saved, arriving when he did—was deserving of the humblest acknowledgement.

He rose, showing no signs of a strenuous day, or his years, and formally blessed the man kneeling beside him in prayer. He reclaimed his wine cup, subsiding happily onto the stool nearest the window. It was generally believed that the night air was noxious, carrying poisons and unholy spirits, but Ceinion had spent too many years sleeping out of doors, on walks across the three provinces and beyond. He found that he slept better by an open window, even in winter. It was springtime now, the air fragrant, night flowers under his window.

"I feel badly for the man who yielded me his bed."

His companion shifted his considerable bulk up from the floor and grasped his own cup, refilling it to the brim, without water. He took the other, sturdier chair, keeping the flask close by. "And well you should," Brynn ap Hywll said, smiling through his moustache. "Brynnfell's bursting. Since when do you travel with an escort?"

Ceinion eyed him a moment, then sighed. "Since I found a Cadyri raiding party looking at your farm."

Brynn laughed aloud. His laugh, like his voice, could overflow a room. "Well, thank you for deciding I'd sort out that much." He drank thirstily, refilled his cup again. "They seem good lads, mind you. Jad knows, I did my share of raiding when young."

"And their father."

"Jad curse his eyes and hands," Brynn said, though without force. "My royal cousin in Beda wants to know what to do about Owyn, you know."

"I know. I'll tell him when I get to Beda. With Owyn's two sons beside me." The cleric's turn to grin this time.

He leaned back against the cool stone wall beside the window. Earthly pleasures: an old friend, food and wine, a day with some good unexpectedly done. There were learned men who taught withdrawal from the traps and tangles of the world. There was even a doctrinal movement afoot in Rhodias to deny marriage to clerics now, following the eastern, Sarantine rule, making them ascetics, detached from distractions of the flesh—and the complexities of having heirs to provide for.

Ceinion of Llywerth had always thought—and had written the High Patriarch in Rhodias, and others—that this was wrong thinking and even heresy, an outright denial of Jad's full gift of life. Better to turn your love of the world into an honouring of the god, and if a wife died, or children, your own knowledge of sorrow might make you better able to counsel others, and comfort them. You lived with loss as they did. And shared their pleasures, too.

His words, written and spoken, mattered to others, by Jad's holy grace. He was skilled at this sort of argument but didn't know if he would be on the winning side of this one. The three provinces of the Cyngael were a long way from Rhodias, at the edge of the world, the misty borders of pagan belief. North of the north wind, the phrase went.

He sipped his wine, looking at his friend. Brynn's expression was sly at the moment, amusingly so. "Happen to see the way Dai ab Owyn looked at my Rhiannon, did you?"

Ceinion took care that his own manner did not change. He had, in fact, seen it—and something else. "She's a remarkable young woman," he murmured.

"Her mother's daughter. Same spirit to her. I'm an entirely beaten man, I tell you." Brynn was smiling as he said this. "We solve a problem that way? Owyn's heir handled by my girl?"

Ceinion kept his look noncommittal. "Certainly a useful match."

"The lad's already lost his head, I'd wager." He chuckled. "Not the first to do so, with Rhiannon."

"And your daughter?" Ceinion asked, perhaps unwisely.

Some fathers would have been startled, or offered an oath—what mattered the girl's wishes in these things? But Brynn ap Hywll didn't do that. Ceinion watched, and by the lamplight saw the big man, his old friend, grow thoughtful. Too much so. The cleric offered an inward, mildly blasphemous curse, and immediately sought—also silently—the god's forgiveness for that.

"Interesting song the younger one sang before the meal, wasn't it?"

There it was. A shrewd man, Ceinion thought ruefully. Much more than a warrior with a two-handed sword.

"It was," he said, still keeping his own counsel. This was all too soon. He temporized. "Your bard was out of countenance."

"Amund? It was too good, you mean? The song?"

"Not that. Though it was impressive. No, Alun ab Owyn breached the laws for such things. Only licensed bards are allowed to improvise in company. Your harper will need appeasing."

"Spiky man, Amund. Not easily softened, if you are right."

"I am right. Call it a word offered the wise."

Brynn looked at him. "And your other question? About Rhiannon? What sort of word was that?"

Ceinion sighed. It had been a mistake. "I wish you weren't clever, sometimes."

"Have to be. To keep up in this family. She liked the . . . song, you think?"

"I think everyone liked the song." He left it at that.

Both men were still awhile.

"Well," Brynn said finally, "she's of age, but there's no great rush. Though Amren wants to know what to do about Owyn and Cadyr, and this . . ."

"Owyn ap Glynn isn't the problem. Neither's Amren, or Ielan in Llywerth. Except if they cling to these feuds that will end us." He'd spoken with more fire than he'd intended.

The other man stretched out his legs and leaned back, unruffled. Brynn drank, wiped his moustache with a sleeve, and grinned. "Still riding that horse?"

"And I will all my life." Ceinion didn't smile this time. He hesitated, then shrugged. Wanted to change the subject, in any case. "I'll tell you something before I tell it to Amren in Beda. But keep it close. Aeldred's invited me to Esferth, to join his court."

Brynn sat up abruptly, scraping the chair along the floor. He swore, without apologizing, then banged his cup down, spilling wine. "How *dare* he? Our high cleric he wants to steal now?"

"I said he'd invited me. Not an abduction, Brynn."

"Even so, doesn't he have his own Jad-cursed holy men among the Anglcyn? Rot the man!"

"He has a great many, and seeks more . . . not cursed, I hope." Ceinion left a pointed little pause. "From here, from Ferrieres. Even from Rhodias. He is . . . a different sort of king, my friend. I think he feels his lands are on the way to being safe now, which means new ambitions, ways of thinking. He's arranging to marry a daughter north, to Rheden." He looked steadily at the other man.

Brynn sighed. "I'd heard that."

"And if so, there goes *that* rivalry on the other side of the Wall, which we've relied upon. Our danger is if we remain . . . the old sort of princes."

There were three oil lamps burning in the room, one set in the wall, two brought in for a guest: extravagance and respect. In the mingling of yellow lamplight, Brynn's gaze was direct now. Ceinion, accepting it, felt a wave of memory crash over him from a terrible, glorious summer long ago. This happened more and more as he grew older. Past and present colliding, simultaneous visions, the present seen with the past. This same man, a quarter-century ago, on a battlefield by the sea, the Volgan himself and the Erling force they'd met by their boats. There had been three princes among the Cyngael that day but Brynn had led the centre. A full head of dark hair on him then, far less bulk, less of this easy humour. The same man, though. You changed, and you did not change.

"You said he's after clerics from Ferrieres?" Picking up the other thing that mattered.

"So he wrote me."

"It starts with clerics, doesn't it?"

Ceinion gazed affectionately at his old friend. "Sometimes. They are notoriously aloof, my colleagues across the water."

"But if not? If it works, opens channels? If the Anglcyn and Ferrieres join to push away the Erling raiders on both sides of the Strait? And mayhap a marriage that way, too . . . ?"

"Then the Erlings come here again, I would think." Ceinion finished the thought. "If we remain outside whatever is happening. That's my message to Beda, when I get there." He paused, then added the thought he'd been travelling with: "There are times when the world changes, Brynn."

A silence in the room. No noises from the corridor either, now; the household abed, or most of them. Some of the warband likely dicing in the hall still, perhaps with the young Cadyri, money changing hands by lantern light. He didn't think there would be trouble; Brynn's men were extremely well trained, and they were hosts tonight. The night breeze came through the window, sweetened with the scent of flowers. Gifts of the god's offered world. Not to be spurned.

"I hate them, you know. The Erlings and the Anglcyn, both."

Ceinion nodded, said nothing. What was there to say? A homily about Jad, and love? The big man sighed again. Drained his cup one more time. He showed no effects from the unwatered wine.

"Will you go to him? To Aeldred?" he asked, as Ceinion had expected.

"I don't know," he said, which had the virtue of being honest.

BRYNN LEFT, not down the corridor to his own bedchamber, but for one of the outbuildings. A young serving lass waiting for him, no doubt, ready to slip out wrapped in a cloak as soon as she saw him go through the door. Ceinion knew it was his duty to chastise the other man for this. He didn't even consider it; had known ap Hywll and his wife for too long. One of the things about living in and of the world: you learned how complex it could be.

He doused two of the lamps, disliking the waste. A habit of frugality. He left the door a little ajar, as a courtesy. With Brynn outside, the lord of the manor would not be his own last visitor of the night. He'd been here, and in ap Hywll's other homes, before.

Somewhat as an afterthought, while he waited, he went to his pack and drew from it the letter he was carrying with him north-west to Beda on the sea. He took the same seat as before, by the window. No moons tonight. The young Cadyri princes would have had a good, black night for a cattle raid . . . and they'd have been slaughtered. Bad luck for them that Brynn and his men would have been here, but you could die of bad luck.

Jad of the Sun had allowed him to save lives today, a different sort of gift, one that might have meaning that went beyond what a man was permitted to see. His own prayer, every morning, was that the god see fit to make use of him. There was something—there had to be something—in his arriving when he did, looking up the slope, seeing movement in the bushes. And following, for no very good reason besides a *knowing* that sometimes came to him. More than he deserved, that gift, flawed as he knew he was. Things he had done, in grief, and otherwise. He turned his head and looked out, saw stars through rents in moving clouds, caught the scent of the flowers again, just outside in the night.

Needful as night's end. Needful as night.

Two subtle offerings in the triad game, then a song, improvised as they listened. Three young people here, on the cusp of their real existence, the possible importance of their lives. And two of them would very likely have been lying dead tonight, if he'd been a day later on the road, or even a few moments.

He ought to kneel and give thanks again, feel a sense of blessing and hope. And those things were there, truly, but they lay underneath something else, more undefined, a heaviness. He felt tired suddenly. The years could creep up on you, if a day lasted too long. He opened the letter again, the red, broken seal crumbling a little.

"Whereas it has for some time been our belief that it is the proper duty of an anointed king under Jad to pursue wisdom and teach virtue by example, as much as it is our task to strengthen and defend . . ."

With the lamps doused, there wasn't enough light to read by, particularly for a man no longer young, but he had this committed to memory and was communing with it more than actually considering the contents again, the way one might kneel before a familiar image of the god on one's own stone chapel wall. Or, the thought came to him, the way one might contemplate the name and stone-carved sun disk over a grave visited so many times it wasn't really *seen*, only apprehended, as one lingered one more time until twilight fell, and then the dark.

In the dark, from the corridor, she knocked softly then entered, taking the partially open door for the invitation it was.

"What?" said Enid, setting down the tall candle she carried. "Still dressed and not in the bed? I'd hoped you'd be waiting for me there."

He stood up, smiling. She came forward and they kissed, though she was kind enough to let it be a kiss of peace on each cheek, and not more than that. She wore some sort of perfume. He wasn't good at naming these woman-scents but it was immediately distracting. He was suddenly aware of the bed. She'd intended that, he knew. He knew her very well.

Enid looked at the wine cups and the wide-necked flask. "Did he leave any for me?"

"Not much, I fear. There may be some, and water to mix."

Enid shook her head. "I don't really need."

She took the seat her husband had so recently vacated to go out with whichever girl had been waiting for him. In the softer light she was a presence sitting near to him, a scent, a memory of other nights—and other kisses of peace when peace had not been what she'd left behind when she went away. His restraint, not hers, or even Brynn's, for these two had their own rules in this long marriage and Ceinion had, years ago, been made to understand that. His restraint. A woman very dear.

"You are tired," she said after a moment's scrutiny. "He gets the best of you, coming first, and then I arrive—always hoping—and find . . ."

"A man not worthy of you?"

"A man not susceptible to my diminishing charms. I'm getting old, Ceinion. I think my daughter fell in love tonight."

He took a breath. "I'll say, in sequence, no, and no, and . . . perhaps."

"Let me work that out." He could see she was amused. "You are finally yielding to me, I am not yet old in your sight, Rhiannon might be in love?"

There was something about Enid that always made him want to smile. "No, alas, and yes, indeed, and perhaps she is, but the young always are."

"And those of us not young? Ceinion, will you not kiss me? It has been a year and more."

He did hesitate a moment, for all the old reasons, but then he stood up and came forward to where she sat and kissed her full upon the lips as she lifted her head, and despite his genuine fatigue he was aware of the beating of his heart and the swift presence of desire. He stepped back. Read her mischievous expression an instant before she moved a hand and touched his sex through the robe.

He gasped, heard her laugh as she withdrew her touch.

"Only exploring, Ceinion. Fear me not. No matter what you say to be kind, there will come a night when I can't excite you any longer. One of these visits . . ."

"The night I die," he said, and meant it.

She stopped laughing, made the sign of the sun disk, averting evil.

Or trying to. They heard a cry from outdoors. Through the window, as he quickly turned, Ceinion saw the arc of a thrown and burning brand.

Then he saw horsemen in the farmyard and screaming began.

ALUN THOUGHT HE'D SEEN his brother this way before, if not *quite* like this. Dai was restless, irritable, and afraid. Gryffeth, staking out the left side of the just-wide-enough bed, made the mistake of complaining about Dai's pacing in the dark and received a blister-inducing torrent of profanity in return.

"That wasn't called for," Alun said.

Dai wheeled on him, and Alun, in the middle of the bed (having drawn the short straw), stared back at his brother's straining, rigid outline through the darkness. "Come to bed, get some sleep. She'll still be here in the morning."

"What are you talking about?" Dai demanded.

Gryffeth, unwisely, snorted with laughter. Dai took a step towards him. Alun actually thought his brother might strike their cousin. This anger was the part that wasn't quite as it had been before, whenever Dai had been preoccupied with a girl. That, and the fear.

"Doesn't matter," Alun said quickly. "Listen, if you can't sleep, there's sure to be dicing in the hall. Just don't take all the money and don't drink too much."

"Why are you telling me what to do?"

"So we can get some rest," Alun said mildly. "Go with Jad. Win something."

Dai hesitated, a taut form across the room. Then, with another flung, distracted curse, he jerked the door open and went out.

"Wait," Alun said quietly to Gryffeth. They waited, side by side in the bed.

The door swung open again.

Dai strode back in, crossed to his pack, grabbed his purse, and went back out.

"Now," said Alun, "you can call him an idiot."

"He's an idiot," Gryffeth said, with feeling, and turned over in bed.

Alun turned the other way, determined to try to sleep. It didn't happen. The tapping at their door—and the woman's voice from the corridor—came only moments later.

IT WAS OBVIOUS from Helda's expression, and her darting glances at Rhiannon, that she was concerned. Their young cousin had thrown herself on her bed as soon as the four of them had returned from the hall to her chambers. She lay there, still in the green, belted gown, an extravagance of light blazing in the two rooms (with Meredd away, forever now, among the Daughters of Jad, Rhiannon had claimed the adjoining chamber for the other three women). She looked, if truth were told, genuinely unwell: feverish, bright-eyed.

Without a word spoken the three had resolved to humour her, and so nothing had been said in opposition to her immediately voiced demand for all the lights to be lit, or the next request, either.

Rania had the purest voice, in chapel and banquet hall, and Eirin the best memory. They'd gone off to the other room together, murmuring, and now returned through the connecting doorway, Eirin smiling, Rania biting her lip, as she always did before singing.

"I won't do very well," she said. "We only heard it once."

"I know," Rhiannon said, unusually mild, her voice at odds with her look. "But try."

They had no harp here with them. Rania sang unaccompanied. It was well done, in truth, a different tone given by a woman's voice in a quiet (too-bright) room, late at night, as compared to the same song heard in the hall as the sun was going down, when the younger son of Owyn ap Glynn had given it to them:

The halls of Arberth are dark tonight,
No moons ride above.
I will sing a while and be done.

The night is a hidden stranger,
An enemy with a sword,
Beasts in field and wood.

The stars look down on owl and wolf,
All manner of living creature,
While men sleep safe behind their walls.

The halls of Arberth are dark tonight,
No moons ride above.
I will sing a while and be done.

The first star is a longed-for promise,
The deep night a waking dream,
Darkness is a net for the heart's desire.

The stars look down on lover and loved,
All manner of delight,
For some do not sleep in the night.

The riddle of the darkest hours
Has ever and always been thus,
And so it is we can say:

Needful as night's end,
Needful as night,
By the holy blessed god, they are both true.

The halls of Arberth are dark tonight,
No moons ride above.
I have sung a while and I am done.

Rania looked down shyly when she finished. Eirin
clapped her hands, beaming. Helda, older than the other
three, sat quietly, a faraway look on her face. Rhiannon
said, after a moment, "By the holy blessed god."

It was unclear whether she was echoing the song, or
speaking from the heart . . . or whether both of these
were true.

They looked at her.

"What is happening to me?" Rhiannon said, in a small
voice.

The others turned to Helda, who had been married
and widowed. She said, gently, "You want a man, and it
is consuming you. It passes, my dear. It really does."

"Do you think?" said Rhiannon.

And none of them would ever have matched this voice
to the tones of the one who normally controlled them
all—the three of them, her sisters, all the young women
of household and kin—the way her father commanded
his warband.

It might have been amusing, it *should* have been, but the change cut too deeply, and she looked disturbingly unwell.

"I'm going to get you wine." Eirin rose.

Rhiannon shook her head. Her green cap slipped off. "I don't need wine."

"Yes, you do," said Helda. "Go, Eirin."

"No," said the girl on the bed, again. "That isn't what I need."

"You can't *have* what you need," Helda said, walking over to the bed, amusement in her voice, after all. "Eirin, a better thought. Go to the kitchen and have them make an infusion, the one for when we can't sleep. We'll all have some." She smiled at the other three, ten years younger than she was. "Too many men in the house tonight."

"Is it too late? Could we have him come here?"

"What? The singer?" Helda lifted her eyebrows.

Rhiannon nodded, her eyes beseeching. It was astonishing. She was pleading, not giving a command.

Helda considered it. She wasn't sleepy at all, herself. "Not alone," she said finally. "With his brother and the other Cadyri."

"But I don't need the other two," Rhiannon said, a hint of herself again.

"You can't have what you need," Helda said again.

Rania took a candle and went for the infusion; Eirin, bolder, was sent to bring the three men. Rhiannon sat up in the bed, felt her own cheeks with the backs of her hands, then rose and went to the window and opened it—against all the best counsel—to let the breeze cool her, if only a little.

"Do I look all right?" she asked.

"It doesn't matter," said Helda, maddeningly.

"I feel faint."

"I know."

"I *never* feel this way."

"I know," said Helda. "It passes."

"Will they be here soon?"

ALUN DRESSED AT SPEED and went to find Dai in the banquet hall, leaving Gryffeth in the corridor with the girl and the candle. Neither of them seemed to mind. They *could* have gone to the women's rooms around the corner and waited there, but they didn't seem inclined to do that.

He carried his harp in its leather case. The woman had specifically said that the daughter of Brynn ap Hywll wanted the singer. The brown-haired girl, telling him this at the door, before Gryffeth got out of bed, had smiled, her eyes catching the candlelight she carried.

So Alun went to get Dai. Found him dicing at a table with two of their own friends and three of the ap Hywll men. He was relieved to see that Dai had a pile of coins in front of him already. His older brother was good at dice, decisive in betting and calculating, and with a wrist flick that let him land the bones—anyone's bones—on the short side more often than one might expect. If he was winning, as usual, it meant he might not be too badly disturbed after all.

Perhaps. One of the others noticed Alun in the doorway, nudged Dai. His brother glanced up, and Alun motioned him over. Dai hesitated, then saw the harp. He got up and came across the room. It was dark except for lamps on the two tables where men were awake and gaming. Most of those bedding down here were asleep by now, on pallets along the walls, the dogs among them.

"What is it?" Dai said. His tone was curt.

Alun kept his own voice light. "Hate to take you from winning money from Arberthi, but we've been invited to the Lady Rhiannon's rooms."

"What?"

"I wouldn't make that up."

Dai had gone rigid, Alun could see it even in the shadows.

"We? All of . . . ?"

"All three of us." He hesitated. Told truth, better here than there. "She, um, asked for the harp, I gather."

"Who said that?"

"The girl who fetched us."

A short silence. Someone laughed loudly at the dicing table. Someone else swore, one of the sleepers along the wall.

"Oh, Jad. Oh, holy Jad. Alun, *why* did you sing that song?" Dai asked, almost whispering.

"What?" said Alun, genuinely taken aback.

"If you hadn't . . ." Dai closed his eyes. "I don't suppose you could say you were sleepy, didn't want to get out of bed?"

Alun cleared his throat. "I could." He was finding this difficult.

Dai shook his head. Opened his eyes again. "No, you're already out of bed, carrying the harp. The girl saw you." He swore then, to himself, more like a prayer than an oath, not at Alun or anyone else, really.

Dai lifted both his hands and laid his fists on Alun's shoulders, the way he sometimes did. Lifted them up and brought them down, halfway between a blow and an embrace. He left them there a moment, then he took his hands away.

"You go," he said. "I don't think I am equal to this. I'm going outside."

"Dai?"

"Go," said his brother, at some limit of control, and turned away.

Alun watched him walk across the room, unbar the heavy front doors of Brynn ap Hywll's house, open one of them, and go out alone into the night.

Someone got up from the gaming table and barred the doors behind him. Alun saw one of their own band look over at him; he gestured, and their friend swept up Dai's purse and winnings for him. Alun turned away.

And in that moment he heard his older brother scream an urgent, desperate warning from the yard outside. The last word he ever heard him speak.

Then the hoofbeats of horses were out there, drumming the hard earth, and the war cries of the Erlings, and fire, as the night went wild.

CHAPTER III

S he is curious and too bold. Always has been, from first awakening under the mound. A lingering interest in the other world, less fear than the others, though iron's presence can drain her as easily as any of them.

Tonight there are more mortals than she can remember in the house north of the wood; the aura is inescapable. No moons to cast a shadow: she has come away to see. Passed a green *spruaugh* on the way, seethed at him to stop his chattering, knows he will go now, to tell the queen where she is. No matter, she tells herself. They are not forbidden to look.

The cattle are restless in their pen. First thing she knows, an awareness of that. The lights almost all doused in the house now; shining only in one chamber window, two, and in the big room beyond the heavy doors. Iron on the doors. Mortals sleep at night, fearfully.

She feels hooves on the earth, west of them.

Her own fear, before sight. Then riders leaping the fence, smashing through it into the farmyard below and fire is thrown and iron is drawn, is everywhere, sharp as death, heavy as death. She hasn't come for *this*, almost flees, to tell the queen, the others. Stays, up above, unseen flicker in the dark-leaved trees.

Brighter and lesser auras all around the farmyard. The doors bursting open, men running out, from house, from barn, iron to hand in the dark. A great deal of noise, screaming, though she can screen some of that away:

mortals too loud, always. They are fighting now. A feeling of hotness within her, dizziness, blood smell in the yard. She feels her hair changing colour. Has seen this before, but not here. Memories, long ago, trying to cross to where she is.

She feels ill, thinned by the iron below. Clings to a beech, draws sap-strength from that. Keeps watching, cold and shivering now, afraid. No moons, she tells herself again, no shadow or flicker of her to be seen, unless a mortal has knowledge of her world.

She watches a black horse rear, strike a running man with hooves, sees him fall. There is fire, one of the outbuildings ablaze now. A confusion of dark and roiling mortal forms. Smoke. Too much blood, too much iron.

Then something else comes to her. And on the thought—quick and bright as a firefly over water—between her shoulders, where they all had wings once, she feels a spasm, a trembling of excitement, like desire. She shivers again, but differently. She spies out more closely: the living and the dead in the chaos of that farmyard below. And yes. Yes.

She knows who died first. She can tell.

He is face down on the churned, trampled earth. First dead of a moonless night. Could be *theirs,* if she moves quickly enough. Has to be fast, though, his soul fading already, very nearly gone, even as she watches. And such a long time since a mortal in his prime has come to them. To the queen. Her own place in the Ride forever changed if she can do this.

It means going down into that farmyard. Iron all around. Horses thundering, sensing her, afraid. Their hooves.

No moons. The only time this can be done. Nothing of her to be seen. Tells herself that, one more time.

None of them has wings any more or she could fly. She lets go of the tree, finger by finger, and goes forward and down. She sees someone on the way. He is hurrying up the slope, breathing hard. He never knows that she is there, a faerie passing by.

ೲ

He had to get to his sword. Dai screamed a warning, and then he did it again. Men sprang from pallets, roaring, seizing weapons. The double doors were thrust open, the first of their people hurtling into the night. Alun heard the cries of the Erlings, Brynn's warband shouting in reply, saw their own men from Cadyr rushing out. But his own room, and his sword, were back along the corridor the other way. Terribly, the other way.

Alun ran for all he was worth, heart pounding, his brother's voice in his ears, a fist of fear squeezing his heart.

When he got to the room, Gryffeth—who knew battle sounds as well as any of them—had already claimed his own blade and leather helm. He came forward, handed Alun his, wordlessly. Alun dropped the harp where they were; he unsheathed the sword, dropped the scabbard, too, pushed the helmet down on his head.

The woman with Gryffeth was not wordless, and was terrified.

"Dear Jad! There are no guards where we are. Come! *Hurry!*"

Alun and Gryffeth looked at each other. Nothing to be said. The heart could crack. They ran the other way, farther down the same dark hallway, the brown-haired girl beside them, her hand somehow in Alun's, candle fallen away. Then north, skidding at the hall's turning, up the far wing to the women's rooms.

Away from the double doors, from the fighting in the farmyard. From Dai.

The girl pointed, breathing in gasps. They burst in. A woman screamed, then saw it was them. Covered her mouth with the back of a hand, backing up against a table. Alun took a fast look, sword out. Three women here, one of them Brynn's daughter. Two rooms, a connecting door. He went straight across to the eastern window, which was, inexplicably, open. Moved to close the shutters, slide down the wooden bar.

The Erling hammer, descending, splintered wood, shattered the sill, barely missed breaking Alun's extended arm like so much kindling. A woman screamed. Alun stabbed through the wreckage of the window, blindly into the dark. Heard a grunt of pain. Someone shouted a high warning; he twisted hard, a wracking movement, back and away. Horse hooves loomed, thrust for the splintered window frame, smashed it in—and then a man hurtled through and into the room.

Gryffeth went for him, swearing, had his thrust taken by a round shield, barely dodged the axe blow that followed. The women pressed back, screaming. Alun stepped up beside his cousin—then had to wheel back the other way as a second man came roaring through the window, hammer in hand. They'd figured it out, where the women were. Erlings. Here. Nightmare on a moonless night; a night made for an attack.

But what were they doing so far inland? Why here? It made no sense. This was not where the raids came.

Alun swung at the second man, had his sword blocked, wrenchingly. He was bleeding from the splintered wood, so was the Erling. He stepped back, shielding the women. Heard a clattering noise, boots behind him, and then longed-for words.

"Drop weapons! There are two of you, five of us, more coming."

Alun threw a glance back, saw one of Brynn's captains, a man almost as big as the Erlings. *Jad be thanked for mercy,* he thought. The captain had spoken

Anglcyn, but slowly. It was close to the Erling tongue; he'd be understood.

"You may be ransomed," Brynn's man went on, "if someone cares enough for you. Touch the women and you die badly, and will wish you were dead before you are."

A mistake, those words, Alun later thought.

Because, hearing them, the first man moved, cat-quick in a crowded room, and he seized Rhiannon mer Brynn—whose warning had been the one that had drawn Alun back from the window—and wrenched her away from the others. The Erling gripped her in front of him as a shield, her arm behind her back, twisted high, his axe gripped short, held to her throat. Alun caught his breath on a curse.

One of the other women dropped to her knees. The room was crowded with men now, smell of sweat and blood, mud and muck from the yard. They could hear the fighting outside, dogs barking frantically, the cattle lowing and shifting in their pen. Someone cried out, and then stopped.

"Ransom, you say?" the Erling grunted. He was yellow-bearded, wearing armour. Eyes beneath a metal helmet, the long nosepiece. "No. Not so. You drop weapons now or this one's breast is cut off. You want to see? I don't know who she is, but clothing is fine. Shall I cut?"

Brynn's captain stepped forward.

"I said drop weapons!"

A silence, taut, straining. Alun's mouth was dry, as if full of ashes. Dai was outside. *Dai was outside.* Had been there alone.

"Let him do it," said Rhiannon, the daughter of Brynn ap Hywll. "Let him do it, then kill him for me."

"*No!* Hear me," Alun said quickly. "There are better than fifty fighting men here. You will not have so many for a raid. Your leader made a mistake. You are losing out there. Listen! There is nowhere for you to go. Choose your fate here."

"Chose it when we took ship," the man rasped. "Ingavin claims his warriors."

"And his warriors kill women?"

"Cyngael whores, they do."

One of the men behind Alun made a strangled sound. Rhiannon stood, the one arm twisted behind her back, the axe fretting at her throat. Fear in her eyes, Alun saw; none in her words.

"Then die for this Cyngael whore. Kill him, Siawn! Do it!"

The axe, gripped close to the blade, moved. A tear in the high-necked green gown, blood at her collarbone.

"Dearest Jad," said the woman on her knees.

A heartbeat without movement, without breath. And then the other Erling, the second man in through the window, dropped his shield with a clatter.

"Leave her, Svein. I've been taken by them before."

"Be a woman for the Cyngael, if you want!" the man named Svein snarled. "Ingavin waits for me! *Drop weapons, or I cut her apart!*"

Alun, looking at pale, wild eyes, hearing battle madness in the voice, laid down his sword, slowly.

There was blood on the girl. He saw her staring back at him. He was thinking of Dai, outside, that shouted warning before the hooves and fire. No weapon at all. His heart was crying and there was a need to kill and he was trying to find a space within himself to pray.

"Do the same," he said to Gryffeth, without turning his head.

"Do not!" Rhiannon said, whispering it, but very clear.

Gryffeth looked at her and then at Alun, and then he dropped his blade.

"He will kill her," said Alun to the men behind him, not looking back. His eyes were on the girl's. "Let his fellows be defeated outside, and then we will settle with these two. They have nowhere on Jad's earth to go from here."

"Then he *will* kill her," said the man named Siawn, and he stepped forward, still with his sword. Death in his voice, and an old rage.

The axe moved again, another rip in the green, a second ribbon of blood against white skin. One of the women whimpered. Not the one being held, though she was biting her lip now.

They stayed like that, a moment as long as the one before Jad made the world. Then a hammer was thrown.

The yellow-bearded Erling was wearing his iron helmet or his head would have been pulped like a fruit by that blow. Even so, the sound of the impact was sickening at close range in a crowded room. The man crumpled like a child's doll stuffed with straw; dead before his body, disjointed and splayed, hit the floor. The axe fell, harmlessly.

It seemed to Alun that no one in the room breathed for several moments. Extreme violence could do that, he thought. This wasn't a battlefield. They were too close together. Such things should happen . . . outdoors, not in women's chambers.

The woman in whose chambers they were standing remained where she'd been held, motionless. The flying hammer had passed near enough to brush her hair. Both arms were at her sides now, and no one was holding an axe to her. Alun could see two streams of blood on her gown, the cuts at throat and collarbone. He watched her draw one slow breath. Her hands were shaking. No other sign. Death had touched her, and turned away. One might tremble a little.

He turned away, to the Erling who had thrown that hammer. Reddish beard streaked with grey; long hair spilling from the helmet bowl. Not a young man. His throw, the slightest bit awry, would have killed Brynn's daughter, crushing her skull. The man looked around at all of them, then held out empty hands.

"All men are fools," he said in Anglcyn. They could make it out. "The gods gave us little wisdom, some less than others. That man, Svein, angered me, I confess. We all go to our gods, one way or another. Little profit in hurrying there. He'd have killed the girl, and both of us. Foolish. I will not bring a great deal in ransom, but I do yield me, to you both and to the lady." He looked from Alun to Siawn behind him, and then to Rhiannon mer Brynn.

"Shall I kill him, my lady?" said Siawn grimly. You could hear the wish in him.

"Yes," said the brown-haired woman, still on her knees. The third woman, Alun saw, had just been sick, on the far side of the room.

"No," said Rhiannon. Her face was bone-white. She still hadn't moved. "He's yielded. Saved my life."

"And what do you think he would have done if there'd been more of them here?" the man named Siawn asked harshly. "Or fewer of us in the house tonight, by Jad's mercy? Do you think you'd still be clothed, and standing?" Alun had had the same thought.

They were speaking Cyngael. The Erling looked from one of them to the other, then he chuckled, and answered in their own language, heavily accented. He had been raiding here before; he'd said as much.

"She would have been claimed by Mikkel, who is the only reason we are so far from the ships. Or by his brother, which would have been worse. They'd have stripped her and taken her, in front of all of us, I imagine." He looked at Alun. "Then they'd have found a bad way to kill her."

"Why? Why that? She's . . . just a woman." Alun needed to leave, but also needed to understand. And another part of him was afraid to go. The world, his life, might change forever when he went outside. As long as he was here, in this room . . .

"This is the house of Brynn ap Hywll," said the Erling. "Our guide told us that."

"And so?" Alun asked. They'd had a guide. He registered that. Knew the Arberthi would, as well.

Rhiannon was breathing carefully, he saw. Not looking at anyone. Had never once screamed, he thought, only that one warning to him, when the horse smashed the window.

The Erling took off his iron helmet. His red hair was plastered to his skull, hung limply to his shoulders. He had a battered, broken-nosed face. "Mikkel Ragnarson leads this raid, with his brother. One purpose only, though I did try to change his mind for those of us who came for our own sakes, not his. He is the son of Ragnar Siggurson, and grandson of Siggur, the one we named the Volgan. This is vengeance."

"*Oh, Jad!*" cried the man named Siawn. "Oh, Jad and all the Blessed Victims! Brynn was outside when they came! Let's go!"

Alun had already picked up his sword, had turned, twisted through the others, was flying as fast as he could down the corridor for the double doors. Siawn's desperate cry came from behind him.

Brynn ap Hywll hadn't been the only one outside.

He hadn't killed anyone yet, the thought came. A need was rising, with his terror.

TERROR WENT AWAY like smoke on a wind as soon as he was out through the doors and saw what there was to see. Its passing left behind a kind of hollowness: a space not yet filled by anything. He had been quite certain, in fact, from the moment he'd heard Dai's first cry, but there was knowing, and knowing.

The attack was over. There hadn't been enough of the Erlings to cope with Brynn's warband here and their own Cadyri, even with the element of surprise. It was obviously to have been a raid on an isolated farmhouse—a large, specifically chosen farmhouse, but even so, this had been meant to kill Brynn ap Hywll, not meet his gathered force. Someone had erred, or had very bad luck. He'd said that himself, inside. Before he'd come running out into the yard to see the body lying here not far from the open doors. Not far at all.

He stopped running. Others were moving, all around him. They seemed oddly distant, vague, blurred somehow. He stood very still, and then, with an effort that took a great deal out of him, as though his body had become extremely heavy, Alun went forward again.

Dai hadn't had anything but the knife in his belt when he'd gone out, but there was an Erling sword in his hand now. He was face down in the grass and mud, a dead raider beside him. Alun went over to that place, where he lay, and he knelt in the mud and put down his own blade, and took off his helmet and set it down, and then, after another moment, he turned his brother over and looked at him.

Not cheap, the selling of his life, the "Lament for Seisyth" went. The one the bards sang, at one point or another, in the halls of all three provinces during those winter nights when men longed for spring's quickening and the blood and souls of the younger ones quickened at the thought of bright, known deeds.

The axe blow that killed Dai had fallen from behind and above, from horseback. Alun saw that by the light of the torches moving through the yard now. His blood and soul did not quicken. He held a maimed body, terribly loved. The soul was . . . elsewhere. He ought to pray now, Alun thought, offer the known, proper words. He couldn't even remember them. He felt old, weighted by grief, the need to weep.

But not yet. It was not over yet. He heard shouting still. There was an armed Erling in the yard some distance away, his back to the door of one of the outbuildings, holding a sword to a nearly naked figure in a half-ring made by the Arberthi warband and Alun's own companions.

Still on his knees, his brother's head in his lap now, blood soaking into his leggings and tunic, Alun saw that the captive figure was Brynn ap Hywll, being held—in the most savage irony he could imagine—exactly as his daughter had been, moments before.

The clerics taught in chapel (and text, for those who could read) that Jad of the Sun did battle in the night under the world for his children, that he was not cruel or capricious as the gods of the pagans were, making sport of mortal men.

You would not have known it tonight.

Riderless horses moving in the yard among the dead; servants running after them, taking their reins. Wounded men crying. The flames seemed to have been put out except for one shed, burning down at the other end of the farmyard, nothing near it to be claimed by fire.

There had been more than fifty fighting men sleeping here tonight, with weapons and armour. The northmen could not have known or expected that, not in a farm-house. Bad luck for them.

The Erlings had fled or were taken, or were dead. Except one of them held Brynn now, with nowhere to go. Alun wasn't sure what he wanted to do, but he was about to do something.

You go. I don't think I am equal to this. Not the voice, the brother, he'd known all his life. And for a very last word, a command, torn from him: *Go!*

Sending Alun away, at the end. And how could that be their last shared moment in the god's world? In a life Alun had lived with his brother from the time he was born?

He set Dai's head gently down and rose from the mud and started over towards that torchlit half-circle of men. Someone was speaking; he was too far away yet to hear. He saw that Siawn and Gryffeth and the others had come out now, the big, red-bearded Erling gripped between two of them. He looked over at his cousin, and then away: Gryffeth had seen him kneeling beside Dai, so he knew. He was using his sword for support, point down in the earth, looked as if he wanted to sink into the dark, trampled grass. They had grown up together, the three of them, from childhood. Not so long ago.

Rhiannon mer Brynn was in the yard as well now, beside her mother, who was standing straight as a Rhodian marble column, not far from the arc of men, gazing at her captive husband through the smoke and flames.

HE SAW OWYN'S YOUNGER SON—Owyn's *only* son now, a sorrow under Jad—moving too quickly towards the other men, sword in hand, and he understood what was working in him. It could be like a poison, grief. Ceinion went forward swiftly, at an angle, to intercept him. A necessary life was still in the balance. It was too dark to read faces, but you could sometimes tell a man's intention from the way he moved. There was death around them in the farmyard, and death in the way the young Cadyri prince was going forward.

Ceinion spoke, almost running, calling his name. Alun kept going. Ceinion had to catch him, lay a hand on the young man's arm—and received a look that chilled him, for his pains.

"Remember who you are!" the cleric snapped, deliberately cold. "And what is happening here."

"I know what happened here," said the boy—he was still something of that, though his father's heir as of tonight. And there were ripples that might flow from that, for all of them. Princes mattered, under Jad.

"It is still happening. Wait, and pray. That man with the sword is the Volgan's grandson."

"I thought as much," said Alun ab Owyn, a bleakness in his voice that was a sorrow of its own to the cleric hearing it. "We learned he was leading them, inside." He drew a breath. "I need to kill him, my lord."

There were things you were supposed to say to that, in the teachings, and he knew what they were, he had even written some of them. What Ceinion of Llywerth, high cleric of the Cyngael, anchor and emblem of his people's faith in Jad, murmured amid the orange flickering of torches and the black smoke was: "Not yet, my dear. You can't kill him yet. Soon, I hope."

Alun looked at him, and after a stiff moment nodded his head, once. They went forward together into that half-circle of men and were in time to see what happened there.

࿓

The taken-away sword had struck the tumbled raider first, but a second Erling's axe from behind and above had killed the Cyngael sooner.

She crouches by the fence until those first two bodies are left alone again—the one who knelt beside one of them standing and walking away—and then, not allowing any time for fear to take hold of her, she goes straight in, at speed, and claims a soul for the queen.

A moonless night. *Only* on a moonless night.

Once it was otherwise and easier, but once, also, they were able to fly. She lays hands on the body, and speaks the words they are all taught, says them for the first time, and—*yes, there!*—she sees his soul rise from blood and earth to her summoning.

It hovers, turning, drifting, in a stray breath of wind. She exults fiercely, aroused, her hair changing colour, again and then again, body tingling with excitement, even amid the fear of shod hooves and the presence of iron, which is weakening and can kill her.

She watches the soul she's claimed for the Ride float above the sprawled, slain mortal body and she sees it turn to go, uncertain, insubstantial, not entirely *present* yet in her world, though that will come, it will come. She didn't expect to feel so much desire. This isn't hers, though, this is for the queen.

He turns completely around in the air, moves upwards, then comes slowly back down, touches ground, already gathering form again. He looks towards her, sees, doesn't see—not quite yet—and then to the south he turns and begins to go, pulled towards the wood . . . as if to a half-remembered home.

He will reach them in the forest soon, taking surer, stronger form as he goes, a shape in *their* world now, and the queen will see him when he arrives, and will love him, as a precious gift, shining by water and wood and in the mound. And she herself, when she rejoins the others, will be touched by the glory of doing this as silver moonlight touches and lights pools in the night.

No moons tonight. A gift she has been given, this mortal death in the dark, and so beautiful.

She looks around, sees no one near, goes out then from that farmyard, from iron and mortals, living and dead, springing over the fence, up the slope, stronger as she leaves blades and armour behind. She pauses at the crest of the ridge to look back down. She always looks when near to them. Drawn to this other, mortal half of the world. It happens among the Ride, she isn't the only one. There are stories told.

The auras below are brighter than torches for her: anger, grief, fear. She finds all of these, takes them in, tries to distill them and comprehend. She looks down from the same beech tree as before, fingers upon it, as before. Two very big men in the midst of a ring; one holding iron to the other, who came bursting out of the small structure, roaring for a weapon. It frightened her, the red heat in that voice. But he was seen by the raider before his own men could reach him, and pinned by a sword to the wall. Not killed. She was not sure why, at first, but now she sees. Or thinks she does: other men arrive, freeze like carvings, then more come, gather, and are there now, like stone, torchlight around two men.

One of the two is afraid, but not the one she would have thought. She doesn't understand mortals well at all. Another world, they live in.

It is quiet now, the battle over except for this, and one other thing they will not know, down below. She listens. Has always liked to listen, and watch. Trying to understand.

"Understand me," the Erling said again, in his own tongue. "I kill him if anyone moves!"

"Then do it!" snapped Brynn ap Hywll. He was barefoot in the grass, only a grey undertunic covering his belly and heavy thighs. Another man would have looked ridiculous, Ceinion thought. Not Brynn, even with a sword to him and the Erling's left hand bunching his tunic tightly from behind.

"I want a horse and an oath to your god that I will be allowed passage to our ships. Swear it or he dies!" The voice was high, almost shrill.

"One horse? Pah! A dozen men you led are standing here! You stain the earth with your breathing." Brynn was quivering with rage.

"Twelve horses! I want twelve horses! Or he dies!"

Brynn roared again. "No one swear that oath! No one *dare!*"

"I *will* kill him!" the Erling screamed. His hands were shaking, Ceinion saw. "I am the grandson of Siggur Volganson!"

"Then do it!" Brynn howled back. "You castrate coward! Do it!"

"No!" said Ceinion. He stepped forward into the ring of light. "No! My friend, be silent, in Jad's name. You do not have permission to leave us!"

"Ceinion! Don't swear that oath! Do not!"

"I *will* swear it. You are needed."

"He won't do it. He's a coward. Kill me and die with me, Erling! Go to your gods. Your grandfather would have gutted me like a fish by now! He'd have ripped me open." There was a white-hot, spitting fury in his voice, near to madness.

"You killed him!" the Erling snarled.

"I did! *I did!* I chopped off his arms and cut his chest open and ate his bloody heart and laughed! So carve me now and let them do the same to you!"

Ceinion closed his eyes. Opened them. "This must not be. Erling, hear me! I am high cleric of the Cyngael. *Hear me!* I swear by holiest Jad of the Sun—"

"No!" roared Brynn. "Ceinion, I forbid—"

"—that no harm will come to you when you release—"

"*No!*"

"—this man, and that you will be allowed—"

The small door to the outbuilding—it was the brewhouse—banged open, right behind the two men. The Erling startled like a nervous horse, looked frantically back over his shoulder, swore.

Died. Brynn ap Hywll, in the moment his captor half turned, hammered an elbow viciously backwards and up into the other man's unprotected face beneath the nosepiece, smashing his mouth open. He twisted hard away from the sword thrust that followed. It raked blood from his side, no more than that. He stepped back quickly, turned . . .

"*Here!*"

Ceinion saw a sword arcing through the torchlight. Something beautiful in that flight, something terrible. Alun ab Owyn's blade was caught by Brynn at the hilt. Ceinion saw his old friend smile then, a grey wolf in winter, at the Cadyri prince who had thrown it. *I ate his heart.*

He hadn't. Might have done, though, the way he'd been that day. Ceinion remembered that fight—against this one's grandfather. A meeting of giants, crashing together on a blood-slick morning battlefield by the sea. In battle this fury happened to Brynn, the way it did to the Erlings of Ingavin's bear cult: a madness of war, claiming a soul. *If you became what you fought, what were you?* Not the night for that thought. Not here, good men dead in the dark farmyard.

"He swore an oath!" the Erling bubbled, spitting teeth. Blood in the broken mouth.

"Jad curse you," said Brynn. "My people died here. And my guests. Rot your ugly soul!" He moved, barefoot, half-naked. The Cadyri blade in his hand flicked right. The Erling moved to block it. The younger man wore armour, was big, rangy, in his prime.

Had been. The annihilating backhand blow swept down like a falling of rocks from a mountain height, crashing through his late parry, biting so deeply into his neck between helmet and breastplate that Brynn had to plant a foot on the fallen man, after, to lever and jerk it out.

He stood back, looked around slowly, flexing his neck and shoulder muscles, a bear in a circle of fire. No one moved, or said a word. Brynn shook his head, as if to clear it, to release fury, come back to himself. He turned to the door of the brewhouse. A girl stood there, in an unbelted tunic, flushing in the torchlight, her dark hair loose, for bed. For being bedded. Brynn looked at her.

"That was bravely done," he said, quietly. "Let all men know it."

She bit at her lower lip, was trembling. Ceinion was careful not to look to where Enid stood beside her daughter. Brynn turned around, took a step towards him, then another. Stopped squarely in front of the cleric, feet planted wide on his own soil.

"I'd never have forgiven you," he said, after a moment.

Ceinion met that gaze. "You'd have been alive to not forgive me. I spoke truth: you do not have leave to go from us. You are needed still."

Brynn was breathing hard, the coursing rage not yet gone from him, the big chest heaving, not from exertion but from the force of his anger. He looked at the young Cadyri behind Ceinion. Gestured with the blade.

"I thank you for this," he said. "You were quicker than my own men."

Owyn's son said, "No thanks need be. At least my sword is blooded, though by another. I did nothing at all tonight but play a harp."

Brynn looked down at him a moment from his great height. He was bleeding from the right side, Ceinion saw, the tunic ripped open there; he didn't seem aware of it. Brynn glanced away into the shadows of the farmyard, west of them. The cattle were still lowing on the other side in their pen. "Your brother's dead?"

Alun nodded his head, stiffly.

"Shame upon my life," said Brynn ap Hywll. "This was a guest in my house."

Alun made no reply. His own breathing was shallow, by contrast, constricted. Ceinion thought that he needed to be given wine, urgently. Oblivion for a night. Prayer could come after, in the morning with the god's light.

Brynn bent down, wiped both sides of the blade on the black grass, handed it back to Alun. He turned towards the brewhouse. "I need clothing," he said. "All of you, we will deal with . . ."

He stopped, seeing his wife in front of him.

"We will deal with the dead, and do what we can for the wounded," Enid said crisply. "There will be ale for the living, who were so valiant here." She looked over her shoulder. "Rhiannon, have the kitchen heat water and prepare cloths for wounds. Fetch all my herbs and medications, you know where they are. All of the women are to come to the hall." She turned back to her husband. "And you, my lord, will apologize tonight and tomorrow and the next day to Kara, here. You likely gave her the fright of a young life, more than any Erling would have, when she came to fetch ale for those still dicing and found you sleeping in the brewhouse. If you want a night's sleep outside the doors, my lord, choose another place next time, if we have guests?"

Ceinion loved her even more, then, than he had before.

Not the only one, he saw. Brynn bent down and kissed his wife on the cheek. "We hear and obey you, my lady," he said.

"You are bleeding like a fat, speared boar," she said. "Have yourself attended to."

"Am I permitted the slight dignity of trousers and boots first?" he asked. "Please?" Someone laughed, a release of strain.

Someone else moved, very fast.

Siawn, a little tardy, cried out, following. But the red-bearded Erling had torn free of those holding him and, seizing a shield from one of them—not a sword— crashed through the ring around Brynn and his wife.

He turned away from them, looking up and south, raised the shield. Siawn hesitated, confused. Ceinion wheeled towards the slope and the trees. Saw nothing at all, in the black night.

Then he heard an arrow strike the lifted shield.

"There he goes!" said the Erling, speaking Cyngael very clearly.

He was pointing. Ceinion, whose eyes were good, saw nothing, but Alun ab Owyn shouted, "I see him. Same ridge we were on today! Heading down the other way."

"Don't touch the arrow!" Ceinion heard. He spun back. The big Erling, not a young man, grey in his hair and beard, set down the shield carefully. "Not even the shaft, mind."

"Poison?" It was Brynn.

"Always."

"You know who it was, then?"

"Ivarr, this one's brother." He jerked his head towards the one on the ground. "Black-souled from birth, and a coward."

"This one was brave?" Brynn snarled it.

"He was here with a sword," said the Erling. "The other one uses arrows, and poison."

"And Erlings should be *much* too brave to do that," Brynn said icily. "Can't rape a woman with a bow and arrow."

"Yes, you can," said the Erling quietly, meeting his gaze.

Brynn took a step towards him.

"He saved your life!" Ceinion said quickly. "Or Enid's."

"Buying his own," Brynn snapped.

The Erling actually laughed. "There's that," he said. "Trying to, at any rate. Ask someone what happened inside."

But before that could be done, they heard another sound. Drumming hooves. An Erling horse thundered through the yard, leaped the fence. Ceinion, seeing the rider, cried out after him, hopelessly.

Alun ab Owyn, pursuing a foe he was unlikely ever to see or find, disappeared almost immediately on the dark path that curved around the ridge.

"Siawn!" said Brynn. "Six men. Follow him!"

"A horse for me," cried Ceinion. "That is the heir of Cadyr, Brynn!"

"I know it is. He wants to kill someone."

"Or be killed," said the red-bearded Erling, watching with interest.

THE ARCHER HAD a considerable start and poison on his arrows. It was pitch black on the path among the trees. Alun had no knowledge of the Erling horse he'd seized and mounted, and the horse wouldn't know the woods at all.

He cleared the fence, landed, kicked the animal ahead. They pounded up the path. He had a sword, no helmet (on the ground, in mud, beside Dai), no torch, felt a degree of unconcern he couldn't ever remember in himself before. A branch over the path struck his left shoulder, rocked him in the saddle. He grunted with pain. He was doing something entirely mad, knew it.

He was also thinking as fast as he could. The archer would come out and down from the slope—almost certainly—at the place they had reached earlier today, with Ceinion. The Erling was fleeing, would have a horse waiting for him. Would anticipate pursuit and head back into the trees, not straight along the path to the main trail west.

Alun lashed the horse around a curve. He was going too fast. It was entirely possible that a stump or boulder would break the animal's leg, send Alun flying, crack his neck. He flattened himself over the mane and felt the wind of another branch pass over his head. There was a body behind him, on the churned-up earth of a farmyard far from home. He thought of his mother and father. Another blackness there, darker than this night. He rode.

The only good thing about the moonless sky was that the archer would have trouble finding his way, too—and seeing Alun clearly, if he came close enough for a bowshot. Alun reached the forking trail where the slope came out on the path south-west. Remembered, only this afternoon, climbing up with Dai and then both of them coming down with the high cleric.

He drew a breath and left the path right there, not hesitating, plunging into the woods.

It was impossible, almost immediately. Swearing, he pulled the horse to a stop and listened in blackness. Heard—blessed be Jad—a sound through leaves, not far ahead. It could be an animal. He didn't think it was. He twitched the reins, moved the horse forward, carefully now, picking his way, sword out. A semblance of a trail, no more than that. His eyes were adjusting but there was no light at all. An arrow would kill him, easily.

He dismounted on that thought. Looped the reins around a tree trunk. His hair was slick with sweat. He heard sounds again—something ahead of him. It wasn't an animal. Someone unused to being silent in a forest, an unknown wood, far from the sea, amid the terror of pursuit, a raid having gone entirely wrong. Alun gripped his sword and followed.

He came upon the four Erlings too quickly, before he was ready for them, stumbling through beech trees into a sudden, small space, seeing them there, shadows—two kneeling to catch their breath, one slumped against a tree, the fourth directly in front of him, facing the other way.

Alun killed that one from behind, kept moving, slashed away the sword of the one leaning by the tree, gripped him and turned him with an arm twisted behind his back, snarled, "Drop blades, both of you!" to the kneeling pair.

A triad, he thought suddenly, remembering Rhiannon held, then Brynn. *Third time tonight*. The thought was urgent, sword-swift.

He remembered what had happened to the other two men who had held their captives this way, and even as the thought came he broke the pattern. He killed the man he was using as a shield, pushing him hard away to fall on the earth, and he stood alone to face two Erlings in a clearing in a wood.

He had never actually killed before. Two now, in moments.

"Come on!" he screamed at the pair before him. Both bigger than him, hardened sea-raiders. He saw the nearer one's head jerk suddenly, looking past Alun, and without any actual thought Alun dove to his right. The arrow from behind flew past him and hit the Erling in the sword arm.

"*Ivarr, no!*" the man screamed.

Alun rolled, scrambled up, turned his back on the two of them, sprinting immediately east into the thicket where the bowman would be. He heard him running through to the other side, then mounting up. The horse was there!

He wheeled back, running hard, swearing savagely. The fourth of those he'd surprised here was running the

other way, towards the path. The wounded man was on
his knees, clutching the arrow in his arm, making small,
queer sounds. He was as good as dead, they both knew
it: poison on the arrowhead, the shaft. Alun ignored him,
pushed through to his horse, clawed free the reins,
mounted, forced his way back through the trees and then
the clearing again to the other side. He could still hear
the archer's horse ahead of them, that rider swearing too,
fighting to find a path through in thick, treed blackness.
He felt a surging in his blood, fury and hardness and
pain. His sword was red, his own doing this time. It
didn't help. It didn't help.

He broke through, the horse thrashing into open space,
saw water, a pool in the wood, the other rider going
around it to the south. Alun roared wordlessly; galloped
the Erling horse into the shallow water, splashing through
at an angle to shorten the way, cut off the other man.

He was almost thrown over the animal's head as it
halted, stiff-legged.

It reared straight back up, neighing, clawing at the air
in terror, and then it came down and did not move at all,
as if anchored so firmly it might never stir again.

The entirely unexpected will elicit very different
responses in people, and the sudden intrusion of the
numinous—the vision utterly outside one's range of
experience—will exaggerate this, of course. One person
will be terrified into denial, another will shiver in delight
at a making manifest of dreams held close for a lifetime.
A third might assume himself intoxicated or bewitched.
Those who ground their lives in a firm set of beliefs about
the nature of the world are particularly vulnerable to such
moments, though not without exception.

Someone who—like Owyn's younger son that night—
had already had his life broken into shards, who was
exposed and raw as a wound, might be said to have been

ready for confirmation that he'd never properly understood the world. We are not constant, in our lives, or our responses to our lives. There are moments when this becomes clear.

Alun's foot came out of one stirrup when the horse reared. He clutched at the animal's neck, fought to stay in the saddle, barely did so as the hooves splashed down hard. His sword fell into the shallow water. He swore again, tried to make the horse move, could not. He heard music. Turned his head.

Saw a growing, inexplicable presence of light, pale as moonrise, but there were no moons tonight. Then, as the music grew louder, approaching, Alun ab Owyn saw what was passing by him, walking and riding on the surface of that water, in bright procession, the light a shimmering, around them and in them. And everything about the night and the world changed then, was silvered, because they were faeries and he could *see* them.

He closed his eyes, opened them again. They were still there. His heart was pounding, as if trying to break free of his breast. He was trammelled, entangled as in nets, between the desperate need to flee from the unholy Jad-cursed demons these must be—by all the teachings of his faith—and the impulse to dismount and kneel in the water of this starlit pool before the very tall, slender figure he saw on an open litter, borne in the midst of the dancing of them all, with her pale garments and nearly white skin and her hair that kept changing its colour in the silvered light that grew brighter as they passed, the music louder now, wild as his heart's beating. There was a constriction in his chest, he had to remind himself to breathe.

If these were evil spirits, iron would keep them at bay, so the old tales promised. He'd dropped his sword in the water. It occurred to him that he ought to make the sign of the sun disk, and with that thought he realized that he couldn't.

He couldn't move. His hands on the horse's reins, the horse rooted in the shallows of the pool, the two of them breathing statues watching what was passing by. And in that growing, spirit-shaped brightness in the depths of a moonless wood at night, Alun saw— for the first time— that the saddle cloth of the Erling horse he rode bore the pagan hammer symbol of Ingavin.

And then, looking at that queen again—for who else could this possibly be, borne across still waters, shining, beautiful as hope or memory?—Alun saw someone next to her, riding a small, high-stepping mare with bells and bright ribbons in its mane, and there came a harder pounding, like a killing hammer against his wounded heart.

He opened his mouth—he could do that—and he began to shout against the music, struggling more and more wildly to move arms or legs, to dismount, to *go* there. He was unable to do anything at all, couldn't stir from where he and the horse were rooted, as his brother rode past him, changed utterly and not changed at all, dead in the farmyard below them, and riding across night waters here, not seeing Alun, or hearing him, one hand extended, and claimed, laced in the long white fingers of the faerie queen.

SIAWN AND HIS MEN knew exactly where they were going, heading up the slope. They also had torches. Ceinion, though he preferred to walk, had been riding all his life. They came to the place where the trail from the ridge met the path, stopped there, the horses stamping. The cleric, though much the oldest, was the first to hear sounds. Pointed into the woods. Siawn led them there, cutting a little north of where Alun had tried to force his way through. There were nine of them. The other young Cadyri, Gryffeth ap Ludh, had joined them, fighting sorrow. They found the two dead Erlings and a dying one almost immediately.

Siawn leaned over in his saddle and killed the wounded man with his sword. He'd needed to do that, Ceinion thought: Brynn's captain had come into the yard too late, after the fighting was done. The cleric said nothing. There were teachings against this, but this wood tonight was not the place for them.

By the light of their smoking torches they saw signs of passage through the far side of that small glade. They went straight through and out the other side, and so came to the wider clearing, the pool of water under stars. Stopped then, all of them, without words. It became very quiet, even the horses.

The man next to Ceinion made the sign of the sun disk. The cleric, a little belatedly, did the same. Pools in the wood, wells, oak groves, mounds . . . the half-world. The pagan places that had once been holy before the Cyngael had come to Jad, or the god had come to them in their valleys and hills.

These forest pools were his enemies, and Ceinion knew it. The first clerics, arriving from Batiara and Ferrieres, had chanted stern invocations, reading from the liturgy beside such waters as this, casting out all presence of false spirits and old magics. Or trying to. People might kneel today in stone chapels of the god and go straight from them to seek their future from a wise woman using mouse bones, or drop an offering in a well. Or into a pool by moonlight, or under stars.

"Let's go," Ceinion said. "This is just water, just a wood."

"No it isn't, my lord," said the man beside him, respectfully but firmly. The one who had made the sign.

"He's here. Look." And only then did Ceinion see the boy on his horse, motionless in the water, and understand.

"Dear Jad!" said one of the others. "He went into the pool."

"No moons," said another. "A moonless night—look at him."

"Do you hear music?" said Siawn abruptly. "Listen!"

"We do *not*," said Ceinion of Llywerth, fiercely, his heart beating fast now.

"Look at him," Siawn repeated. "He's trapped. Can't even move!" The horses were restive now, agitated by their riders, or by something else, tossing their heads.

"Of course he can move," said the cleric, and swung down from his mount and went forward, striding hard, a man used to woods and nights and swift, decisive movement.

"No!" cried a voice from behind him. "My lord, do not—"

That he ignored. There were souls here, to save and defend. His entrusted task for so long. He heard an owl cry, hunting. A normal sound, *proper* in a night wood. Part of the order of things. Men feared the unknown, and so the dark. Jad was Light in his being, an answer to demons and spirits, shelter for his children.

He spoke a swift prayer and went straight into the pool, splashing through the shallows, calling the young prince's name. The boy didn't even turn his head. Ceinion came up beside him, and in the darkness he saw that Alun ab Owyn's mouth was wide open, as though he was trying to speak—or shout. He caught his breath.

And then, terribly, there *was* the sound of music. Very faint it seemed to Ceinion, ahead of them and to the right. Horns and flutes, stringed instruments, bells, moving across the unrippled stillness of the water. He looked, saw nothing there. Ceinion spoke Jad's holy name. He signed the disk, and seized the reins of the Erling horse. It wouldn't move.

He didn't want the others to see him struggling with the animal. Their souls, their belief, were in danger here. He reached up with both arms and pulled Owyn's son, unresisting, from the saddle. He threw the young man over one shoulder and carried him, splashing and staggering, almost falling, out of the pool, and he laid him down on the dark grass at the water's edge. Then he knelt beside him, touched the disk about his throat, and prayed.

After a moment, Alun ab Owyn blinked. He shook his head. Drew a breath and then closed his eyes, which was a curious relief, because what Ceinion saw in his face, even in the darkness, was harrowing.

Eyes still closed, voice low, utterly uninflected, the young Cadyri said, "I saw him. My brother. There were faeries, and he was there."

"You did not," Ceinion said firmly, clearly. "You are grieving, my child, and in a strange place, and you have just killed someone, I believe. Your mind was overswayed. It happens, son of Owyn. I know it happens. We long for those we have lost, we see them . . . everywhere. Believe me, sunrise and the god will set you right on this."

"I saw him," Alun repeated.

No emphasis, the quiet more unsettling than fervour or insistence would have been. He opened his eyes, looking up at Ceinion.

"You know that is heresy, lad. I do not want—"

"I saw him."

Ceinion looked over his shoulder. The others had remained where they were, watching. Too far away to hear. The pool was still as glass. No wind in the glade. Nothing that could be taken for music now. He must have

imagined it himself; would never claim to be immune to
the strangeness of a place like this. And he had a memory
of his own, pushed hard away, always, of . . . another place
like this. He was aware of the shapes of power, the weight
of the past. He was a fallible man, always had been, struggling to be virtuous in times that made it hard.

He heard the owl again; far side of the water now.
Ceinion looked up, stars overhead in the bowl of sky
between trees.

The Erling horse shook its head, snorted loudly, and
walked placidly out of the pond by itself. It lowered its
head to crop the black grass beside them. Ceinion
watched it for a moment, the utter ordinariness. He
looked back at the boy, took a deep breath.

"Come, lad," he said. "Will you pray with me, at
Brynn's chapel?"

"Of course," said Alun ab Owyn, almost too calmly.
He sat up, and then stood, without aid. Then he walked
straight back into the pool.

Ceinion half lifted a hand in protest, then saw the boy
bend down and pick up a sword from the shallows. Alun
walked back out.

"They've gone, you see," he said.

They returned to the others, leading the Erling horse.
Two of Brynn's men made the sign of the disk as they
came up, eyeing the Cadyri prince warily. Gryffeth ap
Ludh dismounted and embraced his cousin. Alun returned
the gesture, briefly. Ceinion watched him, his brow knit.

"The two Cadyri and I will go back to Brynnfell," he
said.

"Two of them escaped from me," Alun said, looking
up at Siawn. "The one with the bow. Ivarr."

"We'll catch him," said Siawn, quietly.

"He went south, around the water," Owyn's son said,
pointing. "Probably double back west." He seemed

composed, grave even. Too much so, in fact. The cousin was weeping. Ceinion felt a needle of fear.

"We'll catch him," Siawn repeated, and cantered off, giving the pool a wide berth, his men following.

Certainty can be misplaced, even when there is fair cause for it. They didn't, in fact, catch him: a man on a good-enough horse, in darkness, which made tracking hard. Some days later, word would come to Brynnfell of two people killed, by arrows—a farm labourer and a young girl—in the thinly populated valley between them and the sea. Both the man and the girl had been blood-eagled, which was an abomination. Nor would anyone ever find the Erling ships moored, Jad alone knew where, along the wild and rocky coastline to the west. The god might indeed know, but he didn't always confide such things to his mortal children, doing what they could to serve him in a dark and savage world.

CHAPTER IV

Rhiannon had known since childhood (not yet so far behind her) that her father's importance did not emerge from court manners and courtly wit. Brynn ap Hywll had achieved power and renown by killing men: Anglcyn and Erling and, on more than one occasion, those from the provinces of Cadyr and Llywerth, in the (lengthy) intervals between (brief) truces among the Cyngael.

"Jad's a warrior," was his blunt response to a sequence of clerics who'd joined his household and then attempted to instill a gentler piety in the battle-scarred leader of the Hywll line.

Nonetheless, whatever she might have known from harp song and meadhall tale, his daughter had never seen her father kill until tonight. Until the moment when he had slashed a thrown and caught sword deep into the Erling who'd been trying to bargain his way to freedom.

It hadn't disturbed her, watching the man die.

That was a surprise. She had discovered it about herself: seeing the sword of Alun ab Owyn in her father's thick hands come down on the Erling. She wondered if it was a bad, even an impious thing that she didn't recoil from what she saw and heard: strangled, bubbling cry, blood bursting, a man falling like a sack.

It gave her, in truth, a measure of satisfaction. She knew that she ought properly to atone for that, in chapel. She had no intention of doing so. There were two gashes on her throat and neck from an Erling axe. There was blood on her body, and on her green gown. She had been expecting to die in her own chambers tonight. Had *told* Siawn and his men to let the Erling kill her. She could still hear herself speaking those words. Resolute then, she'd had to conceal shaking hands after.

Had, accordingly, little sympathy to spare for Erling raiders when they were slain, and that applied to the five her father ordered executed when it became evident they were not going to bring any ransom.

They were dispatched where they stood in the torch-lit yard. No words spoken, no ceremony, pause for prayer. Five living men, five dead men. In the time one might lift and drink a cup of wine. Brynn's men began walking around the yard with torches, killing those Erlings who lay on the ground, wounded, not yet dead. They had come to raid, take slaves, rape and kill, the way they always came.

A message needed to be sent, endlessly: the Cyngael might not worship gods of storm and sword, or believe in an afterworld of endless battle, but they could be— *some* of them could be—as bloody and as ruthless as an Erling when need was.

She was still outside when her father spoke to the older, red-bearded raider. Brynn walked up to the man, held again between two of their people, more tightly than before. He had broken free once—and saved Brynn from an arrow. Her father, Rhiannon realized, was dealing with a great anger because of that.

"How many of you were here?" Brynn bit off the words, speaking quietly. He was never quiet, she thought.

"Thirty, a few more." No hesitation. The man was almost as big as her father, Rhiannon saw. And of an age.

"As many left behind?"

"Forty, to guard the ships. Take them off the coast, if necessary."

"Two ships?"

"Three. We had some horses, to come inland."

Brynn had dressed by now, was holding his own sword, though there was no need for it. He began to pace as they spoke. The red-bearded Erling watched his movements, standing between two men. They were gripping his arms tightly, Rhiannon saw. She was certain her father was going to kill him.

"You rode straight for this farmhouse?"

"Yes, that was the idea. If we could find it."

"How *did* you find it?"

"Captured a shepherd."

"And he is?"

"Dead," said the Erling. "I can take you to him, if you want."

"You expected this house to be undefended?"

The man smiled a little, then, and shook his head. "Not defended by your warband, certainly. Young leaders. They made a mistake."

"You weren't one of them?"

The other man shook his head.

"The one who held me brought you here? Of the line of the Volgan?"

The Erling nodded.

"Elder grandson?" Brynn had stopped in front of him again.

"Younger. Ivarr's the elder."

"But he didn't lead."

The man shook his head. "Yes and no. It was his idea. But Ivarr's . . . different."

Brynn was stabbing his blade into the earth now.

"You came to burn this farm?"

"And kill you, and any of your family here, yes."

He was so calm, Rhiannon thought. Had he made his peace with dying? She didn't think that was it. He'd surrendered, said he didn't want to be killed, back in her chamber.

"Because of the grandfather?"

The man nodded. "Your killing him. Taking the sword. These two decided they were of an age to avenge it, since their father had not. They were wrong."

"And why are you here? You're as old as I am."

First hesitation. In the silence Rhiannon could hear the horses and the crackle of torches. "Nothing to keep me in Vinmark. I made a mistake, too."

Part of an answer, Rhiannon thought, listening closely.

Brynn was staring at him. "Coming, or before you came?"

Another pause. "Both."

"There's no ransom for you, is there."

"No," the man said frankly. "Once there might have been."

Brynn's gaze was steady. "Maybe. Were you ransomed last time you were taken here, or did you escape?"

Again, a silence. "Escaped," the Erling admitted.

He had decided, Rhiannon realized, that there was no hope in anything but honesty.

Brynn was nodding. "I thought so. I believe I remember you. The red hair. You *did* raid with Volganson, didn't you? You escaped east, twenty-five years ago, after he died. Through the hills. All the way to the Erling settlements on the east coast. They chased you, didn't they? You used a cleric as hostage, if I remember."

A murmur, from those listening.

"I did. I released him. He was a decent enough man."

Brynn's voice altered slightly.

"That was a long way to go."

"By Ingavin's blind eye, I wouldn't want to do it again," the Erling said dryly.

Another silence. Brynn resumed his pacing. "There's no ransom for you. What can you offer me?"

"A hammer, sworn loyalty."

"Until you escape again?"

"I said I wouldn't do it again, that journey. I was young then." He looked down and away for the first time, then back up. "I have nothing to go home to, and this place is as good as any for me to end my days. You can make me a slave, to dig ditches or carry water, or use me more wisely, but I will not escape again."

"You will take the oath and come to the faith of Jad?"

Another slight smile, torchlight upon him. "I did that last time."

Brynn didn't return the smile. "And recanted?"

"Last time. I was young. I'm not any more. Neither Ingavin nor your sun god are worth dying for, in my judgement. I suppose I am a heretic to two faiths. Kill me?"

Brynn was standing still again, in front of him.

"Where are the ships? You will guide us to them."

The Erling shook his head. "Not that."

Rhiannon saw her father's expression. He wasn't normally someone she feared.

"Yes that, Erling."

"This is the price of being allowed to live?"

"It is. You spoke of loyalty. Prove it."

The Erling was still a moment, considering. Torches moved in the yard around them. Men were being carried inside, or helped if they could walk.

"Best kill me then," the red-bearded man said.

"If I must," said Brynn.

"No," said someone else, stepping forward. "I will take him as a man of mine. My own guard."

Rhiannon turned, her mouth falling open.

"Let me be clear on this," her mother went on, coming to stand beside her husband, looking at the Erling. Rhiannon hadn't realized she was even with them. "I believe I understand. You would fight an Erling band that came upon us now, but will not reveal where your fellows are?"

The Erling looked at her. "Thank you, my lady," he said. "Certain things done for life make the life unworthy. You become sick with them. They poison you, your thoughts." He turned back to Brynn. "They were shipmates," he said.

Brynn's gaze held that of the Erling another moment, then he looked to his wife. "You trust him?"

Enid nodded her head.

He was still frowning. "He can easily be killed. I will do it myself."

"I know you will. You want to. Leave him to me. Let us get to our work. There are wounded men here. Erling, what is your name?"

"Whatever name you give me," the man said.

The Lady Enid swore. It was startling. "What is your name?" she repeated.

A last hesitation, then that wry expression again. "Forgive me. My mother named me Thorkell. I answer to it."

RHIANNON WATCHED the Erling go with her mother. He'd said before, in her rooms, that he could be ransomed. A lie, it now emerged. From the look of him—an old man still raiding—Helda had said she doubted it. Helda was older, knew more about these things. She was the calmest of them, too, had helped Rhiannon simply by being that way. They had almost died. They *could* have died tonight. The one named Thorkell had saved her father and herself, both.

Rhiannon, hands steady as she gathered linens and carried heated water with Helda for the wounded in the hall, remembered the wind of that hammer flying past her face. Realized—already—that she would likely do so all her life, carrying the memory like the two scars on her throat.

Tonight the world had altered, very greatly, because there was also the other thing, which ought to have been pushed away or buried deep or lost in all the bloodshed, but wasn't. Alun ab Owyn had ridden an Erling horse out of the yard, pursuing the archer who'd shot at her father. He hadn't yet come back.

Brynn ordered a pit to be dug in the morning, beyond the cattle pen, and the bodies of the slain raiders shovelled in. Their own dead—nine so far, including Dai ab Owyn—had been taken into the room attached to the chapel, to be cleansed and clothed, laid out for the rituals of burial. Woman's work after battle, when it could be done. Rhiannon had never performed these rites before. They had never been attacked at home before. Not in her lifetime. They didn't live near the sea.

They tended the wounded in the banquet hall, the dead in the room by the chapel, lights burning through Brynnfell. Her mother stopped by her once, long enough to look at her neck and then lay a salve—briskly, expressionlessly—and wrap the two wounds with a linen cloth.

"You won't die," she said, and moved on.

Rhiannon knew that. She would never now be sung for a pure white, swan-like neck, either. No matter. No matter at all. She carried on, following her mother. Enid knew what to do here, as in so many things.

Rhiannon helped, as best she could. Bathing and wrapping wounds, speaking comfort and praise, fetching ale with the servant girls for the thirsty. One man died on a table in their hall, as they watched. A sword had taken off most of one leg, at the thigh, they couldn't stop the bleeding. His name was Bregon. He'd liked fishing, teasing the girls, had freckles on his nose and cheeks in summer. Rhiannon found herself weeping, which she didn't want but couldn't seem to do much about. Not very long ago, when tonight had begun, there had been a feast, and music. If Jad had shaped the world differently, time could run backwards and make it so the Erlings had never come. She kept moving a hand, touching the cloth around her neck. She wanted to stop doing that, too, but couldn't.

Four men carried Bregon ap Moran from the hall on a table board, out the doors and across the yard to the room by the chapel where the dead men were. She looked at Helda and they followed. He used to make jokes about her hair, Rhiannon remembered, called her Crow when she was younger. Brynn's men had not been shy with his children, though that had changed when she came into womanhood, as did much else.

She would lay him out for burial—with Helda's help, for she didn't know what to do. There were half a dozen women in the room, working among the dead by lantern light. The cleric, Cefan, was kneeling with a sun disk between his hands, unsteadily intoning the ritual words of the Night Passage. He was young, visibly shaken. How could he not be, Rhiannon thought.

They set Bregon's board down on the floor. The tables were covered with other bodies already. There was water, and linen clothing. They had to wash the dead first, everywhere, comb out their hair and beards, clean their fingernails, that they might go to Jad fit to enter his halls if the god, in mercy, allowed. She knew every man lying here.

Helda began removing Bregon's tunic. It was stiff with blood. Rhiannon went to get a knife to help her cut

it away, but then she saw that there was no one by Dai ab
Owyn, and she went and stood over the Cadyri prince
where he lay.

Time didn't run backwards in the world they had.
Rhiannon looked down at him, and she knew it would be
a lie to pretend she hadn't seen him staring at her when
she'd walked into the hall, and another lie to say it was
the first time something of that sort had happened. And
a third one (a failing of the Cyngael, threes all the time?)
to deny that she'd enjoyed having that effect on men.
The passage from girl to woman being negotiated in
pleasure, an awareness of growing power.

No pleasure now, no power that meant anything at all.
She knelt beside him on the stone floor and reached out
and brushed his brown hair back. A handsome, clever
man. *Needful as night's end,* he had said. No ending to
night now, unless the god allowed it for his soul. She
looked at the wound in him, the dark blood clotted
there. It occurred to her that it was proper that Brynn's
daughter be the one to attend to a prince of Cadyr, their
guest. Cefan, not far away, was still chanting, his eyes
closed, his voice wavering away from him like the smoke
from the candles, rising up. The women whispered or
were silent, moving back and forth, doing their tasks.
Rhiannon swallowed hard, and began to undress the
dead man.

"*What are you doing?*"

She'd thought, actually, that she would know if he
came into a room; that already she would know when
that happened. She turned and looked up.

"My lord prince," she said. Rose and stood before
him. Saw the cousin, Gryffeth, and the high priest
behind, his face grave, uneasy.

"What are you doing?" Alun ab Owyn repeated. His
expression was rigid, walled off.

"I am . . . attending to his body, my lord. For . . . laying out?" She heard herself stammering. She never did that.

"Not you," he said flatly. "Someone else."

She swallowed. Had never lacked courage, even as a child. "Why so?" she said.

"You dare ask?" Behind, Ceinion made a small sound and a gesture, then stood still.

"I must ask," Rhiannon said. "I know of nothing I might ever have done to Owyn's house to cause this to be said. I grieve for our people, and for your sorrow."

He stared at her. It was difficult, in this light, to see his eyes, but she had seen them in the hall, before.

"Do you?" he said finally, blunt as a hammer. She couldn't stop thinking of hammers. "Do you even begin to grieve? My brother went outside alone and unarmed because of you. He died hating me because of you. I will live with that the rest of my days. Do you realize this? At all?"

There was something hot, like a fever, coming off him now. She said, desperately, "I believe I understand what you are saying. It is unjust. I didn't *make* him feel—"

"A lie! You wanted to make every man love you, to play at it. A game."

Her heart was pounding now. "You are . . . unjust, my lord." Repeating herself.

"Unjust? You tested that power every time you entered a room."

"How do you know any such thing?" How *did* he know?

"Will you deny it?"

She was grieving, her heart twisting, because of *who* it was, saying these words to her. But she was also Brynn's daughter, and Enid's, and not raised to yield, or to cry.

"And you?" she asked, lifting her head. Her bandage chafed. "You, my lord? Never tested yourself? Never went on . . . cattle raids, son of Owyn? Into Arberth, perhaps? Never had someone hurt, or die, when you did that? You *and* your brother?"

She saw him check, breathing hard. She was aware that he was, amazingly, near to striking her. How had the world come to this? The cousin stepped forward, as if to stop him.

"It is wrong!" was all Alun could manage to say, fighting for self-control.

"No more than the things a boy does, becoming a man. I cannot steal cattle or swing a sword, ab Owyn!"

"Then go east to Sarantium!" he rasped, his voice altered. "If you want to deal in power like that. Learn . . . learn how to poison like their empresses, you'll kill so many *more* men."

She felt the colour leave her face. The others in the room had stopped moving, were looking at them. "Do you . . . hate me so much, my lord?"

He didn't reply. She had thought, truly, he would say yes, had no idea what she'd have done if he did so. She swallowed hard. Needed her mother, suddenly. Enid was with the living, in the other room.

She said, "Would you wish the Erling hadn't thrown his hammer to save my life?" Her voice was level, hands steady at her sides. Small blessings, he wouldn't know how much this cost her. "Others died here, my lord prince. Nine of us now. Likely more, before sunrise. Men we knew and loved. Are you thinking only of your brother tonight? Like the Erling my father killed, who demanded one horse when he had men taken with him?"

His head snapped back, as from a blow. He opened his mouth, closed it without speaking. Their eyes locked. Then turning, blundering past the cleric and his cousin, he rushed from the room. Ceinion called his name. Alun never broke stride.

Rhiannon put a hand to her mouth. There was a need to weep, and a greater need not to do so. She saw the cousin, Gryffeth, take two steps towards the door, then stop and turn back. After a moment, he went and knelt beside the dead man. She saw him extend a hand and touch the place where the blade had gone in.

"Child," whispered the high cleric, her father's friend, her mother's.

She didn't look at him. She was staring, instead, at the open doorway. The emptiness of it, where someone had gone out. Had walked into the night, hating her—the way he'd said his brother had left him. A pattern? Set and sealed with iron and blood?

You can't have what you want, Helda had said, even before everything else.

"How did this happen?" she asked, of the cleric, of the world.

Holy men usually spoke of the mysterious ways of the god.

"I do not know," Ceinion of Llywerth murmured, instead.

"You're *supposed* to know," she said, turning to look at him. Heard her voice break. Hated that. He stepped forward, drew her into his arms. She let him, lowered her head. Didn't weep, at first, and then she did. Heard the cousin praying over the body on the floor beside them.

❦

Three things not well or wisely done, the triad went. *Approaching a forest pool by night. Making wrathful a woman of spirit. Drinking unwatered wine alone.*

They did things by threes in this land, Alun thought savagely. Obviously it was time for him to claim one of the wine jars and carry it off, drain it by himself until oblivion came down.

He wished in that moment, striding through the empty farmyard without the least idea where he meant to go, that the Erling arrow had killed him in the wood. The world was unassuageably awry. His heart had a hollow inside it where Dai had been. It was not going to fill; there was nothing to fill it with.

He saw a glimmering of light on the treed slope beyond the yard.

Not a torch. It was pale, motionless, no flickering.

He found himself breathing shallowly, as if he were hiding from searchers. He squeezed shut his eyes. The glow was still there when he opened them. There was no one else in the farmyard now. A spring night, the breeze mild, dawn a long way off still. The stars brilliant overhead, in patterns that told their stories of ancient glory and pain, figures from before the faith of Jad came north. Mortals and animals, gods and demigods. The night seemed heavy and endless, like something into which one fell.

A shining on the slope. Alun undid his belt, let fall his sword, walked through the gate of the yard and up the hill.

SHE SEES HIM drop the iron. Knows what that means. He can see her now. He has been in the pool with them. For some of them, after that, the faeries can be seen. Her impulse, very strong, is to flee. It is one thing to hover near, to watch them, unseen. This is something else.

She makes herself stay where she is, waiting. Has a sudden, fearful thought, scans with her mind's eye: the *spruaugh,* who might tell of this, is curled asleep in the hollow of a tree.

The man comes through the gate, closes it behind him, begins to climb the slope. He can *see* her. She almost does fly away then, though they can't really fly, not any more. She is trembling. Her hair shivers through its colours, again and again.

SHE WAS SMALLER than the queen, half a head smaller than he was. Alun stopped, just below where she stood. They were beside the thicket, on the mostly open slope. She'd been half hidden behind a sapling, came out when he stopped, but touching it. Utterly still, poised for flight. A faerie, standing before him in the world he'd thought he'd known.

She was slender, very long fingers, pale skin, wide-set eyes, a small face, though not a child's. She was clad in something green that left her arms free and showed her legs to the knee. A belt made of flowers, he saw. Flowers in her hair—which kept changing colour as he looked, dizzyingly. The wonder of that, even under stars. He could only see clearly by the light she cast. That, as much as anything, telling him how far he'd come, walking up from the farmyard. The half-world, they named it in the tales. Where he was now. Men were lost here, in the stories. Never came back, or returned a hundred years after they'd walked or ridden away, everyone they knew long dead. He could see her small breasts through the thinness of what she wore. Did they feel the cold, faeries?

There was an ache in his throat.

"How . . . how am I seeing you?" He had no idea if she could even speak, use words. His words.

Her hair went pale, nearly white, came back towards gold but not all the way. She said, "You were in the pool. I . . . saved you there." Her voice, simply speaking words, made him realize he had never, really, made music with his harp, or sung a song the way it should be sung. He felt that he would weep if he were not careful.

"How? Why?" He sounded harsh to his own ears, after her. A bruising of the starlit air.

"I stopped your horse, in the shallows. They would have killed you, had you come nearer the queen."

She'd answered one question, not the other. "My brother was there." It was difficult to speak.

"Your brother is dead. His soul is with the Ride."

"Why?"

Reddened hair now, crimson in summer dark. Her shining let him see. "I took it for the queen. First dead of the battle tonight."

Dai. No weapon, when he had gone out. First dead. Whatever that meant. But she was telling him. Alun knelt on the damp, cool grass. His legs were weak. "I should hate you," he whispered.

"I do not know what that means," she said. Music.

He thought about that, and then of the girl, Brynn's daughter, in that room by the chapel, where his brother's body lay. He wondered if he would ever play the harp again.

"What . . . why does the queen . . . ?"

Saw her smile, first time, a flashing of small, white teeth. "She loves them. They excite her. Those who have been mortals. From your world."

"Forever?"

The hair to violet. The slim, small body so white beneath the pale green garment. "What could be forever?"

That hollow, in his heart. "But after? What happens . . . to him?"

Grave as a cleric, as a wise child, as something so much older than he was. "They go from the Ride when she tires of them."

"Go where?"

So sweet a music in this voice. "I am not wise. I do not know. I have never asked."

"He'll be a ghost," Alun said then, with certainty, on his knees under stars. "A spirit, wandering alone, a soul lost."

"I do not know. Would not your sun god take him?"

He placed his hands on the night grass beside him. The coolness, the needed *ordinariness* of it. Jad was beneath the world now, they were taught; doing battle with demons for his children's sake. He echoed her, without her music. "I do not know. Tonight, I don't know anything. Why did you . . . save me in the pool?" The question she hadn't answered.

She moved her hands apart, a rippling, like water. "Why should you die?"

"But I am going to die."

"Would you rush to the dark?" she asked.

He said nothing. After a moment, she took a step nearer to him. He remained motionless, kneeling, saw her hand reach out. He closed his eyes just before she touched his face. He felt, almost overwhelmingly, the presence of desire. A need: to be taken from himself, from the world. To never come back? She had the scent of flowers all about her, in the night.

Eyes still closed, Alun said, "They tell us . . . they tell us there will be Light."

"Then there will be, for your brother," she said. "If that is so."

Her fingers moved, touched his hair. He could feel them trembling, and understood, only then, that she was as afraid, and as aroused as he was. Worlds that moved beside each other, never touched.

Almost never. He opened his mouth, but before he could speak again he felt a shockingly swift movement, an absence. Never said what he would have said, never *knew* what he would have said. He looked up quickly. She was already ten paces away. In no time at all. Standing against a sapling again, half turned, to fly farther. Her hair was dark, raven black.

He looked back over his shoulder. Someone was coming up the slope. He didn't feel surprise at all. It was as if the capacity to feel that had been drained from him, like blood.

He was still very young that night, Alun ab Owyn. The thought that actually came to him as he recognized who was climbing—and was gazing past him at the faerie—was that nothing would ever surprise him again.

Brynn ap Hywll crested the ridge and crouched, grunting with the effort, beside Alun on the grass. The big man plucked some blades of grass, keeping silent, looking at the shimmering figure by the tree not far away.

"How do you see her?" Alun asked, softly.

Brynn rubbed the grass between his huge palms. "I was in that pool, most of a lifetime ago, lad. A night when a girl refused me and I went walking my sorrow into the wood. Did an unwise thing. Girls can make you do that, actually."

"How did you know I . . . ?"

"One of the men Siawn sent to report. Said you killed two Erlings, and were mazed in the pond till Ceinion took you out."

"Does he . . . did Siawn . . . ?"

"No. My man just told me that much. Didn't understand any of it."

"But you did?"

"I did."

"You've . . . seen them all these years?"

"I've been *able* to. Hasn't happened often. They avoid us. This one . . . is different, is often here. I think it's the same one. I see her up here sometimes, when we're at Brynnfell."

"Never came up?"

Brynn looked over at him for the first time. "Afraid to," he said, simply.

"I don't think she'll hurt us."

The faerie was silent, still by the slender tree, still poised between lingering and flight, listening to them.

"She can hurt you by drawing you here," Brynn said. "It gets hard to come back. You know the tales as well as I do. I had . . . tasks in the world, lad. So do you, now."

Ceinion, down below, before: *You do not have leave to go from us.*

Alun looked at the other man in the darkness, thought about the burden in those words. A lifetime's worth. "You dropped your sword, to climb up here."

He saw Brynn smile then. A little ruefully, the big man said, "How could I let you be braver than me, lad?" He grunted again, and rose. "I'm too old and fat to crouch all night in the dark." He stood there, bulky against the sky.

The shimmering figure by the tree moved back, another half a dozen paces.

"Iron," she said, softly. "Still. It is . . . pain."

Brynn was motionless. He'd never have heard her, Alun realized. Not ever have known the music of this voice, through all the years. *Most of a lifetime ago.* He wondered at someone with the will to know of this, and not speak of it, and stay away.

"But I left my . . ." Brynn stopped. Swore, though quietly. Reached down into his boot and pulled free the knife that was hidden there. "My sorrow," he said. "It was not intended, spirit." He turned away, and stepping forward strongly, hurled the blade, arcing it through the night air, all the way down the hill and over the fence into the empty yard.

A very long throw. *I couldn't have done that,* Alun thought. He stared at the figure beside him: the man who'd killed the Volgan long ago, in the days when the Erlings were here every spring or summer, year after year. A harder, darker time, before Alun had been born, or Dai.

But if you were slain in a small, failed raid today, you were just as dead as if it had been back then at the hands of the Volgan's own host, weren't you? And your soul . . . ?

Brynn turned to him. "We should go," he said. "We must go."

Alun didn't move from where he knelt on the cool grass. *And your soul?*

He said, "She isn't supposed to exist, is she?"

"What man would say that?" Brynn said. "Were they fools, our ancestors who told of the faerie host? The glory and peril of them? Her kind have been here longer than we have. What the holy men teach is that they endanger our hope of Light."

"Is that what they teach?" Alun said.

Heard his own bitterness. Dark here, in the starry night, except for the light where she was.

He turned his head again, almost against his will, looked at her, still backed away from the tree. Her hair was pale again. Since the knife had gone, he thought. She hadn't come nearer, however. He thought of her fingers, touching him, the scent of flowers. He swallowed. He wanted to ask her again about Dai, but he did not. Kept silent.

"You know it is true, what they teach us," said Brynn ap Hywll. He was looking at Alun, not over at the figure that stood beyond the tree, shimmering, her hair the colour now of the eastern sky before the morning sun. "You can feel it, can you not? Even here? Come down, lad. We'll pray together. For your brother and my men, and for ourselves."

"You can . . . just walk away from this?" Alun said. He was looking at the faerie, who was looking back at him, not moving, not saying a word now.

"I have to," said the other man. "I have been doing it all my life. You will begin doing it now, for your soul's sake, and all the things to be done."

Alun heard something in the voice. Turned his head, looked up again. Brynn gazed back at him, steadily, a looming figure in the dark of the night. Thirty years with a sword, fighting. *The things to be done.* Had either of the moons been shining tonight—if the old tales told true— none of this would have happened.

Dai would still be dead, though. Among all the other dead. Brynn's daughter had challenged him with that, driven him out of doors because there was . . . no answer for her, and no release from this hollowness within.

Alun turned back to the faerie. Her wide-set eyes held his. Maybe, he thought, there was a release. He drew a slow breath and let it out. He stood up.

"Watch over him," he said. Not more than that. She would know.

She came forward a few steps, to the tree again. One hand on it, as if embracing, merging into it. Brynn turned his back and started resolutely down and Alun followed him, not looking back, knowing she was there, was watching him from the slope, from the other world.

When he reached the farmyard, Brynn had already reclaimed their swords. He handed Alun his, and his belt.

"I'll get my knife in the morning," ap Hywll said.

Alun shook his head. "I saw where it fell, I think." He walked across the yard. The lanterns inside did not cast their glow this far, only lit the windows, showing where people were, the presence of life among the dying and the dead. He found the knife almost immediately, though. Carried it back to Brynn, who stood for a moment, holding it, looking at Alun.

"Your brother was our guest," he said at length. "My sorrow is great, and for your mother and father."

Alun nodded his head. "My father is a . . . hard man. I believe you know it. Our mother . . ."

Their mother.

Let the light of the god be yours, my child,
Let it guide you through the world and home to me . . .

"My mother will want to die," he said.

"We live in a hard world," Brynn said after a moment, reaching for words. "They will surely find comfort in having a strong son yet, to take up the burdens that will fall to you now."

Alun looked up at him in the darkness. The bulky presence. "Sometimes people . . . don't take up their burdens, you know."

Brynn shrugged. "Sometimes, yes."

No more than that.

Alun sighed, felt a great weariness. He was the heir to Cadyr, with all that meant. He shook his head.

Brynn bent down and slipped the dagger into the sheath in his boot. He straightened. They stood there, the two of them in the yard, as in a halfway place between the treed slope and the lights.

Brynn coughed. "Up there you said . . . you asked her to take care of him. Um, what did . . . ?"

Alun shook his head again, didn't answer. Would never answer that question, he decided. Brynn cleared his throat again. From inside the house, beyond the double doors, they heard someone cry in pain.

Neither of them, Alun realized, was standing in such a way that they could see if there was still a shimmering above them on the hill. If he turned his head . . .

The big man abruptly slapped his hand against his thigh, as if to break a mood, or a spell. "I have a gift for you," he said brusquely, and whistled.

Nothing for a moment, then out of the blackness a shape appeared and came to them. The dog—he was a wolfhound, and huge—rubbed its head against ap Hywll's thigh. Brynn reached down, a hand in the dog's fur at its neck.

"Cafall," he said calmly. "Hear me. You have a new master. Here he is. Go to him." He let go and stepped away. Nothing again, at first, then the dog tilted its head—a grey, Alun thought, though it was hard to be sure in the darkness—looked at Brynn a moment, then at Alun.

And then he came quietly across the space between.

Alun looked down at him, held out one hand. The dog sniffed it for a moment, then padded, with grace, to Alun's side.

"You gave him . . . that name?" Alun asked. This was unexpected, but ought to have been trivial. It didn't feel that way.

"Cafall, yes. When he was a year old, in the usual way."

"Then he's your best dog."

He saw Brynn nod. "Best I've ever had."

"Too great a gift, my lord. I cannot—"

"Yes, you can," said Brynn. "For many reasons. Take a companion from me, lad."

That was what the name meant, of course. *Companion.* Alun swallowed. There was a constriction in his throat. Was *this* what would make him weep tonight, after everything? He reached down and his hand rested on the warmth of the dog's head. He rubbed back and forth, ruffling the fur. Cafall pushed against his thigh. The ancient name, oldest stories. A very big dog, graceful and strong. No ordinary wolfhound, to so calmly accept this change with a spoken word in the night. It wasn't, he knew, a trivial gift at all.

Not to be refused.

"My thanks," he said.

"My sorrow," said Brynn again. "Let him . . . help keep you among us, lad."

So that was it. Alun found himself blinking; the lights in the farmhouse windows blurring for a moment. "Shall we go in?" he asked.

Brynn nodded.

They went in, to where lanterns were burning among the dead in the room beside the chapel, and among all the wounded children of Jad—wounded in so many different ways—within the house.

The dog followed, then lay down by the chapel door at Alun's murmured command. Outside, on the slope to the south, something lingered for a time in the dark and then went away, light as mist, before the morning came.

CHAPTER V

It had not been a good spring or summer for the traders of Rabady Isle, and there were those quite certain they knew why. The list of grievances was long.

Sturla Ulfarson, who had succeeded Halldr Thinshank as governor of the island's merchants and farmers and fisherfolk, might have only one hand but he possessed two eyes and two ears and a nose for the mood of people, and he was aware that men were comparing the (exaggerated) glories of Thinshank's days with the troubles and ill omens that had marked the beginning of his own.

Unfair, perhaps, but no one had *made* him manoeuvre for this position, and Ulfarson wasn't the self-pitying sort. Had he been so, he'd have been inclined to point out that the notorious theft of Thinshank's grey horse and the marring of his funeral rites last spring—the start of all their troubles—had happened before the new governor had been acclaimed. He'd have noted that no man, whatever kind of leader he might be, could have prevented the thunderstorm that had killed two young people in the night fields shortly after that. And he might also have bemoaned the fact that it was hardly within the power of a local administrator to control events in the wider world: warfare among Karch and Moskav and the Sarantines couldn't help but impact upon trade in the north.

Sturla One-hand did make these points decisively (he was a decisive man, for the most part) when someone dared challenge him directly, but he also set about doing what he could do on the isle, and as a result he discovered something.

It began with the families of the young man and woman killed in the storm. Everyone knew Ingavin sent the thunder and all manner of storms, that there was nothing accidental if people were killed or homes ruined by such things (a world where the weather was utterly random was a world not to be endured).

The girl had been doing her year of service to the *volur* at the compound by the edge of the forest. The young women of Rabady Isle took this duty, in turn, before they wed. It was a ritual, an honourable one. Fulla, the corn goddess, Ingavin's bride, needed attention and worship too, if children were to be born healthy and the fields kept fertile. Iord, the seer, was an important figure here on the isle: in her own way, as powerful as the governor was.

Sturla One-hand had paid a formal visit to the compound, bringing gifts, shortly after his election by the *thring*. He hadn't liked the *volur*, but that wasn't the point. If there was magic being used, you wanted it used for you, not against you. Women could be dangerous.

And that, in fact, is what he discovered. The families of the young man and the girl were elbowing each other towards a feud over their deaths, each blaming the other's offspring for the two of them being out by the memorial cairn, lying together when the lightning broke. Sturla had his own thoughts as to who had inveigled whom, but it was important to be seen to be conducting an inquiry first. His principal desire was to keep a blood feud from Rabady, or, at the least, to limit the casualties.

He set about speaking with as many of the young ones as he could, and in this way came to have a conversation with a yellow-haired girl from the mainland, the newest member of the circle of women in the compound. She had come (properly) in response to his summons and had knelt before him, shy, eyes suitably downcast.

She had little assistance, however, to offer concerning the two lightning-charred young ones, claiming to have seen Halli with the lad only once, "the evening before Bern Thorkellson came to the seer with Thinshank's horse."

The new governor of Rabady Isle, who had been leaning back in his seat, an ale flask in his one good hand, had leaned forward. The lightning storm, the two dead youngsters, and a possible feud became less compelling.

"Before he what?" said Sturla One-hand.

He put the flask down, reached out with his hand and grabbed the girl by her yellow hair, forcing her to look up at him. She paled, closed her eyes, as if overwhelmed by his powerful nearness. She was pretty.

"I . . . I . . . should not have said that," she stammered.

"And why not?" growled Ulfarson, still gripping her by the hair.

"She will kill me!"

"And why?" the governor demanded.

She said nothing, obviously terrified. He tugged, hard. She whimpered. He did it again.

"She . . . she did a magic-working on him."

"She what?" said Sturla, struggling, aware he was not sounding particularly astute. The girl—he didn't know her name—suddenly rocked forward and threw her arms around his legs, pressing her face to his thighs. It was not actually unpleasant.

She said, weeping, "She hated Thinshank . . . she will kill me . . . but she uses her power for . . . for her own purposes. It is . . . wrong!" She spoke with her mouth against him, arms clutching his legs.

Sturla One-hand let go of her hair and leaned back again. She remained where she was. He said, "I will not hurt you, girl. Tell me what she did."

In this way, the governor—and later the people of Rabady—learned of how Iord the seer had made a black *seithr* spell, rendering young Thorkellson her helpless servant, forcing him to steal the horse, then making him invisible, enabling him to board the southern ship that had been in the harbour—board it with the grey horse—and sail away unseen. It was done by the *volur* to spite Halldr Thinshank, of course, which was not an unreasonable desire, by any means. But it was a treachery that had unleashed—obviously—malevolent auras upon the isle (Halldr's, one had to assume), causing the calamities of the season, including the lightning storm that killed two innocent youths.

Erling warriors were not, by collective disposition, inclined to nuanced debate when resolving matters of this sort. Sturla One-hand might have been more thoughtful than most, but he'd lost his hand (and achieved some wealth) raiding overseas. You didn't *ponder* when attacking a village or sanctuary. You drank a lot beforehand, prayed to Ingavin and Thünir, and then fought and killed—and took home what you found in the fury and ruin you shaped.

An axe and sword were perfectly good responses to treachery, in his view. And they would serve the useful additional purpose of displaying Sturla's resolution, early in what he hoped would be a prosperous tenure as governor of the isle.

Iord the seer and her five most senior companions were taken from the compound early the next morning, stripped naked (bony and slack-breasted, all of them, hags fit for no man), bound to hastily erected posts in the field near the cairn stone where the two youngsters had died.

When they came for her, the seer tried—babbling in terror—to say that she'd *deceived* young Thorkellson. That she'd only pretended to cast a spell for him, had sent him back into town to be found.

Sturla One-hand had not lived so many years by being a fool. He pointed out that the lad had *not* been found. So either the seer was lying, or the boy had seen through her deception. And though young Thorkellson had been known to be good with blade and hammer (Red Thorkell's son would be, wouldn't he?), he was barely grown. And where was he? And the horse? She had her magic, what answer would she give?

She never did answer.

The six women were stoned to death, the members of the two feuding families invited to throw—standing together—the first volleys of stone and rock, as the most immediately aggrieved. The wives and maidens joined the men, one of the times they were permitted to do that. It took some time to kill six women (stoning always did).

The ale was good that night and the next, and a second ship from Alrasan in the south—where they worshipped the stars—appeared in the harbour two days later, come to trade, a clear blessing of Ingavin.

The yellow-haired girl from the mainland had stood at the edges of the stoning ground; they'd made the younger ones from the compound come watch. She'd had a fearsome serpent coiled about her body, darting a venomous tongue. She was the only one not terrified of it. No one stood near her as they watched the old women die. The governor couldn't remember (he'd drunk a good deal that day and night) just how he'd learned about her having been bitten back in the spring. Perhaps she had told him herself.

The snake was noticed in the field. Not surprisingly. Serpents held the power of the half-world within the skin they sloughed, rebuilding it anew. A snake would devour the world at the end of days. It was much talked about that night. A sign, it was agreed to be, a harbinger of power.

The girl was named by Sturla Ulfarson as the new *volur* of Rabady Isle a few days later, after the southern

ship had done its trading and gone. Normally the men of
Rabady didn't make this choice, but these weren't
normal times. You didn't stone a seer every year, did you?
Maybe this change would prove to be useful, bring the
power of women, *seithr* and night magic, the compound
itself, more under control.

Sturla One-hand wasn't sure about that, and he couldn't
actually have traced with precision the thoughts or conversations that had led to any of these decisions. Events had
moved quickly, he had been . . . riding them . . . the way
longships rode a wave, or a leader on a battlefield rode the
sweep of the fight, or a man rode his woman after dark.

She was young. What of it? All the old ones were
dead. They could have sent for a woman across the
water to Vinmark, even to Hlegest itself, but who knew
what that might have brought them, or when? Better
not draw the attention of increasingly ambitious men
there, in any case. The girl had saved them from the
effects of an angry spirit and seemed to have been
already chosen by the snake. Men had been saying that,
in the taverns. Sturla could read a rune-message if it was
spelled out for him.

He did know her name by then. Anrid. They called
her "the Serpent," though, by summer's end. She hadn't
come to him in the town again nor, in fact, did it occur
to him to ask her to do so. There were enough girls
about for a governor, no need to get entangled in *that*
way with seers who kept snakes by their beds in the dark
or wrapped them around their bodies to watch stones
split flesh and crack bone in the morning light.

Jormsvik was more a fortress than a city.

For one thing, only the mercenaries themselves and their
servants or slaves lived within the walls. The rope-makers,

sailmakers, armourers, tavern-keepers, carpenters, metal-smiths, fishermen, bakers, fortune-tellers all lived in the unruly town outside the walls. There were no women allowed inside Jormsvik, though prostitutes were scattered through the twisting streets and alleys just outside. There was money for a woman to make here, beside a large garrison.

You had to fight someone to become one of the men of Jormsvik, and fight steadily to stay in. Until you became a leader, when your battles might reasonably be expected to be all for hire and profit—if you stayed out of the tavern brawls.

For three generations the mercenaries of this fortress by the sea had been known and feared—and employed—through the world. They had fought at the triple walls of Sarantium (on both sides, at different times) and in Ferrieres and Moskav. They had been hired (and hired away) by feuding lords vying for eminence here in the Erling lands, as far north as the places where the sky flashed colours in the cold nights and the reindeer herds ran in the tens of thousands. One celebrated company had been in Batiara, joining a Karchite incursion towards fabled Rhodias forty years ago. Only six of them had returned—wealthy. You received your fee in advance, and shared it out beforehand, but then you divided the spoils of war among the survivors.

Survivors could do well.

First, you had to survive getting in. There were young men desperate or reckless enough to try each year, usually after the winter ended. Winter defined the north-lands: its imminent arrival; the white, fierce hardness of the season; then the stirring of blood and rivers when it melted away.

Spring was busiest at the gates of Jormsvik. The procedure was known everywhere. Goatherds and slaves knew it. You rode up or walked up to the walls. Shouted a name—sometimes even your real one—to the watch, issued a challenge to let you in. That same day, or the next morning, a man drawn by lot would come out to fight you.

The winner went to bed inside the walls. The loser was usually dead. He didn't *have* to be, you could yield and be spared, but it wasn't anything to count on. The core of Jormsvik's reputation lay in being feared, and if you let farmboys challenge you and walk away to tell of it by a winter's turf fire in some bog-beset place, you weren't as fearsome as all that, were you?

Besides which, it made sense for those inside to deter challengers any way they could. Sometimes the sword rune could be drawn from the barrel on a morning by a fighter who'd been too enthusiastically engaged in the taverns all night, or with the women, or both, and sometimes it wasn't just a farmboy at the gates.

Sometimes, someone came who knew what he was doing. They'd all gotten in that same way, hadn't they? Sometimes you could die outside, and then the gate swung open and a new mercenary was welcomed under whatever name he gave—they didn't care in Jormsvik, *everyone* had a story in his past. He'd be told where his pallet was, and his mess hall and captain. Same as the man he'd replaced, which could be unpleasant if the dead man had friends, which was usually the case. But this was a fortress for the hardest men in the world, not a warm meadhall among family.

You got to the meadhalls of Ingavin by dying with a weapon to hand. Time then for easiness, among ripe, sweet, willing maidens, and the gods. On this earth, you fought.

BERN WAS AWARE that he'd made a mistake, almost immediately after stooping through the low door of the alehouse outside the walls. It wasn't a question of thieves—the fighting men of Jormsvik were their own brutal deterrent to bandits near their gates. It was the mercenaries themselves, and the way of things here.

A stranger, he thought, a young man arriving alone in summer with a sword at his side, could only be here for one reason. And if he was going to issue a challenge in the morning, it made nothing but sense for any man in this ill-lit room (which was nonetheless bright enough to expose him for what he was) to protect himself and his fellows in obvious ways against what might happen on the morrow.

They could kill him tonight, he realized, rather too late, though it didn't even have to come to that. Those on the benches closest to where he'd sat down (too far from the doorway, another mistake) smiled at him, asked after his health and the weather and crops in the north. He answered, as briefly as he could. They smiled again, bought him drinks. Many drinks. One leaned over and offered him the dice cup.

Bern said he had no money to gamble, which was true. They said—laughing—he could wager his horse and sword. He declined. At the table they laughed again. Big men, almost all of them, one or two smaller than himself, but muscled and hard. Bern coughed in the dense smoke of the room. They were cooking meat over two open fires.

He was sweating; it was hot in here. He wasn't used to this. He'd been sleeping outdoors for a fortnight now, riding south into Vinmark's summer, trees green and the young grass, salmon leaping in the still-cold rivers. He'd been riding quickly since he'd surprised and robbed a man for his sword and dagger and the few coins in his purse. No point coming to Jormsvik without a weapon. He hadn't killed the man, which might have been a mistake, but he'd never yet killed any man. Would have to, tomorrow, or he'd very likely die here.

Someone banged down another tin cup of ale on the board in front of him, sloshing some of it out. "Long life," the man said and moved on, didn't even bother to stay to share the toast. They wanted him rendered senseless tonight, he realized, slack-limbed and slow in the morning.

Then he thought about it again. He had no *need* to challenge tomorrow. Could wake with a pounding head and spend the day clearing it, challenge the day after, or the morning after that.

And they'd know it, he realized, every man in this room. They'd all done this before. No, his first thought had been the wiser one: they wanted him drunk enough to make a mistake tonight, get into a brawl, be crippled or killed when there was nothing at stake—for them. Should he be flattered they thought he was worth it? He wasn't fooled. These were the most experienced soldiers-for-hire in the north: they didn't take chances when they didn't need to. There was no glory in winning a wall-challenge when the sword rune was drawn, only risk. Why take it, if you didn't have to? If the foolish traveller came into an ale room the night before, showing his sword?

At least he'd hidden the horse, among the trees north of town. Gyllir was accustomed to being tied in the woods now. He wondered if the stallion still remembered Thinshank's barn. How long did horses remember things?

He was afraid. Trying not to let them see it. He thought of the water then, that dead-black night, guiding the grey horse into the sea from the stony beach. Expecting to die. Ice-cold, end of winter, whatever lay waiting in the straits, under the water: what he'd survived. Was there a reason he'd lived? Did Ingavin or Thünir have a purpose in this? Probably not, actually. He wasn't . . . important enough. But there was still no need to walk open-eyed into a different death tonight. Not after coming out of the sea alive on a Vinmark strand as a grey day dawned.

He lifted the new cup and drank, just a little. A bad mistake, coming in here. You died of mistakes like that. But he'd been tired of solitude, nights alone. Had thought to at least have a night among other men, hear human voices, laughter, before he died in the morning fighting a mercenary. He hadn't thought it through.

A woman stood up, came over towards him, hips swaying. Men made way in the narrow space between tables for her, though not without squeezing where she could be reached. She smiled, ignored them, watched Bern watching her. He felt dizzy already. Ale after not drinking for so long, the smoke, smells, the crowd. It was so hot. The woman had been sitting with a burly, dark-bearded man clad in animal skins. A bear-warrior. They had them here in Jormsvik, it seemed. He remembered his father: *Some say the* berserkirs *use magic. They don't, but you never want to fight one if you can help it.* Bern saw, through fire smoke and lantern light, that the man was watching him as the woman approached.

He knew this game, too, suddenly. Stood up just as she stopped in front of him, her heavy breasts swinging free beneath a loose tunic.

"You're a pretty man," she said.

"Thank you," Bern muttered. "Thank you. Need to piss. Right back."

He twisted past her. She grabbed deftly for his private parts. With an effort, Bern refrained from glancing guiltily at the very big man she'd just left.

"Hurry back and make me happy," she called after him.

Someone laughed. Someone—big, blond, hard-eyed—looked up then, from the dicing.

Bern slapped a coin on the counter and ducked outside. He took a deep breath; salt in the night air here, sound of sea, stars overhead, the white moon high. The nearer ones in the room would have seen him pay. Would know he wasn't coming back.

He moved then, quickly. He could die here.

It was very dark, no lights to speak of outside the inns and the low, jumbled wooden dwellings and the rooms where the whores took their men. A mixed blessing, the darkness: he'd be harder to find, but might easily run headlong into a group of people, trying to make his way north and out from this warren of buildings. A fleeing stranger, Bern was certain, would be happily seized to be questioned at leisure.

He ran up the first black alley he came to, smelled urine and offal, stumbled through a pile of garbage, choking. Could he just walk, he wondered? Avoid being seen to be running from something?

He heard noises behind him, from the alehouse door. No, he couldn't just walk. Needed to move. It would be a sport for them. Something to enliven a night outside the fortress walls, waiting for a new contract and a journey somewhere. A way to keep in fighting trim.

In the blackness he bumped into a barrel lying on its side. Stooped, groped, righted it. No top. Grunting, he turned it over, sweating now, and clambered up, praying the bottom was solid enough. He stood, gauged distance as best he could in the dark, and jumped for the slanting roof of the house above. Caught a purchase, levered a knee up, awkward with the sword at his hip, and pulled himself onto the roof. If there was someone inside they'd hear him, he knew. Could raise an alarm.

When you had no obvious choices, you acted as if what you needed to do could be done.

Why was he remembering so many of his father's words tonight?

Prone on the roof above the alley, he heard three or four men go by in the street. He was being hunted. He was a fool, the son of a fool, deserved whatever fate he met tonight. He didn't *think* they'd kill him. A broken leg or arm would spare someone the need to fight him tomorrow with a risk involved. On the other hand, they were drunk, and enjoying themselves.

Wiser to surrender?

More sounds, a second group. "Pretty-faced little shit-eater," he heard someone say, at the entrance to the alley. "I didn't like him."

Someone laughed. "You don't like anyone, Gurd."

"Do yourself with a hammer," Gurd said. "Or do it to that little goatherd who thinks he can join us." There came the unmistakable sound of a blade being drawn from a scabbard.

Bern decided that surrender was not a promising option.

Carefully, holding his own sword out of the way, he backed along the roof. He needed to go north, get beyond these houses and into the fields. He didn't think they'd care enough to leave drinking and go looking for him out there in the night. And come morning, once he rode up to the gates and issued a challenge, he'd be safe. Although that probably wasn't the best way to describe what would follow then.

He could have stayed at home, a servant for two more years. He could have hired himself out on a farm some-where on the mainland, invented a name for himself, been a servant or a labourer there.

That wasn't what he'd ridden the grey horse into the sea to become. Everyone died. If you died before the walls of Jormsvik, perhaps the sword in your hand would get you to Ingavin's halls.

He didn't actually believe that, truth be told. If it were so, any farmhand could get himself run through by a mercenary and drink mead forever with smooth-skinned maidens among the gods, or until the Serpent devoured the Worldtree and time came to a stop.

It couldn't be that easy.

Neither was moving on this roof, which slanted too much. They all slanted, to let the snow slide in winter. Bern skidded sideways, dug in fingers and boots to stop himself, heard the sword scrape. Had to hope, could *only* hope, no one else heard it. He lay still again, sweat trickling down his sides. No sounds below except for running feet. He slowly manoeuvred himself around to look the other way.

There was a ramshackle, two-storey wooden house on the other side of another narrow alley. Just the one, the others were all one-level, like the house he was on. One of the new-style stone chimneys ran up an outside wall, set back from the street, he saw. They didn't have these on the isle. It was meant to allow a hearth, warmth and food, on a second floor. It looked as if it was going to fall over. There was a window in that second storey, overlooking his rooftop. The wooden shutters were open. One hung crookedly, needing repair. He saw a candle burning on the ledge, illuminating a room—and the face of the girl watching him.

Bern's heart lurched. Then he saw her put a finger to her lips.

"Gurd," she called down, "you coming up?"

A laugh below. They had gone right around, were in the street on the other side now. "Not to you. You hurt me last time, you're wild when I do you."

Someone else laughed. The girl across the way swore tiredly. "How 'bout you, Holla?"

"I go with Katrin, you know that. She hurts me when I *don't* do her!"

Gurd laughed this time. "You see a stranger?" He was right below. If Bern moved to the roof's edge he could look down on them. He heard the question and closed his eyes. Everyone died.

"Didn't," said the girl. "Why?"

"Pretty farmboy thinks he's going to be a mercenary."

Her voice was bored. "You find him, send him up. I need the money."

"We find him, he's no good to you. Trust me."

The girl laughed. The footsteps moved on. Bern opened his eyes, saw her turn her head to watch the men below go down the lane. She turned back and looked at him. Didn't smile now, nothing like that. She moved back, however, and gestured for him to come across the way.

Bern looked. A small window in a flat wall, above his level. A slanting roof where he was, no purchase to run and jump. He bit his lip. The heroes of the Days of Giants would have made this jump.

He wasn't one of them. He'd end up clattering down the face of the wall to the street below.

Slowly he shook his head, shrugged. "Can't," he mouthed, looking across at her.

She came back into the window frame, looked left and right down the lane. Leaned out. "They're around the alley. I'll get you at the door. Wait till I open."

She hadn't given him up. She could have. He couldn't stay on this roof all night. He had two choices, as he saw it. Jump down, keep to shadows and alleys, try to get north and out of town with a number of fighting men— he didn't know how many—prowling the streets for him. Or let her get him at the door.

He pulled himself nearer the edge. The sword scraped again. He swore under his breath, looked over and down.

Saw where the door was. The girl was still at the window, waiting. He looked back at her and he nodded his head. A decision. You came over into the world—crossed from an island on a stolen horse—you had decisions to make, in the dark sometimes, and living until morning could turn on them.

She disappeared from the window, leaving the candle there, so small and simple a light.

He stayed where he was, watching it, this glimmer in darkness. There was a breeze. Up here on the roof he could smell the sea again, hear the distant surge of water beneath the voices and laughter of men. Always and ever beneath those things.

An idea came to him, the beginnings of an idea.

He heard a sound. Looked down. She carried no light, was a shadow against the shadows of opened door and house wall. No one in the laneway, at least not now. He seemed to have decided to do this. Bern slid himself to the lowest point on the pitched roof, held his scabbard with one hand, and dropped. He stumbled to his knees, got up, went quickly to her, and in.

She closed the door behind him. It creaked. No bolt or bar, he saw. Two other doors inside, off the narrow corridor: one beside them, one at the back.

She followed his glance. Whispered, "They're in the taverns. Upstairs is mine. Step over the fourth stair, it's missing."

In the dark, Bern counted, stepped over the fourth stair. The stairs creaked, as well. Each sound made him wince. Her door was ajar. He went in, she was right behind him. This one she closed, slid down a bar to lock it. Bern looked at it. A kick would splinter lock and door.

He turned, saw the candle in the window. A strangeness, to be looking at it now from this side. Not a feeling he could explain. He crossed and looked out at the roof across the lane, where he'd been moments before, the white moon above it, and stars.

He turned back into the room and looked at her. She wore an undyed tunic belted at the waist, no jewellery, paint on her lips and cheeks. She was thin, legs and bones, brown hair, very large eyes, her face thin, too. Not really what a man would want in a woman for the night, though some of the soldiers might like them young, an illusion of innocence. Or like a boy. An illusion of something else.

She wasn't innocent, not living here. There was no furniture to speak of. Her bed, where she worked, was a pallet on the floor in a corner, the coverings spread over it neatly enough. A bundle against the wall beside it would be her clothing, another pile of cooking things, and food. That shouldn't be on the floor, he thought. There'd be rats. A basin, a chamber pot, both on the floor as well. Two wooden stools. A black pot hooked on an iron bar stretched across the fireplace he'd seen from outside. Firewood by that wall. The candle on the window ledge.

She went to the window, took the candle, put it on one of the stools. She sank down on the bedding, crossed her legs, looked up at him. Said nothing, waiting.

Bern said, after a moment, "Why hasn't anyone fixed that stair?"

She shrugged. "We don't pay enough? I like it. If someone wants to come up they need to know the hole's there. No surprises."

He nodded. Cleared his throat. "No one else in here?"

"They will be later. In and out. Told you. Both of 'em at the taverns."

"Why . . . aren't you?"

The same shrug. "I'm new. We go later, after the others start their night. They don't like it if we get there too soon. Beat us up, make scars, you know . . ."

He didn't, not really. "So . . . you'll go out soon?"

She raised her eyebrows. "Why? Got a man here, don't I?"

He swallowed. "I can't be found, you know that."

"'Course I know. Gurd'll kill you for fun of it."

"Do . . . any of them . . . just come up?"

"Sometimes," she said, failing to reassure.

"Why did you help me?" He wasn't used to talking. Not since leaving the isle.

She shrugged again. "Don't know. You want me? What can you pay?"

What could he pay? Bern reached into his trousers and took the purse looped inside them, around his waist. He tossed it to her. "All I have," he said.

He'd had it off the careless merchant north of here. Perhaps the gods would look kindly on his giving it to her.

That vague, new-formed idea that had come to him on the roof was still teasing at the edges of his mind. No use or meaning to it, unless he survived tonight.

She was opening the purse, emptied it on the bedding. Looked up at him.

First glimmering of youth, of surprise, in her. "This is too much," she said.

"All I have," he repeated. "Hide me till morning."

"Doing it anyhow," she said. "Why'd I bring you?"

Bern grinned suddenly, a kind of light-headedness. "I don't know. You haven't told me."

She was looking at the coins on her bed. "Too much," she said again.

"Maybe you're the best whore in Jormsvik," he said.

She looked up quickly. "I'm not," she said, defensively.

"A jest. I'm too afraid right now to take a woman, anyhow."

He doubted she was used to hearing that from the fighters in Jormsvik. She looked at him. "You going to challenge in the morning?"

He nodded. "That's why I came. Made a mistake, going to an inn tonight."

She stared at him, didn't smile. "That's Ingavin's truest truth, it is. Why'd you?"

He tilted the sword back, sat carefully on the stool. It held his weight. "Wasn't thinking. Wanted a drink. A last drink?"

She appeared to be thinking about that. "They don't *always* kill, in the challenges."

"Me they will," he said glumly.

She nodded. "That's a truth, I guess. After tonight, you mean?"

He nodded. "So you might as well have the purse."

"Oh. That's why?"

He shrugged.

"I should at least do you then, shouldn't I?"

"Hide me," Bern said. "It's enough."

She looked at him. "It's a long night. You hungry?"

He shook his head.

She laughed, for the first time. A girl, somewhere in there with the Jormsvik whore. "You want to sit and *talk* all night?" She grinned, and began untying the knotted belt that held her tunic. "Come here," she said. "You're pretty enough for me. I can earn some of this."

Bern had thought, actually, that fear would strip away desire. Watching her begin to undress, seeing that unexpected, amused expression, he discovered that this was wrong. It had been, he thought, a long time since he'd had a woman. And the last one had been Iord, the *volur*, in her cabin on the isle. The serpent coiling somewhere in the room. Not a good memory.

It's a long night. After a moment, he started to remove his sword-belt.

He was later to consider—sometimes soberly, sometimes not so—how a man's life could turn on extremely small things. Had he turned up another alley when he'd left that tavern, found a different roof to climb. Had they begun to disrobe even a little sooner . . .

"Thira!" they heard, from downstairs. "You still up there?"

He knew that voice now. *Gurd'll kill you for fun of it,* she had said.

"In the fireplace!" she whispered urgently now. "Push up a ways. Hurry!"

"You can turn me in," he said, surprising himself.

"No to that," she said, retying her belt quickly. "Get in there!" Turning to the door, she shouted, "Gurd! Watch fourth step!"

"I know!" Bern heard.

He hurried to the chimney space, bending down and stepping over the rod that held the black pot. Awkward, especially with the stolen sword. He scraped his shoulder on the rough stone, swore. He straightened up inside, cautiously. It was pitch black and very tight. He was sweating again, heart hammering. Should he have stayed in the room, fought the man when he came up? Gurd would kill him, or simply step back and call for friends. Bern would have nowhere to go.

And the girl would die, as well, if he was found here. A bad death, with these men. Should he care about that, if he wanted to be a Jormsvik mercenary? No matter, too late now.

The chimney widened a little, higher up, more than he'd thought. He reached overhead with both hands, scrabbling at stone. Pebbles fell, rattling. He found places to grip, levered himself, got his boots on either side of the bar that stretched across, pushed the sword to hang straight down. He needed to get higher but couldn't see a thing in the blackness of the chimney, no way to check for footholds. He put his boots right to the edges, pressing against the stone. The bar held. For how long, he didn't know, or want to think. Imagined himself crashing down, unable to move in the chimney, spitted like a squealing pig by the man in the room. A glorious death.

Gurd banged on the door; the girl crossed and opened it. He hoped—abruptly—that she'd thought to hide the purse.

He heard her voice. "Gurd, I didn't think you'd—"

"Out of the way. I want your window, not your skinny bones."

"What?"

"No one's seen him in the streets, there's ten of us looking. Shit-smeared goatboy may be on a roof."

"I'd have seen him, Gurd." Bern heard her footsteps cross behind the mercenary's to the window. "Come to bed?"

"You'd see nothing but one of us to screw. Ingavin's blood, it *pisses* me to have a farmhand escape us!"

"Let me make you feel better, then," the girl named Thira said in a wheedling voice. "Long as you're here, Gurd."

"Slipped coins, all you want. Whore."

"Not *all* I want slipped, Gurd," she said. Bern heard her laugh softly and knew it wasn't real.

"Not now. I might come back later if you're dying for it. No money, though. I'd be doing you a favour."

"No to that," said Thira sharply. "I'll be down in Hrati's getting a man who takes care of a girl."

Bern heard a blow, a gasp. "Decent tongue in your head, whore. Remember it."

There was a silence. Then, "Why would you cheat me, Gurd? A man oughtn't do that. What I do bad to you? Do me and pay me for it."

Bern felt a cramping in his arms, held almost straight over his head, clutching the stone wall. If the man in the room turned to the fire and looked, he'd see two boots, one on either side of the cooking pot.

The man in the room said, to the woman, "Get your tunic up, don't take it off. Turn over, on your knees."

Thira made a small sound. "Two coins, Gurd. You know it. Why cheat me for two coins? I need to eat."

The mercenary swore. Bern heard money land on the floor and roll. Thira said, "I knowed you was a good man, Gurd. I knowed it. Who you want me be? A princess from Ferrieres? You captured me? Now you got me?"

"Cyngael," the man grunted. Bern heard a sword drop. "Cyngael bitch, proud as a goddess. But not any more. Not now. Put your face down. You're in the mud. In the . . . field. I got you. Like. This." He grunted, so did the girl. Bern heard shifting sounds where the pallet was.

"Ah!" Thira cried. "Someone save me!" She screamed, but kept it soft.

"All dead, bitch!" Gurd growled. Bern heard the sounds of their movements, a hard slap on skin, the man grunting again. He stayed where he was, eyes closed, though it didn't matter in this blackness. Heard the mercenary again, breath rasping now: "All carved up. Your men. Now you find . . . what an Erling's like, cow! Then you die." Another slap.

"No!" cried Thira. "Save me!"

Gurd grunted again, then groaned loudly, then the sounds ceased. After a moment, Bern heard him stand up again.

"Worth a coin, not more'n that, Ingavin knows," Gurd of Jormsvik, a captain there, said. "I'll take the other back, whore." He laughed.

Thira said nothing. Bern heard the sword being picked up, boots crossing the floor again to the door. "You see anyone on a roof, you shout. Hear?"

Thira made a muffled sound. The door opened, closed. Bern heard boots on the stairs, then a clatter, and swearing. Gurd had forgotten the fourth stair. A brief, necessary flicker of pleasure at that. Then gone.

He waited a few more moments, then stepped carefully down from the bar, stooped almost double, and squeezed out from the chimney. He scraped his back this time.

The girl was on the pallet, face down, hidden by her hair. The candle burned on the stool.

"He hurt you?" Bern asked.

She didn't move, or turn. "He took a coin back. He oughtn't cheat me."

Bern shrugged, though she couldn't see him. "You have a full purse from me. What's a coin matter?"

She still didn't turn. "I earned it. You can't understand that, can you?" She said it into the rough blanket of the pallet.

"No," said Bern, "I guess I can't." It was true, he didn't understand. But why should he?

She turned then, sat up, and quickly put a hand to her mouth—a girl's gesture again. Began to laugh. "Ingavin's eye! Look at you! You're black as a southern desert man."

Bern looked down at his tunic. Ash and soot from the fireplace were all over him. He turned up his hands. His palms were coal black from the fireplace walls.

He shook his head ruefully. "Maybe I'll scare them in the morning."

She was still laughing. "Not them, but sit down, I'll wash you." She got up, arranged her tunic, and went to a basin by the other wall.

It was a long time since a woman had tended him. Not since they'd had servants, before his father had killed his second man in an inn fight and been exiled, ruining the world. Bern sat on the stool as she bade him, and a whore by the walls of Jormsvik cleaned and groomed him the way the virgins in Ingavin's halls were said to minister to the warriors there.

Later, without speaking, she lay down on the pallet again and took off her tunic and he made love to her, distracted a little now by the noisy sounds of other love-making in the two rooms below. With a memory of what he'd heard from within the fireplace, he actually tried to be gentle with her, but afterwards he didn't think it had mattered. He'd given her a purse, and she was earning it, in the way she did that.

She fell asleep, after. The candle on the stool burned down. Bern lay in the darkness of that small, high room, looking out the unshuttered window at the summer night, waiting for first light. Before that came, he heard voices and drunken laughter in the street below: the mercenaries going back to their barracks. They slept there, always, whatever they did out here in the nights.

Her window faced east, away from the fortress and the sea. Watching, listening to the girl breathe beside him, he caught the first hint of dawn. He rose and dressed. Thira didn't move. He unbarred the door and went softly down the stairs, stepping over the fourth one from the bottom, and came out into the empty street.

He walked north—not running, on this morning that might be the last of his unimportant life—and passed the final straggling wooden structures, out into fields beyond. A chill, grey hour, before sunrise. He came to the wood. Gyllir was where he'd left him. The horse would be as hungry as he was, but there was nothing to be done about that. If they killed Bern they'd take the stallion, treat him well: he was a magnificent creature. He rubbed the animal's muzzle, whispered a greeting.

More light now. Sunrise, a bright day, it would be warm later. Bern mounted, left the wood. He rode slowly through the fields towards the main gates of Jormsvik. No reason to hurry now. He saw a hare at the edge of the trees, alert, watching him. It crossed his mind to curse his father again, for what Thorkell had done to bring him here, to this, but in the end he didn't do that, though he wasn't sure why. It also occurred to him to pray, and that he did do.

There were guards on the ramparts above the gates, Bern saw. He reined the horse to a halt. Sat silently a moment. The sun was up, to his left, the sea on the other side, beyond a stony strand. There were boats—the dragon-headed ships—pulled up on the shore, a long, long row of them. He looked at those, the brightly painted prows, and at the grey, surging sea. Then he turned back to the walls and issued a challenge to be admitted to the company of Jormsvik, offering to prove his worth against any man sent out to him.

A CHALLENGE COULD BE entertaining, though usually only briefly so. The mercenaries prided themselves on dealing briskly with country lads and their delusions of being warriors. A trivial, routine aspect of their life. Draw the rune with a sword on it, ride out, cut someone up, come back for food and ale. If a man took too long to handle his lot-drawn task he could expect to be a source of amusement to his fellows for a time. Indeed, the likeliest way to ensure being killed—for a challenger—was to put up too much of a fight.

But why come all the way to Jormsvik-on-the-sea at the bottom of Vinmark just to surrender easily, in the (probably vain) hope of having your life spared? There might be some small measure of accomplishment back home for a farmer in having fought before these walls and come away alive, but not *that* much, in truth.

Only a few of the mercenaries would bother to climb the ramparts to watch, mostly companions of the one who'd drawn the sword-lot. On the other hand, for the artisans and fishermen and merchants of the town sprawling outside the walls, daily life offered little enough in the way of recreation, so it was generally the case that they'd suspend activity and come watch when a challenger was reported.

They wagered, of course—Erlings always wagered—usually on how long it would take for the newest victim to be unhorsed or disarmed, and whether he'd be killed or allowed to limp away.

If the challenge came early in the morning—as today—the whores were usually asleep, but with word shouted through the lanes and streets many of them would drag themselves out to see a fight.

You could always go back to bed after watching a fool killed, maybe even win a coin or two. You might even take a carpenter or sailmaker back with you before he returned to his shop, make another coin that way. Fighting excited the men sometimes.

The girl called Thira (at least partly Waleskan, by her colouring) was among those who came down towards the gates and the strand when word ran round that a challenge had been issued. She was one of the newer whores, having arrived from the east with a trading party in spring. She had taken one of the rickety, fire-prone upper-level rooms in the town. She was too bony and too sharp-tongued (and inclined to use it) to have any real reason to expect a rise in her fortunes, or enough money to lower her bed to a ground-floor room.

These girls came and went, or died in winter. It was a waste of time feeling sorry for them. Life was hard for everyone. If the girl was fool enough to put a silver coin on the latest farmer who'd shown up to challenge, all you wanted to do was bite the coin, ensure it was real, and be quick as you could to cover part of the wager—even at the odds proposed.

How she got the coin was not at issue—all the girls stole. A silver piece was a week's work on back or belly for a girl like Thira, and not much less than that, at harder labour, for the craftsmen of the town. It took several of them, mingling coins, to match the wager. The money was placed, as usual, with the blacksmith, who had a reputation for honesty and a good memory, and who was also a very large man.

"Why you doing this?" one of the other girls asked Thira.

It had created a stir. You didn't bet on challengers to win.

"They spent half last night trying to find him. Gurd and the others. He was in Hrati's and they went for him. I figure if he can dodge a dozen of them for a night, he might handle one in a fight."

"Not the same thing," said one of the older women. "You can't hide out here."

Thira shrugged. "If he loses, take my money."

"Well aren't you the easy one with silver?" the other woman sniffed. "What happens if Gurd come out his self, to finish what he couldn't?"

"Won't. Gurd's a captain. I ought to know. He comes to me now."

"Hah! He come up those broken stairs to you only when someone he wants is busy. Don't get ideas, girl."

"He was with me last night," Thira said, defensively. "I know him. He won't fight . . . it's beneath him. As a captain and all."

Someone laughed.

"Is it?" someone else said.

The gates had opened. A man was riding out. There were murmurs, and then more laughter, at the girl's expense. People were fools sometimes. You couldn't pity them. You tried to gain from it. Those who hadn't been quick enough to be part of the wager were cursing themselves.

"Give over the money now," a pockmarked sailmaker named Stermi said to the blacksmith, elbowing him. "This farmer's a dead man."

Seabirds wheeled, dove into the waves, rose again, crying.

"Ingavin's eye!" exclaimed the girl named Thira, shaken. The crowd eyed her with raucous pleasure. "Why'd he *do* this?"

"Oh? Thought you said you knew him," the other whore said, cackling.

They watched, a largish, buzzing group of people, as Gurd Thollson—a captain for two years now, excused from having to do this any more unless he chose to— rode out in glorious chain mail from the open gates of Jormsvik and moved past them, unsmiling, eyes hidden under helm and above bright yellow beard, towards the farmboy waiting on the stony strand astride a grey horse.

HE HAD PRAYED. Had no farewells to make. There was no one who would lose anything at all if he died. This was a choice. You made choices, in the sea and on land, or somewhere between the two, on the margins.

Bern backed Gyllir up a little as the mercenary who had drawn the battle lot approached. He knew what he wanted to do here, had no idea if he could. This was a trained warrior. He wore an iron helm, chain-mail armour, a round shield hooked on the saddle of his horse. Why would he take any kind of chance? Though this was where Bern saw his own chance lying, small as it might be.

The Jormsvik fighter came nearer; Bern retreated a little more along the stony beach, as if flinching backwards. Edge of the surf now, shallow water.

"Where'd you hide last night, goatboy?"

This time, the retreat back into the water was genuine, instinctive. He knew the voice. Hadn't known which man in the alehouse last night was Gurd. Now he did: the big, yellow-haired dice player at the next table over, who had seen him pay and hurry out.

"Answer me, cowshit. You're dying here anyhow." Gurd drew his sword. There came a sound from those watching outside the walls.

Something rare came into Bern Thorkellson in that moment, with the deriding, confident voice and a memory of this man the night before. It actually took Bern a moment to identify the feeling. Normally he was controlled, careful, only son of a man too well known for his temper. But a shield wall broke inside him on that strand before Jormsvik, with the sea lapping at the fetters of his horse. He danced Gyllir a little farther backwards into the water—deliberately this time—and he felt, within, the heat of an unexpected fury.

"You're a sorry excuse for an Erling, you know that?" he snapped. "If I'm supposed to be a shit-smeared farmhand, why couldn't you find me last night, Gurd? I didn't go far, you know. Why's it take a captain to kill a goatboy today? Or be killed by one? I beat you last night, I'll beat you now. In fact, I like that sword of yours. I'll enjoy using it."

A silence; a man stunned. Then a stream of obscenity. "You beat no one, you lump of dung," the big man snarled, edging his horse forward in the water. "You just hid, and wet yourself."

"Not hiding now, am I?" Bern raised his voice to be heard. "Come on, little Gurd. Everyone's watching."

Again he backed up. His boots in the stirrups were in the water now. He could feel the horse reach for footing. The shelf sloped here. Gyllir was calm. Gyllir was a glory. Bern drew his stolen sword.

Gurd followed, farther into the sea. His horse danced and shifted. Most Erling warriors fought on foot, riding to battle if they had a horse and dismounting there. Bern was counting on that. For one thing, Gurd couldn't use the shield and sword *and* control his mount.

"Get down and fight!" the captain rasped.

"I'm here, little Gurd. Not hiding. Or is this Erling afraid of the sea? Is that why you're not raiding? Will they even let you back in when they see it? Come get me, mighty captain!"

Again he shouted it, to let those watching on the grass hear him. Some of them had begun drifting nearer the strand. He was surprised at how little fear he felt, now that it had come to this. And the anger in him was fierce and warming, a blaze. He thought of the girl last night: this massive, bearded captain stealing a coin from her out of sheer malice. It shouldn't matter—he'd told *her* that—but it did. He couldn't say why, didn't have time to decide why.

Gurd pointed with his blade. "I'm going to hurt you before I let you die," he said.

"No you aren't," said Bern, quietly this time, for no one else's ears but their own—and the gods', if they were listening. "Ingavin and Thünir led me through the sea on this horse in the dark of a night. They are watching over me. You die here, little Gurd. You're in the way of my destiny." He surprised himself, again—hadn't any idea he would say that, or what it meant.

Gurd rapped his helm down hard, roared something wordless, and charged. More or less.

It is difficult to charge in surf at the best of times. Things are not as one expects, or as one's horse expects. Movements slow, there is resistance, footing shifts—and then, where sand and stones slide away, it disappears entirely, and one is swimming, or the horse is, wild-eyed. One cannot charge at all, swimming, wearing armour, heavy and unbalanced.

But this, on the other hand, was a Jormsvik fighter, a captain, and he was not—taunting aside—afraid of the sea, after all. He was quick, and his horse was good. The first angled blow was heavy as a battle-hammer and Bern barely got his own blade across his body and in front of it. His entire right side was jarred by the impact; Gyllir rocked with it, Bern gasped with the force, pulled the horse back to his right in the sea, by reflex, more than anything.

Gurd pushed farther forward, still roaring, took another huge downward swing. This one missed, badly. They were deeper now, both of them. Gurd nearly unhorsed himself in the waves, rocking wildly as his mount, legs thrashing, struggled beneath him.

Bern felt an improbable mixture of ice and fire within him: fury and a cold precision. He thought of his father. Ten years of lessons with all the weapons Thorkell knew. How to block a downward forearm slash. His inheritance?

He said, watching the other man struggle and then right himself, "If it makes you feel better, dying here, I'm not a farmboy, little Gurd. My father rowed with the Volgan for years. Thorkell Einarson. Siggur's companion. Know it. Won't get you to Ingavin's halls this morning, though." He paused; locked eyes with the other man. "The gods will have seen you steal that coin last night."

If he died now, the girl did too, because he'd said that. He wasn't going to die. He waited, saw awareness—of many things—flicker and ripple in the other man's blue eyes. Then he steered Gyllir forward at an angle with his knees and he stabbed Gurd's horse with a leaning, upward thrust just above the waterline.

Gurd cried out, pulled at reins uselessly, waved his sword—for balance more than anything—slipped from the tilting saddle.

Bern saw him, weighted with chain mail, up to his chest in water, fighting to stand. His dying horse thrashed again, kicked him. Bern actually had a moment to think about pitying the man. He waited until Gurd, fighting the weight of his armour, was almost upright in the waves, then he angled Gyllir again, smoothly in the sea, and he drove his sword straight into the captain's handsome, bearded face just below the nosepiece. The blade went through mouth and skull bone, banged hard against the metal of the helm at the back. Bern jerked it out, saw blood, sudden and vivid, in the water. He watched the other man topple into white, foaming surf. Dead already. Another angry ghost.

He dismounted. Grabbed for the drifting sword, better by far than his own. He took hold of Gurd by the ringed neckpiece of his armour and pulled him from the sea, blood trailing from the smashed-in face. He threw the two swords ahead of him, used both hands to drag the heavy body up on the strand. He stood above it, dripping, breathing hard. Gyllir followed. The other horse did not, a carcass now, in the shallow water. Bern looked at it a moment, then walked back into the sea. He bent and claimed the dead man's shield from the saddle. Walked back out onto the stones again.

He looked over at the crowd gathered between sea and walls, and then up at the soldiers on the ramparts above the open gates. Many of them up there this sunlit summer morning. A captain riding out, claiming the fight: worth watching, to see what he did to the challenger who'd offended him. They'd seen.

Two men were walking out through the gates. One lifted a hand in greeting. Bern felt the anger still within him, making a home, not ready to leave.

"This man's armour," he called, lifting his voice over the deeper voice of the tumbling sea behind him, "is mine, in Ingavin's name."

It wouldn't fit him but could be altered, or sold. That's what mercenaries did. That's what he was now.

At the margins of any tale there are lives that come into it only for a moment. Or, put another way, there are those who run quickly through a story and then out, along their paths. For these figures, living their own sagas, the tale they intersect is the peripheral thing. A moment in the drama of their own living and dying.

The metalsmith, Ralf Erlickson, elected to return to his birthplace on Rabady Isle at the end of that same summer after ten years on the Vinmark mainland, the last four of which had been spent in the town outside the walls of Jormsvik. He'd made (and saved) a decent sum, because the mercenaries had needed his services regularly. He'd finally decided it was time to go home, buy some land, choose a wife, beget sons for his old age.

His parents were dead, his brothers gone elsewhere— he wasn't certain where any more, after ten years. There were other changes on the isle, of course, but not so many, really. Some taverns had closed, some opened, people dead, people born. The harbour was bigger, room for more ships. Two governors had succeeded each other since he'd left. The new one—Sturla One-hand, of all people—had just begun serving. Ralf had a drink or three with One-hand just after arriving. They traded stories of a shared childhood and divergent lives after. Ralf had never gone raiding; Sturla had lost a hand overseas . . . and made a small fortune.

A hand was a fair trade for a fortune, in Ralf's estimation. Sturla had a big house, a wife, land, access to other women, and power. It was . . . unexpected. He kept quiet about that thought, though, even after several cups. He was coming home to live, and Sturla was the governor. You wanted to be careful. He asked about unmarried women, smiled at the predictable jests, made a mental note of the two names Sturla did mention.

Next morning he went out from the walls, walking through remembered fields to the women's compound. There was an errand he'd promised to do. No need to ask directions. The place wouldn't have moved.

It was in better repair than he recalled. Sturla had told him a bit about that: the stoning of the old *volur,* emergence of a new one. Relations, the governor had allowed, were good. The witch-women had even taken to bringing food and ale for the harvesters at end of day. They never spoke, Sturla had told him, shaking his head. Not a word. Just walked out, in procession, a line of them, carrying cheese or meat and drink, then walked back. In procession.

Ralf Erlickson had spat into the rushes on the governor's floor. "Women," he'd said. "Just their games."

One-hand had shrugged. "Less than before, maybe." Ralf got the feeling he was taking credit for it.

The details of the town's reciprocation were evident as he approached the compound. The fence was in good condition; the buildings looked sturdy, doors hanging properly; wood was stacked high already, well before winter. There were signs of construction, a new outbuilding of some kind going up.

A woman in a grey, calf-length tunic watched him approach, standing by the gate.

"Ingavin's peace on all here," Ralf said, routinely. "I have a message for one of you."

"All peace upon you," she replied, and waited. Didn't open the gate.

Ralf shifted his feet. He didn't like these women. He vaguely regretted accepting the errand, but he'd been paid, and it wasn't a difficult task.

"I am to speak with someone whose name I don't know," he said.

She laughed, surprisingly. "Well, you don't know mine."

He wasn't used to laughter in the seer's compound. He'd come twice in his youth, both times to offer support to friends seeking a *seithr* spell from the *volur*. There'd been no amusement, on either occasion.

"Were you ever bit by a snake?" he asked, and was pleased to see her startle.

"Is that the one you need to see?"

He nodded. After a moment, she opened the gate.

"Wait here," she said, and left him in the yard as she went into one of the buildings.

He looked around. A warm day, end of summer. He saw beehives, an herb garden, the locked brewhouse. Heard birdsong from the trees. No sign of any other women. He wondered, idly, where they were.

A door opened and someone else came out, alone: wearing blue. He knew what that meant. Under his breath he cursed. He hadn't expected to deal with the *volur* herself. She was young, he saw. One-hand had told him that, but it was disconcerting.

"You have a message for me," she murmured. She was hooded, but he saw wide-set blue eyes and pulled-back yellow hair. You might even have called her pretty, though that was a dangerous thought with respect to a *volur*.

"Ingavin's peace," he said.

"And Fulla's upon you." She waited.

"You . . . the snake . . . ?"

"I was bitten, yes. In the spring." She put a hand inside her robe and withdrew it, gripping something. Erlickson stepped back quickly. She wrapped the creature around her neck. It coiled there, head up, looking at him from above her shoulder, then flicked an evil tongue. "We have made our peace, the serpent and I."

Ralf Erlickson cleared his throat. *Time,* he thought, *to be gone from here.* "Your kinsman sends greetings. From Jormsvik."

He'd surprised her greatly, he realized, had no idea why. She clasped her hands at her waist.

"That is all? The message?"

He nodded. Cleared his throat again. "He . . . is well, I can say that."

"And working for the mercenaries?"

Ralf shook his head, pleased. They didn't know everything, these women. "He killed a captain in a challenge, midsummer. He's inside Jormsvik, one of them now. Well, in truth, he isn't inside, at the moment."

"Why?" She was holding herself very still.

"Off raiding. Anglcyn coast. Five ships, near two hundred men. A big party, that. Left just before I did." He'd seen them go. It was late in the season, but they could winter over if they needed to. He had made and mended weapons and armour for many of them.

"Anglcyn coast," she repeated.

"Yes," he said.

There was a silence. He heard the bees.

"Thank you for your tidings. Ingavin and the goddesses shield you," she said, turning away, the serpent still about her neck and shoulders. "Wait here. Sigla will bring you something."

Sigla did. Generous enough. He spent some of it at an inn that night, on ale and a girl. Went looking for property the next morning. Not that there was so much of it on the isle. Rabady was small, everyone knew everyone. It might have helped if his parents had still been living, instead of buried here, but that was a waste of a wish. One of the names Sturla had given him was that of a widow, no children, young enough to still bear, he'd been told, some land in her own name, west end of the isle. He brushed his clothes and boots before going to call.

His son was born the next summer. His wife died in the birthing. He buried her back of the house, hired a wet nurse, went looking for another wife. Found one, and younger this time: he was a man with a bit of land now. He felt fortunate, as if he'd made good choices in life. There was an oak tree standing by itself near the south end of his land. He left it untouched, consecrated it to Ingavin, made offerings there, lit fires, midsummer, midwinter.

His son, fourteen years later, cut it down one night after a bad, drunken fight the two of them had. Ralf Erlickson, still drunk in the morning, killed the boy in his bed with a hammer when he found out, smashed in his skull. A father could deal with his family as he chose, that was the way of it.

Or it had been once. Sturla One-hand, still governor, convened the island's *thring*. They exiled Ralf Erlickson from Rabady for murder, because the lad had been asleep when killed, or so the stepmother said. And since when had the word of a woman been accepted by Erlings in a *thring*?

No matter. It was a done thing. He left, or they'd have killed him. Well on in years by then, Ralf Erlickson found himself on a small boat heading back to the mainland, landless (One-hand had claimed the exile's property for the town, of course).

Eventually, he made his way back down to Jormsvik, for want of a better thought. Worked at his old trade, but his hand and eye weren't what they had been. Not surprising, really, it had been a long time. He died there a little while after. Was laid in the earth outside the walls in the usual fashion. He wasn't a warrior, no pyre. One friend and two of the whores saw him buried.

Life, for all men under the gods, was uncertain as weather or winter seas: the only truth worth calling true, as the ending of one of the sagas had it.

PART TWO

CHAPTER VI

When the king's fever took him in the night there was not enough love—or mercy—in the world to keep him from the fens and swamps again.

Drenched with sweat upon the royal bed (or pallet, if they were travelling), Aeldred of the Anglcyn would cry out in the dark, not even aware he was doing it, so piteously it hurt the hearts of those who loved him to know where he was going.

They all thought they knew where, and when, by now.

He was seeing his brother and his father die long years ago on Camburn Field by Raedhill. He was riding in icy rain (a winter campaign, the Erlings had surprised them), wounded, and shivering with the first of these fevers at the end of a brutal day's fighting; and he was king, as of twilight's coming down upon that headlong, fever-ravaged flight from the northmen who had broken them at last.

King of the Anglcyn, fleeing like an outlaw to hide in the marshes, the *fyrd* broken, lands overrun. His royal father hideously blood-eagled on the wet ground at Camburn in blood and rain. His brother cut in pieces there.

He didn't know about them until later. He did know it now, a late-summer night in Esferth so many years after, tossing in fever-dream, reliving the winter twilight when Jad had abandoned them for their sins. The blades and axes of the Erlings pursuing them in the wild dark, the northmen triumphantly crying the accursed names of Ingavin and Thünir like ravens on the rain wind . . .

It is difficult to see with the rain lashing their faces, a heavy blanket of cloud, night coming swiftly now. Both good and bad: they will be harder to hunt down, but can easily miss their own way, not able to use torches. There are no roads here across moor and tor. There are eight of them with Aeldred, riding west. It is Osbert who is nearest the king (for he is the king now, last of his line), as he always is, and Osbert who shouts them to a jostling halt by the pitiful shelter of a handful of elms. They are soaked to the bone, chilled, most wounded, all exhausted, the wind lashing.

But Aeldred is shivering with fever, slumped forward on his horse, and he cannot speak in answer to his name. Osbert moves his mount nearer, reaches out, touches the king's brow . . . and recoils, for Aeldred is burning hot.

"He cannot ride," he says, leader of the household troop.

"He must!" Burgred snaps, shouting it over the wind. "They will not be far behind us."

And Aeldred lifts his head, with a great effort, mumbles something they cannot hear. He points west with one hand, twitches his reins to move forward. He slips in the saddle as he does so. Osbert is near enough to hold him, their horses side by side.

The two thegns look at each other over the wracked body of the man who is now their king. "He will die," Osbert says. Aeldred, son of Gademar, is twenty years old, just.

The wind howls, rain slashes them like needles. It is very dark, they can hardly see each other. After a long moment, Burgred of Denferth wipes water from his face and nods. "Very well. The seven of us carry on, with the royal banner. We will try to be seen, draw them west. You find a farmhouse somewhere, and pray."

Osbert nods his head. "Meet in Beortferth, on the island itself, among the salt fens. When we can."

"The marshes are dangerous. You can find your way through?"

"Maybe not. Have someone watch for us."

Burgred nods again, looks over at their boyhood friend, this other young man, slumped on his horse. Aeldred in battle was deadly, commanding the left flank of the *fyrd* with his household guard. It was not the left flank that crumbled, not that it mattered now.

"Jad curse this day," Burgred says.

Then he turns and six men follow him across an open field in the dark, one carrying their banner, moving west again, but deliberately, not as quickly as before.

Osbert, son of Cuthwulf, left alone with his king, leans over and whispers, tenderly, "Dear heart, have you even a little left? We ride for shelter now, and should not have far to go."

He has no idea if this is true in fact, no clear sense of where they are, but if there are farms or houses they should be north of here. And when Aeldred, with another appalling effort, pushes himself upright and looks vaguely towards him and nods—shivering, still unable to speak—it is northward that Osbert turns, leaving the elms, heading into the wind.

He will remember the next hours all his life, though Aeldred, lost in that first-ever fever, never will. It grows colder, begins to snow. They are both wounded, sweat-drenched, inadequately clothed, and Aeldred is using the last reserves of an iron will just to stay on his horse. Osbert hears wolves on the wind; listens constantly for horses, knowing, if he hears them, that the Erlings have come and it is over. There are no lights to be seen: no charcoal burner by the woods, no farmers burning candles or a fire so late on a night like this. He strains his eyes into the dark and prays, as Burgred had said he should. The king's breathing is ragged. He can hear it, the rasp and draw. There is nothing to see but falling snow, and black woods to the west, and the bare, wintry fields through which they ride. A night fit for the world's end. Wolves around, and the Erling wolves hunting them in the dark.

And then, still shivering uncontrollably, Aeldred lifts his head. A moment he stays thus, looking at nothing, and then speaks his first clear words of the night's flight. "To the left," he says. "West of us, Jad help me." His head drops forward again. Snow falls, the wind blows, more a hammer than a knife.

Aeldred will claim, ever after, to have no recollection of saying those words. Osbert will say that when the king spoke he heard and felt the presence of the god.

Unquestioningly, he turns west, guiding Aeldred's horse with one hand now, to stay beside his own. Wind on their right, pushing them south. Osbert's hands are frozen, he can scarcely feel the reins he holds, his own or the king's. He sees blackness ahead, a forest. They cannot ride into that.

And then there is the hut. Directly in front of them, close to the trees, in their very path. He would have ridden north, right past it. It takes him a moment to *understand* what he is seeing, for his weariness is great, and then Osbert begins to weep, helplessly, and his hands tremble.

Holy Jad has not, after all, abandoned them to the dark.

THEY DARE NOT LIGHT A FIRE. The horses have been hidden out of sight in the woods, tied to the same tree, to keep each other warm. The snow is shifting and blowing; there will be no tracks. There can be no signs of their passage near the house. The Erlings are no strangers to snow and icy winds. Their *berserkirs* and wolf-raiders flourish in this weather, wrapped in their animal skins, eyes not human until the fury leaves them. They *will* be out there, in the wind, hunting, for the northmen know by now that one of the line of Athelbert left Camburn Field alive. In some ways it ought not to matter. With a land taken and overrun, an army shattered, what can a king matter, alone?

But in other ways, it means the world, it *could* mean the world, and they will want Aeldred killed, in a manner as vicious as they can devise. So there is no fire in the swineherd's house where a terrified man and his wife, awakened by a pounding on their door in the wild night, have abandoned a narrow bed to pile threadbare blankets and rags and straw upon the shivering, burning man who—they have been told—is their king under holy Jad.

Whether it is the relative stillness within these thin walls, out of the howling wind, or some portent-laden deepening of his sickness (Osbert is no leech, he does not know), the king begins to cry out on the swineherd's bed, shouting names at first, then a hoarse rallying cry, some words in ancient Trakesian, and then in the Rhodian tongue of the holy books—for Aeldred is a learned man and has been to Rhodias itself.

But his shouting might kill them tonight.

So in the darkness and the cold, Osbert, son of Cuthwulf, lies down beside his friend and begins whispering to him as one might murmur to a lover or a child, and each time the king draws a wracked breath to cry out in oblivious agony, his friend clamps a bloodstained hand over his mouth and stifles the sound, again and again, weeping as he does so, for the pity of it.

Then they do hear cries, from outside in the white night, and it seems to Osbert, lying beside his king in that frigid hut (so cold the lice are probably dead), that their ending has come indeed, the doom no man can escape forever. And he reaches for the sword beside him on the earthen floor, and vows to his father's spirit and the sun god that he will not let Aeldred be taken alive from here to be ripped apart by Erlings.

He moves to rise, and there is a hand on his arm.

"There are going by," the swineherd whispers, toothless. "Hold, my lord."

Aeldred's head shifts. He drags for breath again. Osbert turns quickly, grips the other man's head with one hand (hot as a forge it is) and covers the king's mouth with his other, and he murmurs a prayer for forgiveness, as Aeldred thrashes beside him, trying to give utterance to whatever pain and fever are demanding that he cry.

And whether because of prayer or a moon-shrouded night or the northmen's haste or nothing more than chance, the Erlings do pass by, how many of them Osbert never knew. And after that the night, too, passes, longer than any night of his life had ever been.

Eventually, Osbert sees, through unstopped chinks in wall and door (wind slashing through), that the flurries of snow have stopped. Looking out for a moment, he sees the blue moon shining before clouds slide to cover it again. An owl cries, hunting over the woods behind them. The wind has died down enough for that.

Towards dawn, the king's terrible shivering stops, he grows cooler to the touch, the shallow breathing steadies, and then he sleeps.

OSBERT SLIPS INTO THE WOODS, feeds and waters the horses . . . precious little, in truth, for the family's only nurture in winter is carefully rationed salted pork from their swine and unflavoured, mealy oatcakes. Food for animals is an impossible luxury. The pigs are in the forest, left to forage for themselves.

Amazed, he hears laughter from inside as he returns, ducking through the doorway. Aeldred is taking a badly blackened cake for himself, leaving the others, less charred. The swineherd's wife is blushing, the king smiling, nothing at all like the man who'd shivered and moaned in the dark, or the one who'd screamed like an Erling *berserkir* on the battlefield. He looks over at his friend and smiles.

"I have just been told, gently enough, that I make a deficient servant, Osbert. Did you know that?"

The woman wails in denial, covers her crimson face with both hands. Her husband is looking back and forth, his face a blank, uncertain what to think.

"It is the only reason we let you claim rank," Osbert murmurs, closing the door. "The fact that you can't even clean boots properly."

Aeldred laughs, then sobers, looking up at his friend. "You saved my life," he says, "and then these people saved ours."

Osbert hesitates. "You remember anything of the night?"

The king shakes his head.

"Just as well," his friend says, eventually.

"We should pray," Aeldred says. They do, giving thanks on their knees, facing east to the sun, for all known blessings.

They wait until sunset and then they leave, to hide among the marshes, besieged in their own land.

BEORTFERTH IS A LOW-LYING, wet islet, lost amid dank, spreading salt fens. Only the smaller rodents live there, and marsh birds, water snakes, biting insects in summer. It was the bird-catchers who first found the place, long ago, making their precarious way through the fens, on foot, or poling flat-bottomed skiffs.

It is almost always foggy here, tendrils of mist, the god's sun a distant, wan thing, even on the clear days. You can see strange visions here, get hopelessly lost. Horses and men have been sucked down in the stagnant bogs, which are deep in places. Some say there are nameless creatures down there, alive since the days of darkness. The safe paths are narrow, not remotely predictable, you must know them exactly, ride or walk in single file, easy to ambush. Groves of gnarled trees rise up in places, startling and strange in the greyness, roots in water, leading the wanderer to stray and fall.

In winter it is always damp, unhealthy, there is desperately little in the way of food, and that winter—when the Erlings won the Battle of Camburn Field—was a cruelly harsh one. Endless freezing rain and snow, thin, grey-yellow ice forming in the marsh, the wet wind slashing. Almost every one of them has a cough, rheumy eyes, loose bowels. All of them are hungry, and cold.

It is Aeldred's finest hour. It is this winter that will create and define him as what he will become, and some will claim to have sensed this as it was happening.

Osbert is not one of them, nor Burgred. Concealing their own coughs and fluxes as best they can, flatly denying exhaustion, refusing to acknowledge hunger, Aeldred's two commanders (as young as he was, that winter) will each say, long afterwards, that they survived by *not* thinking ahead, addressing only the demands of each day, each hour. Eyes lowered like a man pushing a plough through a punishing, stony field.

In the first month they arrange and supervise the building of a primitive fort on the isle, more a windbreak with a roof than anything else. When it is complete, before he ever steps inside, Aeldred stands in a slanting rain before the forty-seven men who are with him by then (a number never forgotten, all of them named in the *Chronicle*) and formally declares the isle to be the seat of his realm, heart of the Anglcyn in their land, in the name of Jad.

His realm. Forty-seven men. Ingemar Svidrirson and his Erlings are inside Raedhill's walls, foraging unopposed through a beaten countryside. Not a swift sea raid for slaves and glory and gold. Here to settle, and rule.

Osbert looks across sparse, patchy grass in rain towards Burgred of Denferth, and then back at the man who leads them in this hunted, misty refuge, with salt in the biting air, and for the first time since Camburn Field he allows himself the *idea* of hope. Looking up from the plough. Aeldred kneels in prayer; they all do.

That same afternoon, having given thanks, in piety, their first raiding party rides out from the swamps.

Fifteen of them, Burgred leading. They are gone two days, to make a wide loop away from here. They surprise and kill eight Erlings foraging for winter provisions in a depleted countryside, and bring their weapons and horses (and the provisions) back. A triumph, a victory. While they are out, four men have come wandering in through the fens, to join the king.

Hope, a licence to dream. The beginnings of these things. Men gather close around a night fire in Beortferth Hall, walls and a roof between them and the rain at last. There is one bard among them, his instrument damply out of tune. It doesn't matter. He sings the old songs, and Aeldred joins in the singing, and then all of them do. They take turns on watch outside, on the higher ground, and farther out, at the entrances to the marshes, east and north. Sound carries here; those on watch can hear the singing sometimes. It is a warming for them, amazingly so.

That same night, Aeldred's fever comes again.

They have their one singer, and a single aged cleric with bad knees, some artisans, masons, bird-catchers, fletchers, farmers, fighting men from the *fyrd*, with and without weapons. No leech. No one with knives and cups to bleed him, or any sure knowledge of herbs. The cleric prays, kneeling painfully, sun disk in his hands, where the king lies by the fire and Osbert—for it is seen as his task—tries, in anguish, to decide whether Aeldred, thrashing and crying out, oblivious, lost to them and to Jad's created world, needs to be warmed or cooled at any given moment, and his heart breaks again and again all the long night.

BY SPRINGTIME THERE ARE almost two hundred of them on the isle. The season has brought other life: herons, otters, the loud croaking of frogs in the marsh. There are more wooden structures now, even a small chapel, and they have organized, of necessity, a network of food suppliers, hunting parties. The hunters become more than that, if Erlings are seen.

The northmen have had a difficult winter of their own, it appears. Short of food, not enough of them to safely extend their reach beyond the fastness of Raedhill until others come—*if* they come—when the weather turns. And their own foraging parties have been encountering, with disturbing frequency, horsed Anglcyn fighters with murderous vengeance in their eyes and hands, emerging from some base the Erlings cannot find in this too-wide, forested, hostile countryside. It is one thing to beat a royal army in a field, another to hold what you claim.

The mood on the isle is changing. Spring can do that, quickening season. They have a routine now, shelter, birdsong, greater numbers each day.

Amid all this, those of the Beortferth leaders not taking parties out from the fens are . . . learning how to read.

It is a direct order of the king's, an obsession. An idea he has about the kingdom he would make. Aeldred himself, stealing time, labours at a rough-hewn wooden table at a translation into Anglcyn of the single, charred Rhodian text someone found amid the ruins of a chapel west and south of them. Burgred has not been shy about teasing the king about this task. It is entirely uncertain, he maintains, what ultimate good it will be to have a copy in their own tongue of a classical text on the treatment of cataracts.

The consolations of learning, the king replies, airily enough, are profound, in and of themselves. He swears a good deal, however, as he works, not seeming especially consoled. It is a source of amusement to many of them, though not necessarily to those engaged, at a given moment, in sounding out their letters like children under the cleric's irritable instruction.

Among the new recruits making their way late in winter, through the fens to Beortferth was a lean grey man claiming training in leechcraft. He has bled the king by cup and blade, achieving little, if anything. There is also a woman with them now, old, stooped like a hoop—and so safe among so many restless men. She has wandered the marshes, gathered herbs (spikemarrow, wortfen), and spoken a charm into them—when the pinch-mouthed cleric was not nearby to mutter of heathenish magics—and has applied these, pounded into a green paste, to the king's forehead and chest when his fever takes him.

This, too, as best Osbert can judge, does nothing beyond causing angry-looking reddish weals. When Aeldred burns and shivers Osbert will take him in his arms and whisper, endlessly, of summer sunlight and tended fields of rye, of well-built town walls and even of learned men discoursing upon eye diseases and philosophy, and the Erling wolves beaten back and back and away, oversea.

In the mornings, white and weak, but lucid, Aeldred remembers none of this. The nights are harder, he says more than once, for his friend. Osbert denies that. Of course he denies it. He leads raiding parties in search of game, and northmen. He practises his letters with the cleric.

And then one day, the ice gone, birds around and above them, Aeldred son of Gademar, who was the son of Athelbert, sends twenty men out in pairs, riding in different directions, each pair with the image of a sword carved upon a block of wood.

Change is upon them, with the change of season. The gambler's throw of a kingdom's dice. If something is to happen it must be before the dragon-ships set sail from the east to cross the sea for these shores. The king on his isle in the marsh summons all that is left of the *fyrd,* and all other men, the host of the Anglcyn, to meet him on the next night of the blue full moon (spirits' moon, when the dead wake) at Ecbert's Stone, not far from Camburn Field.

Not far at all from Raedhill.

OSBERT AND BURGRED, comparing in whispers, have judged their number at a little under eight hundred souls, the summoned men of the west. They have reported as much to the king. There are more, in honesty, than any of them expected. Fewer than they need.

When has any Anglcyn army had the men it needed against an Erling force? They are aware, by starlight, of risk and limitation, not indifferent to these things, but hardly affected by them.

The sun has not yet risen; it is dark and still here at the wood's edge. A clear night, little wind. This is a forest once said to be haunted by spirits, faeries, the presence of the dead. Not an inappropriate place to gather. Aeldred steps forward, a shadow against the last stars.

"We will do the invocation now," he says, "then move before light, to come upon them the sooner. We will pass in darkness, to end the darkness." That phrase, among many, will be remembered, recorded.

There is an element of transgression in doing the god's rites before his sun rises, but no man there demurs. Aeldred, his clerics beside him (three of them now), leads that host in morning prayer before the morning comes. *May we always be found in the Light.*

He rises, they move out, before ever the sun strikes the Stone. Some horsed, mostly on foot, a wide array of weapons and experience. You could call them a rabble if you wanted. But it is a rabble with a king in front of it, and a knowledge that their world may turn on today's unfolding.

There is an Erling force south-east of them, having come out from Raedhill at the (deliberately offered) rumour of a band of Anglcyn nearby, possibly led by Gademar's last son, the one who could still dare call himself king of these fields and forests, this land the northmen have claimed. Ingemar could not but respond to this bait.

Aeldred rides at the front, his two friends and thegns on either side. The king turns to look back on his people who have gathered here during the dark of a blue moon night.

He smiles, though only those nearest can see this. Easy in the saddle, unhelmed, long brown hair, blue eyes (his slain father's eyes), the light, clear voice carrying when he speaks.

"It begins now, in Jad's holy name," he says. "Every man here, whatever his birth, will be known for the whole of his life as having been at Ecbert's Stone. Come with me, my darlings, to be wrapped in glory."

IT IS GLORIOUS, in the event: as told by myriad chroniclers, sung so often (and variously), woven into legend, or into tapestries hung on stone walls, warming winter rooms. Osbert will live to hear his exploits of the day celebrated—and unrecognizable.

He is at the king's side when they leave the wood and move south towards Camburn where their outliers have reported the Erlings camped by a field they know. Burgred, at Aeldred's command, takes one hundred and fifty men east, along the black line of the trees, to angle south as well, between Camburn and the walls of Raedhill.

The Erlings are not yet awakened under the raven banners, are not yet ready for a day's promised hunting of an Anglcyn band when that band—and rather more than that—appear from the north, moving at speed.

The northmen have their watchmen, of course, and some brief warning. They are not, by any measure, cowards, and the numbers are near to even. Amid screamed orders they scramble into armour, seizing hammers and spears and axes; their leaders have swords. There is, however, much to the elements of surprise and speed in any fight, and disarray can turn a battle before it starts, unless leaders can master it.

They have not expected even numbers today, or the ferocity of the charge that roars into their camp as the first hues of sunlight appear in the east. The northmen form urgent ranks, stand, buckle, hold again for a time. But only for a time.

There is sometimes knowledge that can subvert men's ardour on a battlefield: the Erlings here in Esferth know that they have walls not far away at Raedhill, behind which they can shelter, deal with these Anglcyn at leisure, without the chaos caused by this heavy, venomous, pre-dawn assault.

Responding to the unspoken, their leaders order a pull-back. Not an entirely wrong course. There is some distance to cover to Ingemar and the others back in Raedhill, but in the past the Anglcyn have been content to force the northmen to retreat. After which they would regroup to consider a next step. There is reason, there-fore, to believe it will be so again as the sun comes up this bright spring morning, lighting meadow flowers and young grass.

Then there is reason to understand that they are wrong. The men of the Anglcyn are not stopping to debate among themselves, to consider options and alternatives. They are following hard, some of them on horse, some with bows. The withdrawal becomes, in the way of these things, all too often, a flat-out retreat.

And as the Erling escape from their abandoned camp and position becomes a clamorous rout, a flight east towards distant Raedhill, just about at the moment when fear will invest the body and soul of even a brave man, the northmen discover another host of the Anglcyn between them and the walls of safety—and the world, or that small corner of it, changes.

Amid cries of *Aeldred and Jad,* withdrawal, retreat, rout turn into slaughter, very near the same wet, wintry plain that saw King Gademar blood-eagled as a winter's wet, grey twilight came down.

Less than half a year ago. The time it took Aeldred of Esferth to evolve from a fleeing refugee hiding in a swine-herd's bed, shivering with fever, to a king in the field, avenging his father and brother, cutting the northmen to pieces by the blood-soaked field that saw their own defeat.

They even take the raven banner, which has never happened in these lands before. They kill Erlings all the way to the walls of Raedhill and make camp there at sunset, and there they pray with lifted voices at the long day's end.

In the morning the northmen send out emissaries, to offer hostages and sue for peace.

IN THE MIDST of the last of the seven days and nights of feasting in Raedhill that accompany King Aeldred's conversion of the Erling leader, Ingemar Svidrirson, into the most holy faith of Jad of the Sun, Burgred of Denferth, the king's lifelong companion, finds that the black bile rising in his gorge is simply too strong.

He leaves the banquet hall, walks alone into the beclouded night past the spearmen on guard, away from the spill of torchlight in the hall and the sounds of revelry, seeking a darkness to equal the one he finds within.

He hawks and spits into the street, trying to dispel the clawing sickness he feels, which has nothing to do with too much ale or food and is, instead, about the desire to commit murder and the need to refrain.

The noise is behind him now and he wants it there. He walks towards the town gates, away from the feasting hall, finds himself in a muddy laneway. Leans against a wooden wall there—a stable, from the sounds within—and draws a deep breath of the night air. Looks up at the stars showing through rents in the swift clouds. Aeldred told him once that there are those in distant lands who worship them. So many ways for men to fall into error, he thinks.

He hears a cough, turns his head quickly. There is no danger here now, except, perhaps, to their souls because of what is happening in the banquet hall. He expects it to be a woman. There are many of them about, with all the soldiers in Raedhill. There's money to be made by night, in rooms with a pallet, or even in the lanes.

It isn't a woman, following.

"Windy out here. I brought us a flask," Osbert says mildly, leaning back against the stable wall beside him. "The Raedhill brewhouse is run by a widow, it seems. Learned all her husband had to teach. King's asked her to join his court, brew for us. I approve."

Burgred doesn't want another drink but takes the flask. He has known Osbert as long as he's known Aeldred, which is to say most of his life. The ale's strong and clean. "Best ale I ever had was made by women," he murmurs. "Religious house in the north, by Blencairn."

"Never been there," Osbert says. "Hold the flask a bit." He turns around. Burgred hears his friend urinating against the wall. Absently he drinks, looking up at the sky again. Blue moon over west, waning towards a crescent above the gates. It was full the night they won the second battle of Camburn Field and camped before these walls: not even a fourteen-night ago. They had Ingemar and his remnant penned in here like sheep, and a dead, unspeakably mutilated king to avenge. Burgred still wants to kill, an urge deeper than desire.

Instead they are feasting that same Erling remnant, offering them gifts and safe passage east across the rivers to that part of these Anglcyn lands that has long been given over to the northmen.

"He doesn't think like we do," Osbert murmurs, as if reading his mind. He takes back the flask.

"Aeldred?"

"No, the miller upstream. Of course Aeldred. You understand that Ingemar knelt before him, kissed his foot in homage, swore fealty, accepted Jad."

Burgred swears, viciously. "Carved his father open from the back, cracked his ribs apart and draped his lungs out on his shoulders. Yes, I know *all* these things." His hands are fists, just saying it.

The other man is silent for a time. The wind carries the sounds of the banquet to them. Someone is singing. Osbert sighs. "We were less than seven hundred men at the gates. They had two hundred left inside, and the season turning, which could mean dragon-ships, soon. We had no easy way of smashing into a walled, defended town. One day we might, but not now. My friend, you know all *these* things, too."

"So instead of starving them out, we feast, and honour them?"

"We feast, and honour the god and their coming to his light."

Burgred swears again. "You speak that way, but in your heart you feel as I do. I know it. You want the dead avenged."

Sounds carry to them from the distant hall. "I believe," says the other man, "that it is tearing him apart to do this, and he is doing it nonetheless. Be glad you are not a king."

Burgred looks over at him, the face hard to see in darkness. He sighs. "And these foul Erlings will *stay* with Jad? You really think so?"

"I have no idea. Some of them have, before. Here's what I do think: the world will know that Ingemar Svidrirson, who wanted to be a king here, has knelt and sworn loyalty to Aeldred of Esferth and accepted a sun disk and royal gifts from him, and will leave him eight hostages, including two sons—and we gave them nothing in exchange. *Nothing*. And I know that has never happened since first the Erlings came to these shores."

"You call the gifts nothing? Did you see the horses?"

"I saw them. They are the gifts of a great lord to a lesser. They will be seen as such. Jad did defeat Ingavin here, and took the raven banners, too. My friend, come back and drink with me. We have won something important here, and it is just a beginning."

Burgred shakes his head. There is still pain, a congestion in his chest. "I would . . . follow him under the world to battle demons. He knows that. But . . ."

"But not if he makes peace with the demons?"

Burgred feels the heaviness, a weight like stones. "It was . . . easier on the isle, in Beortferth. We knew what we had to do."

"Aeldred still knows. Sometimes . . . with power . . . you do things that fall against your heart."

"I may not be suited for power, then."

"You have it, my dear. You will have to learn. Unless you leave us. Will you leave us?"

The wind dies down, faint music fades. They hear horses through the stable wall.

"You know I won't," Burgred says, finally. "He knows I won't."

"We must trust him," Osbert says, softly. "If we can keep him healthy and alive for long enough, they will not take us again. We will leave a kingdom to our children, one they can defend."

Burgred looks at him. Osbert is a shadow in the blackness of the laneway, and a voice forever known. Burgred sighs again, from the heart. "And they will learn how to read Merovius on cataracts, in Trakesian, or he'll slaughter them all."

There is a pause, and then Osbert's laughter in the darkness, rich as southern wine.

⁓

Fevers were tertian, quartan, daily, or hectic. They stemmed—almost always—from imbalances in the four humours, the alignment of coldness, heat, moisture, dryness in all men. (There were other concerns peculiar to women, each month, or when they gave birth.)

The fevered could be bled, with knife and cup, with leeches, in locations and in degrees according to the teachings followed by the physician. Sometimes the patient died of this. Death walked near to the living at all times. It was known. It was generally considered that a good physician was one who didn't kill you sooner than whatever afflicted you would have.

Those suffering from acute fever might be comforted (or not) by prayer, eased by poultices, wet sheets, warm bodies next to them, music, or silence. They were treated with hydromel and oxymel (and physicians had divergent views as to which sort of honey was best, in the mixing), or with aconite and wild celery when it was thought that witchery lay at the root of their burning. Lemon balm and vervain and willow would be compounded, or buck-thorn to purge them inside, sometimes violently. Coltsfoot and fenugreek, sage and wormwood, betony, fennel, hock and melilot were all said to be efficacious, at times.

Valerian might help a sufferer sleep, easing pain.

Fingernails could be clipped and buried under an ash tree by blue moon's light, though not, of course, if any cleric were about to know of it. And that same caution applied to remedies involving gemstones and invoca-tions in the night wood, though it would be foolish to deny that these took place all over the kingdom of the Anglcyn.

At one time or another, all of these remedies and more had been brought to bear in the matter of King Aeldred's fevers, whether they were countenanced by the king and his clergy or not.

None of them were able to reorder the marred world in such a way as to end the fires that still seized him some nights, so many long years after that first one had.

"WHY IS IT DARK?"

It was always predictable how the king would emerge, but, more recently, not how long it would take. What was certain was that he would be pale, weak-voiced, lucid, precise, and angry.

Osbert had been dozing on the pallet they always made for him. He woke to the voice.

"It is the middle of the night, my lord. Welcome back."

"I lost a whole day this time? Dear Jad. I haven't got days to lose!" Aeldred was never profane, but the fury was manifest.

"I dealt with the reports as they came. Both new *burhs* on the coast are on time, nearly complete, fully manned. The shipyard is at work. Be easy."

"What else?" Aeldred was not being easy.

"The taxation officers went out this morning."

"The tribute from Erlond—Svidrirson's? What word?"

"Not yet, but . . . promised." It was never wise to be less than direct with the king when he returned from wherever the fever took him.

"Promised? How?"

"A messenger rode in after midday. The young one, Ingemar's son."

Aeldred scowled. "He only sends the boy when the tribute's late. Where is he?"

"Housed properly, asleep, I'd imagine. It is late. Be at ease, my lord. Athelbert received him formally in your stead, with his brother."

"On what excuse for my not being there?"

Osbert hesitated. "Your fevers are . . . known, my lord."

The king scowled again. "And where was Burgred, come to think of it?"

Osbert cleared his throat. "We had rumour of a ship sighted. He went with some of the *fyrd* to find out more."

"A ship? Erling?"

Osbert nodded. "Or ships."

Aeldred closed his eyes. "That makes little sense." There was a silence. "You have been beside me all the time, of course."

"And others. Your daughters were here tonight. Your lady wife sat with you before going to chapel to pray for your health. She will be relieved to hear you are well again."

"Of course she will."

That had nuances. Most of what Aeldred said had layers, and Osbert knew a great deal about the royal marriage.

The king lay still on his pillow, eyes shut. After a moment, he said, "But you never left, did you?"

"I . . . went to the audience chamber to take the reports."

Aeldred opened his eyes, turned his head slightly to look at the other man. After a silence, he said, "Would you have had a better life had I driven you away, do you think?"

"I find that hard to imagine, my lord. The better life *and* being driven away."

Aeldred shook his head a little. "You might walk properly, at least."

Osbert brought a hand down to his marred leg. "A small price. We live a life of battles."

Aeldred was looking at him. "I shall answer for you before the god one day," he said.

"And I shall speak in your defence. You were right, my lord, Burgred and I were wrong. Today is proof, the boy coming, the tribute promised again. Ingemar has kept his oath. It let us do what needed to be done."

"And here you are, unmarried, without kin or heir, on one leg, awake all night by the side of the man who—"

"Who is king of the Anglcyn under Jad, and has kept us alive and together as a people. We make our choices, my lord. And marriage is not for every man. I have not lacked for companionship."

"And heirs?"

Osbert shrugged. "I'll leave my own name, linked—if the god allows—with yours, in the shaping of this land. I have nephews for my own properties." They had had this conversation before.

Aeldred shook his head again. There was more grey in his beard of late, Osbert saw. It showed in the lamplight, as did the circles under his eyes, which were always there after fever. "And I am, as ever when this passes, speaking to you as a servant."

"I *am* a servant, my lord."

Aeldred smiled wanly. "Shall I say something profane to that?"

"I would be greatly alarmed." Osbert returned the smile.

The king stretched, rubbed at his face, sat up in the bed. "I surrender. And I believe I will eat. Would you also send for . . . would you ask my lady wife to come to me?"

"It is the middle of the night, my lord."

"You said that already."

Aeldred's gaze was mild but could not be misconstrued. Osbert cleared his throat. "I will have someone send—"

"Ask."

"Ask for her."

"Would you be so good as to do it yourself? It is the middle of the night."

A small, ironic movement of the mouth. The king was back among them, there was no doubting it. Osbert bowed, took his cane, and went out.

HE LOOKED AT HIS HANDS in the lamplight after Osbert left. Steady enough. He flexed his fingers. Could smell his own sweat in the bedsheets. A night and a day and this much of another night. More time than he had to yield, the grave closer every day. These fevers were a kind of dying. He felt light-headed now, as always. That was understandable. Also physically aroused, as always, though there was no easy way to explain that. The body's return to itself?

The body was a gift of Jad, a housing in this world for the mind and immortal soul, therefore to be honoured and attended to—though not, on the other hand, over-loved, because that was also a transgression.

Men were shaped, according to the liturgy, in a distant image of the god's own most-chosen form, of all those infinite ones he could assume. Jad was rendered by artists in his mortal guise—whether golden and glorious as the sun, or dark-bearded and careworn—in wood carving, fresco, ivory, marble, bronze, on parchment, in gold, in mosaic on domes or chapel walls. This truth (Livrenne of Mesangues had argued in his *Commentaries*) only added to the deference properly due to the physical form of man—opening the door to a clerical debate, acrid at times, as to the implications for the form and status of woman.

There had been a period several hundred years ago when such visual renderings of the god had been interdicted by the High Patriarch in Rhodias, under pressure from Sarantium. That particular heresy was now a thing of the past.

Aeldred thought, often, about the works eradicated during that time. He'd been very young when he'd made the journey over sea and land and mountain pass to Rhodias with his father. He remembered some of the holy art they'd seen but also (having been a particular sort of child) those places in sanctuary and palace where the evidence of smashed or painted-over works could be observed.

Waiting now in the lamplit dark of a late-summer night for his wife to come, that he might undress her and

make love, the king found himself musing—not for the
first time—on the people of the south: people so ancient,
so long established, that they had works of art that had
been *destroyed* hundreds of years before these northlands
even had towns or walls worthy of the name, let alone a
sanctuary of the god that deserved to be called as much.

And then, tracking that thought, you could walk even
further back, to the Rhodians of the era before Jad came,
who had walked in these lands too, building their walls and
cities and arches and temples to pagan gods. Mostly rubble
now, since the long retreat, but still reminders of . . .
unattainable glory. All around them here, in this harsh
near-wilderness that he was pleased to call a kingdom
under Jad.

You *could* be a proper child of the god, virtuous and
devout, even in a wilderness. This was taught, and he
knew it in his heart. Indeed, many of the most pious
clerics had deliberately withdrawn from those same jaded
southern civilizations in Batiara, in Sarantium, to seek the
essence of Jad in passionate solitude.

Aeldred wasn't a man like one of those. He knew what
he'd found in Rhodias, however ruined it was, and in the
lesser Batiaran cities all the way down through the penin-
sula (Padrino, Varena, Baiana—music in the names).

The king of the Anglcyn would not have denied that
his soul (housed in a body that wracked and betrayed
him so often) had been marked from childhood during
that long-ago journey through the intricate seductions
of the south.

He was king of a precarious, dispersed, unlettered
people in a winter-shaped, beleaguered land, and he
wanted to be more. He wanted *them* to be more, his
Anglcyn of this island. And given three generations of
peace, he thought it possible. He had made decisions, for
more than twenty-five years, denying his heart and soul

sometimes, with that in mind. He would answer to Jad for all of it, not far in the future now.

And he didn't think three generations would be allowed them.

Not in these northern lands, this boneyard of war. He lived his life, fighting through impediments, including these fevers, in defiance of that bitter thought, as if to *will* it not to be so, envisaging the god, in his chariot under the world, battling through evils every single night, to bring back the sun to the world he had made.

ELSWITH CAME BEFORE his meal arrived, which was unexpected.

She entered without knocking, closed the door behind her, moved forward into lamplight.

"You are recovered, by the god's grace?"

He nodded, looking at her. His wife was a large woman, big-boned, as her warrior father had been, heavier now than when she'd come to marry him—but age and eight confinements could do that to a woman. Her hair was as fair as it had been, though, and unbound now—she had been asleep, after all. She wore a dark green night robe, fastened all the way up the front, a sun disk (always) about her neck, pillowed upon the robe between heavy breasts. No rings, no other adornment. Adornments were a vanity, to be shunned.

She had been asking, for years now, to be released from their marriage and this worldly life, to withdraw to a religious house, become one of the Daughters of Jad, live out her days in holiness, praying for her soul, and his.

He didn't want her to go.

"Thank you for coming," he said.

"You sent," she said.

"I told Osbert to say—"

"He did."

Her expression was austere but not unfriendly. They *weren't* unfriendly with each other, though both knew that was the talk.

She had not moved from where she'd stopped to look down at him in the bed. He remembered his first sight of her, all those years ago. Tall, fair-haired, well-made woman, not yet eighteen when they'd brought her south. He hadn't been much older than that, a year from the battles of Camburn, swift to wed because he needed heirs. There had been a time when they were both young. It seemed, occasionally, a disconcerting recollection.

"They are bringing a meal," he said.

"I heard, outside. I told them to wait until I left." From any other woman, that might have been innuendo, invitation. Elswith didn't smile.

He was aroused, even so, even after all these years. "Will you come to me?" he asked. Made it a request.

"I have," she murmured dryly, but stepped forward nonetheless, a virtuous, honourable woman, keeping a compact—but wanting with all her heart to leave him, leave all of them behind. Had her reasons.

She stood by the bed, the light behind her now. Aeldred sat up, his pulse racing. All these years. She wore no perfume, of course, but he knew the scent of her body and that excited him.

"You are all right?" she asked.

"You know I am," he said, and began unfastening the front of her robe. Her full, heavy breasts swung free, the disk between them. He looked, and then he touched her.

"Are my hands cold?"

She shook her head. Her eyes were closed, he saw. The king watched her draw a slow breath as his hands moved. It was not lack of pleasure in this, he knew, with a measure of satisfaction. It was piety, conviction, fear for their souls, a yearning towards the god.

He didn't want her to leave. His own piety: he had married this woman, sired children with her, lived through the tentative reshaping of a realm. Wartime, peacetime, winter, drought. Could not have claimed there was a fire that burned between them, but there was life, a history. He didn't want another woman in his bed.

He slipped the robe past her ample hips, drew his wife down beside him and then beneath. They made love whenever he recovered from his sickness—and only on those days or nights. A private arrangement, balancing needs. The body and the soul.

After, unclothed beside each other, he looked at the marks of red flushing her very white skin and knew that she would—again—be feeling guilt for her own pleasure. The body housed the soul, for some; imprisoned it, for others. The teachings varied; always had.

He drew a breath. "When Judit is married," he said, very softly, a hand on her thigh.

"What?"

"I will release you."

He felt her involuntary movement. She looked quickly at him, then closed her eyes tightly. Had not expected this. Neither had he, in truth. A moment later, he saw the tears on her cheeks.

"Thank you, my lord," she said, a catch in her throat. "Aeldred, I pray for you always, to holy Jad. For mercy and forgiveness."

"I know," said the king.

She was weeping, silently, beside him, tears spilling, hands gripping her golden disk. "Always. For you, your soul. And the children."

"I know," he said again.

Had a sudden, oddly vivid image of visiting one day at her retreat, Elswith garbed in yellow, a holy woman among others. The two of them old, walking slowly in a quiet place. Perhaps, he thought, she was to be his example, and a withdrawal to the god was his own proper course before the end came and brought him either light or dark through the spaces of forever.

Perhaps before the end. Not yet. He knew his sins, they burned in him, but he was in this offered world, and of it, and still carried a dream.

In time, the king and queen of the Anglcyn rose from the royal bed and dressed themselves. Food was sent for and brought in. She kept him company at table while he ate and drank, ravenous, as always, after recovery. The body's appetites. In and of the world.

They slept, later, in their separate bedchambers, parting with the formal kiss of the god on cheeks and brow. Dawn came not long after, arriving in summer mildness, ushering a bright day, enormous with implication.

CHAPTER VII

Hakon Ingemarson, by ten years his father's youngest son, enjoyed being called upon to ride west across three rivers and the vague border as an emissary to King Aeldred's court at Esferth (or wherever else it might be) from their own settlements in the southern part of Erlond.

Aside from the pleasure he took in this very adult responsibility, he found the Anglcyn royal children exhilarating, and was infatuated with the younger daughter.

He was aware that his father was only disposed to send him west when their pledged payments were late, or about to be, taking shrewd advantage of evidence of friendship among the younger generation. He also knew that those at the Anglcyn court were conscious of this, and amused by it.

An ongoing joke, started by Gareth, the younger son, was that if Hakon ever did arrive with the annual tribute, they'd have Kendra sleep with him. Hakon always struggled not to flush, hearing this. Kendra, predictably, ignored it each time, not even bothering with the withering glance her older sister had perfected. Hakon did ask his father to allow him to lead the actual tribute west, when it eventually went, but Ingemar reserved that journey for others, the money well guarded, saving Hakon for explaining—as best he could—their too-frequent delays.

They were sprawled in the summer grass south of Esferth town, near the river, out of sight of the wooden walls. Had eaten here out of doors, four of them, and were idling in late-morning sunshine before returning to town to watch the preparations for the fair continue.

No one spoke. Birdsong from the beech and oak woods to the west across the stream and the rising and falling drone of bees among the meadow flowers were the only sounds. It was warm in the sun, sleep-inducing. But Hakon, reclining on one elbow, was too aware of Kendra beside him. Her golden hair kept coming free of her hat as she concentrated on interweaving grasses into something or other. Athelbert, king's heir of the Anglcyn, lay beyond his sister, on his back, his own soft cap covering his face. Gareth was reading, of course. He wasn't supposed to take parchments out of the city, but he did.

Hakon, lazily drifting in the light, became belatedly aware that he could be accused of staring at Kendra, and probably would be with Athelbert around. He turned away, abruptly self-conscious. And sat up quickly.

"Jad of the Thunder!" he exclaimed. His father's oath. Not an invocation anyone but Erlings new to the sun god were likely to use.

Gareth snorted but didn't look up from his manuscript. Kendra did, at least, glance at where Hakon was looking, briefly raised both eyebrows, and turned calmly back to her whatever-it-was-going-to-be.

"What?" Athelbert said, evidently awake but not moving, or shifting the hat that covered his eyes.

"Judit," said Kendra. "She's angry."

Athelbert chuckled. "Aha! I know she is."

"You're in trouble," Kendra murmured, placidly plaiting.

"Oh, probably," said her older brother, comfortably sprawled in deep grass.

Hakon, wide-eyed, cleared his throat. The approaching figure, moving with grim purpose through the summer meadow, was quite close now. In fact . . .

"She, ah, has a sword," he ventured, since no one else seemed to be saying it.

Gareth did glance up at that, and then grinned with anticipation as his older sister came towards them. Kendra merely shrugged. On the other hand, Prince Athelbert, son of Aeldred, heir to the throne, heard Hakon's words, and moved.

Extremely swiftly, in point of fact.

As a consequence, the point of the equally swift sword, which would *probably* have plunged into the earth between his spread legs a little below his groin, stabbed into grass and soil just behind his desperately rolling form.

Hakon closed his eyes for an excruciating moment. An involuntary, protective hand went below his own waist. Couldn't help it. He looked again, saw that Gareth had done the very same thing, and was wincing now, biting his lip. No longer amused.

It wasn't entirely certain the blade, thrust by someone moving fast on uneven ground, would have missed impaling the older prince in an appalling location.

Athelbert rolled two or three more times, and scrambled to his feet, white as a spirit, cap gone, eyes agape.

"Are you *crazed*?" he screamed.

His sister regarded him, breathing hard, her auburn hair seeming afire in the sunlight, entirely free of any decent restraint.

Restraint was not the word for her at all. She looked murderous.

Judit jerked the sword free of the earth, levelled it, stepped forward. Hakon thought it wisest to scramble aside. Athelbert withdrew rather farther than that.

"Judit . . ." he began.

She stopped, held up an imperious hand.

A silence in the meadow. Gareth had set down his reading, Kendra her grass-plaiting.

Their red-headed sister said, controlling her breathing with an effort, "I sat up with father, beside Osbert, for part of last night."

"I know," said Athelbert quickly. "It was a devout, devoted—"

"He is well now. He wishes to see Hakon Ingemarson today."

"The god be thanked for mercy," Athelbert said piously, still very white.

Hakon saw Judit glance at him. Ducked his head in an awkward half-bow. Said nothing. He didn't trust his voice.

"I went," said the older daughter of Aeldred the king and his royal wife, Elswith, "back to my own chambers in the middle of the night." She paused. Hakon heard the birds, over by the woods. "It was dark," Judit added. Her self-control, Hakon judged, was precarious.

Among other things, the sword was quivering in her hand.

Athelbert backed up another small step. Had probably seen the same thing.

"My women were asleep," his sister said. "I did not wake them." She glanced to one side, regarded Athelbert's bright red cap lying in the grass. Went over to it. Pierced it with the sword, used her free hand to tear the cap raggedly in two along the blade, dropped it back into the grass. A butterfly flitted down, alighted on one fragment, flew away.

"I undressed and went to bed," Judit went on. She paused. Levelled the blade at her brother again. "Jad rot your eyes and heart, Athelbert, there was a dead man's skull in my bed, with the mud still on it!"

"And a rose!" her brother added hastily, backing up again. "He had a rose! In his mouth!"

"I did not," Judit snarled through gritted teeth, "observe that detail until after I had screamed and awakened all three of my women and a guard outside!"

"Most skulls," said Gareth thoughtfully, from where he sat, "belong to dead people. You didn't actually have to say that it was a—"

He stopped, swallowed, as his sister's lethal, green-eyed gaze fell upon him. "Do not even *think* of being amusing. Were you," she asked, in a voice suddenly so quiet it was frightening, "in any possible way, little brother, a part of this?"

"He wasn't!" said Athelbert quickly, before Gareth could reply. And then made the mistake of essaying a placating smile and gesture.

"Good," said Judit. "I need only kill you."

Kendra held up her grass plaiting. "Tie him up with this, first?" she murmured.

"Be careful, sister," Judit said. "Why did you not awaken when I screamed?"

"I'm used to it?" Kendra said mildly.

Gareth snorted. Unwisely. Tried, urgently, to turn it into a cough. Judit took a step towards both of them.

"I'm a . . . deep sleeper?" Kendra amended hastily. "And perhaps your courage is such that what seemed a piercing scream to you was really only—"

"I tore my throat raw," her sister said flatly. "It was the middle of the Jad-cursed night. I was exhausted. I lay down upon a cold, hard, muddy skull in my bed. I believe," she added, "the teeth bit me."

Hearing that last, ruminative observation, Hakon suddenly found himself in extreme difficulty. He looked over at Gareth and took comfort in what he saw: the thrashing desperation of the younger prince's suppressed hilarity. Gareth was weeping with the effort of trying not to howl. Hakon found that he was no longer able to stay upright. He sank to his knees. His shoulders were shaking. He felt his nose beginning to run. Whimpering sounds came from his mouth.

"Oh, my, *look* at those two," said Kendra in a pitying voice. "All right, this is what we will do. Judit, put down the sword." She was displaying, Hakon thought, what was, under the circumstances, an otherworldly composure. "Athelbert, stay exactly where you are. Close your eyes, hands at your sides. That was a craven, despicable, unworthy, *extremely* amusing thing to do and you must pay a price or Judit will make life intolerable for all of us and I don't feel like suffering for you. Judit, go and hit him as hard as you can, but not with the sword."

"You are judge here, little sister?" Judit said icily.

"Someone has to be. Gareth and Hakon are peeing in their hose," Kendra said. "Father would be displeased if you killed his heir and you'd probably regret it afterwards. A little."

Hakon wiped at his nose. These things did *not* happen back home. Gareth was flat on his back, making strangled noises. *"Teeth!"* Hakon thought he heard him moan.

Judit looked at him, then at Kendra, and finally over at Athelbert. After a long moment, she nodded her head, once.

"Do it, fool," Kendra said promptly to her older brother.

Athelbert swallowed again. "She needs to drop the sword first," he said, cautiously. He still looked ready to flee.

"She will. Judit?"

Judit dropped the sword. There remained an entirely forbidding bleakness to her narrowed gaze. She pushed windblown hair back from her face. Her tunic was green, belted with leather above the riding trousers she liked to wear. She looked, Hakon thought suddenly, like Nikar the Huntress, swordbride of Thünir, whom, of course, his family no longer worshipped at all, having come from bloody sacrifices to the . . . less violent faith of Jad.

Athelbert took a breath, managed an almost indifferent shrug. He closed his eyes and spread his legs, braced to absorb a blow. Gareth managed to lever himself into a sitting position to watch. He wiped at his eyes with the back of one hand. Kendra had an odd look to her ordinarily calm, fair features.

Judit, who would one day be saluted the length of the isle and across the seas as the Lady of Rheden, be honoured through generations for courage, and mourned in poets' laments long after the alignments and borders of the world had changed and changed again, walked across the sunlit morning grass, not breaking stride, and kicked her brother with a booted foot, hard (very hard) up between the legs where the sword had almost gone.

Athelbert made a clogged, whistling sound and crumpled to the ground, clutching at himself.

Judit gazed down at him for only a brief moment. Then she turned. Her eyes met Hakon's. She smiled at him, regal, gracious and at ease in a summer-bright meadow. "Did you four drink *all* the wine?" she asked, sweetly. "I have a sudden thirst, for some reason."

It was while Hakon was kneeling, hastily filling a cup for her, splashing the wine, that they saw the Cyngael come walking up from the south, on the other side of the stream.

Four men and a dog. They stopped, looking towards the royal party on the grass. Athelbert was lying very still, eyes squeezed shut, breathing thinly, both hands between his legs. Looking across the river at the dog, Hakon suddenly shivered as if chilled. He set down Judit's cup, without handing it to her, and stood up.

When your hair rose like this, the old tale was that a goose was walking over the ground where your bones would lie. He looked over at Kendra (he was always doing that) and saw that she was standing very still, gazing across the river, a curious expression on her face. Hakon wondered if she, too, was sensing a strangeness about the animal, if this awareness might even be something the two of them shared.

You might have called the wolfhound beside the youngest of the four men a dark grey, if you'd wanted to. Or you could have said it was black, trees behind it, sun briefly in cloud, the birds momentarily silenced by that.

CEINION OF LLYWERTH SQUINTED, looking east into sunlight. Then a cloud passed before the sun and he saw Aeldred's older daughter recognize him first and, smiling with swift, vivid pleasure, come quickly towards them across the grass. He made his way through the stream, which was cool, waist-deep here, that she might not have to enter the water herself. He knew Judit; she would have waded in. On the riverbank, she came up to him and knelt.

With genuine happiness he made the sign of the disk over her red hair and offered no comment at all on its unbound disarray. Judit, he had told her father the last time he'd been here, ought to have been a Cyngael woman, so fiercely did she shine.

"She doesn't shine," Aeldred had murmured wryly. "She burns."

Looking beyond her, he saw the younger sister and brother, and what appeared to be an Erling, and belatedly noted the crumpled figure of Aeldred's heir in the grass. He blinked. "Child, what happened here?" he asked. "Athelbert . . . ?"

His companions had crossed the stream now, behind him. Judit looked up, still kneeling, her face all calm serenity. "We were at play. He took a fall. I am certain he will be all right, my lord. Eventually." She smiled.

Even as she was speaking, Alun ab Owyn, the dog at his heels, walked over towards Aeldred's other children, before Ceinion had had a chance to introduce them formally. The high cleric knew a brief but unmistakable moment of apprehension.

Owyn's son, brought east on impulse and instinct, had not been an easy companion on the journey to the Anglcyn lands. There was no reason to believe he would become one now that they'd arrived. A blow had fallen on him earlier this year, almost as brutal as the one that had killed his brother. He had been direly wounded within, riding home to tell his father and mother that their first-born son and heir had been slain and was buried in Arberthi soil, then drifting through a summer of blank, aimless days. There had been no healing for Owyn's son. Not yet.

He had agreed, reluctantly and under pressure from his father, to be an escort to the Anglcyn court for the high cleric on the path between the sea and the dense forest that lay between the Cyngael and the Anglcyn lands.

Ceinion, watching him surreptitiously as they went, grieved for the living son almost as much as for the dead. Surviving could be a weight that crushed the soul. He knew something about that, thought about it every time he visited a grave overlooking the sea, at home.

KENDRA WATCHED the young Cyngael come over to them, the grey hound beside him. She knew she ought to go to the cleric, as Judit had, receive his blessing, extend her own glad greetings.

She found that she could not move, didn't understand, at all. A sense of . . . very great strangeness.

The Cyngael reached them. She caught her breath. "Jad give you greeting," she said.

He went right past her. Not even glancing her way: straight brown hair to his shoulders, brown eyes. Her own age, she guessed. Not a tall man, trimly made, a sword at his side.

He knelt beside Athelbert, who lay motionless, curled up like a child, hands still clutching between his legs. She was near enough, just, to hear her older brother murmur, eyes closed, "Help me, Cyngael. A small jest. Tell Judit I'm dead. Hakon will help you."

The Cyngael was still for a moment, then he stood. Looking down at the heir to the Anglcyn throne, he said, contemptuously, "You have the wrong playmate. I find nothing amusing about telling someone their brother is dead, and would lie in torment eternally before I let an Erling . . . *help* me . . . with anything. You may choose to eat and drink with them, Anglcyn, but some of us remember blood-eaglings. Tell me, where's your grandfather buried, son of Aeldred?"

Kendra put a hand to her mouth, her heart thudding. Across the meadow, in morning light, Judit was standing with Ceinion of Llywerth, out of earshot. They might have been figures in a holy book, illuminated by clerics with loving care and piety. Part of a different picture, a different text, not this one.

This one, where they were, was not holy. The lash of the Cyngael's words was somehow the worse for the music in his voice. Athelbert, who was, in fact, considerably more than simply a jester, opened his eyes and looked up.

Hakon had gone red, as he was inclined to do when distressed. "I think you insult both Prince Athelbert and myself, and in great ignorance," he said, impressively enough. "Will you retract, or need I chastise you in Jad's holy name?" He laid a hand on his sword hilt.

Aeldred's younger daughter was considerably milder of manner than her sister, and was thought, therefore (though not by her siblings), to be softer. Something peculiar seemed to be happening to her now, however. A feeling, a sensation within . . . a presence. She didn't understand it, felt edgy, angry, threatened. A darkness in the sunlight here, beside it.

Fists clenched at her sides, she walked towards her brother and their longtime friend and this arrogant Cyngael, whoever he was, and, as the stranger turned at her approach, she swung up her own booted foot to kick him in the selfsame way Judit had kicked Athelbert.

Without the same result. This man did not have his eyes closed, and was in the state of heightened awareness that cold fury and a journey into unknown country can both instill.

"Cafall! *Hold!*" he rasped, and in the same moment, as the dog subsided, the Cyngael twisted deftly to one side and caught Kendra's foot as she kicked at him. He gripped it, waist high. Then he pushed it higher.

She was falling. He wanted her to fall.

She would have, had the other, older man not arrived, moving quickly to support her. She hadn't heard the cleric coming over. She stayed that way, her boot gripped by one Cyngael, body held from behind by another.

Outraged, Hakon leaped forward. "You pigs!" he snarled. "Let her go!"

The younger one did so, with pleasing alacrity. Then, less pleasingly, he said, "Forgive me. The proper behaviour here would be . . . what? To let an Erling tutor me in courtesy? I was disinclined to cut her lungs out. What *does* one do when a woman betrays her lineage in this fashion? Accept the offered blow?"

This was difficult, as Hakon had no good answer, and even less of a notion why Kendra had done what she'd done.

"I am entirely happy," the Cyngael went on, in the absurdly beautiful voice they all seemed to have as a gift, "to kill you if you think there's honour to defend here."

"No!" Kendra said quickly, in the same moment Ceinion of Llywerth released her elbows and turned to his companion.

"Prince Alun," he said, in a voice like metal, "you are here as my companion and guard. I am your charge. Remember that."

"And I will defend you with my life from pagan offal," the younger Cyngael said. The words were ugly, the tone eerily mild, flat. *He doesn't care,* Kendra thought suddenly. *He wants to be dead.* She had no least idea how she knew that.

Hakon drew his sword and stepped back, for room. "I am weary of these words," he said with dignity. "Do what you can, in Jad's name."

"No. Forgive me, both of you, but I forbid this."

It was Athelbert, on his feet, clearly in pain, but doing what needed to be done. He stumbled between Hakon and the Cyngael, who had not yet drawn his own blade.

"Ah. Wonderful. You are not dead after all," the one who appeared to be named Alun said, mockingly. "Let's blood-eagle someone in celebration."

At which point, in what might have been the most surprising moment of a profoundly unsettling encounter, Ceinion of Llywerth stepped forward and hammered a short, hard, punishing fist into the chest of his young companion. The high cleric of the Cyngael was not of the soft, insular variety of holy men. The punch knocked the younger man staggering; he almost fell.

"Enough!" said Ceinion. "In your father's name and mine. Do not make me regret my love for you."

Kendra registered that last. And the fact that the dog did not even move despite this attack on his master, and the pain in Ceinion's voice. Her senses seemed unnaturally heightened, on alert, apprehending some threat. She watched the young Cyngael straighten, bring a hand slowly to his chest then take it away. He shook his head, as if to clear it.

He was looking at Ceinion, she saw, ignoring Hakon's blade and Athelbert's intervention. Judit, uncharacteristically, had kept silent, beside Gareth, whose watchful manner was normal, not unusual.

The two Cyngael servants had remained by the stream. It was still morning, Kendra thought, late-summer, a bright day, just south and west of Esferth. No time had passed in the world, really.

"You will note that my sword is still sheathed," Alun said at last, softly, to Ceinion. "It will remain so." He turned to Kendra, surprising her. "Are you injured, my lady?"

She managed to shake her head. "My apologies," she said. "I attacked you. You insulted a friend."

The ghost of a smile. "So I gather. Evidently not wise, in your presence."

"Judit's worse," Kendra said.

"I am not so! Only when—" Judit began.

"*Jad's blood and grief!*" Gareth snarled. "Hakon! Sheathe your blade!"

Hakon immediately did so, then turned with the others and saw why.

"Father!" cried Judit, in a voice that might actually have made one believe she was purely delighted, feeling nothing but pleasure as she stepped forward and made a showy, elaborate, attention-claiming curtsy in the meadow grass.

"Sorry, sorry, sorry," Gareth muttered to the high cleric. "Language. Profane. I know."

"The least of all transgressions here, I'd say," murmured Ceinion of Llywerth, before going forward as well, smiling, to kneel before and rise to be embraced by the king of the Anglcyn.

And then to offer the same hug, and his sun disk blessing, to scarred, limping, large-souled Osbert, a little behind Aeldred and to one side, where he always was.

"Ceinion. Dear friend. This," said the king, "is unlooked for so soon, and a source of much joy."

"You do me, as before, too much honour, my lord," said the cleric. Kendra, watching closely, saw him glance back over his shoulder. "I would present a companion. This is Prince Alun ab Owyn of Cadyr, who has been good enough to journey with me, bearing greetings from his royal father."

The younger Cyngael stepped forward and performed a flawless court bow. From where she stood, Kendra couldn't see his expression. Hakon, on her right side, was still flushed from the confrontation. His sword—thanks be to Gareth and the god—was sheathed.

Kendra saw her father smiling. He seemed well, alert, very happy. He was often this way after his fever passed. Returning to life, as from the grey gates to the land of the dead where judgement was made. And she knew how highly he thought of the Cyngael cleric.

"Owyn's son!" Aeldred murmured. "We are greatly pleased to welcome you to Esferth. Your father and lady mother are well, I trust and hope, and your older brother? Dai, I believe?"

Her father found it useful to let people realize, very early, how much he knew. He also enjoyed it. Kendra had watched him for a long time now, and could see that part, too.

Alun ab Owyn straightened. "My brother is dead," he said flatly. "My lord, he was killed by an Erling raiding party in Arberth at the end of spring. The same party blood-eagled two innocent people, one of them a girl, as they fled to their ships after being defeated. If you have assigned any of your royal *fyrd* to engage the Erlings anywhere in your lands this season, I should be honoured to be made one of them."

The music, still there in his voice, clashed hard with the words. Kendra saw her father absorbing all of this. He glanced at Ceinion. "I didn't know," he said.

He hated not knowing things. Saw it as a kind of assault, an insult, when events took place anywhere on their island—in the far north, in Erlond to the east, even west across the Rheden Wall among the black hills of the Cyngael—without his own swift and sure awareness. A strength, a flaw. What he was.

Aeldred looked at the young man before him. "This is a grief," he said. "My sorrow. Will you allow us to pray with you for his soul, which is surely with Jad?"

From where she stood, Kendra saw the Cadyri stiffen, as if to offer a quick retort. He didn't, though. Only bowed his head in what could have been taken for acquiescence, if you didn't know better. That eerie, inexplicable sensation: she *did* know better, but not how she knew it. Kendra felt an uneasy prickling, a tremor within.

She became aware that Gareth was looking at her, and managed an almost indifferent shrug. He was shrewd, her younger brother, and she had no way of explaining what it was she was . . . responding to here.

She turned back and saw that her father was now gazing at her as well. She smiled, uncertainly. Aeldred turned to study Judit, and then his sons. She saw him register Athelbert's awkward stance and the sword on the grass.

She knew—they all knew—the expression he now assumed. Detached, amused, ironic. He was a much-loved man, Aeldred of the Anglcyn, he had been from childhood, but he dealt out his own affection thoughtfully, and given what he was, how could he not? Their mother was an exception but that, all four children knew, was also complex.

Waiting, anticipating, Kendra heard her father murmur, "Judit, dear heart, don't forget to bring my longsword back."

"Of *course,* Father," said Judit, eyes downcast, her manner entirely subdued, if not her hair.

Aeldred smiled at her. Added gently, "And when you chastise your older brother, and there is no doubt in me he will have deserved it, try to ensure it doesn't affect the likelihood of heirs for the kingdom. I'd be grateful."

"Ah, so would I, actually," Athelbert said, in something approaching his customary voice.

He was not standing normally yet, there was a cramped tilt to his posture, but he was getting closer to upright. Kendra was still in awe, often, at how precisely her father could draw conclusions from limited information. It was something that frightened Athelbert, she knew: a son entirely aware he was expected to be able to follow this man to the throne. The burden of that. You could understand much of what Athelbert did if you thought of it in this way.

"Please come," her father was saying to the two Cyngael. "I walked out to greet Hakon Ingemarson, our young eastern friend, rather than wait for my errant children to bring him back so that he might offer his father's latest explanation for an unsent tribute." Aeldred turned and smiled at Hakon, to take some of the sting from that. The young Erling managed a proper bow.

The king turned back to Ceinion. "This is a gift, your early arrival. We will offer thanks in chapel for a safe journey, and our prayers for the soul of Dai ab Owyn, and then—if you will—we shall feast and talk, and there will be music in Esferth while you tell me you have answered my prayers and are come here to stay."

The cleric made no reply to that last, Kendra saw. She didn't think her father had expected one. Hakon, of course, was red-faced again. She felt sorry for him. A likable, well-meaning boy. She ought to think of him as a man, but that was difficult. It was curious: Athelbert was *far* more childish, but you always knew there was a man there, playing at boy-games because he chose to. And she had seen her brother riding with the *fyrd*.

Aeldred gestured. Ceinion and the younger Cyngael fell into stride with him, walking towards the walls of the town, out of sight north of them. Kendra saw Judit step quietly over and reclaim the sword. She hadn't recognized it as their father's. Athelbert's mutilated cap was left where it had fallen, a redness in the grass. Their own servants, who had hovered cautiously at a distance all this time, now came to gather the remains of their meal. Kendra looked west, saw the two Cyngael servants moving forward from the stream, leading a laden donkey.

It was only then that she saw that one of them was an Erling.

❧

Ebor, the son of Bordis, never minded being posted to night duty on the walls, wherever the court happened to be. He'd even made some friends by taking watches assigned to others, leaving them free for the taverns. A solitary sort of man (much the same when a boy), he took a deep, hard-to-explain comfort from being awake and alone while others feasted or drank or slept, or did the other things one did in the night.

Sometimes a woman, walking near the walls, offering her song to the dark, would call up to him from the bottom of the steps. Ebor would decline while on duty, though not always afterwards. A man had his needs, and he'd never married. Youngest son of a farmer, no land, no prospect of it. He'd joined the standing army of the king. Younger sons did that, everywhere. The way the world was made, no point brooding on it. The army gave you companions, shelter, enough money (usually, not always) for ale and a girl and your weapon. Sometimes you fought and some of you died, though less often of late, as the Erling raiders slowly took the measure of Aeldred of the Anglcyn and the forts and fortified *burhs* he'd been building.

Some of the Erlings were allies now, actually paying tribute to the king. Something deep, passing strange in that, if one thought on it. Ebor wasn't a thinker, exactly, but long nights on watch did give you time for reflection.

Not tonight, however. Tonight, under drifting clouds and the waning blue moon, had been raddled with inter-ruptions, and not from night-walkers offering interludes of love—though one *was* a woman. If you forced a man to make two decisions in haste, Ebor would later tell the king's chamberlain, humble and contrite, chances were he'd make a bad one, or two.

That, Osbert, son of Cuthwulf, would say quietly, is why we have standing orders about the gates at night. To remove the need to make a decision. And Ebor would bow his head, knowing this was so, and that this was not the time to point out that every guard on the wall disobeyed those orders in peacetime.

He would not be punished. The one death in the night was not initially thought to be connected in any way with events at the gate. This was, as it happened, another error, though not his.

༄

The women were beginning to leave the hall, led by Elswith, the queen. Ceinion of Llywerth, placed at the

king's right hand, had the distinct impression that the
older princess, the red-haired one, was disinclined to
surrender the evening, but Judit was going with her lady
mother nonetheless. The younger daughter, Kendra,
seemed to have already left. He hadn't seen her go. The
quiet one, she was less vivid, more watchful. He liked
them both.

His new Erling manservant, or guard (he still hadn't
decided how to think of him), had also gone out; he'd
come and asked permission to do so, earlier. Not a thing
he'd really needed to do, under the circumstances, and
Ceinion wasn't sure what to make of it. A request for
dispensation, in some way. It had felt like that. He'd wanted
to ask more about it, but there were others listening.
Thorkell Einarson was a complex man, he'd decided. Most
men, past a certain age, could be said to be. The young
ones usually weren't, in his experience. The youths in this
hall would want nothing more than glory, any way they
could find it.

There were exceptions. The king, expansive and genial
of mood, had already announced that they would essay
the Cyngael's well-known triad game later, in honour of
their visitors. Ceinion had glanced along the table at Alun
then, wincing, and had known, immediately, that he
would not linger for that. Alun ab Owyn had made his
excuses, prettily, to the queen, asking leave to go to
evening prayer, just before she walked out herself.

Elswith, clearly impressed by the young prince's piety,
had offered to bring him to the royal sanctuary, but Alun
had demurred. No music from him tonight, either, then.
He hadn't brought his harp east on the journey; hadn't
touched it since his brother had died, it appeared. Time
needed to run further, Ceinion decided, a memory
tugging at him from that wood by Brynn's farm. He
pushed that one away.

With the food now being cleared and the restraining presence of the ladies gone, serious drinking could be expected at the long table running down the room. There were dice cups out, he saw. The older prince, Athelbert, had left his seat at the high table and moved farther down to join some of the others. Ceinion watched him set a purse in front of himself, smiling.

Beside Ceinion, King Aeldred leaned back in his cushioned chair, a pleased, anticipatory expression on his face. Ceinion looked past the king and the queen's now-empty seat to where a portly cleric from Ferrieres was brushing at food on his yellow robe, visibly content with the meal and wine he'd been offered in this remote northern place. Ferrieres prided itself, lately, on being next only to Batiara itself, and Sarantium, in cultivating the elements of civilization. They could afford to do so, Ceinion thought without rancour. Things were different here in the northlands. Harsher, colder, more . . . marginal. The edge of the world.

Aeldred turned to him, and Ceinion smiled back at the king, his hands clasped loosely on the tabletop. Alun ab Owyn was ravaged by his brother's death. Aeldred, at the same age, had seen his own brother and father killed on a battlefield, and learned of unspeakable things done to them. And he had accepted homage, not long after, from the man who had slain and butchered them, and let the man live. That same Erling's son was at this table now, in an honoured place. Ceinion wondered if he could talk to Alun about that, if it would mean anything. And then he thought again of the forest pool north of Brynnfell, and wished he'd never been there, or the boy.

He drank from his wine cup. This was the hour when, at a Cyngael feast, the musicians would be summoned to claim and shape a mood. Among the Erlings in Vinmark, too, for that matter, though the songs were not the same, or the mood. There might be wrestlers now, among the Anglcyn, jugglers, knife-throwing contests, drinking bouts. Or all of these at once, in a loud chaos to hold back the night outside.

Not at this court. "I now wish," said Aeldred of the Anglcyn, turning to one and then to the other of the clerics flanking him, "to discuss a translation thought I have, to render into our own tongue the writings of Kallimarchos, his meditations on the proper conduct of a good life. And then I would hear your reasoned opinions on the question of images of Jad and suitable decoration for a sanctuary. I hope you are not fatigued. Do you have a sufficiency of wine, each of you?"

A different sort of king, this one. A different way of pushing back the dark.

Thorkell hadn't wanted to go south from Brynnfell with the cleric and the younger son of Owyn ap Glynn and the dog. And he most emphatically hadn't wanted to continue east with them later in the summer to the Anglcyn lands. But when you cast the gambling bones (as he had) in the midst of a battle, and changed sides (as he had), you lost a large measure of control over your own life.

He could have fled once the eastern journey started. He'd done that once before, after surrendering to the Cyngael and converting to the sun god's faith. That had been a young man's wild flight: on foot, with a hostage, to finally arrive, wounded, bone-weary, among fellow Erlings in the north-east of this wide island.

A long time ago. A different man, really. And without the history he'd accrued, since. Thorkell Einarson would be known now to the survivors of that raiding party as having turned on his companions to save a Cyngael woman—and her father, the man who'd slain the Volgan, the man who was the reason they'd come inland so dangerously far. He was, to put it delicately, unsure of a welcome among his people in the east.

Nor did he feel like cutting alone across this country to find out. He had no hearth to row towards—even if a ship would take him at an oar—having been exiled from his own isle for a bad night's fit of temper after dice.

The young man who'd made that escape alone hadn't had a hip that ached when it rained, or a left shoulder that didn't work well first thing of a morning. The cleric had noticed the second of these on their way here. An observant man, too much so for Thorkell's ease of mind. One morning Ceinion had disappeared into the edge of the oak and alderwood forest that marched along north of them and returned with leaves he'd steeped with herbs in the iron pot the donkey carried. Without saying much, he'd told Thorkell to put the hot leaves on his shoulder, wrap them with a cloth, and leave them there when they set off. He did it the next day, too, even though the wood was known to be accursed, haunted with spirits. He didn't go in far, but he did go far enough to get his leaves.

The poultice helped, which was irritating, in a perverse way. The cleric was older than Thorkell, showed no signs of any stiffness of his own at dawn, kneeling during prayers or rising from them. On the other hand, this man wouldn't have had years of fighting behind him, or manning a longship oar in storms.

It seemed to Thorkell that Jad or Ingavin or Thünir— whatever god or gods you cared to name—had caused him to save that girl, ap Hywll's daughter, and then cast his lot with these Cyngael of the west, an oath-sworn servant to them. There were better fates, but it could also be said there were worse.

He'd had a better one as a free man and a landowner on Rabady, a farm of his own within sound of the sea.

He'd ripped the skein of that destiny himself: killed a man over dice in the tavern by the harbour (his second man, unfortunately), taken with rage like a *berserkir*, using his fists. It had taken four men to pull him off, they told him after.

When you did things like that, Thorkell had lived long enough to know, you surrendered your life into the hands of others, even if the dead man had been cheating you. He shouldn't have had so much to drink that night. Old story.

He'd left the isle, taken work here and there, survived a winter, then found a raiding ship down south when springtime came. He ought to have considered more carefully. Perhaps. Or else a god had been steering his path towards those western valleys.

The lady, Brynn's wife, had claimed him as her own servant, then assigned him as a guard to a reluctant cleric when she'd learned that Ceinion had changed his plans, was journeying south to Cadyr to see Owyn, and from there to Aeldred's court. There was something between the two of them, Thorkell had decided, but he wasn't sure what. Didn't think the cleric was bedding Brynn's wife (amusing as that would have been).

He did know the lady had almost certainly saved his own life after the botched raid and the ensuing discovery that Ivarr Ragnarson had blood-eagled two people during his own flight to the ships. He'd had no business doing that: you used the blood-eagle only for a reason, to make a point. You cheapened it, otherwise. There was no point to be made when you were beaten and running home, and when you did it to a farmhand and a girl.

Ivarr, marked from birth, was strange and dangerous, cold as the black snake that would crush the Worldtree at the end of days and destroy its roots with venom. A coward, too, poison arrows and a bow, which didn't make him less threatening. Not with his grandfather's name to wield.

All of which knowledge did leave open the question of why Thorkell had signed on to that ship, joined a Volgan family raid in the first place. A blood feud two generations down. Ancient history for him, long put behind, or it should have been. Siggur Volganson's grandsons were, very clearly, not what Siggur had been, and Thorkell was no longer what he had been, either. Was it sentiment? Longing for youth? Or just the lack of a better thought in his head?

No good answer. A Cyngael farmhouse inland was a long way to go, and had been unlikely to offer much in the way of plunder. The family's sworn vengeance wasn't his own blood feud, though he'd been there all those years ago when Siggur was killed and his sword taken.

You could say he hadn't seen anything else to do since leaving home, or you could say that in some fashion the dark-hilled, mist-shrouded land of the Cyngael was still entangled with his own destiny. You could say he'd missed the sea, man-killer, fortune-maker. A part-truth, but only that.

Thünir and Ingavin might know how it was, or the golden sun god, but Thorkell wouldn't claim to have an answer himself. Men did what they did.

Right now, in the close, rank darkness of a foetid alley outside a tavern in Esferth, what he was doing was waiting for a man he'd recognized earlier in the day to come out and piss against the wall.

He'd been in the huge, slope-roofed great hall at the king's feast this evening, without formal duties, since Aeldred's servants were attending to their guests. He'd made his way to the high table during an interlude in the serving of courses, to ask permission of the cleric to go outside.

"Why so?" Ceinion of Llywerth had asked him, softly though. The man was no fool.

And Thorkell, who wasn't either, hadn't lied. Murmured, "Saw someone I don't think should be here. Want to check what he's about."

True, as far as it went.

Ceinion, thick grey eyebrows very slightly arched, had hesitated, and then nodded his head. People were looking at them, not a time or place to talk. Thorkell hadn't been sure what he'd have done if the cleric hadn't given his consent, had acted otherwise. He could have slipped out without asking permission in that crowded, noisy hall, probably should have. Wasn't certain why he'd gone up to ask.

His hip was paining him. It sometimes did, at night, even though it hadn't been raining of late. They'd covered a deal of rough ground the past few days, to come out in a meadow this morning where the Anglcyn royal children were having an outing on the grass. Thorkell had actually felt a change in the way of the world, seeing that. It was not the sort of thing the Anglcyn would have even considered, barely a day's ride from the sea, in the years when Thorkell himself was young and he and Siggur and other raiders were beaching longships wherever they pleased along this coast, or on the other side of the channel in Ferrieres. Ingemar Svidrirson had even ruled these lands for a brief time. But he'd failed to capture the youngest son of the king he'd blood-eagled. A mistake. He'd paid for it, though not with his life, surprisingly. His own youngest son was here now, it turned out, an envoy from a tribute-paying Erling. The world had altered greatly in twenty-five years. All old men thought that way, he supposed. Came with the bad hip and the shoulder. You could let yourself be bitter.

He looked towards the mouth of the alley again. Couldn't see much. He'd seen enough when they'd come through the gate today. A well-laid-out, built-up town, Esferth. The court more often here now than in Raedhill. Aeldred was building everywhere, word was. Walled *burhs* within a day's ride of each other, garrisons within them. A standing army, the borders expanding, tribute from Erlond, a marriage planned in Rheden. No easy raiding here. Not any more.

Which was why he was in this rat-skitter alley, instead of in the bright hall, for those truths raised an important question about the man he'd recognized when they had passed into town this afternoon with the king. The *two* men he'd recognized, actually.

The questions that came to you were sometimes (not always) answered, if you waited patiently enough. Thorkell heard a noise from the street, saw a shadow, someone entered the alley. He remained motionless. His eyes had adjusted by now and he saw that this time the figure stumbling out of the tavern to unbutton himself and piss into darkness among the strewn garbage was the man he'd rowed and raided with, twenty-five years before. The one who'd gone off to join the mercenaries at Jormsvik, around the same time Thorkell had escaped home and bought his land on Rabady. Word had come with summer traders and gossip that Stefa had killed his man in the challenge before the gates, which hadn't surprised Thorkell. Stefa had known how to fight. It was all he knew how to do, if you didn't count drinking.

This particular Erling in Esferth tonight was no peaceful trader from the settled eastern end of this island. Not if he was still a Jormsvik mercenary.

Stefa was alone in the alley now. He might not have been—it was a blessing, perhaps. Thorkell coughed, stepped forward, and spoke the man's name, calmly enough.

Then he twisted violently to his right, banging hard against the rough wall as Stefa wheeled, piss spraying, and thrust for his gut with a swiftly drawn knife.

A man who knew how to fight. And drink. A long afternoon and evening's worth of ale, most likely. Thorkell was entirely sober, and seeing better than Stefa in the dark. It allowed him to avoid the knife, pull his own blade in the same motion, and sheathe it between two ribs of the other man, up towards the heart.

He, too, knew how to fight, as it happened. It didn't leave you, that knowing. Your body might slow down, but you knew what you *needed* to do. He'd no idea, by now, how many souls he'd sent to whatever their afterworld might be.

He cursed, afterwards, because he was in some pain, having banged his hip against the wall, dodging, and because he hadn't meant to kill the other man until he'd learned a few things. Principally, what Stefa was doing here.

A mistake, to have used the name. The man had reacted like a frightened sentry to a footfall in the dark. He'd probably changed his name when he got into Jormsvik, Thorkell decided, rather too late. He swore again, at himself.

He dragged the dead man farther back into the alley, hearing the rats scuttle and scurry and the sound of some larger animal moving. He'd just finished doing that—and taking Stefa's purse from his belt—when he heard another man at the mouth of the laneway. He stood still in the blackness and saw him enter, also, to relieve himself. There was enough light at the entrance from the torch outside the tavern for him to see that this was the other man he knew.

He said nothing this time, a lesson learned. Waited until this one was busy with what he'd come out to do, and then moved silently forward. He clubbed the second Erling hard on the back of the head with the bone haft of his knife. Caught him as he slumped.

Then Thorkell Einarson stood for some moments, thinking hard, though not especially clearly, supporting the unconscious body of the son he'd left behind when they exiled him.

Eventually he made a decision, because he had to: perhaps not the best one, but he wasn't sure what the best one would be, given that he'd already killed Stefa. He propped Bern against the wall for a moment, braced him with his good shoulder, and tied his trouser draw-strings, to let him be decent, at least. It was too dark to see his son's face clearly. Bern had grown a beard, seemed bigger across the chest.

Ought to have been more careful, his father thought. Should have known his companion had come out before him, have been looking for Stefa, on the alert when he didn't see him. Thorkell shook his head.

In some endeavours, the lessons you needed to learn might come over time and with no greater risk than a master's reprimand. If you were going to raid on the longships, you could die if you learned too slowly.

On the other hand, if he was understanding this rightly, Bern had managed to get himself into Jormsvik, which said something for a lad who had been condemned to a servant's life by what his father had done. He'd taken himself off the isle, and more than that: you had to kill a fighter to join the mercenaries.

He didn't imagine Bern would feel kindly towards him now, or ever. He thought of his wife, then, wondering about her, though not for long: there wasn't much point. A shared life gone, that one, like the wake of a longship when it moved on through the sea. You needed to steer clear of thoughts like that. They were dangerous as the rocks of a lee shore. *Heimthra,* longing for home, could kill a man from within. He'd seen it happen.

Thorkell hoisted his son's body over his shoulder and headed for the mouth of the alley and the street.

Men passed out all the time near drinking places, everywhere in the world. Woke in grey dawn with rat bites and purses clipped. He had reason to hope the two of them would be seen as a tavern-goer carrying a drunken friend. He was limping with the weight and the pain in his hip. That might help the deception, he thought ruefully.

It didn't, in the event, happen that way. Someone spoke to him as soon as they reached the street.

"Are you going to bring the other one, too? Or is he dead?"

He stopped where he was. A woman's voice. Across the way, from the shadows there. Thorkell stood still, cursing fate and himself: in equal measure, as always.

He looked left and right. No one nearby, no one to have heard her, a small blessing that might save him, and Bern. The tavern's wall torch guttered and smoked in its iron bracket. He heard the steady noise from within. The same sounds from any tavern, everywhere a man might go. But, shouldering the body of his son, hearing a woman address him from the dark, Thorkell Einarson felt a strangeness take hold: as if he'd entered a part of the world that wasn't *quite* the royal city of Esferth in the Anglcyn lands of King Aeldred—a place for which he could not properly have prepared himself, however experienced he might be.

Given that unsettling thought, and being an Erling and direct by nature, he drew a breath and crossed the roadway straight towards the sound of the voice. When he drew near—she didn't back away from him—he saw who this was, and that stopped him again.

He was silent, looking down at her, trying to make some sense of this. "You shouldn't be here alone," he finally said.

"I have no one to fear in Esferth," said the woman. She was young. She was, in fact, the younger daughter of King Aeldred, in a thin cloak, the hood thrown back to reveal her face to him.

"You could fear me," he said slowly.

She shook her head. "You wouldn't murder me. It would make no sense."

"Men don't always do sensible things," Thorkell said.

She lifted her chin. "So you did kill the other one? The first man?"

Not at all sure why, he nodded his head. "Yes. So you see, I might do the same again."

She ignored that, staring at him. "Who was he?"

He was in such a strange world right now. This entire conversation: Aeldred's daughter, Bern on his shoulder, Stefa dead in the alley. A shipmate once. But for the moment, he told himself, he had one goal and the rest had to follow, if he could make it do so. "He was an Erling mercenary," he said. "From Jormsvik, I am almost certain. Not a trader, pretending to be."

"Jormsvik? Surely not! Would they be so foolish? To try raiding here?"

She knew of them. He hadn't expected that, either, in a girl. He shook his head. "I'd not have thought so. Depends who hired them."

Her composure was extraordinary. "And this one?" she asked, gesturing towards the body he carried. "The one you didn't kill?" She was keeping her voice low, not alerting anyone yet. He held to that, as to a spar.

He was going to need her. If only to have her not call the watch and have him seized. He wasn't a man to kill her where she stood; it was true, and she'd guessed it.

Too sure of herself, but not wrong. Thorkell hesitated, then rolled the dice again, with an inward shrug.

"My son," he said. "Though I have no idea why."

"Why he's your son?" He heard amusement, laughed himself, briefly.

"Every man wonders that. But no, why he's here."

"He was with the other?"

"I . . . believe so." He hesitated, threw dice again. There wasn't much time. "My lady, will you help me get him outside the walls?"

"He's a raider," she said. "He's here to report on what he finds." Which was almost certainly true. She was quick, among everything else.

"And he will tell his fellows that he was detected and his companion captured or killed and that you will be ready for them, coming to find them, even. His message will be that they must sail."

"You think?"

He nodded. It was plausible, might be true. The part he didn't tell her wouldn't affect Esferth, only Bern's own life, and not for the better. But there was only so much a father could do once a boy was grown, fledged, out in the world.

The woman looked at him. He heard the tavern behind him again, a rising and subsiding noise. Someone shouted an oath, someone cursed back amid spilling laughter.

"I will have to tell my father, tomorrow," she said finally.

He drew a breath, hadn't realized he'd been holding it. "But you will do that . . . tomorrow?"

She nodded.

"You would really do this?" Thorkell asked, shifting his stance under the weight he carried.

"Because you are going to do something for me," she said.

And so, with a sense that he was still treading some blurred border between known things and mystery, Thorkell drew another breath, this time to ask her the question he probably ought to have asked as soon as he'd seen her out here alone.

He never did ask it; his answer came in another way. She laid a sudden hand on his arm, holding him to silence, then pointed across the street.

Not to the tavern door or the alley, but towards a small, unlit chapel two doors farther up. Someone had stepped outside, letting the chapel door swing shut behind him. He stood a moment, looking up at the sky, the blue moon overhead, and then began to walk away from them. As he did, a shape detached itself from blackness and padded over to him. And with that, Thorkell knew who this was.

"He was praying," Aeldred's daughter murmured. "I'm not sure why, but he'll be going outside now, beyond the walls."

"What?" Thorkell said, a little too loudly. "Why would he do that? He's going to his rooms. Had enough of the celebration. His brother died."

"I know," she said, eyes still on the man and dog moving down the empty street. "But your rooms are the other direction. He is going outside."

Thorkell cleared his throat. She was right about the rooms. "How do you know what he's doing?"

She looked at him. "I'm not certain how, and I *don't* like it, but I do know. So I need someone with me, and Jad seems to be saying it will be you."

Thorkell stared at her. "With you? What is it you want to do?"

"I want to pray, actually, but there isn't time. I'm going to follow him," she said. "And *don't* ask me why."

"Why?" he asked, involuntarily.

She shook her head.

"That's moon-mad. Alone?"

"No. With you, remember? It'll get your son out of Esferth." Her voice changed. "You *swear* you think it will deter them? The raiders? Whoever they are? Swear it."

Thorkell paused. "I'd say yes in any case, you know, but I do think so. I swear it by Jad and Ingavin, both."

"And you won't run away to them? With your son?"

That *would* be a thought she'd have, he realized. He snorted. "My son will want nothing to do with me. And I'd be killed by the raiders for certain, if these are who I think they are."

She glanced down the street again. The man and dog were almost out of sight. "Who are they?"

"The leader's name won't mean anything to you. It's someone who will *want* a report that Esferth and the *burhs* are unassailable."

"We are. But same question back: how are you so sure?"

He was used to this kind of talk, though not with a woman. "Different answer: I'm not certain. This is a raider's guess. My lady, we'd best move if you want to follow that Cyngael."

He saw her take a breath this time, and then nod. She stepped into the street, lifting her hood as she did so. He went with her, along an empty, moonlit lane that seemed of the world and not entirely so. The tavern noises receded, became sea murmur and then silence as they went.

෴

The man below was an honoured guest, a prince, companion of the Cyngael cleric the king had been watching for all summer. Ebor, son of Bordis, up on the wall-walk by the western gate, answered a quiet summons and came down the steps to that lilting voice.

The gates loomed in the dark, seeming higher from down on the ground, newly reinforced this past year. King Aeldred was a builder. Ebor saw a man with a dog, greeted him, heard a courteously phrased request to be allowed outside for a time, to walk under moonlight and stars, feel wind, away from the smoke and noise of the great hall and the town.

He was country-born, Ebor, could understand such a need. It was why he was up here so much of the time himself. It occurred to him, suddenly, to invite the Cyngael up to the wall-walk with him, but that would be a great presumption, and it wasn't what the man had asked of him.

"It isn't quiet out there tonight, all the tents, my lord" he said.

"I'm certain of that, but I wasn't intending to go that way."

Some of the others in the *fyrd* didn't like the Cyngael. Small, dark, devious. Cattle thieves and murderers, they named them. Mostly that came from those Anglcyn north of here, near the valleys or the hills where the ghost wood ended, along which the Rheden Wall had been built to keep the Cyngael out. Years of skirmishing and larger battles could shape such a feeling. But Ebor was from the good farmland east of here, not north or west, and his own dark childhood stories and memories were about Erlings coming up from the dangerous sea. The people of the west were no real enemy compared to longship *berserkirs* drunk on blood.

Ebor had nothing, himself, against the Cyngael. He liked the way they talked.

The night was quiet enough, little wind now. If he listened, he could hear the sounds from outside, though. There were a great many men sleeping in tents (around to the north) with the *fyrd* here and Esferth full to bursting in the run-up to the fair. No danger presented itself to this royal guest out there, unless he found a drunken dice game or took a woman with too-sharp fingernails into a field or hollow, and it wasn't Ebor's task in life to save a man from either of those. The Cyngael had spoken with dignity, no arrogance. He'd offered Ebor a coin: not too much, not too little—a sum fitting the request.

A quiet man, something on his mind. Far from home just now. Ebor looked at him and nodded his head. He took the iron key from his belt and unlocked the small door beside the wide gate and he let them out, the man and the dark grey hound at his side.

A minor encounter in the scheme of things, far from the first time someone had had reason to go out after dark in peaceful times. Ebor turned to go back up to his place on the wall.

The other two called to him before he reached the top.

When he came back down the steps and saw who it was this time, Ebor understood—rather too late—that there was nothing minor unfolding here, after all.

The man this time was an Erling, carrying someone over his shoulder, passed out in drunkenness. That happened every night. The woman, however, was the king's younger daughter, the princess Kendra, and it never even entered Ebor's head to deny her anything she might ask of him.

She asked for the door to be unlocked again.

Ebor swallowed hard. "May . . . may I summon an escort for you, my lady?"

"I have one," she said. "Thank you. Open it, please. Tell no one of this, on pain of my displeasure. And watch for us: to let us back in when we come."

She had an escort. An Erling carrying a drunken man. It didn't feel right. With a sick feeling roiling his guts, Ebor opened the small door for the second time. They went out. She turned back, thanked him gravely, walked on.

He closed the door behind them, locked it, hurried up the stairs, two at a time, to the wall-walk. He leaned out, watching them for as long as he could as they went into the night. He couldn't see very far. He didn't see when the Erling turned south alone, limping, carrying his burden, and the princess went north-west, also alone, in the direction the Cyngael and his dog had gone.

It occurred to Ebor, staring into night, that this might have been a tryst of some kind, a lovers' meeting, the Cyngael prince and his own princess. Then he decided that made no sense at all. They wouldn't have to go outside the walls to bed each other. And the Erling? What was that about? And, rather belatedly, the thought came to Ebor that he hadn't seen any weapon—no sword or even a knife—carried by the young Cyngael who had spoken to him so softly, with music in his voice. It was desperately unwise to go outside without iron to defend yourself. Why would anyone do that?

He was sweating, he realized; could smell himself. He stayed where he was, watching, staring out, as was his duty here, as the princess had told him to do. And in the meantime he began to pray, which was a duty all men had in the night while Jad did battle beneath the world on their behalf, against powers of malign intent.

༺༻

He laid his son down by the bank of the stream. Not far from where they'd come walking this morning and found the royal children idling on the grass. With time now (a little) and a bit more light, with the blue moon reflecting off the river, Thorkell looked down at the unconscious figure, reading what changes he could, and what seemed to be unchanged.

He stayed like that for some moments. He was not a soft man in any possible way, but this had to be a strange moment in a man's life, no one could deny it. He hadn't thought to ever see his son again. His face was unrevealing in the muted moonlight. He was thinking that there was danger for the boy (not a boy any more) if he was left here in the dark, helpless. Beasts, or mortal predators, might come.

On the other hand, there was only so much a father could do, and he'd made a promise that mattered to the girl. He probably wouldn't have made it out without her. Would have tried, of course, but it was unlikely. He looked at Bern by moonlight and spent a moment working out how old his son was. The beard aged him, but he remembered the day Bern was born and it didn't seem so long ago, really. And now the boy was off Rabady, somehow, and raiding with the Jormsvikings, though it made so little sense for them to be here.

Thorkell had his thoughts on that, on what was really happening. His son's breathing was even and steady. If nothing came here before he woke, he'd be all right. Thorkell knew he ought to leave, before Bern opened his eyes, but it was oddly difficult to move away. The strangeness of this encounter, a sense of a god or gods, or blind chance, working in this. It didn't even occur to him to run away with Bern. Where would he go? For one thing, he was almost certain who had paid for the Jormsvik ships, however many there turned out to be. He shouldn't have been quite so sure, really, but he did know a few things, and they fit.

Ivarr Ragnarson had not been caught fleeing from Brynnfell. Two blood-eagled bodies to the west had been the marks of his passage. The Cyngael had never found the ships.

Ivarr had made it home. Stood to reason.

Something else did, too. No thinking man bought mercenaries to raid the Anglcyn coast any more. A waste of money, of time, of lives. Not with what Aeldred had been doing—and was still doing—with his standing army and his *burhs,* and even a fleet of his own being built along this coastline now.

Mercenaries might risk it if you paid them enough, but it didn't make *sense.* You sailed from Vinmark and raided east and south through Karch now, even down to the trading stations of overstretched Sarantium. Or along the Ferrieres coast, or, possibly, you went past here, west to the Cyngael lands. Not much to be gleaned there these days, for the exposed treasure-houses of the sanctuaries had long since been removed inland and inside walls, and the three Cyngael provinces had never had overmuch in the way of gold in any case. But a man, a particular man, might have his reasons for taking dragon-ships and fighting men back there.

The same reasons he'd had at the beginning of summer. And one more now. A brother newly dead, to join a blood feud that had begun long ago.

And if this was so, if it *was* Ivarr, Thorkell Einarson had good reason to expect nothing but a bad death were he to run away now with his son towards the coast, looking for the ships that would be lying offshore or beached in a cove. Ivarr, repellent and deadly as anyone he'd ever known, would remember the man who had blocked the arrow he'd loosed at Brynn ap Hywll from the wooded slope.

He really oughtn't to have been so sure of all this, but he was. Something to do with the night, the mood and strangeness of it. Ghost moon overhead. Nearness to the spirit wood, beyond the margins of which men never went. That girl going out, for no reason that made sense, just following the Cyngael prince. There was something at work tonight. You raided and fought long enough, survived so many different ways of dying, you learned to trust your senses, and this . . . feeling.

Bern hadn't learned enough yet, else he'd not have been so easily taken in an alley. Thorkell grimaced, an expression creasing his features for the first time. Fool of a lad. It was a hard world they lived in. You couldn't *afford* to be a fool.

The boy was making a start, though, had to acknowledge that. Everyone knew how you joined the mercenaries in Jormsvik. The *only* way you could join them. Thorkell looked down at the brown-haired, brown-bearded figure on the grass. A different man might have acknowledged pride.

Thorkell didn't have time to linger, to ask how Bern had done any of this. Nor did he presume that his only son, awakening, would smile in delight and cry his father's name aloud, and Ingavin's in thankfulness.

Bern shouldn't be long from waking. He would have to hope that was so, that this isolated place wouldn't draw wolves or thieves in the next while. The boy had filled out across the chest, he saw. You could almost call him a big man. He still remembered carrying him, years ago. Shook his head at that. Weak thoughts, too soft. Men woke each morning, lay down each night, in a blood-soaked world. You needed to remember that. And he needed to walk back to the girl.

Jaddite now, or not, he murmured an ancient prayer, father's blessing. Habit, nothing else: "Ingavin's hammer, between you and all harm."

He turned to go. Paused, and—berating himself even as he did—took from his belt-purse something he'd removed when he surrendered to the Cyngael for the second time in twenty-five years. He carried it now, instead of wearing

it. The hammer on a chain. You didn't wear the symbols of
the thunder god when you took the faith of Jad.

It was an entirely ordinary, unremarkable hammer.
Thousands like it. Bern wouldn't know it as anything
unique, but he'd realize it was an Erling who had carried
him here, and he'd go back to the ships with the warning
that implied. He'd have some talking to do, to explain his
survival when Stefa never came back, but Thorkell couldn't
help him with that. A boy became a man, had his own stony
way to make on land and sea, like everyone else—then you
died where you died, and found out what happened then.

Thorkell had killed an oar-companion tonight. Hadn't
meant to do that. Not truly a friend, Stefa, but they'd
shared things, covered each other's back in battle, slept
on cold ground, close, for warmth in wind. You did that,
raiding. Then you died where you died. An alley in
Esferth for Stefa, pissing in the dark. He wondered if the
dead man's spirit was out here. Probably was. Blue moon
shining.

He bent and looped the chain into his son's fingers
and closed them over the hammer, and then he went
away along the stream, not looking back, covering
ground towards where he'd seen the princess walking in
her own folly.

There was a snatch of verse in his head as he went.
One his wife used to sing, to all three children when they
were young.

He put it out of his mind. Too soft for tonight, for any
night.

◌

He is coming. She knows it. Is waiting within the
trees, across the stream. He is mortal and can *see* her.
They have spoken under stars (no moons) on the night
she took a soul for the queen. He has watched the Ride

go through their pool in the wood. Then dropped his iron blade and very nearly touched her by the trees on the slope above the farm. It has not left her, that moment, from then until now. No quietude, in wood, in mound, crossing water under stars with the music of the Ride all around.

She trembles, an aspen leaf, her hair violet, then a paler hue. She is far from home, one moon in the sky. A glowing at the wood's edge, waiting.

CHAPTER VIII

Ingavin and Thünir were many things, but they were soul-reapers before all else, and the ravens that followed them, the birds of the battlefield and the banners, were emblems of that.

So was the blood-eagle: a sacrifice and a message. A vanquished king or war-leader stripped naked under the holy sky, thrown on the ground, his face to the churned earth. If he wasn't dead he would be restrained by strong warriors, or with ropes tied to pegs hammered into the earth, or both.

His back would be carved vertically with a long knife or an axe, the bloody opening pulled wide, his ribs cracked back on each side and his lungs drawn out through the opening thus made. They would be draped upon the exposed cage of his ribs: the folded wings of an eagle, blood-crimson, god offering.

It was said that Siggur Volganson, the Volgan, had been so precise and swift in performing the ritual that some of his victims remained alive for a time with their lungs exposed to the watching gods.

Ivarr had not yet been able to achieve this. In fairness, he'd had less opportunity than his grandfather had enjoyed during the years and seasons of the great raids. Times changed.

TIMES CHANGED. Burgred of Denferth, viciously cursing himself for carelessness, nonetheless knew that none of the other leaders at court or of the *fyrd* would have taken more than seven or eight riders to investigate the rumour of a ship, or ships, seen along the coast. He'd had five men, two of them new—using the ride south to assess them.

Three of those men were dead now. Assessment rendered meaningless. But *no one* was raiding the Anglcyn coast these days. How could he have expected what he'd found—or what had found his small party tonight? Aeldred had *burhs* all along the coast, watchtowers between them, a standing army, and—as of this summer—the beginnings of a proper fleet for the first time.

The Erlings themselves were different in this generation: settlers in the eastern lands, half of them (or something like that) were Jaddite now, trimming their sails to the winds of faith. Times changed, men changed. Those still roaming the seas in dragon-ships pursuing sanctuary treasures and ransom and slaves went to Ferrieres now, or east, where Burgred had no idea (and didn't care) what they found.

The lands of King Aeldred were defended, that was what mattered. And if some Erlings remembered this king as a hunted fugitive in wintry swamplands . . . well, those same Erlings were humbly sending their household warriors or their sons with tribute to Esferth these days, and fearing Aeldred's reprisals if they were late.

None of which unassailable truths was of any help to Burgred now.

It was night. Summer stars, ocean breeze, a waning blue moon. They had camped on open ground, less than a day's ride from Esferth, between the *burh* of Drengest, where the new shipyard was, and the watchtower west of it. He could have reached either place, but he was training men, testing them. It was a mild, sweet night. Had been.

The two on guard had shouted their warnings properly. Thinking back, Burgred decided that he and his men had surprised the Erling party as much as they'd been surprised themselves. Unfortunately, there were at least twenty Erlings—almost half a longship's worth—and they were skilled fighters. Disturbingly so, in fact. Commands had been barked, registered, implemented in a night skirmish. It hadn't taken him long to realize where these men were from, and to accept what life and ill fortune had doled out tonight.

He'd ordered his men to drop their weapons, though not before the two guards and one other of his company—Otho, who was a *good* man—lay dead. No great shame surrendering to a score of Jormsvik mercenaries mad enough to be ashore this near to Esferth. He had no idea *why* they were here: the mercenaries were far too pragmatic to offer themselves for raids as foolhardy as this one would be. Who would pay them enough to even consider it? And why?

It made too little sense. And it was not a puzzle worth having more men die while he tried to solve it. Best surrender, much as it burned to do that, let them sell him back to Aeldred for silver and safe passage to wherever they were really going.

"We yield ourselves!" he cried loudly, and dropped his sword on the moonlit grass. They would understand him. The two languages borrowed from each other, and the older Jormsvik raiders would have been here many times in their youth. "You have been foolish beyond all credit to come here, but sometimes folly is rewarded, for Jad works in ways we do not understand."

The largest of the Erlings—eyes behind a helm— grinned and spat. "Jad, you say? I think not. Your name?" he rasped. He already knew what this was about.

No reason to hide it. Indeed, the whole point was his name, and what it was worth. It would save his life, and the lives of his three surviving men. These were mercenaries.

"I am Burgred, Earl of Denferth," he said. "Captain of King Aeldred's *fyrd* and his Household Guard."

"Hah!" roared the big man in front of him. Laughter and shouts from the others, raucous and triumphant, unable to believe their good fortune. They knew him. Of course they knew him. And experienced men would also know that Aeldred would pay to have him back. Burgred cursed again, under his breath.

"What are you doing here?" he asked, angrily. "Do you not know how little you can win along this coast now? When did the men of Jormsvik begin selling themselves for small coin and certain battle?"

He had spent his entire life, it seemed, fighting them and studying them. He was aware of a hesitation.

"We were told Drengest could be taken," the man in front of him said, finally.

Burgred blinked. "*Drengest*? You are mocking me."

There was a silence. They weren't mocking him. Burgred laughed. "What fool told you that? What fools listened to him? Have you *seen* Drengest yet? You must have."

The Erling planted his sword in the earth, removed his helm. His long yellow hair was plastered to his head. "We've seen it," he said.

"You understand there are nearly one hundred men of the *fyrd* in there, over and above the rest of the people inside the walls? You've seen the walls? You've seen the fleet being built? You were going to attack *Drengest*? You know how close you are to Esferth here? What do you have, thirty longships? Forty? Fifty? Is Jormsvik emptied for this folly? Are you all summer-mad?"

"Five ships," the Erling said at length, shifting his feet. A professional, not a madman, aware of everything Burgred was saying, which made this even harder to understand.

Five longships meant two hundred men. Fewer, if they had horses. A large raid, an expensive one. But not nearly enough to come here. "You were led to believe you could take that *burh,* where our fleet's being built and guarded, with five ships? Someone lied to you," Burgred of Denferth said flatly.

Last words spoken in a worthy life.

He had time to recall, bewildered again, that the Erlings had always seen bows as the weapon of a coward, before the moonlight left his eyes and he went to seek the god with an arrow in his chest.

GUTHRUM SKALLSON BLINKED in the moonlight, not quite believing what he'd just seen. Then he did believe it, and turned.

He wasn't a *berserkir,* had never been that wild on a battlefield, was happy to wear armour, thank you, but the rage that filled him in that moment was very great and he moved swiftly with it. Crossed to the man with the bow and swung his arm in a full backhanded sweep, smashing it into the archer's face, sending him sprawling in the blue-tinted grass.

He followed, still in a fury, swearing. Bent over the crumpled form, seized the fallen bow, cracked it over his knee, then grabbed the belt-quiver and scattered the arrows with one furious, wide, wheeling motion in an arc across the summer field. He was breathing hard, at the edge of murder.

"You'll die for doing that," the man on the ground said, through a smashed mouth, in his eerie voice.

Guthrum blinked again. He shook his head, as if stunned. It was not to be borne. He lifted the man with one hand; he weighed less than any of them, by a good deal. Holding him in the air by the bunched-up tunic, so his feet swung free, Guthrum pulled the knife from his belt.

"No!" shouted Atli, behind him. Guthrum ignored that.

"Say it to me again," he grunted to the little man dangling in front of him.

"I will kill you for that blow," said the man he held at his mercy. The words came out half a whistle, through bleeding lips.

"Right, then," said Guthrum.

He moved the knife, in a short, practised motion. And was brought up hard by a heavy hand seizing his wrist, gripping fiercely, pulling it back.

"We won't get final payment if he dies," Atli grunted. "Hold!"

Guthrum swore at him. "Do you know how much silver he just cost us?"

"Of course I know!"

"You heard the white-faced coward threaten my life? Mine!"

"You struck him a blow."

"Ingavin's blood! He killed our ransom, you thick-headed fool!"

Atli nodded. "Right. He's also paying us. And he's a Volganson. The last one. You want to go home with that blood on your blade? We'll settle this on the ships. Best get out of here now, and off this coast. Aeldred'll be coming soon as they find these bodies."

"Of *course* he will."

"Then let's go. We kill the last two?" Atli awaited orders.

"Of course we kill them," gasped the little man Guthrum was still holding in the air. Guthrum threw him away, into the grass. He lay there, crumpled and small, not moving.

Guthrum swore. What he *wanted* to do was send the last two Anglcyn back to Esferth to explain, to say the killing was unintended. That they were leaving these shores. There were a great many Erlings hereabouts, or living not far east of here. The last thing Jormsvik needed was their own people enraged because the Anglcyn had cut off trading rights, or raised the tribute tax, or decided to kill a score of them and display the heads on pikes for the death of Aeldred's earl and friend. It could happen. It *had* happened.

But he couldn't let them go back. There was no explanation that would achieve anything useful. Living men would name the Jormsvik raiders as the men who'd killed an earl of the Anglcyn with a coward's bow, after he'd surrendered. It wouldn't do at all.

He sighed, glared at the figure in the grass again.

"Kill them," he said, reluctantly. "Then we move."

It is a truth hardly to be challenged that most men prefer not to have others decree the manner and time of their dying. Jormsvik mercenaries, responsible on an individual and collective basis for so many deaths, were not unaware of this. At the same time, the engrossing and unsettling events in that moonlit meadow, from the time the Anglcyn was shot to the moment Guthrum issued that last order, had compelled attention—and diverted it.

One of the captive Anglcyn twisted, in the moment Guthrum spoke, grabbed a boot-top knife, stabbed the nearest of the men guarding him, ripped free of the belated clutch of another, and tore off into the night. Not, normally, a problem. There were twenty of them here, they were swift and experienced fighters.

They did not, however, have horses.

And a moment later the fleeing Anglcyn did. Six mounts had been tethered nearby. They ought to have been claimed already. They hadn't been. The arrow, the loss of an earl's ransom, Guthrum's assault on the man paying them. There were reasons, obviously, but it was a mistake.

Running hard, they reached the other horses. Five of them mounted up without an order spoken. No need for orders here. They gave chase. They were not horsemen, however, these Erlings, these dragon-ship raiders, scourges of the white wave, sea foam. They could ride, but not as an Anglcyn did. And he had chosen the best horse—the earl's, almost certainly. The dead earl's, their lost ransom. It was all bad. Then it got worse.

They heard his horn sound, shattering the night.

The riders reined up hard. The others on foot behind them in the meadow looked at each other, and then at Guthrum, who was leading this party. Every man there knew they were in enormous peril suddenly. Inland. On foot, all but five of them. A full day from the ships, at least, with a fortified *burh* and a guard tower nearby, and Esferth itself just to the north. It would be day, bright and deadly, long before they got back to the shore.

Guthrum swore again, viciously. He killed the last Anglcyn himself, almost absently, a sword in the chest, ripped out as soon as it went in, wiped dry on the grass, sheathed again. The riders came back. The accursed horn was still sounding, shredding the dark.

"You five ride back," he rasped. "Tell Brand to land a ship's worth of men, start this way. You guide them. Look for us. We'll be coming fast as we can, the way we came. But if we're chased we might be caught, and we'll need more men in a fight."

"Forty enough?" Atli asked.

"No idea, but I can't risk more. Let's go."

"I want a horse!" said the small, vicious man who'd caused all this, sitting up now on the grass. "I'll lead them back."

"Fuck that forever!" said Guthrum savagely. "You wanted to come ashore with us, you'll run back with us. And if you can't keep up we'll leave you for Aeldred.

They'd like a Volganson, I imagine. Get on your feet. Steady run, all of you. Riders, go!"

The horn was still blowing, fading east as they started back west themselves. Ivarr got up promptly enough, Guthrum saw. Ragnarson wiped at his mouth, spat blood, then started running with them. He was light-boned, quick-footed. Kept spitting blood for a time, but said nothing more. In the moonlight his features were stranger than ever, the whiteness not entirely human. Ought to have been exposed at birth, Guthrum thought grimly, looking like that as he came into the middle-world. Would have been, in any other family. He'd been threatened with death by this one, Siggur Volganson's heir. It didn't occur to him to be afraid but he did regret not killing him.

An earl, he kept thinking, as they went. An *earl!* Aeldred's friend from childhood. They could have taken the prodigious ransom for Burgred of Denferth, turned straight around, and rowed home for a rich and easy winter in the Jormsvik taverns. Instead, they had a hard, dangerous run ahead; the horn would bring riders in the dark—riders who would learn what had happened, and who knew the terrain far better than they did. They could die here.

He might have been a farmer by now, Guthrum thought. Repairing fences, eyeing rainclouds before harvest time. He actually amused himself, briefly, with the thought, running through night in Anglcyn lands. It had never been likely. Farmers didn't go to Ingavin's halls, or drink from Thünir's horn when they were called from the middle-world. He'd chosen his life a long time ago. No regrets, under the blue moon and the stars.

∽

The moon was over the woods, Bern saw, awakening. Then he grasped that he was lying on grass, looking up at trees, beside a river in the dark.

He'd been pissing in the alley and . . .

He sat up. Too quickly. The moon lurched, stars described arcs as if falling. He gasped. Touched his head: a lump, the stickiness of blood. He cursed, confused, his heart hammering. Looked around, too quickly again: the dizziness assaulted him, blood loud in his ears. He seemed to be holding something. Looked down at the object in his hand.

Knew his father's neck chain and hammer, immediately.

No doubt, no hesitation, even here, so far away from home, from childhood. Small sons could be like that, memorizing each and every thing about the father, a figure larger than anything in the world, filling the house, then emptying it when he left, on the dragon-ships again. There were thousands of necklaces like this one, and there was not one like it in the world the gods had made.

He was very still, listening to the river running over stones, the crickets and frogs. There were fireflies above the water and the reeds. The forest was black beyond the stream. Something had just happened that he could never even have imagined.

He tried to think clearly, but his head was hurting. His father was here. Had been in Esferth, had knocked him out—or rescued him?—and taken him outside the walls and left . . . this.

As a sign of what? Bern swore again. His father had never been a man to make anything clear or easy. But if he could take any idea from being here and holding Thorkell's necklace, it was that his father wanted him out of Esferth.

Suddenly, belatedly, he thought about Ecca, who was—significantly—*not* here outside the walls. Bern stood up then, wincing, unsteady. He couldn't stay where he was. There were always people outside a city, especially now with the king present, and all his household, and a late-summer fair beginning soon. There was a second city's worth of tents around to the north. They'd seen them earlier, when they'd come up.

Finding so many people here had been a large issue. Ecca had wrestled with considerable anger as they'd come to understand what was happening in Esferth and near it. That supposedly unfinished *burh* on the coast, Drengest, was entirely complete, walls secure, defended, a number of ships already built in the harbour.

Not even remotely a place where five ships' worth of men could raid and run, which is what they'd been told they could do. And Esferth itself, which was supposed to be half empty, exposed to an attack that would shape a legend, was thronged with merchants and the Anglcyn *fyrd,* and Aeldred himself was here with his household guard. It was not a mistake, not a misreading of signs, Ecca had snarled. It appeared they had been lied to, by the man who'd paid them to come.

Ivarr Ragnarson, the Volgan's heir. The one everyone whispered ought surely to have been killed when he came out of his mother's womb white as a spirit, hairless, a malformed freak of nature, unworthy of life and his lineage.

It was that lineage that had saved him. Everyone knew the tale: how a *volur* in her trance had spoken to his father and forbidden him to expose the child. Ragnar Siggurson, hesitant by nature, too careful, never the strongest man (following a father who *had* been the strongest of men), had let the child live, to grow up strange and estranged, and vicious.

Bern had his own thoughts about *volurs* and their trances. Not that it mattered. He was desperately unsure what to do. Ecca was a shipmate, his companion on this scouting mission. A Jormsvik raider didn't leave companions behind unless he had no choice at all; they were bound to each other, by oath and history. But this was Bern's first raid, he didn't know enough yet, didn't know if this was a time when you *did* leave to carry an urgent message back. Should he return to Esferth when the gates opened at sunrise and look for Ecca, or find Gyllir in the wood where they'd left the horses and hurry to the ships with a warning?

Was that the meaning in Thorkell's necklace, in his being out here alone? Was Ecca taken? Dead? And if not, what would happen if he returned to the ships after Bern did and asked why his companion had left without him? And just how, in fact, Bern had gotten outside the walls? How he'd explain that, Bern had no idea. And what if Ecca rode back and the ships were gone because Bern had told them it was wiser to cast off?

Too many conflicting needs, conjured thoughts. Hesitations of his own devising (another son of a strong father?). He didn't know, standing unsteadily alone by the water, if he was . . . *direct* enough for this raiding life. He'd be dealing more easily with all of this, he thought, if his head didn't hurt so much.

Something caught his eye, south and east. A bonfire burning on a hill. He watched that light in the darkness, saw it occluded, reappear, vanish again, return. He realized, after a moment, that this was a message. Knew it could not possibly be good for him, or for those waiting by the ships . . . or for Guthrum's party ashore to the south.

The bonfire made his decision for him. He placed his father's necklace over his head and slipped it inside his tunic. The necklace was meant to tell him that it was a friend (his father a friend, the irony in that) who'd taken him out of Esferth. If he was *supposed* to be out of Esferth, that meant trouble inside. And he knew there was trouble, they'd seen it this morning, passing through the gates amid the crowds for the fair. They had planned

244 GUY GAVRIEL KAY

to stay only tonight, learn what they could in the taverns, ride back to the coast in the morning, carrying their message—and warning.

And now a message in fire was lighting the night. This was, in no possible way, a safe place to be coming ashore to raid. The *burh* was walled and garrisoned, they already knew that, and Esferth was thronged to bursting. He had that message to deliver, above anything else. He took a breath, put aside, as best he could, the fierce, hard awareness that his father was out here somewhere in the night not far away, and had, evidently, carried him to this place like a child. Bern turned his back on torchlit Esferth and entered the stream to cross it.

He was midway into the river, which wasn't cold, when he heard voices. He dropped down instantly, silent amid reeds and lilies, only his head above water in the dark, and listened to the voices and the pounding of his heart.

༺༻

Alun had seen the glimmering twice on the journey east, travelling here with Ceinion. Once in the branches of a tree, when they'd camped by a stream running out of the wood and he awoke in the night, and once on a hillside behind them, when he looked back after dark: a shining at twilight, though the sun had set.

He'd known it was her. Wasn't sure if he'd been meant to see, or if she'd come closer than she'd intended. Cafall had been restless all through that coastal journey. The Erling had thought it was the nearness of the spirit wood.

She was following him. He ought, perhaps, to have been afraid, but that wasn't what he felt. Alun had thought about Dai, the night he died, that pool in the wood, souls lost and taken, and it had occurred to him that he might never make music again.

His mother had taken to her chambers when he and Gryffeth and the cleric had brought the tidings home. She had stayed there a fourteen-night, opening only to her women. When she'd come out her hair had changed colour. Not as a faerie's did, shimmering through hues, but as a mortal woman's did, when grief has come too suddenly.

Owyn had covered his face with a hand, Alun remembered, and turned and walked away, at first word of Dai's death. He had drunk a great deal for two days and nights, then stopped. Had spoken after, privately, with Ceinion of Llywerth. There was a history there, not entirely a benign one, but whatever lay behind the two men seemed altered by this. Owyn ap Glynn was a hard man, everyone knew that, and he was a prince with tasks in the world. Brynn had said that same thing to Alun, too. He had a new role, himself. He was heir to Cadyr.

His brother was dead. More than that. Those who told him that time and faith would assuage, meaning well, drawing on experience and wisdom—even his father, even King Aeldred, here—were unaware, *had* to be unaware, of what Alun knew about Dai.

Armoured in faith, as Ceinion and the Anglcyn king were, you could anneal the burning of loss with a belief that the souls of those who had gone were with Jad and would be until all the worlds ended and the god's purposes were revealed and fulfilled.

Faith was no help at all when you knew your brother's soul had been stolen by faeries on a moonless night.

Alun prayed, as required, morning and evening, with urgency. It seemed to him sometimes that he heard his own voice echoing oddly as he chanted the responses of the liturgy. He *knew* things, had seen what he had seen. And heard the music in that forest clearing, as the faeries passed him by, moving across the water.

There was a blue moon tonight, spirit moon, high above the woods, hanging over them like some dark blue candle in a doorway. These were part of the same forest they had skirted to the south. A valley sliced westward, pushing the trees back halfway down to the sea, and the old tale was that the colder danger lay in the south, but this was still named a ghost wood, whatever the clerics might say.

He stood a moment, looking at the trees. He needed to walk through this doorway. Had known he would, from first sighting of her that night when he'd woken, and again on the hill two days later, at twilight. *Forbidden, heresy:* words that meant much, but so little to him now. He had seen her. And his brother. Dai's hand in the faerie queen's, walking on water, after he died. Alun was unmoored and knew it, a ship without rudder or sails, no charts by which to navigate.

He had left the king's feast, made his excuses as courteously as he could, aware that the Anglcyn court—alerted by Ceinion—would feel genuine compassion for what they thought was his pain.

They had no idea.

He'd bowed to the king—a compact man, trimmed grey beard, bright blue eyes—and to the queen, made his way from that crowded, loud, smoky room, dense with the living and their concerns, and gone alone to the chapel he'd seen earlier in the day.

Not the royal one. This one was small, dimly lit, almost an afterthought on a street of taverns and inns, and empty this late at night. What he needed. Silence, shadow, the sun disk above the altar barely visible in this still space. He had knelt, and prayed for the god to lend him the power to resist what was pulling him. But in the end, rising, he gave himself dispensation for being mortal, and frail, and so not strong enough. There was a need in him, and there was also fear.

He had a thought, a memory, and paused by the door of the chapel. In that gloom, lit only by a handful of guttering lamps too far apart on the walls, Alun ab Owyn unbuckled his dagger and belt and set them down on a stone ledge in the half-darkness. He'd worn no sword tonight. Not to a royal feast, as an honoured guest. He turned in the chapel doorway, looked back in the gloom a last time to where the sun disk hung.

Then he went out into the night streets of Esferth. Cafall fell in beside him, as always now. He spoke to a guard at the gates and was allowed to pass. He'd known— with certainty—that it would be so. There were forces at work tonight, beyond any adequate understanding.

Alun went into the meadow beyond the Esferth gates and walked steadily west. The direction of home, but not really. Home was too far away. He came to the stream, crossed through, water to his waist, Cafall splashing beside him, and on the other side he stopped and looked at the woods and turned to Brynn's dog—*his* dog—and said quietly, "No farther now. Wait here."

Cafall pushed his head against Alun's wet hip and thigh, but when he said it again, "No farther," the dog obeyed, staying there beside the rushing water, a grey shape, almost invisible, as Alun went alone into the trees.

SHE KNOWS THE INSTANT he enters among the first oaks and alders, apprehending his aura before she sees him. She stands in a glade by a beech tree, as she did the first time, a hand laid on it for sustenance, sap-strength. She is afraid. But not only that.

He appears at the edge of the glade and stops. Her hair goes to silver. Purest hue, essence of what she is, what they all are: silver around them in the first mound, gleaming. Now lost, undersea. They sing to greet the white moon when it rises.

Only the blue one tonight, hidden from where they stand within the wood. She knows exactly where it is, however. They always know where both moons are. The blue is different, more . . . inward; hues one does not always share with others. Just as she has not shared her coming east, this journey. She took a soul for the queen at the beginning of summer, will not suffer for this following. Or not at the hands of the Ride. There are others in the wood, though, nearby and south. To be feared.

She sees him step forward, approaching over grass, amid trees. A dark wood, far from home (for both of them). There is a *spruaugh* somewhere about, which had angered and surprised her, for she dislikes them all, their green hovering. She'd shown her hair violet to him earlier, and seethed, and he'd retreated, chattering, agitated. She scans with the eye of her mind, doesn't find his aura now. Didn't think he would be anywhere near after seeing her.

She makes herself let go of the tree. Takes a step forward. He is near enough to touch, to be touched. Her hair is shining. She is all the light in this glade, the trees in summer leaf occluding stars and moon, shielding the two of them. A shelter, between worlds, though there are dangers all around. She remembers touching his face on the slope above the farm and the blood-soaked yard, as he knelt before her.

The memory changes the colour of her hair again. It is not only fear she feels. He does not kneel this time. No iron about him. He has left it behind, coming to her, knowing.

They are silent, leaves and branches a canopy above, the grass of the glade shimmering. A breeze, slight sound, it dies away.

He says, "I saw you, twice, coming here. Was I meant to?"

She can feel herself tremble. Wonders if he sees it. They are speaking to each other. It is not to happen. It is a crossing-over, a transgressing. She doesn't entirely understand his words. *Meant to?* Mortals: the world they live within, time different for them. The speed of their dying.

She says, "You can see me. Since the pool." Isn't sure if that is what he meant. They are speaking, and alone here. She reaches a hand backwards, after all, touches the tree again.

"I should hate you," he says. Said that, also, the other time.

She answers, as before, "I don't know what that means. Hate."

A word they use . . . fire in how they live. A flame and then gone. That fire a reason she has always been drawn. But unseen, until now.

He closes his eyes. "Why are you here?"

"I followed you." She lets go of the tree.

He looks at her again. "I know. I know that. Why?"

They think in this way. It has to do with time. One thing, then another thing from it, and then a next. The way the world takes shape for them. She has a thought.

ALUN FELT AS IF HIS MOUTH were dry as earth. Her voice, a handful of words, made him despair again of the idea of making music, of ever hearing anything to match. There was a woodland scent to her, night flowers, and the light—changing, always—about her, in her hair, the only illumination here, where they were. She was shining for him in a forest, and he knew all the tales. Mortals entangled and ensnared within the half-world who never made their way back or were found all changed when they did, companions and lovers dead, or aged, bent into hoops.

Dai was with the faerie queen, walking upon water amid music, coupling in the forested night. Dai was dead, his soul stolen away.

"Why are you here?" he managed.

"I followed you."

Not his answer. He looked at her. "I know. I know that. Why?"

She said, "Because you put away . . . your iron when you came up the slope to me? Before?"

A question in it. She was asking him if this was good enough, as an answer. She spoke Cyngael in the old fashion, the way his grandfather had talked. It frightened him to think how old she might be. He didn't *want* to think of that, or ask. How long did faeries live? He felt light-headed. It was difficult to breathe. He said, a little desperately, "Will you do me harm?"

Her laughter then, first time, rippling. "What harm could I do?"

She lifted her arms, as if to show him how delicate she was, slender, her fingers very long. He could not have named the colour of the tunic she wore, could see the pale, sleek curve of her below it. She extended a hand towards him. He closed his eyes just before she touched his face with her fingers for the second time.

He was lost, knew he was, whatever the tales might say in warning. He had been lost when he left the chapel to come out from behind mortal walls and enter this wood where men did not go.

He took her fingers in his hand, and brought them to his mouth and kissed them, then turned her palm to his lips. Felt her trembling, as leaves did in wind. Heard her say, very faintly, music, "Will you do me harm?"

Alun opened his eyes. She was a silver shining in the wood, beyond imagining. He saw the trees around them and the summer grass.

"Not for all the light in all the worlds," he said, and took her in his arms.

∾

There was very little light in the great hall now: amber pools spilling from the two fires, or where a cluster of men continued to throw dice at one end of the room, and another pair of lamps at the head table where two men remained awake and talking and a third listened quietly, A fourth figure slept there, snoring softly, his head on the board among the last uncleared platters.

Aeldred of the Anglcyn looked at the sleeping cleric from Ferrieres and then turned the other way, smiling a little.

"We have exhausted him," he said.

The cleric on his other side set down his cup. "It is late."

"Is it? Sometimes sleep feels wrong. A surrendering of opportunity." The king sipped his own wine. "He quoted Cingalus at you. You were very kind, then."

"No need to embarrass him."

Aeldred snorted. "While he was citing you to yourself?"

Ceinion of Llywerth shrugged. "I was flattered."

"He didn't know you wrote it. He was patronizing you."

"That wouldn't have mattered if he'd been right in what he argued."

A small sound at that, from the third man. Both turned to him, both smiling.

"Not weary of us yet, my heart?" Aeldred asked.

His younger son shook his head. "Weary, but not of this." Gareth cleared his throat. "Father's right. He . . . didn't even have the quotation properly."

"True enough, my lord prince." Ceinion was still smiling, still cradling his wine. "I'm honoured that you knew it. He was doing it from memory, in fairness."

"But he turned the meaning. He argued against you with your own thought turned backwards. You wrote the Patriarch that there was no error in images unless they were *made* to be worshipped, and he—"

"He cited me as saying images *would* be worshipped."

"So he was wrong."

"I suppose, if you agree with what I wrote." Ceinion's expression was wry. "It could have been worse. He might have cited me as saying clerics should live chaste and unmarried."

The king laughed aloud. Young Gareth's brow remained furrowed. "Why didn't he know it was you who wrote it?"

The subject of their conversation remained where he'd slumped, asleep with most of the men in the darkened hall. Ceinion glanced from the son to the father. He shrugged again.

"Ferrieres tends to look down on the Cyngael. Much of the world does, my lord. Even here, if we are being honest. You call us horse thieves and eaters of oats, don't you?" His tone was mild, unoffended. "He would find it alarming that a scholar cited and endorsed by the Patriarch was from a place so . . . marginal. They used a Rhodian name for me, after all, when they put my phrases in the Pronouncement. An easy error for him to make, not knowing."

"You didn't sign it as Cingalus?"

"I sign everything I write," said the other man gravely, "as Ceinion of Llywerth, cleric of the Cyngael."

There was a little silence.

"He wouldn't even have expected you to be able to write in Trakesian, I imagine," Aeldred murmured. "Or you to read it, for that matter, Gareth."

"The prince reads Trakesian? Wonderful," Ceinion said.

"I'm beginning, only," Gareth remonstrated.

"There's no 'only' in that," the cleric said. "Perhaps we shall read together while I am here?"

"I'd be honoured," Gareth said. His mouth quirked. "It'll keep you from our horses."

A startled silence, then Ceinion burst out laughing and so did the king. The cleric mimed a blow at the prince.

"My children are a great trial," Aeldred said, shaking his head. "All four of them, but Gareth reminds me, I have new texts to show you."

Ceinion turned to him. "Indeed?"

Aeldred allowed himself a satisfied smile. "Indeed. In the morning after prayers we shall go see what is being copied."

"And it is?" Ceinion was unable to mask eagerness.

"Nothing so very much," said the king, with a show of indifference. "Only a physician's tract. One Rustem of Esperaña, on the eye."

"Collating Galinus and adding his own remedies? Oh, glorious! My lord, how in the god's name did you—?"

"A ship from Al-Rassan stopped at Drengest earlier this summer on its way back from trading with the Erlings at Rabady. They know I am buying manuscripts."

"Rustem? That's three hundred years old. A treasure!" Ceinion exclaimed, though softly among the sleepers. "In Trakesian?"

Aeldred smiled again. "In two languages, friend. Trakesian . . . and his original Bassanid."

"*Holy Jad!* But who reads Bassanid? The language is gone, since the Asharites."

"No one yet, but with both texts now we will soon be able to. I have someone working on that. The Trakesian text unlocks the other one."

"This is a glory and a wonder," Ceinion said. He made the sign of the disk.

"I know it is. You'll see it in the morning."

"It will give me great joy."

There was another silence. "That opens a doorway for me, actually," the king said; his tone remained light. "The question I've been waiting to ask."

The cleric looked at him, an exchange of glances in the island of light. Far down the room someone laughed as dice rolled and stopped and fortune smiled, however briefly.

"My lord, I cannot stay," Ceinion said quietly.

"Ah. And thus the door closes," Aeldred murmured.

Ceinion held his gaze in the lamplight. "You know I cannot, my lord. There are people who need me. We were speaking of them, remember? The oat-eaters no one respects? At the edge of the world?"

"We're as much at the edge, ourselves," Aeldred said.

"No. You aren't. Not at this court, my lord. All praise to you for that."

"But you won't help me take it further?"

"I am here now," Ceinion said simply.

"And you will come back?"

"As often as I may." Another small, rueful smile. "For the nourishing of my own spirit. Unworthy as that might be. You know what I think of this court. You are a light to us all, my lord."

The king did not move. "You would make us brighter, Ceinion."

The cleric sipped from his cup before answering. "It would nourish my own desires to do so, to sit here and share learning as old age comes. Do not think I am not tempted. But I have tasks in the west. We Cyngael live where the farthest light of Jad falls. The last light of the sun. It needs attending to, my lord, lest it fail."

The king shook his head. "It is all . . . marginal, here in the northlands," Aeldred said. "How do we build anything to last, when it might come down at any time?"

"That is true of all men, my lord. Of everything we do, anywhere."

"And not more so here? Truly?"

Ceinion inclined his head. "You know I agree with you. I merely—"

"Cite text and doctrine. Yes. But if you refrain from doing that? If you answer honestly? What happens here if the harvest fails in a year the Erlings decide to come back in numbers, not just raiding? Do you think I have forgotten the marshes? Do you think any of us who were there lie down at night, any night, without remembering?"

Ceinion said nothing.

Aeldred went on, "What happens to us if Carloman or his sons in Ferrieres quell the Karchites, as they likely will, and decide they want more land for themselves?" He looked at the sleeping man on his other side.

"You'll beat them back," Ceinion said, "or your sons will. I do believe there is that here which will endure. I am . . . less certain of my people, still fighting each other, still seduced by pagan heresies." He paused, looked away again, and then back. He shrugged. "You spoke of the marsh. Tell me of your fevers, my lord."

Aeldred made an impatient gesture, one that served as a reminder—if one were needed—that this was a king. "I have physicians, Ceinion."

"Who have done little enough to ease them. Osbert tells me—"

"Osbert tells you too much."

"And that, you know well, is untrue. I brought something with me. Do I give it to you, or to him, or whichever physician you trust?"

"I trust none of them." This time it was the king who shrugged. "Give it to Osbert, if you must. Jad will ease my affliction when it pleases him to do so. I am reconciled to that."

"Does that mean we who love you must be?" Ceinion's voice carried just enough amusement to make Aeldred look closely at him, and then shake his head.

"I am made to feel like a child sometimes, by these fevers."

"And why not? We are all still children in some fashion. I can remember skipping stones into the sea as a boy. Then learning my letters. My wedding day . . . there is no shame in that, my lord."

"There is in helplessness."

That stopped him. In the silence, young Gareth rose, took the flask—there were no servants near them now— and poured for the cleric and his father.

Ceinion sipped at the wine. Changed the subject, again. "Tell me of the wedding, my lord."

"Judit's?"

"Unless there is another in the offing." The cleric smiled.

"The ceremonies will be there during the midwinter rites. She goes north to Rheden to make babies and bind two peoples again, the way her mother did, marrying me."

"What do we know of the prince?"

"Calum? He's young. Younger than she is."

Ceinion looked down the hall, back to the king. "It is a good union."

"An obvious one." Aeldred hesitated. His turn to look away. "Her mother has asked me to let her go, after the wedding."

It was news. A confiding. "To Jad's house?"

Aeldred nodded. Took up his wine cup again. He was looking at his younger son, and Ceinion realized this would be news for the prince, as well. A time chosen for the telling, late night, by lamplight. "She has wanted this for a long time."

Ceinion said, "And you have agreed now. Or you wouldn't be telling me."

Aeldred nodded again.

It was not uncommon for men or women, nearing their mortal ending, to seek out the god, pulling back and away from the tumult of the world. It *was* rare for royalty. The world not so easily left behind, for many reasons.

"Where will she go?" the cleric asked.

"Retherly, in the valley. Where our infants are buried. She's been endowing the Daughters of Jad there for years."

"A well-known house."

"Will be better known, with a queen, I imagine."

Ceinion listened for, but did not hear, bitterness. He was thinking about the prince on his other side, didn't look that way, giving Gareth time.

"After the wedding?" he said.

"So she intends."

Carefully, Ceinion said, "We are not supposed to grieve, if someone finds her way, or his, to the god."

"I know that."

Gareth suddenly cleared his throat. "Do . . . the others know of this?" His voice was rough.

His father, who had chosen his moment, said, "Athelbert? No. Your sisters might. I'm not certain. You may tell them, if you like."

Ceinion looked from one to the other. Aeldred, it occurred to him, would not necessarily be an easy man to have for a father. Not for a son, at any rate.

He'd had a good deal of wine, but his thinking was still clear, and the name had now been spoken. A doorway of his own. Perhaps. They were as much alone as they were likely to be, and the younger son, listening, had a thoughtful nature. He drew breath and spoke. "I have," he said, "another wedding thought, if you might entertain it."

"You want a wife again?" The king's smile was gentle.

So was the cleric's, responding. "Not this woman. I am too old, and unworthy." He paused again, then said it: "I have in mind someone for Prince Athelbert."

Aeldred grew still. The smile faded. "This is the heir of the Anglcyn, friend."

"I know it, my lord, believe me. You want peace west of the Wall, and I want my people drawn into the world, from their feuds and solitude."

"It can't be done." Aeldred shook his greying head decisively. "If I choose a princess from any of your provinces, I declare war on the other two, destroy the purpose of a union."

The other man smiled. "You *have* been thinking about this."

"Of course I have! It is what I do. But what answer is there, then?"

And so Ceinion of Llywerth said softly, with the voice-music the Cyngael carried with them through the world, "There is this one answer, lord. Brynn ap Hywll, who slew the Volgan by the sea and might have been our king had he wanted it, has a daughter of an age to be wed. Her name is Rhiannon, and she is the jewel of all women I know. Unless that be her mother. The father is known to you, I dare say."

Aeldred stared at him without speaking for a long time. The Ferrieres cleric snored, cheek to the wooden board. They heard laughter again and a muffled curse from down the room. A sleepy servant prodded the nearer fire with an iron rod.

A door opened before the king spoke.

Doors opened and closed all the time, without consequence or weight. This one was behind them, not the double doors at the far end of the hall. A small door, an exit for the king and his family, should they wish one.

A tall man had to stoop to go through. A passage to inner quarters, privacy, the sleep one would have assumed to be coming soon tonight.

Not so, in the event, for it is not given to men and women to know with any surety what is to come.

The doorways of our lives take many shapes, and the arrivals that change us are not always announced by thunderous pounding or horns at the gates. We may be walking a known laneway, at prayer in a familiar chapel, entering a new one and simply looking up, or we may be deep in quiet talk late of a summer's night, and a door will open behind us.

Ceinion turned. Saw Osbert, son of Cuthwulf, Aeldred's lifelong companion, and his chamberlain. Cuthwulf, as it happened, had been a name cursed in the Cyngael lands, a cattle-raider and worse than that, in more violent days. Another reason (if more were needed) the Anglcyn were hated and feared west of the Wall.

The Erlings had killed Cuthwulf by Raedhill, with his king.

The son, Osbert, was a man Ceinion had come to admire without stint or reservation after two sojourns here. Fidelity and courage, judicious counsel, quiet faith and manifest love: these held their message for those who could see.

Osbert moved forward with the limp he had carried away from a battlefield twenty years ago. He came into the lamplight. Ceinion saw his face. And even by that muted illumination he knew that something had come upon them through that door. He set down his wine, carefully.

Peace, ease, leisure to build and teach, to plant and harvest, time to read ancient texts and consider them . . . these were not the coinage of the north. In other lands they might be, to the south, east in Sarantium, or perhaps in the god's other worlds.

Not here.

"What is it?" Aeldred said. His voice had altered. He stood, his chair scraping back. "Osbert, tell me."

Ceinion would remember that voice, and the fact that the king had been on his feet before he'd heard anything. Knowing already.

And so Osbert told them: of signal flares lit on hills towards the south by the sea, running in their chain of telling fire along the ridges with a message. Not a new tale, Ceinion thought, hearing it. Nothing new here at all, only the old dark legacy of these northlands, which was blood.

CHAPTER IX

"Will my own world be there when I leave you?"

"I don't know what you mean. This is the world we have."

She was beside him, very near. The glade would have been dark were it not for the light she cast. Her hair was all around him, copper-coloured now, thick and warm; he could touch it, had been doing so, in a wood on a summer night. They lay in deep grass, at the edge of a clearing. Sounds of the forest around them, murmurous. These woods had been shunned for generations by his people and the Anglcyn, both. His fear was beside him, however, not among the trees.

"We have stories. Those who went with faeries, and came home . . . a hundred years later." Spirit wood, they named this forest. One of the names. Was *this* what it meant?

Her voice was lazy, a slow music. She said, "I might enjoy lying here that long."

He laughed softly, startled. Felt himself suspended, precariously, between too many feelings, almost afraid to move, as if that might break something.

She turned onto an elbow in the grass, looked at him a moment. "You fear us even more than we fear you."

He thought about that. "I think we fear what you might mean."

"What can I . . . mean? I am just here."

He shook his head. Reached for clarity. "But here for so much longer than we are."

Her turn to be silent. He stared at her, drinking slender grace with his eyes, the *otherness* of her. Her breasts were small, perfect. She had arched her body back above him, before, in the light she made. He wondered, suddenly, how he would pray from now on, what words he could use. Did he ask forgiveness of his god for this? For something the clerics taught did not even exist?

She said, finally, "I think the . . . speed of things for you makes the world more dear."

"More painful?"

Her hair had slipped, by invisible degrees, towards silver again. "More dear. You . . . love more, because you lose so quickly. We don't know . . . that feeling." She gestured, one hand, as if reaching. "You live in . . . in the *singleness* of things. Because they go from you."

"Well, they do, don't they?"

"But you come into the world *knowing* that. It cannot be . . . unexpected. We die, as well. It just takes . . ."

"Longer."

"Longer," she agreed. "Unless there is iron."

His belt and dagger were in the chapel in Esferth. He felt a renewed grief: one of the suspended feelings here. What she had just said. Loving more, because losing.

He said, "Is my brother still with the queen?"

She raised an eyebrow. "Of course."

"But he won't be, always."

"Nothing is always."

Born into the world, knowing that.

She saw he was distressed. "It takes a long time," she said, "before she tires. He is honoured, much loved."

"And he will be lost forever, after. *That* is always."

"Why *lost*? Why see it so?"

"Because we are taught that. That there is a harbour for our souls, and his was taken and will not find the god now. Maybe . . . that is what we fear. In you. That you can do this to us. Perhaps long ago we knew it, about the faeries."

"It was different, once," she agreed. And then shyly, after a moment, "We could fly, then."

"What? How?"

She turned, still shy, to show him her back. And so he saw the ridges clearly, hard, smaller than breasts, inside her shoulder blades, and he understood that these were all that now remained of what had been faerie wings.

He imagined it, creatures like her, flying under blue moon or silver, or at sunset. An ache in his throat, the envisaged beauty of it. In the world, once.

"I'm sorry," he said. He reached out, brushed one with a hand. She shivered, turned back to him.

"There it is again. The way you think. Sorrow. It is so much in you. I . . . we . . . do not live with that. It comes with the speed, doesn't it?"

He thought about this, didn't want to even guess how old she was. She spoke Cyngael the way his grand-father had.

He said it: "You speak my language so beautifully. What does your own sound like?"

She looked surprised a moment, then amused, the hair flashing it. "But this *is* my own tongue. How do you think your people learned it?"

He gaped, closed his mouth.

"Our home is in those woods and pools," she said. "West, towards where the sun lies along the sea at day's end. There was not always so much . . . distance between us."

He was thinking, as hard as he could. Men spoke of the music in the voices of the Cyngael. Now he knew. A knowing, like this night, that shifted the world. How *was* he going to pray? She was looking at him, still amused.

He said, "Is this, is tonight . . . forbidden to you?"

She took a moment to answer. Said, "The queen is pleased with me."

He understood, both answer and hesitation. She was protecting him. In her way, a kindness. They could be kind, it seemed. The queen was pleased because of Dai. The taken soul.

He said, looking at her, "But it is still . . . seen as wrong, isn't it? You have some licence because of what you did, but it is still . . ."

"There is to be distance, yes. Just as for you."

He laughed this time. "Distance? You don't *exist*! To say you are even here is heresy. Our clerics would punish me, some would cast me out from chapel and rites, if I even spoke of it."

"The one from the pool wouldn't," she said quietly.

He hadn't realized she'd seen the cleric that night. "Ceinion? He might," Alun said. "He likes me, because of my father, I think, but he wouldn't allow talk of faeries or the half-world."

She smiled again. "Half-world. I haven't heard that in so long." He didn't want to know how far back in the past something would have to be for her to think that way. The slow uncoiling of time for them. She stretched, feral and sleek as a cat. "But you are wrong about that one. He knows. He came to the queen when his woman was dying."

"What?"

She laughed aloud, quicksilver sound, flutter and ripple in the glade. "Softly. I can hear you," she murmured. She touched him, idly, a hand on his leg. He felt desire, again, was very nearly defined by it. She said, "He came to the mound and asked if one of us might come with him, to help her live. She was coughing blood. He brought silver for the queen, and he wept among the trees outside. He couldn't see us, of course, but he came to ask. She pitied him."

Alun said nothing. Couldn't speak. He knew, everyone knew, about Ceinion's young wife and her death.

"So do not say to me," the faerie added, stretching again, "that that one, of all of you, would deny us."

"She didn't send anything, did she?" he asked, whispering.

Both eyebrows arched, she regarded him. "Why think that? She sent eldritch water from the pool and a charm. She is gracious, the queen, honours those who honour her."

"It didn't . . . help?"

She shook her head. "We are only what we are. Death comes. I did what I could."

He almost missed it. "She sent *you?*"

Her eyes on his, no distance between them, in one way. He needed only move a hand to touch her breast again.

"I have always been . . . most curious."

He sighed. So great a strangeness, the world altering moment by moment as the stars turned above them. Was it slow, or fast, that movement overhead? Did it depend on who was asking?

He said, "And tonight is . . . being curious?"

"And for you, is it not? What else is there for it to be?" A different note in her voice now, under the music.

He was gazing at her. Helpless to look away. Small, even teeth in the wide, thin mouth, pale skin, achingly smooth, the changing hair. Dark eyes. And vestiges of wings. Once, they could fly.

"I don't know," he said, swallowing. "I'm not wise enough. I feel as if I could weep."

"Sorrow, again," she said. "Why does it always come to that, for you?"

"Sometimes we can weep for joy. Do you . . . can you understand that?"

A longer silence. Then she shook her head slowly. "No. I would like to, but this is your cup, not ours."

The . . . otherness, again. This sense that he was both in and entirely outside the world he knew. He said, "Tell me Esferth and the others will be there when I go from here?"

She nodded, calmly. "Though some of them won't be."

He stared. A hard thumping of the heart. "What do you mean?"

"They are starting to ride out. There is anger, men taking horse, bearing iron."

He sat up. "Holy Jad. How do you know?"

She shrugged. The question, he realized, was foolish. How could he understand how she knew things? How could she answer him? Even in the tongue they shared, the language her people had taught his.

He stood up. Began putting on his clothes. She watched him. He was aware, might always be aware now, of the haste of his doing this, seen through her eyes. The way he and the others lived. "I *must* go," he said. "If something has happened."

"Someone died," she said gravely. "There is sorrow. The aura of it."

The speed of their dying. He looked at her, holding his tunic in both hands. He cleared his throat. "Don't envy us that," he said.

"But I do," she said simply; small, sleek, shining otherness in the grass. "Will you come back into the wood?"

He hesitated, and then a thought came that could not have come a night before, when he was younger.

"Will you sorrow if I do not?"

Her eyebrows lifted again, but in surprise this time. She moved a hand, same gesture as before, as if reaching for something. Then, slowly, she smiled, looking up at him.

He pulled on his tunic. No belt, because of the iron. He turned to leave. He hadn't answered her question, either. He had no answer to give.

He looked back from the glade's dark edge. She was still sitting there on the grass, unclothed, in her element, sorrowless.

❦

The voices in the darkness began moving away to the north. Bern remained where he was in the stream. He had a thought, broke off a reed; might need to submerge himself. He heard shouting, men running. Someone rasped a curse, an obscenity directed at Erlings everywhere, and the scabrous, pustulent whores who gave them birth.

Not a good time for this Erling to be discovered.

He'd been right, then. The signal fire had meant nothing good at all. It was still burning. More shouting now, farther away, towards Esferth, where the tents were: the tents outside an overflowing city on the eve of a fair. A city they'd been told would be almost empty, one that they might even loot in a raid that would give rise to songs for generations to their glory, and Jormsvik's.

Glory, Bern decided, was going to be hard to come by now.

He thought quickly, keeping his breathing shallow and slow. Skallson's party had gone east from the ships. A waste of time, some had thought—and the same had been said about Bern and Ecca going into Esferth, once they had learned about the fair. But if they were to leave here—and it seemed evident they were—without anything taken at all, at least *learn* something before they went, it had been decided.

Salvage pride, a flagon's worth, by carrying home report of Aeldred's lands. They might be mocked a little less by their fellows for returning empty-handed, swords unreddened, no tales to tell. A wasted journey at raiding season's end. His own first raid.

Right now, Bern thought, mockery might be the best they could hope for, not the worst. There were worse things than fireside jibes in winter. If that bonfire was an alert, it most likely meant Guthrum Skallson's party had been found. And from the fury in the Anglcyn voices (still heading away from him, Ingavin be thanked) something had happened.

And then he remembered that Ivarr had been with Skallson's party. Bern shivered in the water, couldn't help it. You shivered like that when a spirit passed, someone newly dead, and angry. In that same instant he heard a soft splashing as someone entered the stream.

Bern drew his dagger and prepared himself to die: in water again, third time now. Third time was said to mark power, sacred to Nikar the Huntress, wife to Thünir. Three times was a gateway. He had expected death in the night waters off Rabady. And again in the dawn surf outside Jormsvik. He tried to accept it once more, now. An ending waited for all men, no one knew his fate, everything lay in how you went to your dying. He gripped his blade.

"Stay where you are," he heard.

The voice low, terse, barely audible. Utterly and entirely known all the days of his life.

"Spare me the knife," it went on softly. "I've been stabbed at already tonight. And keep silent or they will find and kill you here," his father added, moving, unerringly, towards where Bern was hidden, submerged to his shoulders, invisible in darkness.

Unless you *knew* he was here. Not a mystery, then, this part at least. He'd gone straight into the stream from the place on the bank where his father had left him. Not magic, not some impossible night vision, brilliant raider's instinct.

"I didn't think they'd offer me wine," he murmured. No greeting offered. Thorkell hadn't greeted him.

His father grunted, coming up. "How's your head?"

"Hurts. Want your neck chain back?"

"I'd have kept it if I wanted it. You made a mistake in that alley. You know the saga: *Have thine eyes about you / in hall or darkness. Be wary ever / be watching always.*"

Bern said nothing. Felt his face redden.

"Two horses?" Thorkell asked calmly.

His father's dark bulk was beside him, Thorkell's voice close to his ear. The two of them together in a stream at night in Anglcyn lands. How was this so? What had the gods decided? And how did men take hold of their own lives when this could happen? He realized his heart was thumping, hated that.

"Two horses," he replied, keeping his voice steady. "Where's Ecca?"

Small hesitation. "That what he was calling himself?"

Was calling. "Right," Bern said bitterly. "Of course. He's dead. You know, the same poet says: *No good ever, whatever be thought / was mead or ale to any man.* Are you drunk?"

The backhanded blow caught him on the side of the head.

"By Ingavin's blind eye, show respect. I got you out of a walled city. Think on it. I went to warn him, he drew a blade to kill when I used his real name. I made a mistake. Is your horse a good one?"

A mistake. One could weep, or laugh. Killing the second man on the isle had been the mistake, Bern wanted to say. He was still trying to wrap his mind around what was happening here. "My horse is Gyllir," he said. Struggled to keep anything out of his voice his father might read as youthful pride.

Thorkell grunted again. "Halldr's? He didn't come after you?"

"Halldr's dead. The horse was for his burning."

That silenced his father, for a moment, at least. Bern wondered if he was thinking of his wife, who had become Halldr's, and was widowed now, alone and unprotected on Rabady.

"There's a tale to that, I imagine," was all Thorkell said.

His voice had not changed at all. Why should it change, though all the world Bern knew had been altered entirely? "Leave Stefa's mount," his father said. "They'll need a horse to find, after they get his body."

Stefa. With an effort Bern kept his hand from going to his head. The stars had swung again with the blow. His father was a strong man.

"They'll see the signs of two horses where we hid them," Bern said. "Won't work."

"It will. I'll find his horse and bring it out. Go now, though, and quickly—some fool killed Burgred of Denferth tonight. Aeldred's riding out himself, I think."

"What?" said Bern, his jaw dropping. "The earl? Why didn't they—?"

"Take him for ransom? You tell me. You're the mercenary. He'd have been worth your raid and more."

But that answer, in fact, he knew. "Ivarr," he said. "Ragnarson's paying us."

"Ingavin's blind eye! I knew it," his father rasped. His old oath, remembered from childhood, familiar as smells and the shape of hands. Thorkell swore again, spat into the stream. He stood waist-deep in the water, thinking. Then: "Listen. That one's going to want you to go west. Don't go. It isn't a raid for Jormsvik."

"West? What's west of here? Just . . ." And then, as his father said nothing, Bern finally thought it through. He swallowed, cleared his throat. "Blood," he whispered. "Vengeance? For his grandfather? And *that's* why he—"

"That's why he bought your ships and men, whatever else he told you, and that's why he wouldn't want a hostage. He wants to go after the Cyngael. But with ransom paid for an earl you'd turn and go home. He was with the shore party, wasn't he?"

Bern nodded. It was sliding into place.

"I'll wager you land we don't own any more they'll find Burgred with an arrow in him."

"He said the *burh* was still unwalled, that Esferth would be almost empty."

Thorkell grunted, spat downstream again. "Empty? During a fair? Serpent-sly, that one. Poisons his arrows."

"How do *you* know that?"

No answer. It occurred to Bern that he'd never spoken in this way with his father in his life. Nothing remotely resembling this terse conversation. He didn't have time, no time at all, to unwind his own held-in rage, the bitterness for lives marred. Thorkell still hadn't asked about his wife. Or Gyllir. Or how Bern had come to be in Jormsvik.

Fireflies darting around them. Bern heard bullfrogs and crickets. No human voices, though; they'd gone north towards the walls and tents. And would be coming out, back this way, heading for the coast. King Aeldred leading them, his father had said.

Guthrum's party was on foot, would be running for the ships right now. If they weren't dead. He had no idea where they'd been when they . . .

"Where are your horses?"

"Just west, in the woods."

"In *those* woods?" Thorkell's voice rose for the first time.

"Are there others?"

"I'll hit you again. Show respect. That's a spirit wood. No Anglcyn or Cyngael will enter it. Stefa ought to have known, if you didn't."

"Well," said Bern, attempting defiance, "maybe he did know. If they don't go in, it's a good place for our mounts, isn't it?"

His father said nothing. Bern swallowed. He cleared his throat. "He only went in a few steps, tethered them, got out right away."

"He did know." Thorkell sounded tired suddenly. "You'd best move," his father said. "Think the rest of it out while you ride."

Bern moved, climbing up the western bank. He said nothing but as he looked around, crouching, Thorkell added, "Don't let Ivarr Ragnarson know you're my son. He'll kill you for it."

Bern stopped, looking down at the dark figure of his father in the stream. A tale there, too, obviously. He wasn't going to ask. He wanted to say something harsh about how late it was for Thorkell to be showing signs of looking after his family.

He turned. Heard his father come out of the water behind him. He walked south, quickly, bent low, went in among the trees to get Gyllir. He shivered, doing so. Spirit wood. He knew Thorkell was watching him, to mark the place. He didn't look back. Offered no farewell and, Ingavin knew, no thanks. He'd die before he did that.

Gyllir whickered at his approach. The horse seemed agitated, tossing his head. Bern rubbed his muzzle, whispering, untied the reins. He left Ecca's horse tethered, as instructed. It wouldn't be for long. Emerged from the woods, mounted, rode, south under stars and the blue moon, pushing Gyllir. There would be mounted men following soon.

The land stretched level, forest to the west, open to the east across the stream, mostly empty at first, uninhabited, then some dark farms over that way, planted barley, rye, the harvest coming soon. A line of low trees, cluster of houses, the ground beginning to slope towards the sea, and their ships. A long way to go. Men following. The bonfire still burning. After a time he saw another one, far off, and then, later, a third, sending its signals, which he couldn't read. The moon was gone by then, behind the woods.

He leaned forward over Gyllir's neck to make his weight easier to bear. *There's a tale, I imagine,* his father had said, learning of the horse. He hadn't asked, though. Hadn't asked.

Heimthra was the word used for longing: for home, for the past, for things to be as they once had been. Even the gods were said to know that yearning, from when the worlds were broken. Bern was grateful, as he rode, that no one on the wide dark earth could see his face, and he had to trust that Ingavin and Thünir would not think the worse of him, if they were watching in the night.

It was Hakon Ingemarson who had recognized Kendra by the stream.

He'd called out to her immediately as he passed with a torch amid a crowd of others heading for the tents. She hadn't wanted to ask how he'd known her so quickly in the dark. Was afraid of his answer. Knew his answer, really.

She'd cursed, silently, the sheer bad luck that had led him past this point, even as she'd turned and achieved a tone of pleased welcome when he came hurrying over.

"My lady! How come you here, unattended?"

"I'm not unattended, Hakon. Ceinion of Llywerth kindly sent his own guard with me." She had gestured, and Thorkell had stepped forward into the light. The dog, thankfully, was across the stream, out of sight. She'd had no least idea how she'd have adequately explained it.

"But there's nothing here at all!" Hakon had exclaimed. She'd realized that he was drunk. They all were. That might make things easier, in fact. "The gathering is over by the tents! Your royal sister and brother are there already. May we escort you?"

Kendra had searched for and failed to find any way to decline. Cursing again, inside, with a ferocity that would have surprised all three of her siblings and utterly disconcerted the young man in front of her, she'd smiled and said, "Of course. Thorkell, wait here for me. I'll likely just stay a short while, and I wouldn't want these men to forgo their entertainment to take me back inside."

"Yes, my lady," the older Erling had said, in the uninflected voice of a servant.

Hakon had looked as if he might protest, but evidently decided to be pleased with what he'd gained so unexpectedly. She'd fallen in with him and the others and they'd made their way to the colourful village of tents that had sprung up north-west of the walls.

When they arrived, they found a boisterous crowd gathered in a wide circle. Hakon pushed through to the front. Inside were two people. It came as no great surprise to Kendra to discover that these were her older brother and sister.

She looked around. To one side of the ring she saw a skull, resting on the grass, a torch set beside it. Kendra winced. She had a fairly good idea, suddenly, what had happened here. Athelbert simply did *not* know when to leave well enough alone.

Judit had a long staff, held crosswise with both hands. She knew how to use it. Athelbert carried a significantly smaller one, a thin switch. Nearly useless, good for swatting at leaves or apples, not much more.

Judit was attempting, with grim purpose and no little skill, to club her brother senseless. Finish the task she'd begun that morning. Athelbert—who had had a great deal to drink, it was clear—was laughing far too much to be at all safe from his sister's assault.

Kendra, eyeing them, listening to the hilarity around her, was thinking about the Cyngael in the woods, and about his dog—the way it had stood on the far side of the stream, rigid and attentive, listening. She didn't know for what. She didn't really *want* to know.

There was nothing to be done now, in any case. No way to turn around and walk away just yet. She had sighed again, fixed a smile on her face, and accepted a cup of watered wine from Hakon, busy on her behalf. She watched her siblings amid a rapturous, howling crowd and smoking torches. A late-summer night, the harvest looking to be good, the fair soon to begin. A time of laughter and celebration.

The entertainment in the ring continued, marked by two pauses for wine on the part of the combatants. Judit's hair was entirely and immodestly unconfined now. Not that she would care, Kendra thought. Athelbert was dodging and ducking without pause. He'd taken two or three blows, including one to the shin that had knocked him sprawling, barely able to roll away from Judit's urgent follow-up. Kendra thought about intervening. She was certainly the only person who could. She wasn't actually sure how much self-control Judit had left. It was sometimes hard to tell.

Then someone shouted loudly, in a different tone, and people were pointing to the south, beyond the city. Kendra turned. A bonfire. They watched the signals begin, and repeat. And then repeat again.

It was Athelbert who decoded the message aloud for all of them. Judit, listening, dropped her staff, went over to stand next to her brother. She began to cry. Athelbert put his arm around her.

Amid the chaos that ensued, Kendra shifted from where Hakon had been hovering at her elbow. Then she slipped away into the dark. Torches were everywhere, shaping patterns in the night. She made her way back to the river. The dog was still there. It didn't seem to have moved, in fact. Thorkell was nowhere to be seen.

Nor was Alun ab Owyn. He ought *not* to matter now, she was thinking. Her mind was in a whirl. One of their own had been slain tonight, if Athelbert had the message right. She was certain that he had.

Burgred. He had been in the marshes with her father, had fought at Camburn, both times, when they lost and when they won. And he had gone chasing a rumour of Erling ships while the king lay wrapped in fever.

Her father, she thought, would be tortured by that knowledge.

There was a movement across the stream. The man she'd followed came out from the trees.

He stopped at the wood's edge, looking lost.

Kendra, heart pounding, saw the dog pad over to him, push his muzzle against the Cyngael's hip. Alun ab Owyn reached down and touched the dog. It was too dark to see his face, but there was something in the way he stood that frightened her. She had been frightened, she realized, all night. All day long, really, from the time the Cyngael party had come into the meadow.

There were noises, men shouting behind her, running towards the city gates, which were open now. Kendra heard a different sound, a footfall, nearer: she looked over, saw Thorkell. His clothes were wet.

"Where were you?" she whispered.

"He's come out," the Erling replied, not answering.

Kendra turned back to the woods. Alun still hadn't moved, except to touch the dog. Uncertainly, she walked towards the river, stood on the bank amid reeds and dragonflies. She saw him look up and see her. Too dark, too dark to know his eyes.

She took a breath. She had no business being here, no understanding of how she knew what she knew.

"Come back to us," she said, fighting fear.

The dog turned to her voice. Blue moon and stars overhead. She heard Thorkell come up behind her. Was grateful for that. She was watching the other man by the trees.

And at length, she heard Alun ab Owyn say, in a voice you had to strain to hear, "My lady, I have a long way to go. To do that."

Kendra shivered. Was close to tears, and afraid. She made herself take another deep breath and said, with courage that perhaps only her father was aware that she had, "I am only this far."

Thorkell, behind her, made an odd sound.

By the trees, Alun ab Owyn lifted his head a little. And then, after a moment, moved forward, walking as if through water even before he reached it. He crossed the stream with the dog. His hair was disordered. He had no belt on his tunic, carried no weapon.

"What . . . are you doing here?" he asked.

Her head high, feeling the breeze in her hair, she said, "I am truly not certain. I felt . . . afraid, from when I saw you this morning. Something . . ."

"You were afraid of me?" His voice was drained of emotion.

Again she hesitated. "Afraid for you," she said.

A silence, then he nodded, as if unsurprised.

I am only this far, she'd said. Where had that come from? But he'd crossed. He'd come across the water from the trees to them. A little behind her, the Erling kept silent.

"Did someone die tonight?" Alun ab Owyn asked.

"We think so," she said. "My brother believes it was Earl Burgred, leading a party south of here."

"Erlings?" he asked. "Raiders?"

He was looking past her now, at Thorkell. The dog was beside him, wet from the river, standing very still.

"It appears so, my lord," said the big man behind her. And then, carefully, "I believe . . . we both know the one who leads them."

And that made a change. Kendra saw it happen. The Cyngael seemed to be *pulled* back to them, snapped like a leash or a whip, away from whatever had happened in the trees. The thing she didn't want to think about.

"Ragnarson?" he asked.

Not a name Kendra knew; it meant nothing to her.

The Erling nodded. "I believe so."

"How do you know this?" ab Owyn asked.

"My lord prince, if it is Ragnarson, he will want to take their ships west from here. King Aeldred is riding out now, after them."

He was very good, Kendra was realizing, at not replying to questions he didn't want to answer.

In the darkness, she looked at the Cyngael prince. Alun was rigid, so taut he was almost quivering. "He'll go for Brynnfell again. They won't be ready, not so soon. I need a horse!"

"I'll get you one," said Thorkell calmly.

"What? I think not," came a slurred, angry voice. Kendra wheeled, white-faced. Saw Athelbert coming across the grass. "A mount? So he can ride my sister and then ride home to boast of it?"

Kendra felt her heart pound, with fury this time, not fear. Her fists were clenched at her sides. "Athelbert, you are drunk! And entirely—"

He went right past her. He might jest and tumble with Judit, letting her buffet him about for the amusement of others, but her older brother was a hard, trained, fighting man, king-to-be in these lands, and enraged right now, for more than one reason.

"Entirely what, dear sister?" He didn't look back at her. He had stopped in front of Alun ab Owyn. He was half a head taller than the Cyngael. "Look at his hair, his tunic. Left his belt in the grass, I see. At least you made yourself presentable before getting off your backside."

Thorkell Einarson took a step forward. "My lord prince," he began, "I can tell you—"

"You can shut your loathsome Erling mouth before I kill you here," Athelbert snapped. "Ab Owyn, draw your blade."

"Have none," said Alun, mildly. And launched himself, in a lithe, efficient movement, at Athelbert. He feinted left, and then his right fist hammered hard at her brother's heart. Kendra's hands flew to her mouth. Athelbert went backwards in a heap, sprawled on the grass. He grunted, shifted to get up, and froze.

The dog, Cafall, was directly above him, a large grey menace, growling in his throat.

"He didn't *touch* me, you Jad-cursed clod!" Kendra screamed at her brother. She was close to tears, in her fury. "I was over watching you and Judit make fools of yourselves!"

"You were? You, er, saw that?" Athelbert said. He had a hand to his chest, was careful to make no sudden movements.

"I saw that," she echoed. "*Must* you take such pains to be an idiot?"

There was a silence. They heard the noises from behind them, towards the gates.

"Less difficult than you think," her brother murmured, finally. Wry, already laughing at himself, a gift he had, in fact. "Where," he said looking up at Alun ab Owyn, "did you learn to do that?"

"My brother taught me," said the Cyngael, shortly. "Cafall, hold!" The dog had growled again as Athelbert shifted to a sitting position.

"Hold is a good idea," agreed Athelbert. "You might want to tell him again? Make sure he heard you?" He looked over at his sister. "I appear to have—"

"Erred," said Kendra, bluntly. "How unusual."

They heard horns, from the city.

"That's Father," said Athelbert. A different tone.

Alun looked over. "We'll need to hurry. Thorkell, where's that horse?"

The big man turned to him. "Downstream. I killed an Erling raider in town tonight. Tracked his horse to the wood just now. If you need a mount quickly you can—"

"I need a mount quickly, and a sword."

"Killed an Erling raider?" Athelbert snapped in the same breath.

"Man I used to know. With Jormsvik now. I saw him in the—"

"*Later!* Come on!" said Alun. "Look!" He pointed. Kendra and the two men turned. She gripped her hands together tightly. The *fyrd* of King Aeldred was streaming out of the gates amid torches and banners. She heard the sound of horses' harness and drumming hooves, men shouting, horns blowing. The glorious and terrible panoply of war.

"My lady?" It was Thorkell. Asking leave of her.

"Go," she said. He wasn't her servant.

The two men began running along the riverbank. The dog growled a last time at Athelbert, then went after them.

Kendra looked down at her brother, still sitting on the grass. She watched him stand, somewhat carefully. He'd had a painful day. Tall, fair-haired as an Erling, graceful, handsome, reasonably near to sober, in fact.

He stood before her. His mouth quirked. "I'm an idiot," he said. "I know, I know. Adore you, though. Remember it."

Then he went quickly away as well, towards the gates, to join the company riding out, leaving her unexpectedly alone in darkness by the stream.

That didn't happen often, being left alone. It was not, in fact, unwelcome. She needed some moments to compose herself, or try.

What are you doing here? he'd asked. The too-obvious question. And how was she to answer? Speak of an aura almost seen, a sound beyond hearing, something never before known but vivid as faith or desire? The sense that he was marked, apart, and that she'd somehow known it, from his first appearance in the meadow that morning?

I have a long way to go, he'd said, across the stream. And she'd known, somehow, what he really meant, and it was a thing she didn't *want* to know.

Jad shield me, Kendra thought. *And him.* She looked towards the trees, unwillingly. Spirit wood. Saw nothing there, nothing at all.

She lingered, reluctant to surrender this quiet. Then, like a blade sliding into flesh, it came back to her that the tumult she was hearing was a response to the death of someone she'd known from childhood.

Burgred of Denferth lifting her onto his horse, so far above the ground, for a canter around the walls of Raedhill. She'd been three, perhaps four. Terror, then pride, and a hiccoughing laughter, giddy breathlessness. Her father's softened, amused face when Burgred brought her back and, leaning in the saddle, set her down, red-faced, on chubby legs.

Did you remember things because they'd happened often, or because they were so rare? That one had been rare. A stern man, Earl Burgred, more so than Osbert. A figure of action, not thought. Carried the marks of the past in a different way. Her father's fevers, Osbert's leg, Burgred's . . . anger. He'd been with Aeldred, and had been loved, when they'd all been very young, even before Beortferth.

An Erling had killed him tonight. How did one deal with that, if one was king of the Anglcyn?

Her father was riding out. Could die tonight. They had no idea how many Erlings were south of them. How many ships. Jormsvik, Thorkell Einarson had said. She knew who they were: mercenaries from the tip of Vinmark. Hard men. The hardest of all, it was said.

Kendra turned then, away from woods and stream and solitude, to go back. She saw her younger brother, standing patiently, waiting for her.

She opened her mouth, closed it. Athelbert would have sent him, she realized. In the midst of chasing down his horse and armour and joining the *fyrd* amid chaos, he'd have done that.

It was too easy to underestimate Athelbert.

"Father wouldn't let you both go?" she asked quietly. Knew the answer before she asked.

Gareth shook his head in the darkness. "No. What happened here? Are you all right?"

She nodded. "I suppose. You?"

He hesitated. "I wouldn't mind killing someone."

Kendra sighed. Others had sorrows, too. You needed to remember that. She came forward, took her brother's arm. Didn't squeeze it or anything like that; he'd bridle at obvious sympathy. Gareth knew the Rhodian and

Trakesian philosophers, had read them aloud to her, modelled himself (or tried) on their teachings. *Conduct yourself in the sure knowledge that death comes to all men born. Be composed, accordingly, in the face of adversity.* He was seventeen years old.

They walked back together. She saw the guard at the gate, white-faced. The one who had let her out. She nodded reassuringly at him, managed a smile.

She and Gareth went to the hall. Osbert was there, amid a blaze of lanterns, giving instructions, men coming and going in front of him. Something he'd done all Kendra's life. His face looked seamed and gaunt. None of them was young any more, she thought: her father, Osbert, Burgred. Burgred was dead. Were the dead old, or young?

There was nothing for her to do, but it was too late to go to bed. They went to morning prayers when sunrise came. Her mother joined them, large, calm, a ship with the wind behind her, sure in her faith. Kendra didn't see Judit in the chapel, but her sister found them later, back in the hall, soberly garbed, hair properly pinned but with a wild fury in her eyes. Judit did not subscribe to the doctrines of composure advocated by Rhodian philosophers. She wanted a sword right now, Kendra knew. Wanted to be on a horse, riding south. Would never, ever, be reconciled to the fact that she couldn't do that.

By then, someone had found the dead Erling in the alley and had reported it to Osbert. Kendra had expected that, had been thinking about it when she was supposed to be praying.

Waiting for a pause in the flow of messages to and from, she went over and told Osbert, quietly, what she knew. He listened, considered, said nothing by way of reproach. That was not his way. He sent a messenger running for the guard who had been on the wall, who came, and another one for the Erling servant of Ceinion of Llywerth, who did not.

Thorkell Einarson, they discovered, had gone south with the *fyrd*. So had the Cyngael cleric, though that had been known: a night ride beside Aeldred on a horse they'd given him. A different sort of holy man, this one. And Kendra knew Alun ab Owyn was also with them, and why.

Someone named Ragnarson. She remembered the way he'd looked, coming out of the wood. She still didn't want to acknowledge what it was she seemed to know about this, about him—without any idea *how* she knew. The world, Kendra suddenly thought, heretically, was not as well-made as it might have been.

She pictured him riding, and the grey dog running beside the horses towards the sea.

∽

Earlier that same night, a woman was making her way carefully across the fields of Rabady Isle, not precisely sure of her direction in the dark, and more than a little afraid to be abroad after moonrise alone. She could hear the sea and the waving grain at the same time. Harvest was coming, the grain fields were high, making it harder to see her way.

A little before, under the same waning blue moon, her exiled husband and only son had spoken together in a stream near Esferth. A coming-together that could only having been shaped—she would have said—by the gods for their own purposes, which were not to be understood. The woman would have been grateful for tidings of the son; would have denied interest in the father.

Her daughters were also away, across the strait on the Vinmark mainland. Neither had sent word for some time. She understood. A family disgrace could make ambitious husbands cautious about such things. There was a king in Hlegest now with increasingly clear ambitions of his own to rule all the Erlings, not just some of them in the north. Times were changing. It meant, among other things, that young men had reason to think carefully, mind their tongues, be discreet with family connections. Shame could come to a man through his wife.

Frigga, daughter of Skadi, once wife to Red Thorkell, then to Halldr Thinshank, now bound to no man and therefore without protection, was not bitter about her daughters.

Women had only so much control over their lives. She didn't know how it was elsewhere. Much the same, she imagined. Bern, her son, ought to have stayed by her when Halldr died instead of disappearing, but Bern had been turned from a landowner's heir into a servant by his father's exile, and who could, truly, blame a young man for rejecting that?

She'd assumed he was dead, after they'd gone looking for him and the horse in the morning and found neither. Had spent nights mourning, not able to let anyone see how much she grieved, because of what he'd obviously done, taking the dead man's funeral horse.

Then, a short while ago, at summer's end, had come tidings that he hadn't died. They'd stoned the *volur* for helping Bern Thorkellson get off the isle.

Frigga didn't believe it. It made no sense at all, that tale, but she wasn't about to say that to anyone. There was no one to whom she could talk. She was alone here, and still had no true idea if her son was alive.

And then, a few days ago, they had named the new *volur*.

One-handed Ulfarson, now governor, did the naming, which was a new thing. There were always new things, weren't there? But the young *volur* was kin to her, nearly, and Frigga had offered some small kindnesses when the girl had first arrived to serve in the women's compound. It seemed now to have been a wise thing to have done, though that wasn't why she'd done it. A woman's road was hard, always, stony and bleak. You helped each other, if and when you could. Her mother had taught her that.

She needed help herself now. It had brought her into the night (windy, not yet cold) and these whispering fields. She was afraid of animals, and spirits, and of living men doing what they were likely to do if they had been drinking and came upon a woman alone. She feared the moment, and what the future held for her in the world.

Frigga stopped, took a deep breath, looked around her by moonlight, and saw the boulder. They had done the stoning here. She knew where she was. Another breath, and a murmured thank-you to the gods. She had been to the women's compound four times in her life, but the last visit had been twenty years ago, and she had come by daylight, each time with an offering when she was carrying a child, and three of her children had lived. Who understood these things? Who dared say they did? It was Fulla, corn goddess, who decreed what happened to a woman when her birth pangs came. It made sense to seek intercession. Frigga moved to the stone. Touched it, murmured the proper words.

She didn't know if what she was doing now could be said to be sensible, but she was, it seemed, no more willing to be a servant than her son had been—to be ordered to bed any man-guest at the behest of Thinshank's first wife, the widow who'd inherited, with her sons.

Second wives had little in the way of rights, unless they'd had time to establish their ground in the house. Frigga hadn't. She wasn't far, in fact, from being cast out, with winter coming. She had no property, thanks to Thorkell's second murder. Nor was she young enough to readily persuade any proper man to take her to wife. Her breasts were fallen, her hair grey, there were no children left waiting in her womb.

She had lingered through a spring and summer, endured what she'd known would come from the day Halldr died, followed by that disastrous funeral: burning him without the horse, the omen of it, the unquiet spirit. She had hoped troubles would pass her by, seen they would not, and finally decided to come out tonight. Much the same path—though she did not know this— her son had taken with a dead man's horse in the spring. A roll of the gambling dice.

Women were not actually allowed to touch the dice, of course, for fear of putting a curse on them.

She saw the first trees, and the light, at the same time.

ANRID WASN'T ASLEEP. She hadn't been sleeping since the stoning. The images that came when she closed her eyes. It was wearing her away. Her elevation to *volur* hadn't changed this; it hadn't even been a surprise. She'd seen the unfolding of events in her mind, as if played out on some raised platform, from the time she'd gone to the governor. In truth, from the time she'd devised her course of action after he'd summoned her to come to him.

It had happened as she'd seen it, including the stoning, when she'd worn the serpent about her body for all of them to see.

She hadn't known this about herself: that anger could make her cause people to die. But the *volur* had had the snake bite her *before* knowing if its poison was gone. Anrid had been the newest girl, and alone here. Her dying wouldn't have mattered to anyone in the world. They had made her stand still, eyes closed in sick terror, and had goaded the released serpent with sticks, and it had bitten her. Then they'd sent her back out on watch duty, waiting curiously to see if she died. Anrid had been sick to her stomach in the yard, and then limped out through the gate to where she was supposed to watch. What else had there been for her to do?

And that night Bern had come. She'd seen him tie the horse and walk into the compound, and the *volur* had arranged to send him to a savage death. No uncertainty about that one, no testing of poison. He'd enter the town at sunrise, thinking he was safe, and would be taken and killed. A man who'd come to the seer for help. She had sheathed him in her wrinkled, dried-out flesh, deceiving him entirely. Laughed about it after. The crude jibes of the other old ones, peering through cracks in the wall, complaining they hadn't had their turn.

Anrid, turning away in disgust to the darkness again, limping, had taken her own first steps towards the stonings (savage death) later that same night when she spoke to the man, warning him. Bern Thorkellson was kin to her, almost. She told herself that now, over and again. You stood by kin in this world because there was no one else to stand by, or who might ever stand by you. A rule of the northlands. You died if you were too much alone.

But she saw stones striking flesh whenever she closed her eyes now.

When they knocked at her door and she rose and opened it and they told her a woman had come, she knew—they would think it was her power—who this had to be, even before her brother's wife's mother was led to her chamber. It wasn't power, it was a quick mind. A different sort of mystery; women weren't ever credited with that.

While she waited, Anrid let the snake coil around her; she did that all the time now. The serpent had been her doorway to this. It was important that the others see her handling it, confront their own fear of doing the same. She was still the newest, still the youngest, and now *volur*. She needed to find a way to survive. *Volurs* could be killed. She knew it.

A knock, the door opened. She gestured for Frigga to enter, closed the door herself, letting no one else in. She had already blocked up the holes through which she and the others used to peek. She put the serpent in the basket they'd made for it.

She hated the snake.

Anrid turned to the older woman, looked at her a moment, opened her mouth to speak, and began to cry. The tears stunned her with how desperately they fell. Her hands were shaking.

"Oh, child," said Frigga.

Anrid couldn't stop weeping. You'd have had to kill her to make her stop. "Will you . . . ?" she began. Choked on her words, tears in her throat. Hands in trembling fists to her mouth. A shuddering of breath. Tried again. "Will you stay with me? Please stay?"

"Oh, child. Have you a place for me?"

Anrid could only nod, again and again, a spasm of the head. The older woman, nearly kin, closest thing she had, came forward and they wrapped each other in arms that had not known or given comfort for so long.

Only the younger one wept, however. Then, later that night, she slept.

CHAPTER X

B rogan the miller, awake as usual before dawn, was thinking, as he pissed into the stream before beginning the day, about some of the things he disliked.

It was a long list. He was a sour, solitary man. Had been drawn to the mill because it gave him a house at the edge of the village, a place removed from (and a stature above) the others. He'd murdered someone to get this mill, but that was an old story and he didn't think or even dream about it often any more. Brogan didn't really like people. They talked too much, most of them.

His servant was, usefully, a mute. He'd been very happy (briefly) when he'd learned that Ord, a farmer with fields east of the village, was looking for work for his youngest son who didn't talk. Brogan had made arrangements to bring the boy to the mill. He was old enough, a broad-shouldered lad. A straw pallet, food, a day a week to help his father. Milk and cheese for Brogan in exchange for that last.

And a decent worker who didn't prattle on when feeding the animals or standing waist-deep in the stream mending the wheel. Brogan, who had come to the mill as a worker himself thirty years ago—and taken certain measures a little later to ensure he'd stay—couldn't understand why people would mar an easy silence with wasted words.

There were still stars in the west. First hint of greyness east. Dawn wind ruffling the reeds in the river. Brogan scratched himself and went to unbolt the mill. A warm day coming. Still summertime, though late in the season, with what that meant.

Brogan didn't like the new end-of-summer fair, third year now. The road west of their hamlet towards the river (of which the millstream was a tributary) became too busy. Steady traffic from coast to Esferth and then back, afterwards.

People on roads signified trouble for Brogan the miller. Nothing good about them at all. Strangers stole things, came looking for women or drink, or just mischief to make or find. Brogan had coins buried in three places around the mill. Would have spent some of them by now, but he'd never wanted anything enough to spend good money on it. A woman, now and again, but you could buy one of those for grain, and many of the farmers paid him with flour and wheels of bread. More than he needed. He left his money buried, but worried about it. Long ago, he'd lain awake wondering if someone would find the old miller in his grave, dig him up, see the crushed skull. Now it was the coins that woke him sometimes in the dark. All over the world men knew that millers made money.

He had three dogs. Didn't like them, their barking, but they offered protection. And Modig, the mute, was a good-sized lad, handy with a cudgel. Brogan himself wasn't a big man, but he'd survived a fight or two in his day.

He'd considered taking a wife, some time ago. Children to do the work as he grew older. The idea had come, lingered a while, and passed: women changed things, and Brogan the miller didn't like change. That was the principal reason he didn't like the king. Even after all these years, Aeldred was always changing things. You had to make bows and arrows for yourself now, or buy them, and you were supposed to practise every week, and be tested by someone from the *fyrd* each spring. Didn't they have other things to do, the *fyrd*? Farmers with bows: that was a stupid, dangerous thought. They'd kill each other before the Erlings had a chance.

It was dark in the mill, but after so many years he knew his way blind. He opened the shutters over the stream, to let in some light and air. Went down the steps, heard the mice skitter from his footfall. He lifted the lock to the sluice, gripped with both hands, put his back to it, and pulled back the chute gate. The water started pouring in. Soon the familiar sounds of the turning wheel and millstones grinding above began. He went back up, took the first sack, opened it, dumped it into the hopper above the turning stones. Through the open window the eastern sky showed brighter. The first women and children would be coming for their flour after sunrise, most of them straight from the dawn prayers in the small chapel.

Brogan was still thinking about changes as he checked the millstones, which were turning easily. A new cleric in the village now. This one could read and write, was supposed to be teaching people. There were new rules for military service, new taxes for the building of the *burhs*. Yes, the *burhs* were supposed to protect them, but Brogan doubted a walled fort at Drengest south and east on the coast, or the other one inland two days east, would do much good for their hamlet or his mill if trouble came. And reading? *Reading?* What in the name of Jad's toes and fingers did that have to do with anything? Might be well enough for a soft man at court where they ate with ale-soddened musicians piping and warbling to spoil good meat. But here? In a farming village? Modig would do *so* much better mending the fence or the waterwheel once he could spell his name! Brogan turned his head to spit expertly out the window into the stream.

The new cleric had called shortly after arriving. Fair enough: the mill was owned by the chapel and the miller together. That was why Brogan was miller, really. When the old one had come to his unexpected end (a sudden fever in midsummer, taken in the one night, buried sadly by his servant at dawn), it had made sense for the cleric to strike a bargain with the dour young man after the funeral rites. The miller's assistant, Brogan by name, had seemed to know what he was doing, and the village couldn't afford to have the mill idle while they considered who should have the position. It was a stroke of good fortune for the young fellow, obviously, but Jad could sometimes bestow generously where you might not have expected it.

Thirty years later, this newest cleric (fifth one Brogan had worked with) had looked around the mill in a cursory sort of way, clearly uninterested in what he saw, and then, growing enthusiastic, had asked Brogan about installing one of the newer-styled vertical wheels. He'd read a letter from a fellow cleric in Ferrieres about them, he said. More power, a better use of the river.

Changes, again. Ferrieres. Brogan, wasting more words than he'd wanted to, had explained about the flow of their small stream, the limited needs of the hamlet, and the cost of having a vertical wheel built and attached.

It was that last, he was sure, that had induced the cleric to nod sagely, stroke a weak, beardless chin, and agree that the simpler ways were often best, fulfilling the god's purposes entirely well.

They left the horizontal wheel alone. Brogan took the chapel's share of the mill's earnings (in coin or kind) to them every second week. He was prompt about that sort of thing; it kept people from coming round and talking.

He did hold back a slightly higher portion for himself. If you set that up from the outset, they were unlikely to have questions. He'd been through this before. The cleric had asked about written records on that first visit, Brogan had explained he didn't know how to write. He'd declined an offer of reading lessons. Leave it to the young ones, he'd said.

People were always wanting to change things. Brogan couldn't understand it. Change was going to come, why hurry it along? The king had even sent around new instructions for farmers at the end of this past winter, with the archers from the *fyrd,* on how to properly handle their fields. Alternating crops. What to grow. As if anyone at court knew anything about farming. Brogan had never been near the king's court (only twice up to Esferth town, which was twice more than enough) but he knew what he thought of it. You didn't need to eat dung to know you wouldn't like the taste.

He leaned out the window and looked upstream to his right. Modig had fed the chickens, was at work in the herb and vegetable garden. A virtue to having a farmer's son here: the garden was looking better than it had in years. Brogan wasn't fussy about what he ate, but he liked turnips and parsnips with his bread and broth and fish, and a decent seasoning as much as the next man, and Modig had a way with the garden. Of course, thought the miller sourly, if he'd had counsel from the courtiers on what seedlings and how much dung to use, it would doubtless be far better.

He spat again into the stream below, saw the pale harbinger of sunrise in the east, and muttered his custom-ary two-sentence version of the rites. His own idea of Jad was not of a god who needed a lot of words. You acknowledged him, gave thanks, and got on with what you had to do. And it didn't need to be done in a chapel. You could pray in a mill over water, gazing out at the fields.

Gazing out at the fields, Brogan the miller saw—in the last near-darkness of a summer night—twenty men or more downstream from him, kneeling beside the water or knee-deep in it, drinking and filling flasks.

He drew his head back quickly, because he saw that they carried weapons. Weapons meant—since they were being quiet and were nowhere near the north-south road—that these were outlaws, or even Erlings, and not simply passing by on their way to trade peacefully at the Esferth fair. Brogan swallowed, his palms suddenly sweaty, scalp prickling. He thought of his coins buried in the yard and just outside it. He thought of death. Armed men across the stream. A large number of men.

Not, in the event, large enough.

From the north, Brogan suddenly heard a dog. His heart lurched. It was a deep, fierce, triumphant howl; not one of his own dogs, though they immediately started their own wild barking in the fenced yard. He looked out, carefully. The men in the stream had begun scrambling from the water, splashing, stumbling, unsheathing swords. They formed, at a shouted string of commands, a tight, disciplined order and began running south.

They *were* Erlings, then. The language gave it away, and no outlaws would be nearly so precise in their formation and movements. Brogan leaned out, looking past where Modig had now stopped working in the garden and was standing rigid, also watching. That howling came again, a sound he would remember. Wouldn't ever want to be hunted by that. Brogan heard hoofbeats and shouting over the barking of his own dogs, and into his field of vision, streaming down from the north, came a galloping company, swords drawn, spears out, hurtling through the stream.

In the pre-dawn light he saw a banner, and Brogan the miller understood that this was the king's *fyrd,* and that they had seen the Erlings and were going to catch up to

them just across the water from his mill. His heart was
pounding as if he, too, were running or riding. He had
been expecting, moments ago, to be killed here, fingers
broken one by one—or worse things—until he told where
his money was. The nightmare that came in his sleep.

Leaning out, he saw the Erlings turn to face the horsemen bearing swiftly down upon them. He didn't like
King Aeldred, all his changes, the new taxes levied to
support *fyrd* and forts, but at this particular moment,
watching those horsemen surround the Erlings, such
feelings were . . . suspended.

Brogan left the mill, went out the door, walked down
to the stream. Modig, holding a spade, opened the
garden gate and came over, stood beside him. The dogs
were still barking. Brogan snapped a command over his
shoulder and they stopped.

There was a grey mist on the millstream, rising.
Through it, as the pale sun came up, they watched what
happened in the meadow on the other side. The mill-
wheel turned.

∽

It occurred to Alun at some point during the night ride
south that he was surrounded now by Anglcyn warriors,
who had traditionally been his enemies, racing to intercept Erlings, who were enemies as well. One of
Athelbert's archers had given him a sword and belt, at the
prince's command. You could name it a friend's gesture.
You had to, really.

For the Cyngael, he thought, friends were hard to
come by in the world. And that, if you stopped to think
about it, really did make the feuds between Arberth and
Cadyr and Llywerth harder to justify. That wasn't something people *did* think about, though, west of the
Rheden Wall. Their endless internal warring was . . . the

way things were. The three provinces raided and goaded each other, fought for primacy, always had. His father, Alun knew, would have preferred stealing a herd of cattle from an arrogant Arberthi and hearing his bard sing about it after, to any foray across the Wall into Rheden, or even mauling Erling raiders.

Though that last might not be true any more, not since Dai was killed. He couldn't be sure, but he thought his father had changed through the spring and summer. Alun was aware of changes within himself, shaped around loss and what he'd seen in that pool by Brynnfell. He didn't know where the changes had taken him, but he knew they were there.

He wasn't sure exactly where he was right now, galloping south-east between copses of trees, but he did know—or believe—that the man who'd led the raid that killed his brother was somewhere ahead of them. Ivarr Ragnarson had eluded pursuit near Brynnfell, fled to his ships and away—and had now killed a good man here. He needed to die. It was . . . important he be killed.

If you stopped to think about it. There was no time to stop tonight—two short rests allowed by the king, no more than a pause to drink at streams, fill flasks, then riding again—but he had plenty of time to think under the summer stars as the blue moon westered through clouds and went down behind the woods. There were riders all around him, but their faces—and his—were shielded from scrutiny. The shelter of darkness, the . . . need for it. And with that, the memory came back to him, inescapable, who had said exactly that, and when: *Needful as night.*

Rhiannon mer Brynn, clad in green at her father's table, the night his brother had died and had his soul stolen away. He realized he hadn't let himself think about her, those words, his own song, since then, as if flinching from too fiercely bright a fire. *Do you hate me so much, my lord?*

Alun looked over towards the woods. More darkness, blurred in distance, the river somewhere between. He thought of the faerie, her hair changing colour, the light she'd made, and he began to wonder, riding, exactly what the world was, how it was crafted, how he'd make his own peace with Jad . . . and the high cleric on the horse ahead of him, beside King Aeldred.

He didn't know if he felt older now, or younger because less sure of things, but he did understand that everything had altered and could not be remade as it had been before. *The speed of things for you,* the faerie had said. He didn't even have a name for her. Did they have names? He hadn't thought to ask before stumbling out of the wood. He had been afraid, as he'd left the trees, wondering if he would come out into different moonlight and find his world gone.

Instead, he'd found an Anglcyn princess, inexplicably, waiting there for him.

I am only this far. As if she'd known of his fear, what he was feeling. No distance at all, just across a quiet stream. The world still his, not altered, yet changed in every way. Her being there another thing to think about, try to understand. He shook his head. There were only so many images, memories, you could deal with at once, Alun decided, before you had to look away.

And then, as the night ended, all changed again.

Thinking back, afterwards, he realized he oughtn't to have been so surprised that they found the Erlings. For one thing, the *fyrd* knew this land as well as he and his brother had known the valleys and fells of Cadyr, every tuck and fold of their province recorded on a mental map, down to the shepherds' huts and the farms where daughters might be willing to rise from their beds, wrapped in a shawl, and come out into the dark, soft and warm, to a known whisper at a night window.

They had been riding along the route that made sense for intercepting a party on foot. The Erlings would be running towards where their ships would have anchored, between the *burh* at Drengest and the steep coastline farther west where they couldn't come ashore. You could figure these things out if you knew where you were and the land around you. Copses and rivers, slopes and hamlets. Aeldred and his *fyrd* would know them all: the places where the Erlings who'd killed Burgred of Denforth would be unable to pass, and the ones they'd try to avoid. They might miss the Erlings in darkness or mist, but they'd find their path.

And they had Cafall with them.

The dog was the part of this night that neither Alun nor Ceinion, and certainly none of the Anglcyns, had thought about. But it was Cafall—hunting dog, Brynn's gift—who howled, a wild sound that could terrify and appall, as they approached a stream in the grey before sunrise. Alun's heart began pounding. Someone near the front raised an arm and pointed, shouting. It was Athelbert, he saw.

They had been intending to pray here, dismount long enough to perform the dawn rites on the riverbank. Instead, they thundered across, west of a village mill, splashing through water, weapons out, and they came up to the Erlings, who were on foot, and surrounded them in a green meadow as the sun came up.

෧෧

There were too many people living here now, too many towns, too many *burhs* with fighting men inside them. Guthrum Skallson, running with fewer than twenty men (five had taken the horses to the ships with a warning, to bring forty of them back), had seen a hill fire burning, and then another to the north, a little later, and had realized that they were in even more danger than he'd thought. They'd run all through the night.

He couldn't say he was surprised when they were found. They'd have taken a different route if the woods and treed slopes had allowed. But they didn't know these lands, and the best he could do was go back west along the same path they'd taken and hope they met their rein-forcements before they were intercepted.

It hadn't happened. He hadn't expected those hilltop flares in the dark, the speed of the Anglcyn response. He'd thought they had a decent chance, that he'd been in worse trouble over the years. Then a dog howled as dawn broke, and the *fyrd* was there.

He had the men circle in the meadow as the Anglcyn riders thundered across the stream. No point running, these were mounted men. He saw the banners in the pale light and understood that King Aeldred hadn't just sent his warriors, he had come himself. They were taken.

It had happened before. There were resources in Jormsvik, Ingavin knew. They could be bought back, for a price and promises. Likely some of them would be hostages for a time. Likely Guthrum would be one of those. He cursed, under his breath.

He had eighteen men; there appeared to be close to two hundred surrounding them, mounted. He wasn't a *berserkir*, he was a mercenary, hired. This wasn't war. He let fall his sword, held up open hands. Stepped forward, that the Anglcyn king might know who led this party.

"How many men did Burgred take south with him?"

A man with a grey beard spoke, in Anglcyn, but not to Guthrum. He understood the words, though; the languages were near enough.

"Six, including himself," said a younger man on a brown horse beside the speaker.

"Shoot six," said the bearded man, who would be Aeldred of the Anglcyn. "Not that one." He pointed to Guthrum.

The younger one spoke. Six arrows flew. Six of Guthrum's men—who had lain down their weapons when he had—fell into the grass.

Guthrum did not fear death. No mercenary could fight as many battles as he had over so many years and live with fear. He didn't *want* to die, however. He liked ale and women, battle and comrades, peril and hardship and ease after. The trappings of a warrior in this middle-world.

He said, "None of them killed your earl. None of them would have."

"Indeed," said the king on the horse in front of him. "So Burgred lives, is coming home even now?"

Guthrum met that gaze. No Erling ought to cower before these people. "We do not use arrows in Jormsvik."

"Ah. So no arrow killed him. Our tidings are false? Good. None will have killed your fellows, if so."

Thought he was clever, this king. Guthrum had heard that of him. Problem was, he *was* clever. In too many ways. Raiding had become impossible here. This journey had been a mistake from the moment they took Ivarr's money and set sail.

Ivarr. Guthrum looked around.

Someone—a younger man, smaller, sitting an Erling horse—had come forward beside the king. He looked down at Guthrum. "Ragnarson was with you?"

Spoke Anglcyn, but you could tell a Cyngael the moment he opened his mouth. How could he know about Ivarr, though? Guthrum considered for a moment, thinking fast, keeping silent.

"Shoot another, Athelbert," said the king.

They shot another. Atli, this time.

Guthrum had come to Jormsvik's walls with Atli Bjarkson fifteen years ago. Walking to the fortress together from homes in the north, meeting on the road, winning their fights on the same morning, joining the same company. A never-forgotten day. The day that split your life into before and after. Guthrum looked down into the grass now in a morning's first light, far from Vinmark, and he spoke the farewell aloud, invoking Ingavin's welcome for a friend in the warriors' halls. Then he turned back to the mounted men surrounding them.

"You were asked a question," said King Aeldred. His voice was calm, flat, but there was no way to mistake the rage in him. This might not be a hostage and ransom circumstance, after all. And Guthrum had men here for whom he was responsible.

"We have surrendered our arms," he said.

"And will you tell me Burgred did not when you found them? When you put an arrow in him?"

"How do you know about that?"

"Athelbert. One more, please."

"Wait!" Guthrum lifted an urgent hand. The prince named Athelbert, more slowly, did the same. No arrow was loosed. Guthrum swallowed, looking up at the Anglcyn, a black rage in his own heart. He could crush any of these in battle, any two of them; he and Atli could have handled half a dozen.

"However you know this," he said, "you are right. Ivarr Ragnarson paid for this raid, and killed the earl. Against my orders and wishes. Do you think we are fools?" He heard the passion in his own voice, moved to master it.

"I think you are, yes, but would not have thought so in that way. Mercenaries killing a nobleman taken. Where is he, then? This Ragnarson?" There was contempt in the voice. Guthrum could hear it.

He would have said he despised Ivarr Ragnarson at least as much as those surrounding them did. He felt no loyalty to him at all. Had been on the edge of killing the man himself. And had that last Anglcyn bowshot taken any man there but Atli, he would likely have pointed back to the stream where Ivarr had obviously remained hidden when they fled. One life surrendered, to save those in his charge. A fair and proper deed.

The flow of time and events is a large river; men and women are usually no more than pebbles in that, carried along. But sometimes, at some moments, they are more. Sometimes the course of the stream is changed, not just for a few people but for many.

They shouldn't have killed Atli, Guthrum Skallson thought, standing in a meadow surrounded by his enemies. *Our weapons were in the grass. We had yielded ourselves.*

"We took five horses," he said. "I sent riders back to the ships."

Aeldred stared down at him for a long time. The arrogance of it was as wormwood, gall, bitterest taste he knew: as if a woman were looking at him this way. Scarcely to be borne.

"Yes," the king said, finally, "you will have done that. And asked for reinforcements to meet you. A ship's worth? Very well. They will be dealt with next. You have all made a terrible mistake. Jad knows, I have no need or desire of ransom for any of you at all. My need, just now, is otherwise. Athelbert."

"My lord!" began another, older man. Another Cyngael. "They have laid down—"

"No words, Ceinion!" said the king of the Anglcyn.

He had spared the life of the man who'd blood-eagled his father. Everyone in the northlands knew the tale. He wasn't doing so now. Aeldred turned away, indifferently, as arrows were notched.

Guthrum nearly got to him.

You didn't let yourself die helplessly in a morning field like a target set up for womanish Anglcyn who dared not fight you properly. Not if you were an Erling and a warrior. He was actually at the king's reins, reaching up, when the sword took him in the throat. It was the young Cyngael who had moved fastest, Guthrum saw with his last sight.

He was dying on his feet, though, in battle, as was proper. The gods loved their warriors, their blood, the dragon-ships, red blades, ravens and eagles called you home to halls where mead flowed freely and forever.

The sun was up, but he couldn't see it, suddenly. There was a long white wave. He named Ingavin and Thünir, and went to them.

⌒

Expressionless, though with his heart beating fast, Brogan the miller stood by the stream and watched his king and warriors kill the Erlings in the meadow.

Fifteen or twenty of them. No hostages, none spared. There was no ferocity or passion in the dispatch of the raiders. They were just . . . dealt with. For more than a hundred years the Anglcyn had lived in terror of these raiders from the sea in their dragon-ships. Now the Erlings were being killed like so many ragged outlaws.

He decided, just then, that he liked King Aeldred after all. And watching the arrows fly, he came also to a reconsideration of his views on the subject of archery. Beside him, Modig stood gripping his spade, his mouth hanging open.

The *fyrd* turned to ride south. As they did, one rider peeled off from the others and came over towards the mill and stream where the two men were. Brogan felt a flicker of apprehension, made himself be calm. These were his defenders, his king.

"You live here?" the mounted man snapped, reining his mount on the other side of the river. "You are the miller?"

Brogan touched a hand to his forehead and nodded. "Yes, my lord."

"Find villagers, farmers, whatever you can. Have these bodies burned before sundown. You yourself are in charge of collecting weapons and armour. Keep them in the mill. There are eighteen Erlings. All were armed in the usual ways. We have a good idea of what should be here when we come back. If anyone steals, there will be executions. We won't stop to ask questions. Understood?"

Brogan nodded again, and swallowed hard.

"Make certain the others here do."

The rider wheeled and set off, galloping now, to catch up with the *fyrd*. Brogan watched him go, a graceful figure in morning light. In the meadow, not far away, lay a number of dead men. Eighteen, the rider had said. His burden now. He cursed himself for coming out to watch. Spat into the stream. It was going to be *very* hard to stop poor men from stealing knives or rings. Surely the *fyrd* wouldn't begrudge—or be able to track—a stray torc or necklace, would they?

It occurred to him that he and Modig might be able to gather most of the arms and store them before anyone else—

No, that wouldn't work. The women would be here soon, for their flour. They would see what had happened. It was impossible to miss: Brogan saw birds already gathering where the bodies lay. He grimaced. This was going to be difficult. He suffered a reversion of his thoughts about king and *fyrd*. The lords were trouble, whenever they came, whenever they noticed you. He ought to have stayed inside. He was turning to Modig, to tell him to make a start, at least, but found his right arm gripped fiercely by his servant.

Modig pointed. Brogan saw a man emerge from the stream to their left—a pale, small figure for an Erling, he would say, later—and begin to run south. He was well behind the *fyrd,* which was almost out of sight. Certainly they were too far away for any call or cry to summon them back to take this last Erling, who'd kept himself hidden, apart from the rest. They'd have to let him go, Brogan thought. Not that he'd get far, alone.

Modig made a sound deep in his chest. He plunged into the stream, splashing through it, then began running, spade in hand.

"Stop!" cried Brogan. "Don't be a fool!"

The Erling was moving fast, but so was young Modig, chasing him. Far away, the dust of the king's men could be seen. Brogan watched the two running men till they were out of sight.

Later that morning he assembled the villagers to gather the weapons and armour—and the rings and arm torcs and belts and boots and brooches and necklaces—of the Erlings. The children ran about, chasing away the birds. Brogan made it very clear, talking more than anyone could remember, that the *fyrd* was coming back, and that death had been promised to anyone known to have taken anything.

The presence of eighteen dead raiders, the shock of them, meant that no one did try to palm or pocket a thing, so far as Brogan could tell. They carried the gear in relays across the water to the mill, piled it in his smaller storeroom. Brogan locked the door, hung the key on his belt.

He picked out only two rings for himself, and a golden torc in the shape of a dragon devouring its own tail. Added three other pieces of jewellery after, when most of the others had gone to bring wood and the two who had stayed behind with him, as guards, were drowsing under the willow by the stream. It was a warm day. Across the water boys were throwing stones at birds and wild dogs near the eighteen dead men.

It was two of the boys who found the body of Modig, the son of Ord, shortly after midday, a little distance to the south. His ears and nose had been hacked off, and his tongue. That last, Brogan the miller thought, was a sad and vicious thing. He was angry. He'd found a perfect servant, finally, and the young fool had gone and gotten himself killed.

Life was an ambush, Brogan thought bitterly, a series of them. Over and over till you died.

Later in the day the villagers began streaming back with armloads and carts of wood, and the cleric. Their women came, too, and all but the youngest children. This was a great event, something unimaginable, never to be forgotten. The king had been here himself, had saved them from Erling raiders, slain them all, right beside the millstream. Their millstream. A tale for the colder nights to come and the long years. Babies not yet born would hear this story, be led to the place where it had happened.

The new cleric spoke under the open sky, invoking Jad's power and mercy, then they lit the pyre, using wood that had been gathered for winter hearths, and they burned the Erlings in the field where they'd died.

After, they dug a grave and buried Modig by the stream and prayed that he might go home to the god, in light.

In a mist before dawn, some distance west, Bern Thorkellson dismounted to relieve himself in a gully. His first halt since leaving his father outside Esferth.

He had spent what remained of the night riding very fast, trying to take his mind from that impossible encounter. What was it the gods were doing with their mortal children? You took a horse across black, frozen waters and lived, fought your way into Jormsvik, went on a raid in Anglcyn lands . . . and were rescued by your father. Twice.

Your accursed father, whose murders were the reason for all of this. For everything that had happened. And he simply showed up where you were—on the other side of the sea—and knocked you out in an alley and somehow carried you outside the walls and then came back to warn you, and order you on your way. It was all . . . hugely difficult. Bern could not have said that much about the world seemed clear to him that night.

He had just finished retying his trousers when a man and woman sat up from a hollow in the ground and stared at him, a handful of paces away.

This, at least, was clear enough.

They stood. It was still quite dark, mist around them, rising off the fields. Their clothing and hair were disordered; it was evident what they'd been doing. The same thing young men and women did in meadows all over the world on a summer night. Bern had done it on the isle, in better days.

He drew his sword. "Lie down again," he said quietly. His own language, but they'd understand him. "And no one is hurt."

"You're an Erling!" the young man said, too loudly. "What are you doing here with a blade?"

"My own business. Attend to yours. Lie down again with her."

"Rot that," said the man, who was broad-shouldered, long-limbed. "My father's the reeve here. Strangers declare themselves when they come by."

"Are you a fool?" Bern asked, calmly enough, he'd have thought.

It was because he was with his girl, Bern later decided, that the Anglcyn did what he did. He reached down, grabbed a thick staff he'd have carried out with him for protection from animals, and stepped forward, swinging it at Bern's head.

The woman cried out. Bern dropped to a knee, heard the whistle of the staff. He rose and levelled a short back-hand slash with his sword to the man's right arm, at the elbow. He felt it hit hard, but not bite.

He'd used the flat of his blade.

Couldn't have said why. A memory of summer fields with a girl? Stupidity such as this man's didn't deserve to be indulged or rewarded. The Anglcyn ought to have lost an arm, his life. Didn't the fool know how the world worked? You met a mounted man with a sword, you did what he instructed you, and prayed, urgently, that you'd live to tell about it.

The staff had fallen to the grass. The Anglcyn's good hand clutched at his elbow. Bern couldn't see his eyes in the darkness.

"Don't kill us!" the girl said, her first words.

Bern looked at her. "I hadn't intended to," he said. She had fair hair, was tall. It was hard to make out more. "I told you to lie down. Do it now. Though if you let this idiot between your legs again you're as much a fool as he is."

The girl's mouth opened. She stared at him, for longer than he'd have expected. Then she reached out and pulled the man down beside her into the hollow again, where they'd been warm together moments ago, young and in summertime.

"Honour your god in the morning," Bern said, looking down at them. He wasn't sure why he'd said that, either.

He went back to Gyllir and rode away.

In the hollow behind him, Druce, the son of Finan who was indeed king's reeve of the lands thereabouts, began swearing viciously, though under his breath, in case.

Cwene, the baker's daughter, put a hand to his mouth. "Hush. Does it hurt?" she whispered.

"Of course it hurts," he snarled. "He broke my arm."

She was clever, understood that his pride was wounded as well, after being so easily subdued in front of her.

"He had a sword," she said. "There was naught you could do. I thought you were very brave."

She thought he'd been a reckless imbecile. She was aware that they ought to have died here. Druce's arm should have been severed, not bruised or broken, by that sword. The Erling could have done anything he wanted to her, after, anything at all, then left them dead in the tall grass with no one ever to know exactly what had happened. She said nothing more, lay there beside Druce, looking up at the last stars as blackness became grey, feeling the breeze that blew.

Eventually they made their way back towards the village, separated in the usual way, went to their homes. Cwene slipped into the house the way she'd come out, through the door that connected to the animal shed. Familiar smells, sounds, everything changed, forever. She should have died in the field. Each breath she took now, for the rest of her days . . .

She got into bed beside her sister, who stirred but did not wake. Cwene didn't sleep. It was too near to morning. She lay there thinking, revisiting what had happened. Her heart was pounding, though she was in bed at home now. She began to weep, silently.

Three months later, in autumn, the baker beat her until she named the reeve's son as the father of the child she was carrying. At that point her father became mightily pleased (it was a very good match) and carried his anger across the village to the reeve's door.

The baker was a large man himself, and not inconsequential. She and Druce were wed before winter. They had two more children before he was killed by someone who didn't want to pay his taxes, or lose his farm. Cwene married twice more; outlived them both. Five children survived childhood, including the daughter conceived in the meadow that summer night.

Cwene had dreams, all her life, of the moment in darkness when an Erling had come upon them, a creature out of nightmare, and had gone away, leaving them their lives as a gift to use or throw away.

We like to believe we can know the moments we'll remember of our own days and nights, but it isn't really so. The future is an uncertain shape (in the dark) and men and women know that. What is less surely understood is that this is true of the past as well. What lingers, or comes back unsummoned, is not always what we would expect, or desire to keep with us.

It was late in a long life, and three husbands had been laid in the earth, before Cwene realized—and acknowledged to herself—that what she had wanted to do, more than anything before or since, was ride away from her home and everyone she knew in the world with that Erling on his grey horse that night long ago.

The clever girl had become a wise woman through the turning years; she forgave herself for that longing before she died.

RIDING SOUTH, Bern was increasingly aware of hunger—he hadn't eaten since late the day before—but he was also conscious of a cold, steady fear in his gut, and he didn't let Gyllir slow as the sun rose, climbing the summer sky. He felt appallingly exposed here in these flat lands running to the sea, knowing the *fyrd* was abroad and looking for Erlings with vengeance in mind.

The Anglcyn worshipped a god of the sun: would that make a difference? Would it help them, under so much summer light? He had never thought such a thing before, and he didn't much like thinking about it now, but he'd never been among Jaddites, either. Rabady Isle seemed very far away; their farm at the village edge, even the straw in the barn behind Arni Kjellson's house. He kept glancing around as he rode, an unceasing sweep of the wide lands to his left.

The signal flares had been farther east, and Aeldred's course had lain on the far side of the river—to begin with. There was nothing to say the king hadn't split his riders in the night, sending some of them this way. Bern, feeling more alone than he had since the night he'd left the isle with Halldr's horse, had a painful sense that the king's men would be very good at knowing where the Jormsvik ships might be.

Gyllir was tired, but there was no help for that. He leaned forward, slapped the horse's neck, spoke to it as a friend. They had to keep moving. For one thing, his might be the only alert the others could get. They had to have five ships offshore before two hundred men came sweeping down upon them. The gods knew, the men of Jormsvik could fight. It might be a close battle if the *fyrd* came. They could easily win it, but if enough of them died, or if the ships were damaged, there was no meaning to such a victory. Glorious or not, they'd die in these Anglcyn lands when Esferth and the accursed *burhs* Aeldred had built sent out the next waves of men. He wasn't quite ready, Bern realized, to go to Ingavin's halls.

He looked east again, no longer into the too-bright sun. Past midday now, the mist had long since burnt away. No hilltop signal fires in this bright daylight. A beautiful afternoon. Birdsong from the forest west, a hawk overhead, circling.

He had no idea what was happening elsewhere. Could only hasten to the sea. His father had done this too, Bern thought suddenly. Had done more, in fact; that journey alone across the Wall and the breadth of the Anglcyn lands, when he'd escaped from the Cyngael after the Volgan died. And now Thorkell was back here. Had even been among the Cyngael again, taken by them a second time. Bern wanted to think of something derisive but couldn't.

I got you out of a walled city. Think on it.

The quiet, assured voice. And a blow to the head when he'd spoken too fast, as if Bern were still a boy on Rabady. But his father had known about Ivarr, had guessed what Ragnarson would say. How did he always know? He cursed Thorkell, as he had so many times since his father's exile, but without fever or fire now. He was too tired, had too many things to think about. He was hungry and afraid. He looked left again, and behind him. Nothing there, a shimmer of heat coming off the ripening fields. Gyllir would have to drink soon. He needed water himself. Not quite yet, he decided. It was too exposed where they were right now.

He didn't recognize the landscape nearly well enough, couldn't tell how far he had yet to ride, though they'd come this way going north to Esferth, he and Ecca, on the other side of the river. There had been a number of people on that road, heading for a royal fair the Erlings hadn't known about. Third year of the fair, someone told them. They hadn't been hiding on the way north, had pretended to be traders. They'd carried sacks on the horses, purporting to hold the goods they'd trade. Ecca's anger had begun on the road, with what they'd heard. If this was the third year of a summer fair, then any tale they'd been told about Esferth being empty was hollow as an emptied ale cask. Ivarr Ragnarson, he'd said to Bern, was either a fool or a serpent, and he suspected the latter.

Bern hadn't paid enough attention on that ride and was suffering for it now; all the endless shallow dips and folds, up and down, up and down, looked exactly the same. The farmland across the river seemed an unimaginable expanse of fertile soil to someone raised on Rabady Isle's stony ground.

He turned in the saddle to look back again. A constant fear of pursuers behind him. The farms began just across the river; anyone in the near fields could see him, a single horseman passing between river and wood. Not alarming in itself, unless they were close enough to see what he was.

The trees on his right were dark, no tracks or paths into them. Sunlight would fail here. There were woods like this in Vinmark. Untamed, unbroken, stretching forever; gods and beasts within them. This forest would be pretty much impenetrable, he guessed, wild and dangerous, an unbroken density of oak and ash, alder and thorn, marching west to the Cyngael lands. Ecca had said that on the way. *A better wall than the Wall* was the saying. And the woods went right down to cliffs above the strait. They'd seen those cliffs from the ships.

The Anglcyn would know all this far better than he did. They'd know the Erling ships had to be east of those sheer bluffs, in one shallow bay or another.

They were. There weren't so many choices and they hadn't been overly subtle about choosing one. Too many mistakes on this end-of-summer raid. Ivarr Ragnarson's raid. They'd anchored, taken hasty counsel, sent Bern and Ecca north to look at Esferth. Ecca had done this many times, knew what he was about, and Bern had a young, reassuring countenance. Brand Leofson had also agreed to let Guthrum and Atli lead a small sweep east, to see what they could find or take while they waited for the report from Esferth, and Ivarr had gone with them.

Bern was the report from Esferth now.

Ivarr Ragnarson would kill him, Thorkell had said, if he learned who Bern's father was. Suddenly, and much too late, Bern understood. *Think the rest of it out while you ride,* he'd been told. And, *He wants to go back west.* Back west. Ivarr had just been there, then. In the Cyngael lands.

And Thorkell had been with him. *That* was how his father knew what had happened. And about poisoned arrows. Something had happened there . . . Thorkell had been taken again. Or else . . .

There was never enough time to think things through. The world didn't seem to work that way. Maybe for women weaving and spinning, maybe for Jaddite clerics in their isolated retreats, waking in the night to pray for the sun. But not for a bound servant on Rabady Isle, or a Jormsvik mercenary, either. Riding towards another gentle, grassy rise, almost identical to the one before and the one before that, Bern heard the sounds of battle ahead of him, across the river.

THE RIDERS GUTHRUM SKALLSON had sent made it back to the ships early in the morning. The help Guthrum requested was dispatched without hesitation by Brand, who was commanding the raid. You didn't leave men behind. It was one of the things that marked Jormsvik.

The riders had spoken feverishly, interrupting each other, more unsettled than raiders ought to be. They told of a clash between Guthrum and Ivarr Ragnarson over the death of an Anglcyn earl. Brand shrugged, hearing of it. These things happened. He'd have sided with Guthrum—earls were worth a great deal, unless out of favour—but sometimes, he had to admit, you just needed to kill someone, especially if it hadn't happened in a long time. That came with the way they lived, with the dragon-ships, with the eagles of Ingavin. And he knew for a fact that Guthrum Skallson had done his share of killing prisoners over the years. They'd sort this when everyone got back.

Forty mercenaries ought to have been more than enough to meet and protect Guthrum and Atli's small party from any likely Anglcyn response, fight their way back to the ships if they did encounter anyone. Brand ordered three ships offshore, to be safe, left two anchored in the shallows, lightly manned, for the returning parties to board and row.

He was being prudent, but was not alarmed. Shore parties met people, incidents happened, sometimes deaths. This was a raid, wasn't it? What did people expect? Jormsvik had been doing this, over the known world, for a long time. Erlings had been coming in longships to these shores for more than a hundred years. Yes, the Anglcyn lands had become harder to raid over the last while, but that had happened at times, too. There were always other places. Three ships had gone last spring out through the straits and down the sea lanes to Al-Rassan, to raid and run before the khalif's men could be there with their curved swords and bows. That would have been a fight to be part of, Brand had thought, hearing the tale. He wanted to go there, see for himself. There was, word had it, wealth beyond description among those desert-born star-worshippers. He wanted to see their women, behind the veils they wore.

It was the life he knew, raiding. The northlands offered no refuge for anyone. Vinmark was a hard place, sent forth hard men. And how else could a man of spirit make his fortune, claim a place by winter hearths and in the skalds' songs, and then the gods' meadhalls? It wasn't as if every man could fish, or find land to farm, or make ale or barrels for ale. It wasn't as if every man wanted to.

You hoped that if you killed someone on a raid you gained something from it, and if some of your own died, that you'd taken even more, to compensate. Then you sacrificed to Ingavin and Thünir, and rowed back out to sea if you had to, or pushed forward inland, depending on where you were and what you were facing. Brand had lost count of the number of times he'd had decisions like this to make.

They had five fully manned ships here, allowing room for horses. Five ships was a large group. This incident might even be useful before it ended, Brand thought. Forty Jormsvik fighters could overwhelm any hasty Anglcyn pursuit of Guthrum from a *burh;* take the leaders hostage— for security first, then gold. Safety and a reward. The oldest tactics of all, just about. Some things never changed, he thought. He kept his own ship as one of the two on shore.

He was wrong, in fact, about a number of things, but had no real way of knowing it. From the bay where the ships were hidden, they hadn't seen the signal fires. A great deal had changed in these lands in the twenty-five years since Aeldred, son of Gademar, had come out from Beortferth and reclaimed his father's throne.

The party dispatched from the ships, guided by two of the (by now exhausted) riders Guthrum had sent back, did find a group of men. Not their returning companions. By then Guthrum and his men were lying dead beside the pyre that would burn them, across a stream from a village mill.

Nor did Brand's relief contingent meet some over-extended, too-quick pursuit from Drengest on the coast. Instead, forty Erlings from the ships, most of them on foot, encountered the mounted *fyrd* of King Aeldred in a field east of the River Thorne, a little past midday.

FROM THE MOMENT he'd heard the name again—Ivarr Ragnarson—spoken by the Jormsvik leader just before he was killed at the king's saddle, Ceinion of Llywerth had felt a terrifying surmise taking shape within him.

He was not a man inclined to flinch from thoughts, or truths, whether of spirit and faith or having to do with the earthly world in which men lived and died. But this growing awareness, as the sun rose and the day wore on, caused him an almost physical pain, a constriction of the heart.

The last of the Volgans had hired this company. Hired them, it seemed, for a raid near Esferth, at the very end of the season. But that made no sense. Aeldred had these lands far too well defended, especially with the fair about to begin. But what if you hadn't really meant to stay here? If you'd lied to the mercenaries about your purpose? What if you'd killed a lucrative hostage to stop them from claiming a vast ransom and happily turning home?

There were compelling reasons why Ivarr Ragnarson might want to lead mercenaries to Cyngael shores, and to a particular farmhouse.

The Jormsvik leaders would regard it as a waste of time, too far to go this time of year. They'd have to be tricked, persuaded. This was a man, Ceinion remembered, who had blood-eagled a girl and a farmhand during his flight last spring. He was said to be deformed in body and spirit, for the two went together, always.

Ceinion had led the dawn prayers south of the meadow where they'd killed the Erlings, had kept them brisk for there was need for haste. He'd mounted with the others and rode again beside the king with the god's sun rising behind them. Aeldred said nothing as they went. Only rasped quick orders to some riders who peeled away from the company and headed east. It was difficult to see this grim-faced, death-dealing figure as the man who'd talked about translated manuscripts and ancient learning in the night just past.

Ceinion kept his distance from Alun ab Owyn as they went. He didn't even want to exchange a glance with the prince, fearful that he might give his thoughts away. If Owyn's son learned what the cleric was thinking he might go wild with helpless panic.

Which was not, in truth, far from a good description of what Ceinion was feeling himself as the morning passed and the countryside rolled beneath horses' hooves. The sun was overhead now. If the dragon-ships of Jormsvik were not found, if they had already cast off with Ragnarson aboard and gone west . . . there would be nothing he or anyone else could do but pray.

Ceinion of Llywerth, high cleric of the Cyngael, believed in his god of light and in the power of holy prayer for almost everything that could be, except the most potent matter of all: the life and death of those he loved. There was a woman lying in a sanctuary grave-yard by the sea, within sound of the surf, beneath a pale grey stone with a simple sun disk carved upon it, and her dying had taken that belief from him. A wound, a rip in the fabric of the world. He had gone a little mad as she died, had done things that still kept him awake some nights. This was not a matter of which he'd written in his long correspondence with Rhodias and the Patriarch.

He was also thinking, in this bright sunlight, of another woman, loved, and her husband, loved, and their daughter, coming into her glory, all of whom might or might not be at Brynnfell now, and he had no way of knowing, and no way of helping them.

Unless they got to the ships in time.

"Can we not go faster?" he asked the king of the Anglcyn.

"No need. He said he sent for help, remember? They will be coming this way," Aeldred said, looking briefly at him. "I am sure of it. We'll stop soon to rest and eat. The river's ahead. I want the *fyrd* fresh for a fight."

"*Some* of them will be coming," said Ceinion. "But we must reach the longships before they get them off from shore."

"They've done that already. Jormsvik knows how to do these things. We'll try to block their way home with the fleet in Drengest. I have six ships. I sent riders to them—they'll be in the water before sundown. Fishing boats out, too, to watch for them. If we find this rescue party, the Erlings will be undermanned at sea. They have horses, which means the wide, slow boats, not the fighting ones. I mean to take them all, Ceinion."

"If they go home, my lord," Ceinion said quietly.

Aeldred threw him a glance.

"What is it I don't know?" the king asked.

The cleric was about to tell him when the horns blew. Then the great grey dog, Alun's dog, sounded his own warning, and ahead of them Ceinion saw the Erlings, with the river just beyond.

One of the outriders was galloping back; he reined hard beside them. "Forty or fifty, my lord! Mostly on foot."

"We have them, then. Get the mounted ones first," the king ordered. "No messages back. *Athelbert!*"

"Going, my lord!" his son shouted over his shoulder, already moving, calling for archers as he went.

Ceinion watched the prince ride, readying his bow, easy in the saddle, his archers swift and smooth to respond to commands: precisely trained, his own contingent here. A very different man than his brother. The sons of Aeldred, he thought, might have divided their father's nature between themselves. That could happen; he had seen it before. He also had a thought, as battle began, about the *way* Aeldred's men were fighting today: from the saddle, with arrows as well as spears, which was new, and immensely difficult. And even more difficult to counter, if they had mastered it. It looked very much as though Athelbert and his archers had done that.

His own people, Ceinion thought, had even more reason to try—to at least *try*—to come together now, and find some way to join the world beyond their hidden valleys. There might be a certain pride in being the last light of the god's sun, where it set in the west, but there were dangers as well.

Such thoughts were for later. Right now he watched a good-sized party of Jormsvik mercenaries form another desperate circle as Athelbert's archers and the others came up to them. The raiders had already crossed the river; bad for them. They couldn't have retreated in any case, outnumbered and facing horsemen in hostile country.

They were brave men. No one on earth could deny or refute that. No swords or axes were thrown down, not even when the command to surrender was given by one of Athelbert's thegns. Ceinion saw two Erling riders racing back west for the river: not cowards, messengers. Athelbert and five of his archers were pursuing them.

Arrows flew from moving horses—and missed. The Jormsvik raiders splashed into the river, which was deeper and wider here than by Esferth. They began fording it. Athelbert came up to the bank of the Thorne. Ceinion watched as the prince took steadier aim and fired. Twice.

He was too far to see what happened in the water, but a moment later Athelbert and his riders turned back. The prince lifted an arm to signal his father. Then he rode calmly to rejoin the *fyrd* surrounding the Erling force. Men had just died here, Ceinion knew, as they had this morning and in the night. What did you make of that? What words and reflections? It was the fate of men and women to die, often before what should have been their time. *Should have been.* Too much presumption in the thought. All rested with Jad, but survivors carried memories.

He moved forward when the king did.

"Have care, my lord," cried a red-haired thegn. "They haven't yielded."

"Shoot ten," said Aeldred.

"My lord!" Ceinion protested.

Ten men were shot where they stood, even as he spoke. Athelbert's archers were really very good. You watched them and you learned something important about the prince, frivolous as he might seem when at play in a meadow.

"You said you want us to get to the ships," the king said tersely, watching the deaths, not looking at him. "If they can send forty in a rescue party, they'll have five, maybe six ships. Might even be seven, depending on how many horses. I'll need my whole company. And good men will die in that fight, if we get to them in time. Don't ask me to linger here, or be merciful. Not this day, cleric."

Cleric. No more than that. A king celebrated for courtesy, suing eloquently for Ceinion's presence at his court. But there was a rage in Aeldred now, Ceinion saw, and the king was hard-pressed to contain it. In fact, he couldn't; it was spilling over. Burgred of Denferth had been a friend from childhood. And beyond that truth, this was a large raid on the eve of the fair in Esferth—threatening to undermine the very idea of the fair. What merchants would come to these shores from abroad, or even overland from north or east, if they had cause to fear attacks from Vinmark?

"Hear me. I am Aeldred of the Anglcyn," the king said, moving his bay horse forward. Two of the *fyrd* shifted to stay between him and the Erlings. Axes could be thrown. "Whichever man leads here, order your men to lay down their arms."

Aeldred waited. Athelbert, Ceinion saw, was looking at his father, bow still to hand. No one moved in the Erling circle, or spoke. Swords and short axes remained levelled outwards. About thirty of them now. If they charged, they'd die; so would some of the Anglcyn. *The king is too close,* he thought.

Aeldred shifted his horse sideways, and even nearer. "Do it now, Erlings. Unless you wish ten more of you executed. The men you were sent to meet are dead behind us. All of them. If you fight you will be killed here without mercy. There are two hundred of us."

"Better die sword in hand than cut down as cowards." A very big man, yellow-bearded to the chest, stepped forward. "You give sworn oath to ransom if we yield ourselves?"

Aeldred opened his mouth. He was rigid again. The idea of a demand . . . He looked at his son.

"No, my lord!" Ceinion cried. "No! They *will* yield!"

Aeldred's mouth snapped shut. His jaw was clenched, his gloved hands fists on his reins. Ceinion saw him close his eyes. After a long moment, the king loosened the fingers of one hand and made the sign of the sun disk. Ceinion drew a ragged breath. His palms were sweating.

"Drop all weapons and tell us where the ships are. You will not be killed."

The yellow-bearded Erling stared at him. It was remarkable, Ceinion thought, the absence of fear in his eyes. "No. We yield ourselves to you, but cannot betray shipmates."

Aeldred shrugged. "Athelbert," he said, before Ceinion could speak.

The Erling leader died, falling backwards, three arrows in his chest, through the leather armour. A fourth went into his cheekbone, below the helmet, quivered there, where he lay in the grass.

"Who is it," Aeldred said after a moment, "who will now speak for you? You have no more time. Weapons down, guides to the longships."

"My lord," Ceinion said again, desperately. "In the holy name of Jad and by all the blessed—"

Aeldred wheeled on him. "Heed your own words! Do you want these ships stopped before they go west and not east? *Do you?*"

"In Jad's name, we do!" came a third, urgent voice.

Ceinion looked over quickly. Alun ab Owyn was moving his horse towards them. "We do, my lord king! Kill them and ride! Surely you know where they might be! High cleric, you heard: Ivarr Ragnarson bought these men. They will be going for Brynnfell, not home! We can't get back in time!"

He'd figured it out, after all.

It seemed he wasn't too young. And he was right, of course, about the timing. Ships from Drengest, out to sea by sundown, ordered to block sea lanes east, would not catch up to trained Erling seamen by the time new orders reached them. Even if they followed them west—and Aeldred had no reason to give such a command—they'd be more than half a day behind, and they wouldn't be as skilled on the water.

"Athelbert, please proceed, if you will be so good," said the king of the Anglcyn. He might have been asking his elder son to comment, in his turn, on a liturgical passage being considered.

Ceinion, in great pain, watched ten more Erlings die. They'd refused to surrender, he told himself. Aeldred had given them that chance. The pain did not lessen. Even after the arrows flew, no one came forward from the now-shrunken circle to yield. Instead, the last twenty of them screamed together, terrifyingly, distilling childhood nightmares for Ceinion in that sound, as they cried the names of their gods to the blue sky and the white clouds. They charged straight into the arrows and blades of two hundred mounted men.

Could childhood fears be expunged in this way, Ceinion wondered, remembering how many chapels and sanctuaries and good, holy men had burned amid those same cries to Ingavin and Thünir.

He watched the first Erlings fall, and then the last, swords and axes gripped, never betraying their fellows. They died in battle, weapons to hand, and so promised a place among eagles in halls of undying glory.

It appalled him, and he never forgot the unspeakable courage of it. Hating every one of those men, and what they made him think.

There was a silence, after, in the field. It all took remarkably little time.

"Very well. Let us go," said the king, after a long moment. "We will leave instructions farther south for men to come gather their weapons and burn them here."

He twitched his reins, turned his horse. Alun ab Owyn, Ceinion saw, was already ahead of them all, desperately impatient. The grey dog was beside him.

"My lord!" said the red-haired thegn. "Look there."

He was pointing back south and east, to where oaks between them and the sea were broken by a valley. Ceinion turned, with Aeldred.

"Oh, my," said Prince Athelbert.

A group of men, eight or ten of them, some mounted, some on foot, with other horses pulling a cart, were coming towards them, waving and calling, voices carrying faintly in the summer air, and then more clearly as they neared.

No one moved. The small party approached. It took some time. Their leader was riding in the cart; he appeared to have a wound, was holding his side. He was

also the one most vigorously shouting, gesticulating with
his free hand, visibly agitated.

Visibly from the south, as well, Ceinion saw. And
speaking a foreign tongue.

"Jad's holy light," said King Aeldred, softly. "They are
Asharite. From Al-Rassan. What is he saying? Someone?"

Ceinion knew fragments of Esperañan, not Asharite.
He tried it. Called a greeting.

Without missing a beat in his tirade, the merchant in
the cart switched languages. The king turned to Ceinion,
expectantly. Forty dead men lay on the grass around
them. Two of Athelbert's men had dismounted, were
efficiently collecting arrows.

"He is outraged, my lord, and unhappy. They declare
themselves to have been assaulted, injured, and robbed
on their way to Esferth Fair. By one man, if I understand
properly. An Erling. He took a horse. A good horse, I
gather. Meant for you, in Esferth. They are . . . they are
displeased with the protection being offered to visitors."

Aeldred looked from the cleric to the man in the cart.
His eyes had widened.

"Ibn Bakir?" he said, looking at the merchant. "My
stud horse? My manuscripts?"

Ceinion translated as best he could. Then, somewhat
belatedly, told the visitors who the man on the bay
horse was.

The Asharite merchant straightened, too quickly.
The cart was a precarious place to stand. He bowed,
almost fell. One of his fellows steadied him. The
merchant had a wound in his right side; blood welled
through what appeared to be green silk. He had a dark
bruise on the side of his head. He nodded energetically,
however. Turned, reached down, still being steadied,
and pulled some parchment scrolls from a trunk behind
him. He waved them in the air, the way he'd waved his

hand before, calling for aid. Someone laughed, then controlled himself.

"Ask him," said Alun ab Owyn, his voice strained, "if the Erling was unusual in his appearance." They hadn't heard him come back.

The king glanced over at Alun. Ceinion asked the question. He didn't know the word for "unusual" but managed "strange." The merchant's effusive manner grew calmer. With the overexcited manner fading, he seemed more impressive, notwithstanding the fluttering green garment. This was a man who had, after all, travelled a long way. He answered gravely, standing on his cart.

Ceinion heard him; felt a wind in his soul.

"He says the Erling was white as a dead spirit, his face, his hair. Not natural. He surprised them rushing out from the trees, took only the horse."

"Ragnarson," said Alun, unnecessarily. He was looking at Aeldred. "My lord king, we must ride. We can beat him there—they lied to you this morning, back in the meadow. He *wasn't* with their messengers to the ships. He's just ahead of us!"

"I believe," said the king of the Anglcyn, "that this is so. I agree with you. We should ride."

Five men were detailed to escort the merchants to Esferth and lodge them with honour. The rest of the *fyrd* turned west and south. They paused only to fill their flasks and let the horses drink. It was Alun ab Owyn who led them splashing into the River Thorne and across, and it was Alun who set the pace after, alongside the woods, until some of those who actually knew where they were going caught up with him.

The king, his bay horse galloping beside Ceinion's, asked only one question on the long ride that followed.

"Ragnarson is the man who led the raid last spring? Brynnfell? When the Cadyri prince was killed?"

Ceinion nodded. There was nothing more to say and a great need for speed.

They never caught up with him, never saw more than the sign of tracks ahead, alone at first, then merging with those of another horse—following it, not side by side. The tracks ran back south-east a little as the river curved between ridges of hills. Both sets, cutting at precisely the place where the Anglcyn outsiders had thought they might. They followed, galloping, between stream and forest, and they came at length to a sheltered strand of stones, and the sea.

Westering sun on the water by then. White clouds on the breeze. Tang of salt. Clear evidence of ships having been beached here, and a large company of men, very recently. Nothing more than those signs; empty the wide sea, in all directions. No way to know, none at all, which way the ships had gone. But Ceinion knew. He knew.

The king ordered the *fyrd* to dismount to let tired horses graze along the beach, up a little way where there was grass. He gave time for riders to rest as well, eat and drink. After which, he called his thegns to council. Invited Ceinion to come, and Alun ab Owyn, a generous gesture.

At which time it was discovered that Alun and his dog and his Erling servant were nowhere to be found.

No man had seen them leave the strand. Half a dozen outriders were dispatched. It wasn't long before they returned. One of them shook his head. Ceinion, standing beside the king, took a step towards them and stopped, without speaking. Owyn of Cadyr, he was thinking, had only the one son living now. He might lose them both.

One of the riders dismounted. "They have gone, my lord." That much was obvious.

"Where?" said Aeldred.

The rider cleared his throat. "Into the forest, I fear."

A stir, then silence among those gathered. Ceinion saw men making the sign of the sun disk. He had just done the same, a habit as old as he was. *What,* he thought, *am I going to say to the father?* A wind was blowing now, from the east. The sun was going down.

"Their horses' tracks go in there," the outrider added. "Into the woods."

Of course they do, Ceinion thought. It was madness, entirely so, what Alun wanted to do. Coming here they'd followed the coastal path all the way, skirting the wood. Of course they had. That was how you went: from the south you travelled along the coast; if you were starting north you went through the watchtower gates of the Wall. But not the forest. No one went through the woods.

But the coastal path would only take you back to Cadyr in the south, and Arberth—and Brynnfell—would be four days beyond that, up the river valleys. Retracing the coast road would be a wasted, meaningless journey. It wouldn't do. Not if you had decided that the Erlings were heading for Brynn ap Hywll's farm again. If you had decided that, and you knew Ivarr Ragnarson was aboard, then you could do something shaped by madness . . .

Ceinion felt old again. That seemed to be happening to him more and more. The man's voice had sounded genuinely regretful just now, reporting the tidings. The young Cyngael prince had saved King Aeldred's life this morning, they had all seen it. They would be sorry to see a young life end in this way.

Someone swore, savagely, breaking the mood. Athelbert. He strode angrily away up the strand. Stones there, some grass, grazing horses, light glittering on the water. It would be dark in the woods, and they stretched all the way to the Cyngael lands, and no one went through them. Ceinion closed his eyes. It was growing cooler, late in the day, edge of the sea, the sun going down.

He would die in there, Owyn's younger son.

I am too old, Ceinion thought again. He was remembering—so vividly—the father as a young man, equally reckless, even more impulsive. And now that man was an aging prince, and his son was about to find his own end trying to go through the untracked woods carrying a warning all the long way home. A desperate, glorious folly. The way of the Cyngael.

CHAPTER XI

Bern backed down on hands and knees from the ridge when he saw the Anglcyn archers begin to shoot. There was a disaster happening, crisp and bright in the sunlight: blue river, green grass, deeper green of trees beyond, the many-coloured horses, the arrows caught by light as they flew. He felt ill, watching.

You didn't abandon shipmates, but he knew what he was seeing. His task was to get back to the coast alive with his warning and these tidings of catastrophe. The Anglcyn were riding for the sea.

Breathing deeply, struggling to calm himself, he led Gyllir away from the battle, to the very edge of the forest. Even in daylight the trees felt oppressive, menacing. Spirits and powers, not to mention hunting cats and wolves and wild boars were in such woods. The *volurs* who put themselves into trances to see along the dark pathways of the dead said that there were animals that housed the spirits of the old gods, and wanted blood.

Looking at the darkness on his right, he could half believe in such creatures. But for all that, a more certain death lay in the other direction with the *fyrd*. They'd ridden at least as fast as he had to get to this place, which was unsettling. Back home, the old women said, *An Erling on a horse of the sea, an Anglcyn on a horse* . . . still, he'd not have thought Gyllir could be matched.

Aeldred's riders were here, though. He couldn't
linger. Waiting would bring them across the river.

Bern used the trees as a backdrop, riding right alongside them, so as not to appear clearly against the sky.
Even so, in the moments when he passed up and then
down along the ridge and had to be in view, his heart felt
painful and loud, as if his chest were a drum. He leaned
low over Gyllir's neck and he whispered a prayer to
Ingavin, who knew the ways of secrecy.

No cry went up. Just as Bern Thorkellson crested that
ridge, an agitated party of merchants from Al-Rassan was
hailing the *fyrd*, coming towards them, loud with indig-
nation. They saved his life, for the outriders turned to see.

It happens this way. Small things, accidents of timing
and congruence: and then all that flows in our lives from
such moments owes its unfolding course, for good or ill,
to them. We walk (or stumble) along paths laid down by
events of which we remain forever ignorant. The road
someone else never took, or travelled too late, or soon,
means an encounter, a piece of information, a memorable
night, or death, or life.

Bern stayed low in the saddle, his neck hairs prickling,
till he was sure he was out of sight. Only then did he
straighten and give Gyllir his head, galloping towards
the sea. He saw gentle, rolling country, rich land. The
sort of soil that made a soft, easy people. Not like
Vinmark, where cliffs crashed jaggedly down in places
where the sea gouged the land like a blade. Where rock-
strewn slopes and icebound winters made farming a
wounding aspiration on farms never large enough.
Where younger sons took to the sea roads with helm and
blade, or starved.

The Erlings were hard with cause, reasons deep and
cold as the black, still waters knifing between cliffs. These
people over here, with their loamy, generous soil and

their god of light, were . . . well, in fact, these people were smashing the best raiders Vinmark had right now. The story didn't seem to hold. Not any more.

The shape and balance of the world had changed. His father (he didn't want to think about his father) had said that more than once on the isle, after he'd decided his raiding days were over.

Thorkell really shouldn't be here, Bern thought. Riding south at speed, he felt too young to sort it through, but not too young to be aware that the changes were happening, had already happened.

There was a distance still to go, but not so much now, as he finally began to recognize where he was. Gyllir was labouring, but so, surely, would be the mounts of Aeldred's *fyrd* behind him. They'd be coming, he knew it. And— sudden thought—they'd see his tracks and realize he was ahead of them. He had to outrace them to the water with enough time to get the ships offshore. He was dripping with sweat in the sunlight, could smell his own fear.

When he saw the valley he remembered it. Gave thanks for that. He followed it south-east and, almost as soon as he did, smelled salt on the wind. The valley opened out. He saw their strand. Only two ships still anchored; the other three already out in the straits beyond.

He began to shout as he galloped up, continued shouting as he leaped from Gyllir's back, stumbling into the midst of the encampment. He tried to be coherent, wasn't sure if he succeeded.

These were Jormsvik men, however. They moved with a speed he'd not have believed possible before he'd joined them. The camp was struck, and the last two ships (undermanned, but no help for that) had oars in place and were pulling to sea before the sun had swung much farther west. This was their life, salt and hardship, dragon-prows. *An Erling on a horse of the sea . . .*

Brand's own ship was last. They were rowing after the others when someone called out to them from shore. Another of those moments when so much may turn one way or another, for they might have been just a little quicker from shore, and so too far out to hear. Bern did hear it, though, looked back from where he stood beside the one-eyed leader of their raid.

"Who is it?" Brand Leofson rasped, squinting.

A rider in the water, waving one arm, forcing a reluctant horse into the sea after them.

"Leave him," said Bern, whose eyes were very good. "Let him be killed by Aeldred. He lied to us. From the start. Ecca kept saying so." He felt fear, and a cold anger.

"Where *is* Ecca?" Brand asked, turning his good eye to Bern.

"Killed in Esferth. Their *king* was there. Hundreds of men. There's an accursed *fair* going on. I told you— Ragnarson lied."

The man beside him, captain, raid leader, veteran of half a hundred battles across the world, chewed one side of his moustache.

"That's him in the water?" Brand said.

Bern nodded.

"I want to talk to that misbegotten bastard," Brand said. "If he's to die, I'll do it myself and report it at home. Back oars!" he cried. "Ramp out! Sling for the horse!"

Precise movements began. *This is a mistake,* Bern was thinking. Couldn't escape the thought as he watched the strange, deadly man on a magnificent, inexplicable horse come closer through the waves. It seemed to him, feeling helpless as a child, that this was a moment in which his life—and not only his own—might be hanging, as in a merchant's balance.

In the afternoon light, under swift, indifferent clouds, Ivarr Ragnarson was taken aboard.

"That," said Brand One-eye, gazing into the sea, "is an Asharite horse."

Bern had no idea if this was true or not, couldn't see why it mattered. The horse was pulled up, a sling drawn under its belly by a man who knew how to swim. They all threw their weight to the far side, to keep the ship in balance as it happened. A difficult exercise, done with ease.

The balance seemed to tilt in Bern's mind as he turned from watching the horse lifted aboard to regarding the twist-mouthed, dripping wet, white-faced, white-haired, pale-eyed grandson of Siggur Volganson, last surviving heir of the greatest of all their warriors.

Ivarr strode to stand directly in front of Leofson.

"How dare you leave shore without me, you worm-eaten lump of dung!" he said. You couldn't get used to his voice. No one else talked like that. It was icy, and it cut.

Brand Leofson, so addressed, looked at Ivarr with what seemed genuine perplexity. This was his ship, he was leader of a Jormsvik raid, a captain of many years' standing, surrounded by his fellows. He shook his head slowly, as if to clear it, then he knocked Ivarr to the deck with a backhanded blow to the face.

"Pull away!" he called over his shoulder. "Hard on the benches, all of you! Out of sight of shore, sail up, whichever way the wind takes us. We'll have a lantern council at darkfall. Signal the others. And you," he said, turning back to Ragnarson, "will stay where you are, on the deck. If you stand up I will knock you down again. If you do it twice I swear by Ingavin's eye and my own I will throw you into the sea."

Ivarr Ragnarson stared up at him but didn't move. The too-pale eyes, Bern decided, held more black rage than he'd have ever thought to see in a man. He looked away.

His father (he didn't want to think about his father) had warned him.

THE YOUNGEST of the mercenaries turned away. Ivarr saw fear in his face. Ivarr was used to both: people avoided looking at him all the time, after furtive glances of horror and fascination, and there was often fear. Ivarr Ragnarson was white as a bone, malformed at one shoulder, his eyes were strange (and not good in bright sunlight)—and men were riddled with fears of the unknown, of spirits, of angry, unassuaged gods.

This young one—he couldn't remember names, people didn't matter enough—had a different quality to his apprehension, though. Something more than the obvious. Ivarr couldn't say what it was, but he could sense it. He had a skill that way.

To be considered later. As was the fact that he was going to kill Brand Leofson. He'd been struck twice today by mongrels from Jormsvik. One of them, Skallson, had already been slain by the Anglcyn, denying Ivarr the pleasure. This one here would have to be allowed to live a little longer: Leofson was needed, if this raid was still going to work. Sometimes pleasures had to be deferred.

Lying on the deck of a ship, salt-soaked, bruised and exhausted and bleeding, Ivarr Ragnarson felt sure of his control of events, even now. It helped that almost everyone you dealt with was a fool, weak, though they might think themselves hard, undermined by needs and desires, friendships and ambitions.

Ivarr had no such weaknesses. He was cut off by his appearance from any possibility of leadership and acceptance. That disposed of ambition. Friendship, as well. And his desires were . . . other than those of most men.

His brother Mikkel—dead in a Cyngael farmyard, one of Ingavin's great hulking fools in life—had actually thought he could be a leader of the Erling people, the way their grandfather was. *That* was why Mikkel had wanted to go to Brynnfell. Revenge, and the sword. With the Volgan's sword in hand, he'd said, ale cup sloshing about, he could rally people around him, to the family's name.

He might have, if he hadn't been thick in the head like a plough ox, and if Kjarten Vidurson—a man Ivarr had to admit he wondered about—hadn't clearly been readying himself for a claim of kingship in Hlegest, with infinitely more weight than Mikkel would ever have had.

Ivarr hadn't said anything about that. He'd wanted Mikkel's raid to happen. His own reasons for going were so much simpler than his brother's: he was bored, and he liked killing people. Vengeance and a raid made killing all right in the eyes of the world. With nothing to aspire to, no status to seek or favour to attain, Ivarr's was an uncomplicated existence, in some ways.

When you looked only to yourself, decisions came more easily. People who harmed or crossed you were to be dealt with without exception. That now included those Cyngael at Brynnfell who had sent him fleeing through a night wood, then desperately back to the ships last spring. That also meant this maggot, Brand One-eye, right here, but only after he'd done what Ivarr needed him to do, which was get him back west.

There were deaths to be accomplished there first. And he still wanted to see if he could grasp and spread someone's lungs out on the red, cracked-open cage of their ribs while they remained alive, bubbling, blood-soaked. It was a *hard* thing to do. You needed opportunities to practise before you could do something so delicate.

When your needs were uncomplicated, it was easy enough to spend a good part of the resources you had (last of the Volgans, heir to all they possessed) buying two hundred mercenaries at the end of a summer.

If people had trouble looking at your face for long it was hardly difficult to lie to them. The Jormsvikings were smug, complacent, full of self-love, beefy and drunken, amusingly easy to deceive, for all their celebrated prowess on ship and in battle. They were what they were, Ivarr thought: tools.

He had dropped gold and silver onto a trestle table in a Jormsvik barracks hall, and told them that Aeldred's coastal *burh* at Drengest was unfinished, under-defended, with ships they might seize for themselves and a newly dedicated sanctuary with too much gold.

He'd seen this, he said, when he and his brother went west in spring. And a watchman they'd taken and killed for information, along the coast, had told them before he died that the king and *fyrd* were spending the summer at Raedhill, hunting north of it, leaving Esferth exposed. Another lie, but Ivarr was good at lying.

Ale went round a smoke-filled room, then round again, and songs were sung about Jormsvik glories in days gone by. And then came another predictable song (Ivarr had heard it too many times, but made himself smile, as if in rue and remembrance) about Siggur Volganson and the great summer of twin assaults on Ferrieres and Karch, and the famous raid on the hidden sanctuary at Champieres, where he'd claimed his sword. More drinking during that, and after. Men asleep at the tables, heads down among spilled ale and guttered candles.

In the morning Ivarr formally paid the mercenaries to make it worth their while to sail, even if they should find little enough for the taking in the Anglcyn lands. He stung their pride—so easily—pointing out how long it had been since they'd challenged Aeldred on his own soil.

There was glory to be won, swords to be reddened, Ivarr said, before dark winter came to the northlands again and closed the wild sea. Make it sound like music, he'd found, and listeners would dance to your song— while not looking at your face.

Simple, really. Men were easy to deceive. You needed only to be clear in your mind about what you wanted them to do. Ivarr always had been, was even more so now. Brynn ap Hywll and any of his family found were to be staked out naked, alive, in the slop and mud of their own farmyard while Ivarr carved them one by one. Ap Hywll was fat as a summer hog, he'd need to cut deep. That was all right, it was not a difficulty.

The blood-eagle rite was a final act of vengeance for his slain brother and grandfather, he would say, sadly. A ritual done in honour of Ingavin's ravens and eagles and in memory of the Volgan line, of which he was the last. After him, they would be no more. And men would hear it and look sorrowful. Would even honour him for it around winter fires.

Amusing. But to make it happen he had to get these ships to Cyngael shores. That was the only uncertain part, if you excepted the fortune that underlay his finding those merchants with a horse earlier today. That, he didn't actually want to think about right now. He'd have missed the ships, otherwise, been left on a hostile coast alone. Perhaps he *should* think about it. Perhaps Ingavin or Thünir was showing his lordly countenance to a pale, small, crooked figure after all. And what could that mean, after so many years?

A distraction. For later. They had to go west, first. That had always been the delicate task. It would have made no sense for Brand Leofson or any other leader to take five ships so late in the year for the feeble returns a Cyngael raid offered these days. Ivarr had known that. So you worked it another way: you told them they were going after Aeldred where he was rich and vulnerable. And when that proved—as you knew it would prove— not to be so after all, you relied on your tongue and their stupid hunger for Ingavin-glory to lure them a little farther west . . . since they'd already come this far, and it would be *such* a terrible loss of face to go back empty-handed.

It was a good plan. Would have been easy, in fact, if Burgred of Denferth hadn't been with the accursed party they'd surprised in the night. The earl had been worth a ransom the raiders could grow fat upon, and they'd known it. Thick-witted and ale-sodden or not, they'd understood who this man was. Aeldred would have paid the taxes from ten cities and a hundred households to have his companion back. And then five Jormsvik ships would have turned around and rowed happily home into the wind, every man singing all the way.

It would have driven him mad.

He'd had no choice but to shoot the man.

An unsatisfying killing, done in haste, no pain involved—except his own when Skallson came near to killing him for it. Ivarr hadn't actually been afraid—he couldn't remember ever being afraid—but he hadn't been ready to die, either.

For one thing, he didn't expect eagles or ravens to escort his spirit to shining halls when death came for him. Ingavin and Thünir loved their tall warriors with bright axes and swords, not twisted, wry-mouthed misfits with death-white skin and eyes that saw better at twilight than in the day's bright sun.

It was less bright now, in fact. They had been pulling steadily from the coast and now the sail was up. The sun was over west. Ivarr waited, as ever, for the evening shadows to come, changing the colour of the sea and sky.

He was happier then, happier in winter. Cold and darkness didn't distress him; they felt like his proper place.

Men thought he was weak. Men were wrong, almost without exception fools beyond the telling. He wondered, sometimes, if his mighty grandfather—never seen or known, killed in Llywerth before Ivarr was born—might have thought the same way, crashing like a wave again and again upon peoples who could do nothing against him for year upon year, until it ended by that western sea.

The gods knew, he had reasons enough to kill Brynn ap Hywll. He would do the women first, Ivarr thought, let the fat man watch, bound and helpless, naked amidst the shit of his yard. It was a pleasing thought. You needed to hold it in mind, point towards it, let nothing distract or divert.

"You will stand up now," said Brand Leofson. A bulky shape above him, suddenly. "Before the council begins you will explain your lies."

He'd expected that. Men were easy to anticipate. All he ever *needed* was a chance to speak.

Ivarr rose slowly to his feet. Rubbed at his jaw where he'd been struck, though there wasn't any pain to speak of now. It was good to look small, though, frail, no danger to anyone.

"I didn't think you'd do what I needed done," he mumbled. Kept his eyes down. Turned his head away, submissive as a beaten wolf. He'd watched wolves in winter snow, learned from them.

"What? You admit you lied?"

Gods! What had the ox-brain *expected* him to do? Deny it? They'd *seen* the finished walls and readied ships in Drengest, which he'd said was empty and exposed. Sixty of them in two parties had been slaughtered today by Aeldred and the *fyrd* out from Esferth—where he'd told them the king would not be.

He hadn't expected those deaths—there was nothing good about losing so many men—but you couldn't let such things affect what you'd had in mind for so long. This entire end-of-summer journey with the Jormsvikings was, after all, a second plan. He was supposed to have taken Brynnfell and the sword in spring, not had his sodden, stupid brother die with almost every man in that yard. Ivarr was all alone in the world now. Shouldn't there be mournful music with that thought? All alone. He'd killed their sister when he was nine; now dear Mikkel had been cut down in an Arberthi farmyard.

Let the skalds make bad songs of it. *Sorrow for Siggur's strong scions/Valour and vaunt among the Volgans* . . .

He didn't feel sorry for himself. What he felt was fury, endlessly, from first awareness of himself, a bent child in a warrior world.

"I lied because we have fallen so far in twenty-five years that even with the warriors of Jormsvik, I was unsure of us."

"We? Us?"

"The Erlings of Vinmark, friend. Ingavin's children of the middle-world."

"What the one-eyed god does that drivel *mean,* you drip-nosed gutter spawn?"

He needed to kill this man. Had to be careful not to let it show. No distractions. Ivarr looked up, then ducked his head again, as if ashamed. Wiped at his nose, placatingly.

"My father died a coward, his own great father unavenged. My brother fell as a hero, trying to do so. I am the only one left. The only one. And Ingavin has seen fit to have me misshapen, unworthy in my poor self to take vengeance for our line and our people."

Brand One-eye spat over the railing of his ship. "I still don't know what raven-shit rubbish you are spewing. Speak plain and—"

"He means he planned to go to Arberth all along, Brand. Never had any thought of Anglcyn lands. He means he tricked us with lies about Aeldred to get us to sea."

Ivarr was careful to keep his eyes lowered. He felt a pulsing in his head, however. This young one, whoever he was, had just become an irritant, and you needed to avoid showing that.

"That the truth?" Brand turned to him. He was a very big man.

Ivarr hadn't wanted things to move this quickly, but part of the skill of these moments was adapting. "Jormsvik has its share of wisdom, even from the young ones who might not be expected to know so much. It is as the boy says."

"Boy's older than you think, maggot, and killed a Jormsvik captain in single combat," said Leofson pompously. A beefy, thick-brained warrior. All he was. Ivarr held back a grimace: he'd made a mistake, these men were famously bound to each other.

"I didn't mean—"

"Shut up, rodent. I'm thinking."

The very halls of Ingavin tremble at such tidings was what Ivarr wanted to say. He kept silent. Composed himself with an image of what he wanted, what he *needed:* the family of Brynn ap Hywll in their own yard— or maybe on a table in their hall under torches, for better light?—naked, all of them, the women soiling themselves with terror, exposed to his red, carving blade. Wife and daughter and the fat man himself. The goal. All else could come later.

"Why you want to get to Arberth so bad?"

They heard sounds across the water; the other ships, moving nearer for the council. They were out of sight of shore, darkness falling soon. Needed to be careful: ships could ram and gouge each other in the sea, riding so nearly. They would rope them together, create a platform of ships, even in open water, in twilight. Jormsvik seamen. They knew how to do such things better than any men alive. A thought, there.

Ivarr took a breath, as if summoning courage. "Why Arberth? Because Kjarten Vidurson in Hlegest seems ready to be a king, and he should have the Volgan's sword again. Or someone should."

He let that last phrase linger, emphasized it just enough. He hadn't *planned* to mention Vidurson, but it worked, it worked. He could feel it. There was a rhythm to these things as ideas came, a dance, as much as any single combat with weapons ever was.

"The sword?" repeated Brand, stupidly.

"My grandfather's blade, taken when ap Hywll killed him. The death never avenged, to my shame—and our people's."

"That was twenty-five years ago! We're mercenaries, for the great gods' sake!"

Ivarr lifted his head, let his pale eyes seem to blaze in the torchlight. "How much glory do you think you'd gain, Brand Leofson, you and every man here, all of Jormsvik, if *you* were the ones to regain that sword?"

A satisfying silence on the deck, and across the water. He'd spoken loudly, ringing it out, that the other boats, approaching, might also hear. He pushed on, next part of the song. "And more: do you not think it might even give you, give all of us, some power and protection from Vidurson should he prove . . . other than some think he is?"

He hadn't planned this, either. He was very happy with it.

"What does *that* mean?" Leofson snarled, now pacing like a bear on the deck.

Ivarr allowed himself to straighten, an equal speaking to an equal. It was necessary to have that status back.

"What does it mean? Tell me, men of Jormsvik, how joyously will a northern man who sets himself as king over all the Erlings—the first in four generations—look upon a walled fortress of fighting men in the south who answer only to themselves?" It was like music, a poem, he was shaping a—

"If this is so," interrupted a voice again, "you might have raised it with us, and let us take counsel at home. You said no single word about Kjarten Vidurson. Or about Arberth, or the Volgan's sword. Instead, tricked to sea with outright lies, sixty good men are dead." It was the boy, the scarcely bearded one. He snorted. "Didn't that watchman you say you captured in spring *tell* you about the new fair starting this year?"

Ivarr's flaring anger calmed quickly. So easy, it was. They made it so easy. He wanted to laugh. They were fools, even when they weren't.

"He *did* say that," he replied, keeping his voice mild. The second question had so nicely taken him off the harder first one. "But he said that because the fair was just beginning—as you say—the king was leaving it to his stewards. That's why I thought there'd be merchants to raid, with few to guard them, rich takings for brave men."

"Just beginning?"

"As you said," Ivarr murmured.

The young one, not as big a man as Leofson but well-enough made, began to laugh. Laughing at Ivarr. With others watching and listening. This was not permitted. He'd killed his sister for laughing like that, when she was twelve and he was nine.

"I will not be made mock of," Ivarr snapped, a hotness in his brain.

"No?" said the other man. His amusement subsided. He had looked away before; he wasn't doing so now. Lights had been hung on the ships' railings, all five of them, and at prow and stern. They were aglow, these ships on the water, marking the presence of mortal men on the wide, darkening sea. "I don't think I'm mocking you, actually. Or not only that."

"What are you saying, Bern?" asked Leofson, quietly.

Bern. The name. To be remembered.

"He's still lying. Even now. You know the peasants' saying. *To trap a fox, you let him trap himself.* He just did. Listen: this is the *third* year of the Esferth Fair, not the first. Every man we met on the road knew it. The city was thronged, Brand, overflowing. Tents in the fields. Guards everywhere, and the *fyrd*. I said 'first year' to see what this fox would do with it. And you heard. Don't call him a maggot. He's too dangerous."

Ivarr cleared his throat. "So the ignorant peasant we captured was wrong about—"

"No," said the one called Bern. "I planted that thought in your head, Ragnarson. You captured no watchman. You never put ashore here. You went straight to Brynnfell in Arberth, and failed. So you wanted to go back—there, nowhere else—for your own blood-hunger. Ingavin's blind eye, sixty men are dead because you lied to us."

"And he killed an earl we took," someone shouted from the ship nearest to them. "An earl!" Voices echoed that.

Greed, thought Ivarr. They were driven by greed. And vanity. Both could be used, always. The hotness was making it harder to think clearly, though, to take back control of this. If the one named Bern would only shut his mouth. If he'd been on one of the other ships . . . such a small change in the world.

Ivarr looked at the man more closely. A ship on either side of theirs now, men lashing them together, practised ease. It had grown darker. His eyes worked better in this twilight with lanterns. *Ingavin's blind eye.*

Something slid into place with that phrase.

"Who is your father?" he said sharply, anger cracking through, with awareness. "I think I know—"

"He's a Jormsviking!" snapped Brand, his voice crashing in, heavy as a smith's hammer. "We are *born* when we pass through the walls into brotherhood. Our histories do not matter, we shed them. Even maggots like you know that of us."

"Yes, yes! But I think I know . . . The way he speaks . . . I think his father was with—"

Brand struck him, a second time, harder than before, on the mouth. Ivarr went down on his back, spat blood, then a tooth. Someone laughed. The hotness went red. He reached towards the dagger in his boot, then stopped, controlling himself to control men. He could be killed here, going for a weapon. Sprawled on his back, he looked up at the big man over him, spat red again, to the side. Spread his hands, to show they were empty.

Saw a sword, then another one, both bright, as if flaming, torchlight upon them. He died there—astonished, it could be said—as Leofson's heavy blade spitted him, biting deep into the deck beneath his body.

BERN REMINDED HIMSELF to breathe. His arm, holding a sword, was at his side. Brand had knocked it away with his own before killing Ivarr with a thrust that had the full force of his body behind it.

Leofson levered his weapon free, with difficulty. There was a silence amid the lanterns, under the first stars. Brand turned to Bern, a curious expression on his scarred countenance.

"You're too young," he said unexpectedly. "Whatever else he was, this was the last of the Volgans. Too heavy a weight to carry all your life. Better it was me."

Bern found it difficult to speak. He managed a nod, though he wasn't sure he really understood what the older man was saying. There was a stillness, a sense of weight all about them, though. This was not an ordinary death.

"Put him overboard at the stern," Brand said. "Attor, do the 'Last Song,' and properly. We don't need any god angry tonight."

Men moved to do his bidding. You put Erlings into the sea if they died on the water. *Last of the Volgans,* Bern thought. The phrase in his head kept repeating itself.

"He . . . he killed sixty men today. As if he'd done it himself."

"True enough," said Brand, almost indifferently.

He was moving on already, Bern realized. Leader of a raid, other things to consider, decisions to be made. He heard a splash. Attor's voice rose. They would be able to hear it on the other boats.

Bern found that his hands were shaking. He looked at his sword, which he was still holding, and sheathed it. He went to the side of the ship, by his own oar, next to the roped ship beside them, and stood there listening as Attar sang, deep-voiced in the dark.

Hard the journey   heavy the waves,
Brief our lingering   on land or sea.
Ingavin ever mind   his Erling-folk,
Thünir remember   who honour you.
Let no angry spirit   still be here,
No soul be lost   without a home.
Salt the sea-foam   by ship's prow,
White the waves   before us and behind.

Bern looked down at the water and then away to the emerging stars, trying to keep his mind empty, to just listen. But then it seemed he was thinking—found himself unable not to think—of his father again. In a stream with him under these same stars last night.

He had felt such anger moments ago, looking down at Ivarr Ragnarson, watching—*knowing*—what the man was doing. The need to kill had crashed over him like nothing in his life before; he'd had his sword out, and driving, before he'd realized what he was doing.

Was this the way it had happened for Thorkell—twice, ten years apart, in two taverns? Was this his father's fury awakening inside him? And Bern was sober as death right now; light-headed with fatigue, but not so much as a beaker of ale since the tavern in Esferth the evening before. Yet even with that, rage had taken him.

If Brand had not been quicker, Bern would have killed the man on the deck and he knew it. His father had done that, twice, exiled for it the second time. *Ruining their lives* was what Bern had always thought, and his heart had been cold as a winter sea, bitter as winter foraging.

Ruining his father's *own* life was more true, he thought now: Thorkell had turned himself, in a moment, from a settled landowner in a place where he had real stature into an exile, no longer young, without hearth or family. How had he felt that day, leaving the isle? And the next day, and in the nights that had followed, sleeping among strangers, or alone? Did he lie down and rise up with *heimthra*, the heart's hard longing for home? Bern had never even put his mind to this.

Are you drunk? he had said to Thorkell in the river. And been struck a blow for that. Open hand, he remembered; a father's admonition.

The wind had died, but now a breeze came again from the east. The lashed ships swayed with it, lanterns bobbing. Jormsvik mariners, best in all the world. He was one of them. A new home, for him. The sky was dark now.

The song came to an end. His hands weren't trembling any more. Thorkell was somewhere north in the night, having crossed the sea again, long past when he'd have thought himself done with raiding. It was a time for home and hearth, wood chopped and piled up for winter winds and snow. Land of his own, fences and tilled fields, tavern fires in town, companionship at night. Gone with one moment's ale-soaked fury. And his youth long gone as well. Not a time of life to be starting again. What was a son—a grown son—to think about all of this? *No soul be lost without a home.*

Bern reached into his tunic and touched the hammer on its silver chain. He shook his head slowly. Thorkell had actually saved *all* of the men here, sending Bern south at speed, with that added warning about Ivarr.

You needed to be strong enough to say these things to yourself, acknowledge them, even through bitterness. And there was more, another thing sliding into awareness now, the way the fainter stars slipped into sight against the darkened sky. *Don't let Ivarr Ragnarson know you're my son.*

He hadn't understood that. He'd asked; his father hadn't answered. Not an answering sort of man. But Ragnarson's pale eyes had seen something here on the deck, in Bern's face by torchlight, or in something he'd said. Some kind of resemblance. He had thought through—fox's mind—to a truth about Bern, and about Thorkell. He'd been about to say it, an accusation, when swords came out and he died. *I think his father was with—*

"Brand! We've rowing to do, best set a course." It was Isolf, at the helm of the ship tied to their starboard side.

"I say south first, head for Ferrieres coast, or Karch coast, whoever holds it this year." That was Carsten, from the other side.

"Ferrieres," said Brand absently. He walked past Bern towards the helm. Attor followed him.

"Aeldred'll have ships in the water by now, certain as Ingavin carries a hammer." Isolf again.

Someone laughed derisively. "They don't know what they're doing. Anglcyn, at sea?" Other voices joining in.

"He'll use Erlings," Brand said. The amusement subsided. "Believe it. Ingemar Svidrirson's his ally here in Erlond, remember? Pays him tribute."

"Fuck him, then!" someone shouted.

A sentiment that found much endorsement, even more crude. Bern stayed where he was, listening. He was too new, had no idea what their best course was. They'd lost almost a third of their company, could manage five ships, but if they ended up in a fight at sea . . .

"We'll do that another time," called Carsten Friddson. "Right now let's just get home with all ships and bodies left. South's best, say I, to the other coast, then we beat back east along it. Aeldred won't venture so far from his own shore just on a chance of finding us at sea."

It did make sense, Bern thought. The new Anglcyn ships at Drengest might be ready, but they wouldn't have had any experience with them yet. And those ships—if they were even on the water—were all that lay between them and home. Surely they could slip past them?

He had a sudden, unexpectedly vivid image of Jormsvik. The walls, gate, barracks, the stony, wave-battered strand, the crooked town beside the fortress where he'd almost died the night before he won his way inside. He thought of Thira. His whore now. He'd killed Gurd, who'd laid claim to her before.

That was how it worked in Jormsvik. You bought your warmth in winter, one way or another. Whores, not wives, was the order of things. But there *was* warmth to be found, a fireside, companionship: he wasn't alone, wasn't a servant, might have a chance, if he was good enough at killing and staying alive, to shape a name for himself in the world. Thorkell had done that.

And it was on that thought of his father that Bern heard Brand Leofson say, with what seemed an unnaturally precise, carrying clarity, "We're not going home yet."

A silence again, then, "What in Thünir's name does that mean?" Garr Hoddson, shouting from the fourth ship.

Brand looked towards him across the other deck. They were all shapes in darkness now, voices, unless standing beside one of the lanterns. Bern had taken a step away from the rail.

"Means the snake said one thing true. Listen. This raid's the worst we've had in years, any of us. It's a bad time for that, with Vidurson making plans up north."

"Vidurson? What of it?" Garr shouted. "Brand, we've lost a full boat of—"

"I know what we've lost! I want to *find*, now. We need to. Listen to me. We're going to go west to get the Volgan's sword back. Or to kill the man who took it. Or both. We're going to that farm, whatever it's called."

"Brynnfell," Bern heard himself saying. His voice sounded hollow.

"That's it," Brand Leofson said, nodding his head. "Ap Hywll's farm. We run enough of us ashore, leave some to the ships, find the place, burn it down, there should be hostages."

"How do we get home, after?" Carsten asking.

Bern could hear a new note in his voice: he was interested, engaged. This had been a disastrous raid, nothing to show for it but their own deaths. No man here wanted to spend a winter hearing about that.

"Decide that when we're done. Back this way, or we go the north route—"

"Too late in the year," Garr Hoddson said. He had stepped across to Carsten's ship, Bern saw.

"Then back this way. Aeldred'll be ashore by then. Or we overwinter west if need be. We've done that before, too. But we'll *do* something before we show our faces home. And if we get that blade back, we have something to show Kjarten Vidurson, too, if that northerner gets ideas we don't like. Anyone here actually decided we need a king, by the way?"

A shout of anger. Jormsvik had its views on this. Kings put limits on you, set taxes, liked to tear down walls that weren't their own.

"Carsten?" Brand lifted his voice over the shouting.

"I'm for it."

"Garr?"

"Do it. We've shipmates to avenge."

But not in the west, Bern thought. *Not there.* It didn't matter. He felt, with genuine surprise, a quickening of his own heartbeat. His father hadn't wanted them to go west, but Ivarr was dead, they weren't listening to his tune, they didn't have to listen to Thorkell's, either.

To get the Volgan's lost sword back from the Cyngael. On his first raid. That would be remembered, it would always be remembered. Bern touched Ingavin's hammer, his father's hammer, at his throat.

There was another part of the verse he'd spoken to his father in the stream; they all knew it, throughout the Erling lands:

Cattle die kinsmen die.
  Every man born will die.
Fierce hearth fires end in ash.
  Fame once won endures ever.

The ships were being unlashed. Bern moved to help. The risen wind was from the east, a message in that. Ingavin's wind, carrying them in the night, dragon-prows on a summer sea.

CHAPTER XII

Jadwina was never quite clear, looking back, whether they received the tidings of the earl's death (she always got his name wrong, but it was difficult to remember things from so long ago) and the slaughtered Erling raiders before or after the evening her life changed—or even that same night, though she didn't think so. It felt as though it had come afterwards. It had been a bad time for her, but she was fairly certain she'd have remembered if it had been that same night.

The troubles had begun a fourteen-night earlier, when Eadyn lost his hand. An accident, an entirely stupid accident, clearing trees with his father, bending a branch for Osca's axe. A clean severing, at the wrist. His life marred, all hope of good fortune spurting from him with his blood. The hand on the grass, fingers still flexed, a thing of its own now. Discarded. A young man, broad-shouldered, fair-haired, picked to marry her, and her own inward choice for that (by Jad's pure grace), turned cripple in a moment's inattention at the edge of wood and scrubland.

He lived. Their cleric, summoned, knew more than most about leechcraft. Eadyn lay in fever for days, his wrist wrapped in a poultice his mother changed at sunrise and sunset. Osca wasn't at the bedside or even at home. He spent those days drinking, swearing, weeping, cursing the god, abusing those who tried to comfort him. What comfort was there under the heavens? He had only the one living son, and a farm that needed Eadyn's strength as his own began to fail.

It was a calamity. Lives turned, lives *ended,* with such moments. The cleric, wisely, kept his distance until Osca had drunk himself into a vomiting stupor and awoke, a day and night later, ashen and heart-scalded. The god had made the world this way, in his unknowable wisdom, the cleric said to the villagers in their small chapel. But it was hard, he conceded. It could be intolerably hard.

Jadwina thought so too. Her own father had shaken his head grimly when he heard the tale. He had politely waited to see if Eadyn would conveniently die, before calling off the proposed match. What else could he do? A cripple was no marriage. He could never swing an axe properly, handle a plough, mend a fence alone, kill a wolf or wild dog. Couldn't even practise with a bow as they were ordered by the king to do now.

It was a sorrow for Eadyn and his family, a lesson for everyone else, as the cleric said, but you didn't have to make it *your* sorrow, too. There were healthy lads in the village, or near enough. You needed to marry daughters usefully. It was a matter of survival. The world, here in the north, or anywhere else probably, wasn't going to make life easy for you.

At some point during that time—it blurred for Jadwina, looking back—Bevin, the smith, had appeared at their door and asked to speak with her father. Gryn had gone walking with him and returned to say that he'd accepted an offer for her.

The younger son of the village smith wasn't the match Eadyn, son of Osca, had been—land was land, after all— but he was better than a one-handed cripple. Jadwina received the tidings and—as best she remembered—she dropped a pitcher on the floor. It might have been on purpose; she couldn't recall. Her father beat her about the back and shoulders, with her mother calling approval. It had been a new-bought pitcher.

Raud, the smith's son, now plighted to her, never even spoke with Jadwina. Not then, at any rate.

Some days later, however, towards twilight, as she was bringing the cow back from the northernmost field, Raud stepped out from a copse by the path. He stood before her. He had come from the forge; there was soot in his clothing and on his face.

"Be wed come harvest," he said, grinning. He had poxed cheeks and long, skinny shanks.

"Not by my will," Jadwina replied, tossing her head.

He laughed. "Wha' matters that? You'll spread legs by will or wi'out."

"Eadyn is two men to your one!" she said. "And you knows it."

He laughed again. "He's one hand to my two. Can't even do this now."

He grabbed at her. Before she could twist away, he had a hand twisted in her hair, spilling her kerchief, and another over her mouth, too tightly for her to bite, or scream. He smelled of ash and smoke. He pulled the hand away quickly and hit her on the side of the head, hard enough for the world to rock and sway. Then he hit her again.

The sun was going down. End of summer. She remembered that. No one on the path, home a long walk from where they were. She couldn't even see the nearest houses of the village.

"Take what's mine now," Raud said. "Get a baby in you, they'll just make me wed you, won' they? What matters that?" She was on the ground by the path, beneath him. He straddled her, a boot on either side, started untying the rope around his trousers, fumbling in his haste. She drew breath to shout. He kicked her in the ribs.

Jadwina gasped, began to weep. It hurt to breathe. He dragged his leggings down around his muddy boots. Lowered himself to his knees then forward onto her. Began pushing, clumsily, at her lower clothes. She hit him, scratching at his face. He swore, then laughed, his hand groped hard at her, down there.

Then his whole body lurched crazily to one side, his head most of all. Jadwina had a confused, frightening sense of wetness. She was in pain, dizzy and terrified. It took her a moment to understand what had happened. Raud's blood was all over her. He'd been hit in the neck from above, behind, by an axe. She looked up.

An axe swung one-handed.

Raud's body, his sex exposed, still erect, his trousers around his ankles, lay sprawled on one side, next to her in the shallow ditch where he'd thrown her down. Instinctively, she shifted away from him. He was, Jadwina saw, already dead. She was afraid she was going to be sick. She put a hand to her side where the worst pain was, then brought it to her face. It came away wet with Raud's blood.

Eadyn, his face ghost-pale, stood above her. She struggled to sit up. Her side felt as if a blade were in it, as if something were broken and sliding within. He stepped back a little. Her cow was behind him, in the grass on the other side of the path, cropping. No sound but that, and the birds flying to branches at end of day; fields and trees, dark green grass, the sun almost down.

"Was out here trying," Eadyn said, finally, gesturing with the axe. "See if I can chop. You know? Saw you."

She seemed able to nod her head.

"Can't do it rightly," he said, lifting the axe a little again, letting it fall. "No good."

Jadwina drew a careful breath, a hand to her side again. She was covered in blood. "Just started, though. You'll get better at it."

He shook his head. "Useless man." She tried not to look at the bandaged stump of his right hand. His good hand, it had been.

"You . . . you were man enough to save me," she said.

He shrugged. "From behind him."

"What matters that?" she said. Her capacity to speak, to think, was coming back. And she had a thought. It frightened her, so she spoke quickly, before fear could take hold. "Lie with me now," she said. "Give me a child. No one else will want me then. You'll have to."

What she saw in him, that moment, in the last fading of the summer daylight, and remembered ever after, was fear, and defeat. It could be read, the way some clerics read words in books.

He shook his head again. "Na, that'll not do. I'm cripple, girl. They'll not wed you to me. And how could I fend for a wife and little ones now?"

"We'll fend the both of us together," she said.

He was silent. The axe—dark with Raud's blood—held in his left hand. "Jad rot it forever," he said finally. "I'm done." He looked at the dead man. "His brothers'll kill me now."

"They'll not that. I'll tell the cleric and reeve what happened here."

"And that'll matter to them?" He laughed, bitterly. "No. I'm away this night, girl. You clean yourself, say nothing. Maybe take a bit of time before they find this. Give me a chance to be gone."

Her heart was aching by then, more than her side, a dull, hard pain, but there was—even in that moment—a part of her that had begun despising him. It was like a death, actually, feeling that.

"Where . . . where will you go?"

"As if I have the least idea," he said. "Jad be with you, girl."

He said that over his shoulder, had already turned away.

He left her there, walked north, back up the grassy path the way that she had come, and then on, beyond the pasture. Jadwina watched until she couldn't see him any more in the twilight. She got herself up, reclaimed her hazel switch, and began leading the cow back home, moving slowly, a hand to her side, leaving a dead man in the grass.

She decided, before she'd reached the first houses, that she wasn't going to listen to Eadyn. He had left her lying there without a backwards glance. They had been pledged to be married.

She went home exactly as she was, Raud's blood on her face and hair and hands, all over her clothing. She saw horror—and curiosity—in people's faces as she took the cow through the village. She kept her head high. Said nothing. They followed her. Of course they followed her. At her door, she told her father and mother, and then the cleric and reeve when they were brought, what had happened, and where. She'd thought she'd be beaten again, but she wasn't. Too many people about.

Men (and boys, and dogs) went running to look. It was well after nightfall that they brought back Raud's body. It was reported how he had been when they'd found him, trousers down, exposed. Two of the older women were instructed by the reeve to examine Jadwina. Behind a door they made her lift her skirts and both of them poked at her and came out, cackling, to report that she was intact.

Her father owned land; the smith was only a smith. There was no one to gainsay her tale. Right there, under torches in front of their door, the reeve declared the matter closed to the king's justice, named the killing a just one. Two of Raud's brothers went north in the morning after Eadyn. They came back without having found any sign of him. Raud was buried in the ground behind the chapel.

And it had been some time during those warm, end-of-summer days that they had learned of the Erling raid and the death of the earl, the king's good friend.

Jadwina hadn't been inclined to care, or listen very much, which is why she was never certain about the course and timing of events. She remembered agitation and excitement, the cleric talking and talking, the reeve riding out and then back. And on one of the days there had been a black billowing of smoke west of them. It turned out to be, they learned, a burning of slain Erlings.

The king himself, it seemed, had been right there, just beyond the trees and the ridges. A battle almost within sight of where they lived. A victory. For those whose lives had not been utterly undone, as Jadwina's had been, it counted as entirely memorable.

Later that same year the smith's wife died, an autumn fever. Two others of the village went to the god as well. Within a fourteen-night of burying his wife, Bevin came to Jadwina's father again, this time for himself. This was the father of the man who had been pledged to her and had assaulted her and been slain for it.

It didn't seem to matter to anyone, certainly not her father. There was a kind of cloud, a stain over Jadwina by then. She was sent to him that same week, to the smithy and the house behind it. The cleric spoke new blessings over them in chapel; they had a cleric who liked to keep abreast of new things. Too much haste, some said of the marriage. Others jested that, with Jadwina's history, her father didn't want to see a third man maimed or killed before getting her off his hands.

No one ever saw Eadyn again, or heard tell of him. Bevin, the smith, as it turned out, was a mild-humoured man. She hadn't expected that in someone so red-faced, and with the sons he had. How could she have expected kindness? They had two children who survived. Jadwina's memories of the year she was wed softened and blurred, overlaid with others as the seasons passed.

In time, she buried her husband; took no other mate. Her sons shared the smithy, after, with their older half-brothers, and she lived with one of them and his wife, tolerably well. As well as such things can ever be, two women in a small house. She was buried herself, when the god called her home, laid in the growing chapel graveyard, next to Bevin, not far from Raud, under a sun disk and her name.

☙

Three things, Alun was thinking, remembering the well-worn triad, *will gladden the heart of a man. Riding to a woman under two moons. Riding to battle, companions at his side. Riding home, after long away.*

He was doing the third, possibly the second. Hadn't thought about the first since his brother died. His heart was not glad.

He saw a sudden branch and ducked. The overgrown path they'd chosen could barely be called such. These woods had no formal name in either tongue, Cyngael or Anglcyn. Men did not enter here, save for the edgings, and only by daylight.

He heard his unwanted companion following. Without turning, Alun said, "There will be wolves in here."

"Or course there will be wolves," Thorkell Einarson said mildly.

"Bears, still, this time of year. Hunting cats. Boars."

"With autumn coming, boars for certain. Snakes."

"Yes. Two kinds, I believe. The green ones are harmless."

They were a fair distance into the forest already, the light entirely gone, even if it might still be twilight outside. Cafall was a shadow ahead of Alun's horse.

"The green ones," Thorkell repeated. Then he laughed—genuine laughter, despite where they were. "How do we tell in the dark?"

"If they bite us and we don't die," Alun replied. "I didn't ask you to come. I told you—"

"You told me to go back. I know. I can't."

This time Alun stopped his horse, the Erling horse Thorkell had found for him. He still hadn't asked about that. They had reached a very small clearing, a little space to face each other. The leaves overhead let a hint of the last evening light come down. It was time for the invocation. He wondered if it had been done before in these woods, if Jad's word had ever reached so far. It seemed to him he felt a humming, just below hearing, but he was aware that that was almost certainly apprehension and no more. There were so many tales.

"Why?" he asked. "Why can't you?"

The other man had also reined his horse. There was just enough light to see his face. He shrugged. "I am neither your servant, nor the cleric's. My life was saved by Lady Enid at Brynnfell and she claimed me as hers. If you are correct, and I believe you are, Ivarr Ragnarson is leading the Jormsvik ships there. I value my life as much as any man, but I gave her my oath. I will try to get back before they do."

"For an oath?"

"For that oath."

There was more, Alun was sure of it. "You understand this is mad? That we have five days, maybe six to survive in these woods?"

"I understand the folly of it better than you do, I suspect. I'm an old man, lad. Trust me, I'm not happy being here."

"Then why—?"

"I answered you. Will you leave it."

The first hint of a temper, strain. Alun's turn to shrug. "I'm not about to fight you, or try to hide. We'll forget rank, though. I think you know more than I do about surviving here." It was easier to say that to this man than to most others, he thought.

"Perhaps a little more. I did bring food."

Alun blinked, and realized, with the words, that his hunger was extreme. He tried to work out the timing. They'd had bread and ale after killing the first Erling party by the stream. Nothing since then. And the *fyrd* had been in the saddle since the middle of the night before.

"Come. Get down," said Thorkell Einarson, as if tracking that thought. "As good a place as any. I need to stretch. I'm old."

Alun dismounted. He'd been a horseman all his life, but his legs were aching. The other man was groping in a saddle pack.

"Can you see my hand?"

"Yes."

"Wedge of cheese. Cold meat coming. I've ale in a flask."

"Jad's blood and grace. When did you . . . ?"

"When we got to the water and saw the ships were gone."

Alun considered this a moment, chewing. "You *knew* I'd do this?"

The other man hesitated. "I knew that I would."

This, too, needed thought. "You were going to come in here alone?"

"Not happily, I promise you."

Alun tore at the chunk of meat the other man passed him, drank thirstily from the offered flask.

"May I ask a question?" The Erling took the ale back.

"Told you, not a servant in here. We need to survive."

"Tell the snakes, the ones that aren't green."

"What's the question?"

"Is this the same wood as north, by Esferth and past it?"

"What? You think I'd be here if there was a break in the trees? Am I a fool?"

"In here? Of course you are a fool. But help me with the question, nonetheless."

A moment, both men silent, then Alun heard his own laughter in that black, ancient wood where the tales he'd known all his life said there were spirits that sought blood and were endlessly angry. Something small skittered, startled by the noise. The dog had gone ahead, now came back to them. Alun gave him some of the meat. He took the ale flask back.

It occurred to Thorkell Einarson, squatting on his haunches beside the young Cyngael, that he hadn't heard the other man laugh before, not once in all their time together, since the night of a spring raid.

Alun said, "You aren't very good at a servant's role, are you? It is the same forest. There's a small valley on this side, I think there's a sanctuary there."

Thorkell nodded. "That's how I remember it, yes." And then, quietly, he added, "So whatever spirit you were with last night might be here as well?"

Alun imagined he felt a wind in his face, though there was none blowing. He was briefly glad of the darkness. He cleared his throat. "I have no idea," he said. "How did you . . . ?"

"I watched you come out of the trees last night. I'm an Erling. My grandmother could see spirits on the roofs of half the homes in our village, summoned them to blight the fields and wells of those she hated. There were enough of those, Ingavin knows. Lad, we can swear an oath to honour the sun god, and wear his disk, but what happens after darkfall? When the sun is down and Jad is under the world, battling?"

"I don't know," Alun said. He still seemed to feel that wind, sense the wood's vibration, so nearly a sound. Five days' journey, maybe more. They were going to die here, he thought. *Three things a brave man remembers at his end . . .*

"None of us knows," Thorkell Einarson said, "but we still have to live through the nights. It is . . . unwise to be so sure we're alone here, whatever the clerics teach. You believe that spirit is kindly disposed?"

Alun took a breath. It was difficult to believe they were speaking of this. He thought of the faerie, shimmering, a light where there was none.

"I believe so."

The other man's turn to hesitate. "You realize that where there is one such power, there may be others?"

"I told you you didn't have to come."

"Yes, you did. Pass the flask. My throat's dry. A sorrow to die with ale to hand and undrunk."

Alun reached the flask across. His calves were sore, the long ride, crouching now. He sat on the grass, wrapped his arms about his knees. "We can't ride all night."

"No. How did you propose to guide yourself, alone?"

"That one I can answer. Think on it."

The other man did. "Ah. The dog."

"He came from Brynnfell. Can find his way home. How were *you* going to do it, alone?"

Thorkell shook his head. "No idea."

"And you thought I was being a fool?"

"You are. So am I. Let us drink to ourselves." Thorkell lifted the flask again, cleared his throat. "Consider sending him ahead? The dog? Ap Hywll would know . . ."

"I did think about it. It seems to make sense to have him with us, and to let him run on alone if we . . ."

"Find a not-green snake or one of the things that are stronger than your spirit and don't like us."

"Should we rest here?" Alun asked. Fatigue was washing over him.

There was an answer given to that question, though not from the man beside him. They heard a sound, movement in the trees.

Larger than a boar, Alun thought, rising, unsheathing his blade. Thorkell was also on his feet, holding his hammer. They stood a moment, listening. Then they heard a different kind of sound.

"Holy Jad," said Alun, a moment later, with considerable feeling.

"I think not, actually," said Thorkell Einarson. He sounded amused. "Not the god. I believe this would be—"

"Be quiet!" said Alun.

The two of them listened, in bemused silence, to a voice, behind them and a little south, moving through the trees where no moonlight could fall. Someone— however improbably—was singing in these woods.

> *The girl for me at the end of the day*
> *Is the one who'd rather kiss than pray,*
> *And the girl for me in the morning light*
> *Is the one who takes and gives delight,*
> *And the girl for me in the blaze of noon*
> *Is the one—*

"Stuff the wailing. We're over here," Thorkell called. "And who knows what else's coming now, the noise you make."

Both men put back their weapons.

Crackling sounds came nearer, branches and leaves, twigs on the forest floor. An oath, as someone collided with something.

"Noise? Wailing?" said Athelbert, son of Aeldred, heir to the Anglcyn throne.

He edged his horse into their small clearing. Straining his eyes, Alun saw that he was rubbing at his forehead. "I hit a branch. Really hard. I also believe I have been insulted. I was singing."

"That what it was?" Alun said.

Athelbert had a sword at his hip, a bow across his back. He dismounted, stood facing the two of them, holding the reins of his horse.

"Sorry," he said ruefully. "To be frank, my sisters and my brother take that same view of my voice. I've decided to leave home, out of shame."

"This," Alun said, "was a bad idea."

"I'm a bad singer," Athelbert replied lightly.

"My lord prince, this is—"

"My lord prince, I know what this is."

Both of them stopped. A moment later, Athelbert was the one who went on. "I know what you are doing. Two men are unlikely to get through this wood alive."

"And three are likely?"

It was Thorkell. He still had that amused tone, Alun realized.

"I didn't actually say that," Athelbert replied. "You do realize where we are? Likelihood? We'll all be killed."

"This is not your concern," Alun said. He forced himself to be gracious. "Generous as the thought might be, my lord, I daresay your royal father—"

"My royal father will have sent outriders after me, as soon as they realized I was gone. They are almost certainly in the trees already, and terrified witless. My father thinks I am . . . irresponsible. There are reasons why he might hold such a view. We'd best move on or they'll find us and say they have to bring me back, and I'll say I won't go, and they'll have to draw weapons against their prince on the orders of their king, which isn't a proper thing to force any man to do, because I'm not going back."

A silence followed this.

"Why?" Thorkell asked finally, the amused tone gone. "Prince Alun is right: this is no Anglcyn quarrel, Erlings raiding west of the Wall."

Alun could see clearly enough to observe Athelbert shaking his head. "That man—Ragnarson?—killed my father's lifelong friend, one of our leaders, a man I knew from childhood. They led a raid into our lands during a summer fair. Word of that will spread. If they get away and—"

Alun's turn to interrupt. "They didn't get away. You killed fifty or sixty of them. A ship's worth. Drove the rest from your shores, running from you. Word of *that* will spread, to the glory of King Aeldred and his people. Why are you here, Prince Athelbert?"

It was almost impenetrably black now, even in the clearing, the trees in summer leaf blocking the stars. Cafall had stood up too, the dark grey dog virtually invisible, a presence at Alun's knee.

After a long time, Athelbert spoke. "I heard what you said, before, by the river. What you believe they intend to do. The farmhouse, women there, ap Hywll, the sword . . ."

"And so? It is still not your—"

"Listen to me, Cyngael! Is *your* father the haven and home of all virtues in the world? Does he rise from a fevered sickbed to make a slaughter of his enemies? Does he translate medical texts from Jad-cursed *Trakesian*? By the time he was my age," said Athelbert of the Anglcyn, speaking with great clarity, "my father had survived a winter hiding in a swamp, had broken out, rallied our scattered people, and retaken his own slain father's realm. To the undying glory of King Aeldred and our land."

He stopped, breathing hard, as if he'd been exerting himself. They heard wings overhead, flapping from one tree to another.

"You are unhappy with him for being a good man?" Thorkell said.

"That is not what I am saying."

"No? Perhaps not. Help me then, my lord. You want some of that same glory," said Einarson. "That is it? Well, that is fairly sought. What young man with a beating heart does not?"

"This one!" said Alun sharply. "You both listen to *me*. I have no interest in any of that. I need to get to Brynnfell before the Erlings. That is all. The coastal path goes to Arberth and it takes almost four days, at speed, then four or five more to get north to Brynn's farm. I *did* that journey this spring, with my brother. The Erlings know exactly where they are going because Ragnarson's with them. No warning we send along the coast will beat them to Brynnfell. I'm here because I have no choice. I'll say it again: I didn't even *want* you to come," he said, turning to Thorkell.

"And I'll say it again, though I shouldn't have to: I am the servant of Lady Enid, wife to Brynn ap Hywll," the Erling replied calmly. "If Ivarr gets to that farm she'll die in the muck of her own yard, hacked apart, and so will any others there, including her daughters. I have *done* such raids. I know what happens. She saved my life. I swore an oath. Ingavin and Jad both know I have not kept every promise I made, but this time I will try."

He was silent. After a moment Alun nodded. "That's you. But this prince is just . . . chasing his father. He's—"

"This prince," said Thorkell, "is entitled to make his own choices in life, reckless or otherwise, as much as we are. A third blade is welcome as a woman in a cold bed. But if he is right and outriders are following him, we need to move."

"He should go back," Alun repeated, stubbornly. "This is not his—"

"Talk to me if you have anything to say. You've said *that* three times," Athelbert snapped. "Make a triad of it, why don't you? Set it to music! I heard you each time. I am not turning back. Will you really refuse aid? Even if it might save lives? Is it so certain you aren't thinking of glory?"

Alun blinked at that. "I swear by Jad's name, it is certain. Don't you see? I do not believe it is *possible* to do this. I expect to die here. We have no idea where water is, or food, what path we might find, or not find. Or what will find us. There are tales of this place going back four hundred years, my lord Athelbert. I have a reason to risk death. You do not."

"I know those stories. The same tales are told on this side. If you go back far enough, we used to sacrifice animals in the valley north of here, to whatever was in the wood."

"If you go back far enough, it wasn't animals," Alun said.

Athelbert nodded his head, unruffled. "I know that, too. It is not for you to judge my reasons. Say that you are here because of your brother, and I because of my father. Leave it and let's go."

Alun still hesitated. Then he shrugged. He'd done what he could. With a hint of wryness in his tone, one that a dead brother would have recognized, he said, "If that is so, this one here breaks the pattern." He nodded towards Thorkell.

"Not really," said the Erling. They heard his amusement. "I'm of a piece with you, in truth. Tell you about it later. Let's move, before we're found and it gets difficult."

"Truly. Some of the outriders sing worse than I do," Athelbert said.

"Jad defend us, if so," said Alun. He reached a hand down, into the fur of the dog's neck. "Cafall, will you lead us home, my heart?"

And with those words Athelbert realized that they weren't as completely without resources as he'd thought, riding into the spirit wood after the two of them, panic and determination warring within him.

They had the dog. Amazingly, it might matter.

The three of them remounted and carefully picked their way out of the small glade, bent low over the horses' necks to stay under branches if they could. They heard sounds as they went. The noises of a wood at night. Owls calling, wingflap of another bird overhead, wood snapping to left and right, sometimes loudly, a scrabbling along branches, scurry, wind. What else each of them heard, or thought he heard, he kept to himself.

Men were avoiding the king, Ceinion saw. He could understand that. Aeldred, philosopher, seeker after the learning of the old schools, shaper of calm devices and stratagems, a man controlled enough to have feasted the Erling who'd blood-eagled his father, was in a rage like a forest fire.

As he'd stalked away across the stones of the beach where the boats had been, his fury had been so intense, it had been as if there were a wave of heat coming off his body. If you were a physician, you feared for a man in such condition; if you were his subject, you feared for yourself.

The king was still down the strand in the gathering dark. Standing close to the crashing surf in the wind, as if together wind and waves might cool him, Ceinion thought. He knew that wasn't going to happen. They had heard from the outriders sent out. Prince Athelbert had gone into the woods.

Fear plainly visible in those reporting this; four exhausted men astride their horses, waiting for the command they would not dare refuse, and could hardly bear to imagine. It never came.

Instead, Aeldred had stood, fighting for control, and then had turned on his heel and gone off to where he was now, his back to all of them, facing the darkening sea under the first stars in the vault of the sky. The blue moon was rising.

Ceinion went after him.

No one else would do it, and the cleric was aware of terrors clinging to what remained of this day, building within himself. He felt trammelled, as in a fisherman's net of sorrows.

Deliberately, he let his approach be heard, scuffling at stones. Aeldred did not turn, stayed as he had been, gazing out at the water. Far off, beyond sight but not sailing, were the shores of Ferrieres. Carloman had taken the coast back from the Karchites in the spring, after two years of campaigning. A disputed, precarious shoreline, that one. It always had been. Everything was precarious, he thought. He was remembering fires in the farmyard at Brynnfell.

"Did you know," said Aeldred, not turning around, "that in Rhodias in the days of its glory there were baths where three hundred men could be bathing in cool water, and as many in the heated pool, and as many again lying at their ease with wine and food?"

Ceinion blinked. The king's voice was conversational, informative. They might have been, themselves, reclining at their ease somewhere. He said, carefully, "My lord. I did hear of such. I have never been there, of course. Did you see this yourself, when you went with your royal father?"

"The ruins of them. The Antae sacked Rhodias four hundred years ago. The baths didn't survive. But you could see . . . what they had been able to make. There are ruins here, too, of course, from when the Rhodians came this far. Perhaps I will show you, some day."

Ceinion thought he could discern the shape of what this was about. Men responded so differently to grief.

"Life was . . . otherwise, then," he agreed, being cautious. It was difficult; he was seeing fires in his mind. The breeze was strong here, but it was pleasant, not cold. It was from the east.

"I was eight years old when my father took me on pilgrimage," Aeldred went on. The same even, casual tone. He still hadn't turned around. It occurred to Ceinion to wonder how the king had known who it was who'd come walking over to him. His particular footfall? Or a simpler awareness that no one else would approach, just then?

"I was excited and impatient, of course," Aeldred went on, "but what you just said . . . that life was otherwise for them . . . that was clear to me, even when I was young. On the way, in one of the cities in the north of Batiara, where the Antae had their own court, we saw a chapel complex. Four or five buildings. In one of them there was a mosaic of the court of Sarantium. The Strategos-Emperor. Leontes."

"Valerius III. They called him 'the Golden.'"

Aeldred nodded. "*There* was a king," he said. A wave crashed and withdrew, grating along stones. "You could see it on that wall. His court around him. The clothing they wore, the jewellery, the . . . *room* they were in. The room they had. In their lives. To make things. I've never forgotten it."

"He was a great leader, by all accounts," Ceinion agreed.

He was letting this unfold. At the back of his mind, his pulse rapid with it, was the awareness of ships, and the east wind.

"I've read one or two chronicles, yes. Pertennius, Colodias. On the other wall I remember another mosaic, less good, I think. An earlier emperor, the one before him. He rebuilt the sanctuary, I think. He was there too, the opposite wall. I remember I wasn't as taken. It looked different."

"Different artisans, very likely," the cleric said.

"Kings depend on that, do you think? The quality of their artisans."

"Not while they live, my lord. After, perhaps, for how they are remembered."

"And what will men remember about—?" Aeldred broke off, resumed again, a different tone. "We shouldn't be forgetting his name," he murmured. "He built Jad's Sanctuary in Sarantium, Ceinion. How are we forgetting?"

"Forgetting is part of our lives, my lord. Sometimes it is a blessing, or we could never move beyond loss."

"This is different."

"Yes, my lord."

"What I was saying . . . about the baths. We have no *space,* no time to make such things."

He had been saying this, Ceinion remembered, at the high table after the banquet last night. Only last night. He said, "Baths and mosaics are not allowed to all of us, my lord."

"I know that. Of course I know. Is it . . . unworthy to feel their absence?"

This was not the conversation he'd been expecting to have. Ceinion thought about it. "I think . . . it is *necessary* to feel that. Or we will not desire a world that lets us have them."

Aeldred was silent, then, "Do you know, I always intended to take Athelbert, his brother, too, to Rhodias. The same journey. To see it again myself, kiss the ring of the Patriarch. Offer my prayers in the Great Sanctuary. I wanted my sons to see it and remember, as I do."

"You were fighting wars, my lord."

"My father took me."

"My lord, I am of an age with you, and have lived through the same times. I do not believe you have anything for which to reproach yourself."

Aeldred turned then. Ceinion saw his face in the twilight.

"Alas, but you are wrong, my lord cleric. I have so much in the way of reproach for myself. My wife wishes to leave me, and my son has gone."

They had arrived. Every man had his own path to such places. Ceinion said, "The queen is seeking to go home to the god, my lord. Not to leave you."

Aeldred's mouth crooked a little. "Unworthy, good cleric. Clever without being wise. Cyngael wordplay, I'd call it."

Ceinion flushed, which didn't happen often. He bowed his head. "We cannot always be wise, my lord. I am the first to say that I am not."

Aeldred's back was to the sea now. He said, "I could have let Athelbert lead the *fyrd* last night. He could have done it. I didn't need to be here."

"Did he ask for it?"

"That is not his way. But he could have dealt with this. I had just come back from my fever. I had no need to ride. I should have left it to him." His hands were fists, Ceinion saw. "I was so angry. Burgred . . ."

"My lord—"

"Do you not understand? My son is dead. Because I did not let—"

"It is *not* for us to say what will be, my lord! We do not have that wisdom. This much I do know."

"In *that* wood? Ceinion, Ceinion, you know where he went! No man has ever—"

"Perhaps no man has tried. Perhaps it was time to lay to rest old fears, in Jad's name. Perhaps a great good will come of this. Perhaps . . ." He trailed off. There was no great good that he could see coming. His words were false in his own ears. There was that image of burning in him, here by the cool sea, as the moon rose.

Aeldred was looking closely at him now. He said, "I have been greatly unjust. You are my friend and guest. These are my own concerns, and you have a grief here. There is a reason Prince Owyn's son went into the spirit wood. My sorrow, cleric. We were too slow, riding. We needed to be here before the ships cast off."

Ceinion was silent. Then he said, as he ought to have said at the beginning, with the dark coming on, "Pray with me, my lord. It is time for the rites."

"There is no piety in my heart," said Aeldred. "I am not in a state to address the god."

"We are never in a state to do so. It is the way of our lives in his world. One of the things for which we ask mercy is that inadequacy." He was on familiar ground, now, but it didn't feel that way.

"And our anger?"

"That too, my lord."

"Bitterness?"

"That too."

The king turned back to the sea. He was still as a monolith, as a standing stone planted on the strand by those who lived here long ago, and believed in darker gods and powers than Jad or the Rhodian pantheon: in sea, in sky, in the black woods behind them.

Ceinion said, again, "We must not presume to know what will come."

"My heart is dark. He . . . should not have done what he did, Athelbert. He is not without . . . duties."

They were back to the son. Not a child any more.

"My lord, the son of a great father might need to shape his own way in the world. If he is to follow you and be more than only Aeldred's child."

The king turned again. He said, "Dying allows no way in the world. They cannot go through that wood."

The cleric let his own voice gain force. A lifetime of experience. So many conversations with the bereaved and the afraid. "My lord, I can tell you that Alun ab Owyn is as capable a man as I know. The Erling . . . is far more than a servant. And I watched Prince Athelbert this past night and day, and marvelled at him. Now I will honour his courage."

"Ah! And you will say this to his mother, when we come back to Esferth? How comforting she will find it!"

Ceinion winced. Behind them, men were gathering wood, lighting night fires on the beach. They would stay until morning. The *fyrd* would be exhausted, ravenous, but they would be feeling pride, deep satisfaction at what they had done. The Erlings were driven off, fleeing them, and threescore of the raiders were dead on Anglcyn soil. The tale would run, would cross these dark waters to Ferrieres, Karch, east to Vinmark itself, and beyond.

For Aeldred and the Anglcyn this could be called a triumphant day, worthy of harp song and celebration after the mourning for an earl. For the Cyngael, it might be otherwise.

"Pray with me," he said again.

There must have been something in his voice, an edge of need. Aeldred stared at him in the last of the light. The wind blew.

It could carry the Erlings tonight. Ceinion could see them in the eye of his mind, dragon-prows knifing black water, rising and falling. Vengeful men aboard. He had lived through such raids, so many times, so many years. He could see Enid, fire at the edges of his vision, pushing inward, as Brynnfell burned and she died.

Always, since his wife had been laid in the ground behind his own sanctuary in Llywerth, there had been that one thing for which he never prayed: the lives of those he loved. He could *see* her, though—all of them at Brynnfell—and the ships in the water like blades, approaching.

Aeldred's gaze was unsettling, as if his thoughts were open to the king. He wasn't ready for that. His role was to offer comfort here.

Aeldred said, "I cannot send the Drengest ships to catch them, friend. They will be too far behind by the time word reaches the *burh,* and if we are wrong, and the Erlings do *not* go west . . ."

"I know it," Ceinion said. Of course he knew. "We aren't even allies, lord. Your soldiers on the Rheden Wall are there against Cyngael raids . . ."

"To keep you out, yes. But that isn't it. I would do this, after last night. But my ships are too new, our seamen learning each other and the boats. They might be able to block the lanes if the Erlings turn home tonight, but—"

"But they cannot catch them going west. I know it."

No words for a time. Ships in his mind, out there somewhere. The beat and withdraw of surf, sound of it, sound of men behind them up the strand, noises of a camp, wind in the gathering night. *Three things the wise man ever fears: a woman's fury, a fool's tongue, dragon-prows.*

"Brynn ap Hywll killed the Volgan, Ceinion. He and his band are very great fighters."

"Brynn is old," Ceinion said. "So are most of his band. That battle was twenty-five years ago. They will have no warning. They may not even be there now. Your men say there were five ships beached here. You know how many men that means, even without those you killed."

"What shall I say?"

Somehow it had been turned around. He had walked over to give comfort. Perhaps he had; perhaps for some men this was the only access they had to being eased.

"Nothing," he said.

"Then we'll pray." Aeldred hesitated, a thinking pause, not an uncertain one. "Ceinion, we will do what we can. A ship to Owyn in Cadyr. They'll sail to him under a truce flag with a letter from me and one from you. Tell him what his son is doing. He might cut off an Erling party on its way back to their ships, if they do go to your shores. And I'll send word north to the Rheden Wall. They can get a message across, if someone is there to receive it . . ."

"I have no idea," Ceinion said.

He didn't. What happened in those lands around the Wall was murky and fog-shrouded, beyond the power and grasp of princes. The valleys and the black hills kept their secrets. He was thinking about something else. *On their way back to the ships.*

If they were doing that, the Erlings, it would be over at Brynnfell. And here he was, knowing it, *seeing* it, unable to do more than . . . unable to do anything. He knew why Alun had gone into the forest. Standing still was very nearly intolerable, it could shatter the heart.

He would pray for Athelbert, and for Owyn's son in the wood, but not for those he most dearly loved. He'd done that once, prayed for her with all the gathered force of his being, holding her in his arms, and she had died.

He was aware of Aeldred's gaze. Told himself to be worthy of his office. The king had lost a lifelong friend and his son was gone.

"They may get through . . . in the forest," he said, again.

Aeldred shook his head, but calmly now. "By the mercy and grace of Jad, I have another son. I was a younger son as well, and my brothers died."

Ceinion looked at the other man, then beyond him at the sea. On that windblown strand he made the sun disk gesture that began the rites. The king knelt before him. Down along the beach where the fires were, the men of the *fyrd* saw this and, one by one, sank to their knees to share the evening invocation, spoken in that hour when Jad of the Sun began his frozen journey under the world to battle dark powers and malign spirits, keeping as many of them as possible away from his mortal children until the light could come to them again, at dawn.

Keeping most of them away. Not all.

It was not the way of things in the world that men and women could ever be entirely shielded from what might seek and find them in the dark.

CHAPTER XIII

Given what followed, it might have been a mistake to stop for what remained of the night, but at the time there hadn't seemed to be much choice.

All three men were hardened and fit and two of them were young, but they'd been awake for two days and nights and in the saddle. In this forest, Thorkell had judged it more dangerous to keep moving in exhaustion, tired horses stumbling, than to stop. They could be attacked as easily while moving, in any case.

He made it easier for the others, asking a respite for himself, though he undermined that somewhat by offering to take the first watch by the pool they found. They filled their flasks. Water was important. Food would become a problem when his small supply ran out. They hadn't decided if they would hunt here; probably they'd have to, though Thorkell knew what his grandmother would have said about killing in a spirit wood.

All three of them drank deeply; the horses did the same. The water was cool and sweet. There was no thought of making a fire. Athelbert hadn't eaten at all; Thorkell gave him bread in the darkness, some of the cold meat. They tethered the horses. Then both princes, Anglcyn and Cyngael, fell asleep almost immediately. Thorkell approved. You needed to be able to do that; it was a skill, a task, your turn on watch would come soon enough.

He stretched out his legs, leaned back against a tree, his hammer across his lap. He was weary but not sleepy.

It was very black, sight was next to useless. He would have to listen, mostly. The dog came over, sank down beside him, head on paws. He could see the faint gleam of its eyes. He didn't actually like this dog, but he had a sense that there would be no hope of achieving this journey without Alun ab Owyn's hound.

He made his muscles relax. Shifted his neck from side to side, to ease the pain there. So many years, so many times he'd done this: night watch in a dangerous place. He'd thought he was through with it. No need to be on guard behind an oak door on Rabady Isle. Life twisted on you—or you twisted it for yourself. No man knew his ending, or even the next branching of his path.

Branching paths. In the quiet of the wood, his mind went back. That often happened when you were awake alone at night.

Once, in fog, on a raid in Ferrieres, he and Siggur and a small band of others had found themselves separated from the main party on a retreat to the coast. They'd gone too far inland for safety, but Siggur had been drinking steadily on that raid (so had Thorkell, truth be told) and they'd been reckless with it. They'd also been young.

They literally stumbled upon a sanctuary they hadn't even known about: a chapel and outbuildings hidden in a knife of a valley east of Champieres. They saw the chapel lights through mist. A sanctuary of the Sleepless Ones, at their endless vigil. There'd have been no lights to see them by, otherwise.

They attacked, screaming Ingavin's name, in the dense, blurred dark. Foolish beyond any words it was, for they were being pursued by the young Prince Carloman, who'd already proven himself a warrior, and it was not a time to be staying to raid, let alone with a dozen men.

But that branching path that had separated them from the body of their company made Thorkell Einarson's fortune. They killed twenty clerics and their cudgel-bearing servants in that isolated valley, seeing terror flare whitely in men's eyes before they fled from the northmen.

Laughing, blood-soaked and blood-drunk, they set fire to the outbuildings and took away all the sanctuary treasure they could carry. Those treasures were astonishing. That hidden complex turned out to be a burial place of royalty, and what they discovered in the recesses of side chapels and surrounding tombs was dazzling.

Siggur had found his sword there.

Being Siggur, he decreed, when they made their way back to the ships and found the others, that this portion of the raid's plunder belonged only to those who had been there. And being Siggur, he had no trouble enforcing his will. Every young man in Vinmark wanted to be one of the Volgan's shipmates in those days. They'd already begun using that name for him.

Thorkell supposed, sitting in darkness, entirely sober, that it could be fairly said that that friendship had shaped his life. Siggur had been very young when they'd started raiding, and Thorkell had been even younger, in awe that such a man seemed to consider him a companion, want him at his side, on a battlefield or tavern bench.

Siggur had never been a thoughtful, considering sort. He'd led by leading, by being at the front of every assault: faster, stronger, a little bit wilder than anyone else—except perhaps for the occasional *berserkir* who'd join them at times. He'd drunk more than any of them, awake and upright after the rest were snoring at benches or sprawled among the rushes of an ale-room floor.

Thorkell remembered—it was a well-known tale—the morning Siggur had come out of an inn with another raider, a man named Leif, after a full night of drinking, and challenged the other to a race—along the oars of their ships, moored side by each in the harbour.

Nothing like it had ever been done before. No one had ever *thought* of such a thing. Amid laughter and wagers flying, they roused and assembled their bleary-eyed men, had them take their places on board and level their oars straight out. Then, as the sun came up, the two leaders began a race, up one side of their ships, leaping from oar to oar, and back down the other side, swinging across by using the dragon-prows.

Leif Fenrikson didn't even make it to the prow.

Siggur went around his ship twice, at speed. That was Siggur at his best: blazoning his own prowess, and also showing that of his chosen companions, for a wobbling or uneven oar would have made him fall, no doubting it. Twice around he ran that course, with Thorkell and every other man on board holding steady for him as he raced alone, bare-chested, around and around them, laughing for the joy of being young and what he was, in morning's first light.

It changed over the years, for so much of youth cannot linger, and ale can bring rage and bitterness as easily as laughter and fellowship. Thorkell realized at some point that Siggur Volganson was never going to stop drinking and raiding, that he couldn't. That there was nothing in Ingavin's offered middle-world for him but cresting white foam waves in sunlight or storm, appearing out of the sea to beach the ships and ride or run inland to burn and kill. It was the *doing* that mattered. Gold, silver, gems, women, the slaves they took—these were only the world's reasons. Access to glory.

Salt spray and lit fires and testing himself again and again, endlessly, those were the things that drove him all his too-short life.

Never saying a word about these thoughts, Thorkell rowed and fought beside him until the end, which came in Llywerth, as everyone knew. Siggur had heard that the Cyngael were gathering a force to meet his ships, and had led them ashore regardless, for the joy of battling what might be there.

They were outnumbered there by the sea, a host assembled from each of the Cyngael's warring provinces. He offered single combat to them, a challenge hurled at all three princes of the Cyngael but taken up by a young man who was no prince at all. And Brynn ap Hywll, big and hard and sober as a Jad-mad cleric on a fasting retreat, had altered the northlands entirely by killing Siggur Volganson on that strand—and taking the sword he'd carried since the raid by Champieres.

It was the death Siggur had always sought. Thorkell knew it, even then, that same day. The only ending Siggur could have imagined. The infirmities of age, sober governing, kingship . . . could not even be conceived. But by then Thorkell already knew it was not his own idea of a life and its iron-swift ending. He'd yielded to the Cyngael, in a sudden stunned emptiness. In time he made his escape, for servitude wasn't his vision of existence either. He crossed the Wall and the Anglcyn lands and then autumn seas home. And then he *made* a home. It was his share of the gems and gold carried away from that chanced-upon valley in Ferrieres that bought him land and a farm on Rabady, in the year he decided it was time.

Rabady Isle was as good a place as any, and better than most, to shape a second life. He found a wife (and no man, living or dead, ever heard him say a word against her), had the two daughters, then his boy. Married the girls off when they were of age, and well enough, across on the mainland. Watched the boy—clever and with some spirit—as he grew. He did some more raiding in those years, chose ships and companions and landings. Salt got in the blood, the Erlings said. The sea was hard

to leave behind you. But no wintering over for him, no
grand designs of conquest. Sober captains, neatly
planned journeys.

Siggur was dead; Thorkell wasn't going back to that
time. He crossed the seas for what there was in it, for
what he could bring home. No man would have said he
was other than prosperous, Thorkell Einarson of Rabady
Isle, once a companion of the Volgan himself. A good-
enough life, with a hearth and a bed at the end, it
seemed, not a blade-death on a distant shore.

No man living knew his end.

Here he was, overseas again, in a wood where no man
should be. And how had that come to pass? The oath
sworn to ap Hywll's wife, yes, but he'd broken oaths over
the years. He'd done so when he first escaped the
Cyngael, hadn't he, after surrendering?

He could have found a way to do the same thing here.
Could do it right now. Kill these two sleeping princes—
in a place where they'd be *expected* to die, where no one
would ever find them—make his way back out of the
wood, wait for the *fyrd* to go north, as they surely would,
start across country to Erlond, where his own people had
settled. In a still-forming colony like that one there
would be many men with stories they didn't want told.
That was how a people's boundaries expanded, how they
moved on from starting points. Questions didn't get
asked. You could make a new life. Again.

He shook his head, to clear it, order his mind. He was
tired, not thinking well. He didn't *have* to kill the other
two. Could just rise up now, while they slept, start back
east. He snorted softly, amused at himself. That still
wasn't right. He didn't even need to sneak away. Could
wake them, bid farewell, invoke Jad's blessing on the two
of them (and Ingavin's, inwardly). Alun ab Owyn had
told him to leave. He didn't have to be here at all. Except

for the one thing. The awareness that lay under the folly of this night like a seed in hard spring ground.

His son was on those dragon-ships, and he was there because Thorkell had killed a man in a tavern a little more than a year ago.

If you were a particular kind of man (Thorkell wasn't) you could probably throw away a good deal of time thinking about fathers and sons; time better spent with an ale flask and honest dice. He couldn't truthfully say he'd put his mind very often to the boy over the years on Rabady. He'd taught him something of fighting, a father owed that duty. If pressed he'd have pointed to a house, land, a position on the isle. Bern was to have had all those when his father died, and wasn't that enough? Wasn't it more than Thorkell had ever had?

He didn't carry many memories of the two of them together as the boy grew up. Some men liked to talk, spin tales at their own hearth or a tavern's—spin them so far from truth you could laugh. His first tavern killing had come about because he *had* laughed at someone doing that. Thorkell wasn't a tale-spinner, never had been. A man's tongue could bring him trouble more quickly than anything else. He kept his counsel, guarded memories. If others in Rabady told the boy tales about his father—truth or lies—well, Bern would learn to sort those for himself, or he wouldn't. No one had taken Thorkell in hand as a boy and taught him how you handled yourself when you came ashore in a thunderstorm on rocks and found armed men waiting for you.

Sitting in that wood that lay like a locked barrier between Cyngael lands and Anglcyn, awake while two young men slept, he did find himself recalling—unexpectedly—an evening long ago. A summer's twilight, mild as a maiden. The boy—eight summers old, ten?—

had come out with him while he repaired a door on the barn. Bern had carried his father's tools, Thorkell seemed to remember, had been amusingly proud to do so. He'd fixed the door then they'd walked somewhere—he didn't remember where, the boundaries of their land—and for some reason he'd told Bern the story of the raid when the Anglcyn royal guard had trapped them too far from the sea.

He really didn't tell many of the old tales. Maybe that's why the evening was with him. The scent of the summer flowers, a breeze, the rock—he remembered now, he'd been leaning against the rock at their northern boundary, the boy looking up at him as he listened, so intent it could make you smile. One evening, one story. They'd walked back to the house, after. No more to it than that. Bern wouldn't even recall the evening, he knew. Nothing of any meaning had taken place.

Bern was bearded and grown. Their land was gone; an exile's house always went to someone else. You could say the boy had made his own choice, but you could also say Thorkell had taken choices away from him, put him in a circumstance where a poisonous serpent like Ivarr Ragnarson might think through whose son this was and take vengeance for what had happened at Brynnfell. You could say his father had put him on that branching path.

Even so, you might even find a reason to chuckle about all of this tonight, if that was the way your humour worked. All you needed to do was think about it. Consider the three of them in this wood. Alun ab Owyn was really here, more than a little maddened, because of a dead brother. Athelbert had come because of his father—the need to make *proof* of himself in Aeldred's eyes and his own. And Thorkell Einarson, exiled from Rabady, was—truthfully—in this forest for his son.

Someone should make a song of it, he thought, shaking his head. He spat into the darkness. He was too tired to laugh, but felt like it, a little.

A small sound. The grey dog had lifted his head, seemed to be watching him. He really was weary, but it almost seemed as if the dog were tracking his thoughts. An unsettling animal, more to it than you'd expect.

He had no idea which way the Jormsvik ships were going, none of them did. This desperate, foolish journey might be entirely unnecessary. You had to come to terms with that. You could be dying for no reason at all. Well, what of that? Reason or no reason, you were just as dead. He'd already lived longer than he'd expected to.

He heard a different sound.

The dog again; Cafall had risen, was standing rigidly, head lifted. Thorkell blinked in surprise. Then the animal whimpered.

And that sound, from that source, frightened him beyond words. He scrambled to his feet. His heart was pounding even before he, too, caught the smell.

That smell first, then sounds, he never saw a thing. The other two men rose, jerked from sleep at the first loud crashing, as if pulled upright like toys on a string. Athelbert began swearing; both unsheathed their swords.

None of them could see anything at all. It was black beyond power of sight to penetrate, stars and moon blocked by the encircling trees and their green-black summer leaves. The pool beside them dark, utterly still.

Such pools, Thorkell thought, rather too late, were where the creatures that ruled the night came to drink, or hunt.

"Jad's holy blood," whispered Athelbert, "what is that?"

Thorkell, had he been less afraid, might have made the easy, profane jest. Because it *was* blood they smelled. And flesh: pungent, rotting, like a kill left in the sun. A smell of earth, too, underneath, heavy, loamy, an animal odour with all of these.

Another sound, sharp in the black, something crack-ing: a small tree, a branch. Athelbert swore again. Alun had not yet spoken. The dog whimpered again, and Thorkell's hand on his hammer began to shake. One of the horses tossed its head and whinnied loudly. No secret to their presence now, if ever there had been.

"Stand close," he snapped, under his breath, though there was hardly a reason to be quiet now.

The other two came over. Alun still had his sword out. Athelbert sheathed his now, took his bow, notched an arrow. There was nothing to be seen, nowhere to shoot. Something fell heavily, north of them. Whatever this was, it was large enough to knock over trees.

And it was in that moment that Thorkell had an image burst within his mind and lodge there, as if rooted. His jaw clenched, to stop himself from crying out.

He had been a fighter almost all his life, had seen brain matter and entrails spilled to lie slippery on sodden ground, had watched a woman's face burn away, melting to bone. He'd seen blood-eaglings, a Karchite hostage torn apart between whipped horses, and never flinched, even when he was sober. These were the northlands, life was what it was. Hard things happened. But his hands were trembling now like an old man's. He actually wondered if he was going to fall. He thought of his grandmother, these long years dead, who had known of such things as the creature out there in the night must be, perhaps even its name.

"Ingavin's blind eye! Kneel!" he rasped, the words forming themselves, forced from him. But when he looked over he saw that the other two were already kneel-ing on that dark ground by the pool. The smell from beyond the glade was overpowering, you could gag or retch; Thorkell apprehended something hideous and immense, ancient, not to be in any way confronted by three men, frail with mortality, in a place where they should not be.

In terror then, weariness entirely gone, Thorkell looked at the shapes of the two men kneeling beside him, and he made a decision, a choice, took a path. The gods called you to themselves—wherever and whatever the gods might be—as it pleased them to do so. Men lived and died, knowing this.

He stayed on his feet.

IN ALL OF US, fear and memory interweave in complex, changing ways. Sometimes it is the thing unseen that will linger and appall long afterwards. Sliding into dreams from the blurred borders of awareness, or emerging, perhaps, when we stand alone, on first waking, at the fence of a farmyard or the perimeter of an encampment in that misty hour when the idea of morning is not quite incarnate in the east. Or it can assail us like a blow in the bright shimmer of a crowded market at midday. We do not ever move entirely beyond what has brought us mortal terror.

Alun would never know it, for it was not a thing that could be shared in words, but the image, the *aura* he had in his mind as he sank to his knees, was exactly what Thorkell Einarson apprehended within himself, and Athelbert was aware of the same thing in the blackness of that glade.

The smell, to Alun, was death. Decay, corruption, that which had been living and was no longer so, not for a long time, and yet was moving as it rotted, crashing in some vast bulk through trees. He had a sense of a creature larger than the woods should, by rights, have held. His heart hammered. Blessed Jad of Light, the god behind the sun: was he not to defend his children from terrors such as this, whatever it was?

He was drenched in sweat. "I'm . . . I'm sorry," he stammered to Athelbert beside him. "This is my doing, my mistake."

"Pray," was all the Anglcyn said.

Alun did so, choking on the rotting stench that filled the grove. He saw Cafall trembling, ahead of him. The horses were steadier, strangely. One had whinnied; now they stood transfixed, statues, as if unable to move or make a sound. And he remembered how he and a different horse had been immobilized like that inside another pool in another wood when the queen of the faeries had passed by.

This was, he knew, another creature from that spirit world. What else could it be? Massive, carrying the odour of decaying animal and death. Not like the faeries. This was . . . something beyond them. "Get *down*!" he said to Thorkell.

The Erling had not knelt, didn't turn his head. Afterwards, Alun would have a thought about that, but in that moment whatever it was that bulked beyond the clearing roared aloud.

The trees shook. It seemed to Alun, ears and mind blasted by immensity of sound, that the stars above the forest had to be swinging in their courses like carried censers in a wind.

Almost deafened, his hands in helpless spasm, he stared into the blank night and waited for this death to claim them. Cafall was on his belly, flat to the ground. Beside the dog, still on his feet, Thorkell Einarson took his hammer and—moving slowly, as if in some dream Alun was having, or pushing into a gale—he laid the shaft across both his palms and he stepped *towards* the sound, and then he set the hammer down, carefully, an offering upon the grass.

Alun didn't understand. He didn't understand anything beyond terror and the awareness of their transgression and the engulfing power just out of sight.

Thorkell spoke then, in the Erling tongue and, his ears still ringing, Alun yet understood enough to hear him say, "We seek only passage, lord. Only that. Will harm no living creature of the wood, if it be thy will to grant us leave." And then there was something else, spoken more softly, and Alun did not hear it.

There came a second roaring, even louder than the first, whether in reply or entirely oblivious to the feeble words of a mortal man, and it seemed to those in the glade as if that noise could flatten trees.

It was Athelbert, of the three of them, who thought he heard another thing within that sound, woven into it. He never put it into words, then or after, but what he sensed while he cowered, stuttering prayers in the gut-harrowing certainty of dying, was pain. Something older than he could even attempt to fathom. The downward reach of his soul didn't go deep enough for that. He heard it, though, and had no idea why this was allowed.

There was no third roaring.

Alun had been waiting for it, instinctively, but then, in the silence, it occurred to him that triads, things in threes, were a shaping of bards, a mortal conceit, a way of the Cyngael, not a grounded truth of the spirit world.

He would take that, with some other things, away from that glade. For it seemed they were going to be allowed to leave. The silence continued. It grew, rippled, reclaimed the woods around. None of them moved. The stars did, ceaselessly, far above, and the blue moon was still rising, climbing the long track laid out for it in the sky. Time does not pause, for men or beasts, though it might seem to us to have stopped at some moments, or we might wish it to do so at others, to suspend a shining, call back a gesture or a blow, or someone lost.

The dog stood up.

THORKELL WAS STILL SHIVERING. The odour was gone, that smell of maggot-eaten meat and fur and old blood. He felt sweat drying on his skin, cold in the night. He found himself eerily calm. He was thinking, in fact, of how many people he had killed in his raiding years. Another in an alley last night, once a shipmate. And of all of them, named or nameless, known, or seen only in the red moment his hammer or axe blade slew them, the one he so much wanted back, the moment he'd reclaim from time if he could, was Nikar Kjellson's killing in the tavern at home a year ago.

In the otherworldly stillness of this glade, he could very nearly *see* himself going out through the low tavern door, stooping under the beam into a soft night, walking home under stars through a quiet town to his wife and son, instead of accepting one more flask of ale and a last round of wagering on the tumbled dice.

He'd have that one back, if the world were a different place.

It *was* different now, he thought, after what had just happened, but not in the way he needed it to be. It occurred to him, with something bordering astonishment, that he might weep. He rubbed a hand through his beard, drew it across his eyes, felt time grip him again, carrying them, small boats on a too-wide sea.

"Why are we alive?" Alun ab Owyn asked. His voice was rough. It was, Thorkell thought, the right question, the only one worth asking, and he had no answer.

"We didn't matter enough to kill," Athelbert said, surprising the other two. Thorkell looked over at him.

They were shapes here, only, all of them. "What did you say to it, at the end? When you put down the hammer?"

Thorkell was trying to decide what to answer when the dog growled, deep in its throat.

"Dear Jad," Alun said.

Thorkell saw where he was pointing. He caught his breath. Something green was shimmering at the edge of their glade, beyond the pool; a human form, or nearly so. He looked the other way, quickly. A second one on their right, then a third, beside that one. No sound at all this time, just the pale green glowing of these figures. He turned back to the Cyngael prince.

"Do you know . . . ? Is this what you . . . ?" he began.

"No," said Alun. And again, "No." Flatly, no hope offered. "Cafall, hold!"

The dog was still growling, straining forward. The horses, Thorkell saw, were agitated now; there was a risk they might break free of their tethers, or hurt themselves trying.

The shapes, whatever they were, were about the height of a man, but the shimmer and glow of them, wavering, made their appearance hard to determine. He wouldn't have seen *anything* if they hadn't cast that faint green illumination. There were at least six of them, perhaps one or two more behind those ringing the glade. His hammer was on the grass, where he'd laid it down.

"Do I shoot?" said Athelbert.

"No!" Thorkell said quickly. "I swore that we'd harm no living thing."

"So we wait till they . . . ?"

"We don't know what this is," Alun said.

"You imagine they're bringing pillows for our weary heads?" Athelbert snapped.

"I have no idea what to imagine. I can only—"

A never-finished thought, that one. Speech can be rendered meaningless sometimes, the sought-after clarity of words. The fierce white light that burst from the pond, shattering darkness like glass, made all three of them throw hands before their eyes and cry aloud.

They were blinded, as unable to see as they had been in the blackness. Too much light, too little light: the same consequence. They were men in a place where they ought not to have been. The sounds in the glade were their own cries, fading in the charged air, the horses' neighing, thrashing of hooves. Nothing from the dog now, no noise at all from the green creatures that had encircled them, or from whatever had made that annihilating flare of light, which was also gone now. It was black again.

Alun, standing rigid and afraid, eyes clenched shut in pain, caught a scent, heard a rustling. A hand claimed his. Then a voice at his ear, music, scarcely a breath, "Drop your iron. Please. Come. I must get away from it. The *spruaugh* are gone."

Fumbling, he let fall his sword and belt, let her lead him, his senses dazzled, eyes useless, heart painful, too large for his chest.

"Wait! I . . . can't leave the others," he stammered, after they'd gone a little distance from the glade.

"Why?" she said, but she did stop.

He'd known she would say that. They were impossibly different, the two of them, beyond his power to even nearly comprehend. The scent of her was intoxicating. His knees felt weak, her touch conjured a kind of madness. She had come for him.

"I *won't* leave the others," he corrected. There were flashes and spirals of light in his field of vision. It was painful when he opened his eyes. He still couldn't see. "What . . . what were . . . ?"

"Spruaugh." He could hear disgust in her voice, could imagine her hair changing colour as she spoke, but he still couldn't see. It occurred to him to be afraid again, to wonder if he would be forever blinded by that shattering flash, but even with the thought came the first hints of returning vision. She was a spilling light beside him.

"What are . . . ?"

"We don't know. Or I don't. The queen might. They are mostly in this forest. A few come into our small one, linger near us, but not often. They are cold and ugly, soulless, without grace. They try, sometimes, to make the queen attend to them, flying to her with tales when we do wrong. But mostly they stay away from where we are, in here."

"Are they dangerous?"

"For you? Everything is dangerous here. You should not have come."

"I know that. There was no choice." He could almost see her. Her hair was an amber glow.

"No choice?" She laughed, rippling.

He said, "Did you feel you had a choice when you rescued me?" It was as if they had to teach each other how the world was made, or seen.

A silence, as she considered. "Is that . . . what you meant?"

He nodded. She was still holding his hand. Her fingers were cool. He brought them to his lips. She traced the outline of his mouth. Amid everything, after everything, here was desire. And wonder. She had come.

"What was it? Before them. The thing that—"

Fingers flat against his mouth, pressing. "We do not name it, for fear it will answer to the name. There is a reason why your people do not come here, why we almost never do. That one, not the *spruaugh*. It is older than we are."

He was silent for a time. Her hand was moving again, tracing his face. "I don't know why we're alive," he said.

"Nor do I." Matter-of-factly, a simple truth. "One of you did make an offering."

"The Erling. Thorkell. His hammer, yes."

She said nothing, though he thought she was about to. Instead, she stepped nearer, rose upon her toes, and kissed him on the lips, tasting of moonlight, though it was dark where they stood, except for her. The blue moon outside, above, shining over his own lands, hers, over the seas. He brought his hands up, touched her hair. He could see the small, shining impossibility of her. A faerie in his arms.

He said, "Will we die here?"

"You think I can know what will come?"

"I know that I can't."

She smiled. "I can keep the *spruaugh* from you."

"Can you guide us? To Brynnfell?"

"That is where you are going?"

"The Erlings are, we think. Another raid."

She made a face, distaste more than anything else. Offended rather than fearful or dismayed. Iron and blood, near to their small wood and pool. And, truly, why should the deaths of mortal men cause a spirit such as this dismay, Alun thought.

Then he had another thought. Before he could back away from it he said, "You could go ahead? Warn them? Brynn has seen you. He might . . . come up the slope, if you were there again."

Brynn had been there with him after the battle. And in that pool in the wood when he was young. He might fight his visions of the spirit world, but surely, surely he would not deny her if she came to him.

She stepped back. Her hair amber again, soft light among tall trees. "I cannot do that and guard you."

"I know," Alun said.

"Or guide."

He nodded. "I know. We are hoping that Cafall can."

"The dog? He might. It is many days for you."

"Five or six, we thought."

"Perhaps."

"And you can be there . . ."

"Sooner than that."

"Will you?"

She was so small, delicate as spray from a waterfall. He could see her chasing a thought, her hair altering as she did, dark, then bright again. She smiled. "I might grieve for you. The way mortals do. I may start to understand."

He swallowed, with sudden difficulty. "I . . . we will hope not to die here. But there are many people at risk. You saw what happened the last time they came."

She nodded, gravely. "This is what you wish?"

It was what he needed. Wishes were another thing. He said, "It will be a gift, if you do this."

So still a place, where they were. There ought to have been more noises in a wood at night, the pad of the animals that hunted now, scurry of those that moved along branches, between roots, fleeing. It was silent. Perhaps the light of her, he thought . . . steering the creatures of the forest away.

She said, serious as children could sometimes be, "You will have taught me sorrow."

"Will you call it a gift?" He remembered what she'd said the night before.

She bit her lip. "I do not know. But I will go home to the hill above Brynnfell and try to tell him there are men coming, from the sea. How do you . . . how do mortals say farewell?"

He cleared his throat. "Many different ways." He bent, with all the grace he could command, and kissed her on each cheek, and then upon the mouth. "I would not have thought my life would offer such a gift as you."

She looked, he thought, surprised. After a moment, she said, "Stay with the dog."

She turned, was moving away, carrying brightness and music. He said, in a panic, sudden and too loud, startling them both, "Wait. I don't know your name."

She smiled. "Neither do I," she said, and went.

Darkness rushed back in her wake. The glade and pond were not far away. Alun made his way there. Called out as he approached, so as not to startle them. Cafall met him at the clearing's edge.

Both men were standing.

"Do we know what *that* was?" Thorkell asked. "The light?"

"Another spirit," Alun said. "This one a friend. She drove them away with it. I don't think . . . we can't stay here. I believe we need to keep moving."

"Tsk. And here I was, imagining you'd gone to fetch those pillows for our heads," said Athelbert.

"Sorry. Dropped them on the way back," Alun replied.

"Dropped your sword and belt, too," said the Anglcyn prince. "Here they are." Alun took both, buckled the belt, adjusted the hang of his sword.

"Thorkell, your weapon?" asked Athelbert.

"It stays here," said the Erling.

Alun saw Athelbert nod his head. "I thought as much. Take my sword. I'll use the bow."

"Cafall?" said Alun. The dog padded over. "Take us home."

They untied and mounted their horses, left glade and silent pond behind, though never the memory of them, pushing westward in the dark on a narrow, subtle track, following the dog, a hammer left behind them in the grass.

⚬⚬

Kendra would have liked to say that it was because of concern for her brother, an awareness of him, that she knew what she knew that night, but it wasn't so.

Word, or a first word, came to Esferth very late. The king's messengers sent from the sea strand to Drengest had carried orders that one ship should go to the Cyngael—to Prince Owyn in Cadyr, who was closest— with word of a possible Erling raid upon Brynnfell.

On the way to Drengest, the three outriders had divided, on orders, one of them racing his tidings to the nearest of the hilltop beacons. From there the message had come north in signal fires. The Erlings were routed, many of them slain. The rest had fled. Prince Athelbert had gone away on a journey. His brother was to be kept safe. The king and *fyrd* would be home in two days' time. Further orders would follow.

Osbert dispatched runners to carry word of victory to the queen and to the city and the tents outside. There was a fair about to begin, men needed reassurance, urgently. The rest of the message was not for others to hear.

It wasn't actually difficult, Kendra thought, as the meaning of the words sank in, to realize what lay beneath the tidings of her brother. You didn't have to be wise, or old.

There were a dozen of them in the hall. She had found it impossible to sleep, and equally difficult to stay all night in chapel praying. This hall, with Osbert, seemed the best place. Gareth had obviously felt the same way; Judit had been here earlier, was somewhere else now.

She looked over at Gareth, saw how pale he had become. Her heart went out to him. Younger son, the quiet one. Had never wanted more than the role life seemed to be offering him. You might even have said what he really wanted was *less* of a role.

But the very specific instructions—*kept safe*—said a great deal about what sort of journey their older brother was taking, though not where. If King Aeldred and the Anglcyn ended up with only one male heir left, life was about to change for Gareth. For all of them, Kendra thought. She looked around. She had no idea where Judit was; their mother was at chapel still, of course.

"Athelbert. In the name of Jad, what is . . . what has he done now?" Osbert asked, of no one in particular.

The chamberlain seemed to have aged tonight, Kendra thought. Burgred's death would be part of it. He'd be moving through memories right now, even as he struggled to deal with unfolding events. The past always came back. In a way you could say that none of those who'd lived through that winter in Beortferth had ever left the marshes behind. Her father's fevers were only the most obvious form of that.

"I have no idea," someone said, from down the table. "Gone chasing them?"

"They have ships," Gareth protested. "He *can't* chase them."

"Some of them might not have made it back to the sea."

"Then he'd have the *fyrd,* they'd all go, and this message wouldn't say—"

"We will learn more soon," Osbert said quietly. "I shouldn't have asked. There's little point in guessing like children at a riddle game."

And that was true enough, as most things Osbert said were. But it was then, in precisely that moment, looking at her father's crippled, beloved chamberlain, that Kendra realized that she knew what was happening.

She knew. As simple and appalling as that. And it was because of the Cyngael prince who had come to them, not her brother. Something had changed in her life the moment the Cyngael had crossed the stream the day before, towards where she and the others were lying on summer grass, idling a morning away.

Just as she had the night before, she knew where Alun ab Owyn had gone. And Athelbert was with him.

As simple as that. As impossible. Had she asked for this? Done something that had brought it upon her as a curse? *Am I a witch?* the thought came, intrusive. Her hand closed, a little desperately, on the sun disk about her neck. Witches sold love potions, ground up herbs for ailments, blighted crops and cattle for a fee, held converse with the dead. Could go safely into enchanted places.

She took her hand from the disk. Closed her eyes a moment.

It is in the nature of things that when we judge actions to be memorably courageous, they are invariably those that have an impact that resonates: saving other lives at great risk, winning a battle, losing one's life in a valiant attempt to do one or the other. A death of that sort can lead to songs and memories at least as much—sometimes more—than a triumph. We celebrate our losses, knowing how they are woven into the gift of our being here.

Sometimes, however, an action that might be considered as gallant as any of these will take its shape and pass unknown. No singer to observe and mourn, or celebrate, no vivid, world-changing consequence to spur the harpist's fingers.

Kendra rose quietly, as she always did, murmured her excuses, and left the hall.

She didn't think anyone noticed. Men were coming and going, despite the hour. The beacon fire's tidings were running through the city. Outside, in the torchlit corridor, she found herself walking a little more quickly than usual, as though she needed to keep moving or she would falter. The guard at the doors, someone she knew, smiled at her and opened to the street outside.

"An escort, my lady?"

"None needed. My thanks. I'm going only back to chapel and my lady mother."

The chapel was to the left so she had to turn that way at the first meeting of lanes. She paused, out of sight, long enough for him to close the door again. Then she went back the other way, heading towards the wall and gates for the second time in as many nights.

Footsteps, a known voice.

"You lied to him. Where are you going?"

She turned. Felt a swift, unworthy flowering of relief, offered thanks to the god. She would be stopped now, would not have to do this after all. Gareth, his face taut with concern, came up to her. She had no idea what to say.

So offered truth. "Gareth. Listen. I can't tell you how, and it frightens me, but I am quite certain Athelbert is in the spirit wood."

He had taken a blow this evening with the tidings, harder than hers. He was still adjusting to it. She saw him step back a little. *A witch! Unclean!* she thought. Couldn't help but think.

Unworthy, that thought. This was her brother. After a moment, he said, carefully, "You feel a . . . sense of him?"

He was close to truth. It wasn't Athelbert, in fact, but that much she wasn't ready to divulge. She swallowed hard, and nodded. "I think he . . . and some others are trying to get west."

"Through that forest? No one . . . Kendra, that's . . . folly."

"That's Athelbert," she said, but it didn't come out lightly. Not tonight. "I think they feel a need to go very fast, or even he wouldn't do this."

Gareth's brow had knitted the way it did when he was thinking hard. "A warning? The Erlings going that way by sea?"

She nodded. "I think that must be it."

"But why would Athelbert care?"

This became difficult. "He might be joining others, making one with them."

"The Cyngael prince?"

He was clever, her little brother. He might also be the kingdom's heir by now. She nodded her head again.

"But how . . . Kendra, how would *you* know?"

She shrugged. "You said it . . . a sense of him." A lie, but not too far from truth.

He was visibly struggling with this. And how should he not? *She* was struggling, and it was inside her.

He took a breath. "Very well. What is it you want to do?"

There it was. She wasn't going to be stopped unless she stopped herself. She swallowed. "Only one thing," she said. "A small thing. Take me outside the walls. It will be easier if I'm with you."

He loved her. His life was altered forever if Athelbert died. And in a different way, she supposed, if she died. Gareth looked at her a moment, then nodded his head. They went to the gate together in the blue moonlight.

A different man on watch, which was good; the last one would have been stricken with fear to see her, after what had happened the night before. There were still hundreds of men (and not a few women, she knew) outside by the tents. They'd have heard glorious tidings by now, a celebration would be beginning.

Gareth had no trouble persuading the guard that they were going out to join in that. Suggested that their sister, the princess Judit, would likely be not far behind, which happened to be—very probably—the case. If she wasn't ahead of them, having gone out another way.

Outside, walking quickly west, not north towards the lights and the tents, Kendra had a tardy thought. She stopped again. "You . . . the message said you were to be kept safe."

Gareth, uncharacteristically, swore. It would have been more impressive if he hadn't sounded as though he were imitating Judit. She might have been amused at any other time. He glared at her. She lowered her gaze.

They moved on, came at length to the river. It all felt oddly like a dream now, a repeating of something done. She had been here last night.

She'd stopped on this side, then, waited for someone to come out of the trees.

Kendra hesitated now, looked up at her brother.

"You are going in, aren't you," he said. "The forest. To . . . spirits there."

Not really a question.

She nodded her head. "Stay for me? Please?"

"I can come."

She touched his hand. That was brave, very much Gareth, would bring her to tears if she wasn't careful. "If you do, I will not go. You may curse all you like at instructions, but I will not lead you into the spirit wood. I won't be long, or go far. Say you'll stay here, or we both go back now."

"That last sounds perfectly good to me."

She didn't smile, though she could see he wanted her to. She waited.

He said, finally, "You are sure of this?"

She nodded again. Another lie, of course, but at least not a spoken one this time.

He leaned forward, kissed her on the forehead. "You are so much better than all the rest of us," he said. "Jad defend you. I'll be here."

Moonlight on the water, reflecting from the stream. Very little breeze, the night mild, late summer. She went quickly, wading in and across, before she could lose what felt like a too-small store of courage, or he could see that she was crying, after all.

The forest here began only a little way beyond the water. It slanted west farther south, and then there was the long knife of the valley half a day's ride that way—and the holy house at Retherly where her mother was going to go after Judit was wed. She knew about that and Judit did. She didn't think her brothers had been told yet.

Marriages and retreats. Kendra couldn't say she'd spent any great amount of time thinking about either, or about boys and men. Perhaps she ought to have. Perhaps this had been a sister's reaction to Judit, whose lifelong defiance of any imposed order or protocol had led her far from the norms of a proper young woman's behaviour.

Kendra was, she supposed, the proper young woman of the family. (An alarming thought, at that particular moment.) It hadn't ever *felt* as though she was, it was more a matter of not enough inclination to pursue such matters, and no one—in truth—alluring or engaging enough to change her mind on the vague but undeniably important subject of men. Her brothers and sisters made jokes about Hakon's interest in her (they weren't kind to him about it), but Kendra considered him a friend, and . . . a boy, really. There wasn't much point thinking about it, in any case. Her father would decide where she wed, just as he had with Judit.

Her sister's fiery recklessness hadn't done much to alter the fact that she was marrying a thirteen-year-old Rheden prince this winter. As far as Kendra was concerned, defiance needed to *get* you somewhere, or it was just . . . being noisy.

She wasn't sure whether what she was doing now was defiant, or mad, or—most alarmingly—if it was something dark and complex and having to do with a man, after all. There was nothing *ordinary* about it, she knew.

She also knew, very near the trees now, that if she even slowed, let alone broke stride here at the wood's edge, fear would take hold of her entirely, so she kept walking— into the darkness of branches and leaves where Alun ab Owyn had gone the night before.

The strangeness, this terrible, unsettling inward strangeness, grew stronger. He was in these woods. She knew it. And she even seemed to know exactly where she needed to go now, where he had been last night. *This is unholy,* she thought, and bit her lip. *I could burn for this.*

It wasn't far, which was a blessing of the god upon her life, and might mean she was not yet entirely cast out from Jad's countenance and protection. She had no time to try to think that through.

Where she stopped was less a clearing than an easing of the press of trees around, where grass might grow. She thought about wolves, then snakes, made herself stop that. She stood very still, because this was the place. She waited.

And nothing happened. A sense of foolishness assailed her. That, too, she pushed away. She might not understand this awareness within, but it would be the worst sort of lie to the self to deny it was in her, and she would not do that. She cleared her throat, too loudly, almost made herself jump.

In the darkness of the spirit wood, Kendra said, very clearly, "If you are here, whatever it is you are, whatever was here last night, that he came to meet . . . you need to know that he's in the woods again now, to the south, which is . . . very dangerous. And with him is my brother, Athelbert. Maybe others. If you mean him well, and I pray to . . . my god that you do, will you help them? Please?"

Silence. Her voice, words spoken, then nothing, as if the sounds had been simply swallowed, absorbed, sinking away into never-having-been. That feeling of foolishness again, hard to push back. They would name her mad or a witch, or both. That Ferrieres cleric visiting had spoken in the royal chapel four days ago of the heresies and pagan rites that still flourished in corners of the Jaddite world, and his voice had hardened when he'd told how such things needed to be burned away, that the light of the god might not be dimmed by them.

This was, she supposed, a corner of the world.

She saw a light, where none had been. Kendra cried out, then covered her mouth quickly. She had *come* here to be heard. Trembling, groping for courage she really wasn't sure she possessed, she saw something green appear in front of her, beside a tree trunk. A little taller than she was. Slender, hairless; it was hard to discern features, or eyes, for the glow was strange, obscuring as much as it illuminated. So this, she thought, was what Alun ab Owyn had come to meet.

In the oddest, almost inexplicable way, seeing this vague, sexless, indeterminate shape, she suddenly felt better—couldn't sort out why that might be. It didn't seem malevolent. Nor should it be, she thought, if Alun had been here to meet it.

"Thank . . . thank you," she managed. "For co . . . coming to me. Did you hear? They are south. Near the coast, I believe. They . . . they are trying to get through the wood. Do . . . do you *understand* anything I say?"

No response, no movement, no eyes to see or read. A green shape, a muted glow in the wood. It was real, however. The spirits were *real*. She was speaking to one. Fear, and wonder, and a sense of . . . very great urgency.

"Can you help them? *Will* you?"

Nothing at all. The creature was motionless, as if carved. Only a slight shimmer of the green aura suggested it was a living thing. But fire glowed and shimmered and was not alive. She might be wrong. She might not understand *any* of this properly.

And that last thought, in fact, was nearest to the truth.

Why should she have understood what was happening? How could she do so? The *spruaugh* stayed another moment and then withdrew, leaving darkness behind it again, deeper for the lost light.

Kendra sensed immediately that this was all she was going to see, all that would happen. The space among the trees felt . . . emptied out. Fear had gone, she realized, replaced by wonder, a kind of awe. The world, she thought, was never going to seem the same again. Going back, she wouldn't be returning to the same stream or moonlight or the city she had left.

There were green shimmering creatures in the woods beside Esferth, whatever the clerics might say. And people had always *known* this was so. Why else the centuries-long fear of this forest? The stories told to frighten children, or around night fires? She stayed where she was another moment, a pause before returning, breathing in the darkness, alone, as she had been last night, but not quite the same.

And so a difficult truth about human courage was played out among those trees. A truth we resist for what it suggests about our lives. But sometimes the most gallant actions, those requiring a summoning of all our will, access to bravery beyond easy understanding or description . . . have no consequence that matters. They leave no ripples upon the surface of succeeding events, cause nothing, achieve nothing. Are trivial, marginal. This can be hard to accept.

Aeldred's younger daughter did something almost unspeakably brave, going alone at night into the blackness of a wood believed to be haunted, *intending* to confront the spirit world—which was the most appalling heresy according to every tenet she had ever learned. And she did do that and spoke a message, the warning she'd come to give—and it signified nothing at all, in the wheel and turn of that night.

The faerie had gone already, long before.

She had, in fact, been tracking Aeldred's *fyrd* all the previous night and through this day and into evening from within the wood. Almost all of the *spruaugh* in the forest were south as well by now, and this one, hearing (and, yes, understanding) Kendra's words, set itself to quickly go that way also, but pursuing its own desires: such desires as those creatures still possessed, which had nothing to do with guarding three mortal men in a forest that had once been named a godwood, in the days when men dissembled less about such things.

A hard truth: that courage can be without meaning or impact, need not be rewarded, or even known. The world has not been made in that way. Perhaps, however, within the self there might come a resonance, the awareness of having done something difficult, of having done . . . *something*. That can ripple, might do so, though in a different way.

Mostly, walking as quickly now as she dared in the root-and-branch darkness, what Kendra felt was relief. A rush of it, like blood to the head when you stand up too quickly. She had no idea what that green spirit had been, but it had come to her. Spirit world, half-world. She had *seen* it, a glowing in the night. Everything altered with that.

She came to the edge of the trees, saw moonlight through the last screening leaves, then unmediated, with stars, as she came out. The stream, the summer grass, her brother on the far bank. And what she felt, emerging, was near to joy.

The world had changed, in ways she couldn't sort through, but it was still, in the main, the place she'd always known. The water, as she waded through, was cool, pleasantly so on a summer night. She could hear music and laughter to her left, north of the city. She could see the walls in the distance, torches for the guards on the ramparts.

She could see her brother, solid and familiar and reassuring. She stopped in front of him. He seemed taller, Kendra thought: somewhere over the summer Gareth had grown. Or was that a sense that came from what she knew about Athelbert?

Gareth touched her shoulder.

"I'm me," she said. "Not spirit-claimed. Shall I kick you to prove it?"

He shook his head. "I'd think Judit's soul had claimed you. Do you want to go to the tents? Be with people?"

He hadn't probed or pressed her at all. She shook her head. "My clothing and boots are wet. I want to change. Then I think I need to go to chapel, if that's all right? You can go over to the—"

"I'll stay with you."

The guard said nothing (what was he going to say?) when they called to come back in so soon after going out. Kendra went to her rooms, woke her women, had two of them help her change (they raised eyebrows but said nothing either—and what were *they* going to say?). Then she went back out to where Gareth had waited (again) and they went to chapel together.

The streets were busy for so late an hour, but Esferth was crowded and jubilant. They could hear the noise from the taverns as they went. Walked past the one where she'd stood across the street last night when Alun ab Owyn had come out with his dog, and she'd called the Erling over to her.

Gareth broke their silence. "Is he all right?"

"Who?"

"Athelbert. Of course."

She blinked. Had made an error there. She managed a shrug. "I think he'll be all right. After all, Judit is nowhere near him."

Gareth stopped for a second, then burst out laughing. He dropped an arm around her shoulder and they continued that way, turning right at the next junction of streets towards the chapel.

"Where *is* Judit, do you think?" she asked.

"I imagine at the tents."

He was probably right, Kendra thought: there *was* cause for wine and celebration with the Erlings slaughtered and driven away.

In the event, however, they were wrong. Entering the royal chapel they saw their sister beside the queen, at prayer. Kendra stopped for a moment in the side aisle, surprised. She found herself gazing at two profiles, candlelight upon them. The queen's face round, fleshy, though still smooth, hints of a nearly lost beauty; Judit in the bright flush of red-haired, fair-skinned glory, on the cusp of her journey north to Rheden and marriage.

Kendra knew she had been avoiding the thought of that. So much would change. Their mother would leave for Retherly, and once Judit was married it would be her turn next. There might be green spirits in the wood, but the way of the world was not going to change for an Anglcyn princess because of them.

Aeldred's two younger children went over and knelt beside their mother and sister, looking towards the sun

disk and the altar and the cleric standing there, leading
the prayers. After a moment they added their voices to
the incantations and responses. Some things at least still
seemed clear enough, and needful: in the nighttime you
prayed for light.

CHAPTER XIV

Sometimes, as events in a given saga or idyll or tale move towards what may be seen as a resolution, those in the midst of what is unfolding will have a sense—even at the time—of acceleration, a breathlessness, urgency, speed.

Often, however, this emerges only in looking back, an awareness long after the fact (sometimes accompanied by belated fear) as to how many strands and lives had been coming together—or breaking apart—at the same time. Men and women will wonder at how they did *not* perceive these things, and be left with a sense that chance, accident, or miraculous intervention (for good or ill) lay at the heart of the time.

It is the humbling, daunting nature of this truth that can lead us to our gods, when pace and press subside. But it also needs to be remembered that sagas and idylls are constructed, that someone has composed their elements, selected and balanced them, bringing what art and inclination they have, as an offering. The tale of the Volgan's raid with a handful of men on a sanctuary of the Sleepless Ones in Ferrieres will be very differently told by a cleric surviving the attack, chronicling the round of a dismal year, and an Erling skald celebrating a triumph. Those inside a story do not usually think of themselves that way, though some may have an eye to fame and those who come after.

Mostly, we are engaged in living.

Riding back from the coast in bright summer daylight on the main road by the River Thorne, birdsong above, harvest-ready fields to the east and the forest receding for a time as a valley cut it away, Ceinion of Llywerth watched the Anglcyn *fyrd* struggle to define a collective state of mind, and he understood their difficulty.

The victory was magnificent, memorable, complete. A considerable Erling force had been shattered, driven away with major losses on the raiders' side and next to none on theirs. No deaths, in fact, after the initial night killings that had sparked the king's ride.

It was a time of glory. There were traders from abroad in Esferth for the fair—the story of Aeldred's riding out at night would be in Ferrieres and Batiara before autumn changed the leaves. It would reach Al-Rassan when the silk-clad horse traders went home.

Glory then, more than enough to share. But the death that had begun it mattered. They all mattered, of course, Ceinion told himself, but it was idle—even for a cleric dispensing pieties—to pretend that some lives did not signify more for their people than others, and Burgred of Denferth had been one of the three great men in these lands.

So there was that, to dim the joy of this homeward ride. There was also the prince, gone into the spirit wood. The madness of that, the death at the heart of it. And so those of the *fyrd* who wished to let their spirits soar kept a distance from King Aeldred and the mask that had become his face this morning.

And so again it seemed to Ceinion, as it had by the sea at twilight, that they were waiting on him. In a way it was an irony. He was only a visitor here, and the Cyngael were far from allies of the Anglcyn. In another sense, the reason Prince Athelbert was in the wood was that Alun ab Owyn had gone there, and Ceinion knew it, and so did the king.

You could say that it properly fell to a Cyngael, to their high cleric, to provide consolation and hope right now. Ceinion didn't know if it was possible. He was very tired. Unused to so much riding, with a body that didn't ease and loosen as it once had in the mornings. He was also heartsick and afraid, picturing the dragon-ships that might even now be cleaving seas to the west. There were blue skies overhead. He had prayed for storms in the night.

These inward sorrows didn't matter, or couldn't be *permitted* to matter, if you accepted the duties of your office. Ceinion twitched his reins and cantered his horse over beside Aeldred's. The king glanced at him, nodded, no more than that. No one was near them. Ceinion took a breath.

"Do you know," he said coldly, "if I were cleric of your royal chapel, I would be ordering you to do penance now."

"And why would this be?" Aeldred's voice was equally cold.

Within, Ceinion quailed at what he heard, but forced himself to push on. "For the thoughts that are written in your face."

"Ah. Thinking now is cause for chastisement?"

"It always has been. Certain kinds of thought."

"How illuminating. And what unspoken reflections of mine amount to transgressions, cleric?"

The title again, not his name. Ceinion looked over at the king, trying not to be obvious about his scrutiny. He wondered if Aeldred were succumbing to one of his fevers. If that might explain . . .

"I am perfectly well," said other man bluntly. "Please answer my question."

Ceinion said, as briskly as he could, "Heresy, a breaking from holy doctrine." He lowered his voice. "You are easily wise enough to know what I am saying. I am glad you are well, my lord."

"Pretend, if you will, that I am not wise at all, that you ride beside a fool, deficient in sense. Explain." The king's face had flushed. Fever, or anger? They said he still denied when his illness was coming on, after twenty-five years. A refusal to accept. That gave Ceinion a thought.

"Let me ask a question. Do you truly believe two royal princes and an Erling who rowed with Siggur Volganson are incapable of contending with wolves and snakes in a wood?"

He saw what he was looking for. The flicker in the other man's eyes, swift awareness of where this was going.

"I would imagine," said King Aeldred, "they ought to be able to defend themselves against such."

"But you decided, even before we set out this morning, that your son is now dead. You have . . . accepted his death. You said as much on the strand last night, my lord."

No reply for a time. The horses cantered, a ground-covering pace, without urgency. It was warm in the sunlight, the weather accursedly benign, a scattering of soft clouds. He needed black storms, the howl of wind, obliterating seas.

Aeldred said, "You are upbraiding me for beliefs about the forest. Tell me, Ceinion, did you come here *through* the wood? Or did you and your companions avoid it?"

"And why," said the cleric, deliberately sounding surprised, "would I choose to risk getting lost in a wood when the coastal path from Cadyr lay open before us?"

"Ah. Good. And it has always been from Cadyr that you set out? It is from that coast that all of the Cyngael coming east have departed? Tell me, high cleric, who it is has made a journey through that wood in living memory, or in your chronicles and songs? Or do not the songs of the Cyngael tell something different, entirely?"

Ceinion felt equal to this, by training and disposition and necessity. He said firmly, "It is my task, and yours, my lord, to steer the people—our people in both lands, where we share the blessing of Jad—away from such pagan fears. If you think your son and his companions equal to wild animals and to not losing their way, you must not surrender hope that they will come out in the west. And there is a chance they will save lives doing so."

Birdsong, horses' hooves, men's voices, laughter, though not near to them. Aeldred had turned his head, was looking directly at him, the eyes bright, clear, no fever, only knowledge. After a moment, he said, "Ceinion, dear friend, forgive me or do not, as you will or must, but I saw spirits close on twenty-five years ago, the night of the battle we lost at Camburn, and then in Beortferth that winter. Lights in the swamp at twilight and at night, moving, taking shape. Not marsh fires, not fever, not dream, though the fevers did begin the night of the battle. High cleric, Ceinion, hear me. I *know* there are powers in that wood who do not mean us well and are not to be mastered by men."

It had taken so little time to say, and to hear. But how much time did a sword stroke take? An arrow's flight? How long was there between the last breath of someone you loved when they were dying, and the breath they did not take?

Ceinion's heart was pounding. An easy ride, their battles over, talking on a summer's day. Even so, he felt himself assaulted, under siege. He was not necessarily equal to this, after all.

You brought your own memories and ghosts to these exchanges, however much you fought to keep them out, to be simply a holy man, a distilled voice for the teachings of the god you served.

He knew what he should say to this, what he was required to say. He murmured, "My lord, surely, you just gave yourself answer: it was the very night your kingdom was lost, after the battle, your father and brother slain . . . the worst night of your life. Is it any wonder that—"

"Ceinion, do me enough courtesy to believe I have thought of this. They were . . . present for me before, long before. From childhood, I have since come to understand. I denied them, avoided, would not accept . . . until the night of Camburn. And in the marshes after."

What had he expected? That his words would shed a dazzling illumination upon a confused soul? He *knew* what this man was. He tried another way, because he had to: "Do you . . . do you not know how arrogant it is to trust our mortal vision over the teachings of faith?"

"I do. But I am not able to deny what I do know. Call it a flaw and a sin, if you will. Could *you* do that denying?"

The question he hadn't wanted. An arrow, flying.

"Yes," he said, finally, "though not easily."

Aeldred looked at him. Opened his mouth.

"No questions, I beg of you," Ceinion said. Raw as an open wound, all these years after.

The king gazed at him a long moment, then looked away and was silent. They rode for a time, through the mild, sweet glory of late summer. Ceinion was thinking as hard he could; careful thought, his refuge.

"The fevers," he said. "My lord, could you not see that they—?"

"That I conceived visions in my fevered state? No. Not so."

Two very clever men, long-lived, and subtle. Ceinion considered this a moment, then realized that he understood something else, as well. He gripped his reins tightly.

"You believe that the fevers are . . . that they come to you as . . ." He reached for words. This was difficult, for many reasons.

"As punishment. Yes, I do," said the king of the Anglcyn, his voice flat.

"For your . . . heresy? This belief?"

"For this belief. My fall from the teachings of Jad, in whose name I live and rule. Do not believe that what I am telling you has come kindly to me."

He couldn't imagine believing that. "Who knows of this?"

"Osbert. Burgred did. And the queen."

"And they believed you? What you saw?"

"The two men did."

"They . . . saw these things as well?"

"No." He said it quickly. "They did not."

"But they were with you."

Aeldred looked at him again. "You know what the old tales tell. Yours and ours, both. That a man who enters the sacred places of the half-world may see spirits there, and if he survives he may see them after, all his days. But it is also told that some are born with this gift. This, I came to believe, was so with me. Not Burgred, not Osbert, though they stood by me in the marsh, and rode with me from Camburn that night."

The sacred places of the half-world. Uttermost heresy. A mound not far from Brynnfell, another summer, long ago. A woman with red-gold hair dying by the sea. He had left her with her sister, taken horse, gone riding in a frenzy, in a madness of sorrow beyond words. No memory, at all, of that ride. Had come to Brynnfell at twilight two days later, bypassed it, entered the small wood—

He made himself—as always—twist his mind away from that moon-shaped memory. It was not to be looked upon. You trusted and believed in the words of Jad, not in your own frail pretense of knowing the truth of things.

"And the queen?" he asked, clearing his throat. "What does the queen say?"

It was the hesitation, Aeldred's delay in replying. A lifetime of listening to men and women tell what was in their hearts, in words, in pauses, in the things not quite said.

The man beside him murmured, gravely, "She believes I will lose my soul when I die, because of this."

It was clear now, Ceinion thought. It was achingly clear. "And so she will go to Retherly."

Aeldred was looking at him. He nodded his head. "To pray each day and night for me until one of us dies. She sees it as her first duty, in love and in faith."

A burst of laughter, off to their right, somewhere behind. Men riding home in triumph, knowing songs and feasting awaited them.

"She might be right, of course," said the king, his tone light now, as if discussing the coming barley harvest or the quality of wine at table. "You should be denouncing me, Ceinion. Is that not your duty?"

Ceinion shook his head. "You seem to have done that to yourself, for twenty-five years."

"I suppose. But then came what I did last night."

Ceinion looked quickly over. He blinked; then this, too, slipped into understanding.

"My lord! You did not *send* Athelbert into that wood. His going there is no punishment of you!"

"No? Why not? Is it not sheerest arrogance to imagine we understand the workings of the god? Did you not tell *me* that? Think! Wherein lies my transgression, and where has my son now gone?"

Wolves and snakes, Ceinion had said, foolishly, moments ago. To this man who was bearing more than two decades of guilt. Trying to serve the god, and his people, and carrying these . . . memories.

"I believe," Aeldred was saying, "that sometimes we are given messages, if we are able to read them. After I taught myself Trakesian, and sent out word I was buying texts, a Waleskan came to Raedhill—this was long ago—with a scroll, not more than that. He said he'd bought it on the borders of Sarantium. I'm sure he looted it."

"One of the plays?"

The king shook his head. "Songs of their liturgy. Fragments. The horned god and the maiden. It was badly torn, stained. It was the first Trakesian writing I ever bought, Ceinion. And all this morning I have been hearing this in my head:

When the sound of roaring is heard in the wood
The children of earth will cry.
When the beast that was roaring comes into the fields
The children of blood must die.

Ceinion shivered in sunlight. He made the sign of the disk.

"I believe," Aeldred went on, "if you will forgive me, and it is not an intrusion, that you did not denounce what I have just said because . . . you also have some knowledge of these things. If I am right in this, please tell me, how do you . . . carry that? How do you find peace?"

He was still half in the spell of the verse. *The children of earth will cry.* Ceinion said, slowly, choosing words, "I believe that what doctrine tells us, is . . . becoming truth. That by teaching it we help it become the nature of Jad's world. If there are spirits, powers, a half-world beside ours, it is . . . coming to an end. What we teach *will* be true, partly because we teach it."

"Believing makes it so?" Aeldred's voice was wry.

"Yes," said Ceinion quietly. He looked at the other man. "With the power we know lies in the god. We are his children, spreading across his earth, pushing back forests to build our cities and houses and our ships and water mills. You know what is said in *The Book of the Sons of Jad*."

"That is new. Not canonical."

He managed a smile. "A little more so than a song of the horned god and the maiden." He saw Aeldred's mouth quirk. "They use it as liturgy in Esperaña where it was written, have begun to do so in Batiara and Ferrieres now. Clerics carrying the word of Jad to Karch and Moskav have been told by the Patriarch to cite that book, carry it with them—it is a powerful tool for bringing pagans to the light."

"Because it teaches that the world is ours. Is it, Ceinion? Is it ours?"

Ceinion shrugged. "I do not know. You cannot imagine how much I do not know. But you asked how I make my peace and I am telling you. It is a frail peace, but that is how I do it."

He met the other man's gaze. He hadn't denied what Aeldred had guessed. He wasn't going to deny it. Not to him.

The king's eyes were clear now, his flush had receded. "The beast dies, roaring, not the children?"

"Rhodias succeeded Trakesia, and Sarantium, Rhodias, under Jad. We are at the edge of the world here, but we are children of the god, not just . . . of blood."

Silence again, slightly altered. Then the king said, "I did not expect to be able to speak of this."

The cleric nodded. "I can believe that."

"Ceinion, Ceinion, I will need you with me. Surely you can see that? Even more, now."

The other man tried to smile but failed. "We will talk of that. But before, we must pray, with all piety we may command, that the Erling ships sailed for home. Or, if not, that your son and his companions pass through the woods, and in time."

"I can do that," said the king.

❧

Rhiannon wondered, often, why everyone still looked at her the way they did, concern written large, vivid as a manuscript's initial capital, in their eyes.

It wasn't as if she spent her days wan and weeping, refusing to rise from her bed (her mother wouldn't have allowed that, in any case), or drifting aimlessly about the farmhouse and yard.

She had been working as hard as anyone else all summer. Helping to bring Brynnfell back from fire and ruin, tending to the wounded in the early weeks, riding out with her mother to the families of those who'd suffered death and loss and taking what steps needed to be taken there. She devised activities for herself and Helda and Eirin, ate at table with the others, smiled when Amund the harper offered a song, or when someone said anything witty or wry. And still those furtive, searching looks came her way.

By contrast, Rania had been allowed to leave. The youngest of her women (with the sweetest voice) had been so terrified in the aftermath of the raid that Enid and Rhiannon had decided to let her go. The farmhouse had too many images of burning and blood for Rania just now.

She had left them early in the summer, weeping, visibly shamed despite their reassurances, with the contingent of men who would spend the summer by their castle towards the wall. The land there needed defending in summertime; there was little love lost between the men of Rheden and the Cyngael of the hills and valleys north of the woods; cattle and horses had been stolen on both sides, sometimes the same ones back and forth, for as long as anyone could remember. That was why Rheden had built the wall, why Brynn (and others) had castles there, not farmhouses. Her parents were here, though, attending to Brynnfell and its people.

So Rania had gone away, and everyone seemed to understand why she had been so distressed, to accept it as natural. But Rhiannon was right here, doing whatever needed to be done, undeterred by night-memories of an Erling hammer smashing her window, or a blade held to her throat in her own rooms by a screaming, blood-smeared man vowing to kill her.

She made her morning visits to the labourers' huts, carried food to the men repairing the farmyard struc-tures, offered a smile and a word of encouragement with their cheese and ale. She attended at chapel twice a day, spoke the antiphonal responses in her clearest voice. She shirked nothing, avoided nothing.

She just wasn't sleeping at night. And surely that was her own affair, not shared, not proper cause for all those thoughtful glances from Helda and her mother?

Besides, these past few days, as the rebuilding drew to a close and preparations for the harvest began, her father seemed to be afflicted in the same way.

Rhiannon, rising quietly—as she had been doing all summer—stepping past her sleeping women to go out into the yard, wrapped in a blanket or shawl, to pace along the fence and think about the nature of a person's life (and was there something wrong in that?), had found her father out there before her for three nights now.

The first two times she'd avoided him, turning back another way, for wasn't he to be allowed his own solitude and thoughts? The third night, tonight, she gathered her green shawl about her shoulders and walked across the yard to where he stood, gazing up at the slope south of them under the stars. The blue moon, a crescent, was over west, almost down. It was very late.

"A breeze tonight," she said, coming to stand beside him at the gate.

Her father grunted, glanced over and down at her. He was clad only in his long nightshirt, and barefoot, as she was. He looked away into the darkness. A nightingale was singing beyond the cattle pen. It had been with them all summer.

"Your mother's troubled about you," Brynn said at length, a finger going to his moustache. He had trouble with these conversations, she knew.

Rhiannon frowned. "I can see she is. I'm beginning to get angry about it."

"Don't. You know she leaves you alone, usually." He glanced at her briefly, then away. "It isn't . . . right for a young girl to be unable to sleep, you know."

She gripped her elbows with both hands. "Why a young girl only? Why me? What about you, then?"

"Just the last few days for me, girl. It's different."

"Why? Because I'm supposed to go singing through the day?"

Brynn chuckled. "You'd terrify everyone if you did."

She didn't smile. Smiles, she'd admit, tended to be forced now, and in the darkness she didn't feel she had to.

"So, why are you awake?" she asked.

"It's different," he repeated.

It was possible he was coming out to meet one of the girls, but Rhiannon didn't think so. For one thing, he obviously knew she was in the yard at night, everyone seemed to know. She didn't like it, being watched that way.

"Too easy an answer," she said.

A long silence this time, longer than she was happy with. She looked over at her father: the bulky figure, more paunch and flesh than muscle now, hair silver-grey, what was left of it. An arrow had been loosed from this slope above them, to kill him that night. She wondered if that was why he kept looking up at the shrubs and trees on the rise.

"You see anything?" he asked abruptly.

She blinked. "What do you mean?"

"Up there. See anything?"

Rhiannon looked. It was the middle of the night. "The trees. What? You think someone's spying on . . . ?" She was unable to keep fear from her voice.

Her father said quickly, "No, no. Not that. Nothing like that."

"What, then?"

He was silent again. Rhiannon stared up. Shapes of trunk and branch, bushes, black gorse, stars above them.

"There's a light," Brynn said. He sighed. "I've seen a Jad-cursed light for three nights now." He pointed. His hand was steady enough.

A different kind of fear, now, because there was nothing at all to be seen. The nightingale was still singing.

She shook her head. "What . . . what kind of light?"

"Changes. It's there now." He was still pointing. "Blue."

She swallowed. "And you think . . . ?"

"I don't think anything," he said quickly. "I just *see* it. Third night."

"Have you told . . . ?"

"Who? Your mother? The cleric?" He was angry. Not with her, she knew.

She stared into emptiness and dark. Cleared her throat. "You . . . you know what some of the farmers say. About the, our woods over up there?"

"I know what they say," her father said.

Only that. No swearing. It frightened her, actually. She was gazing up the slope and there was nothing there. For her.

She saw her father's large, capable hands gripping the top rail of the fence, twisting, as if to break the bar off, make it a weapon. Against what? He turned his head the other way and spat into the darkness. Then he unlatched the gate.

"Can't keep doing this," he said. "Not every night. Stay and watch me. You can pray if you like. If I don't come back down, tell Siawn and your mother."

"Tell them what?"

He looked at her. Shrugged, in the way that he had. "Whatever seems right."

What was she going to do? Forbid him? He swung open the gate, went through, closed it behind him— habits of a farmyard. She watched him begin to climb. Lost sight of him halfway up the slope. He was in his nightshirt, she was thinking, carried no weapon. No iron. She knew that that was supposed to matter . . . if this was what they were so carefully not saying it might be.

She wondered suddenly, though not unexpectedly, since it happened every night, where Alun ab Owyn was now in the world, and if he hated her still.

She stayed by the gate a long time, looking up, and she did pray, like one of the Sleepless Ones in the dark, for her father's life, and the lives of all those in the house, and the souls of all their dead.

She was still there when Brynn came back down.

Something had changed. Rhiannon could see it, even in darkness. She was afraid, before he spoke. "Come, girl," her father said, re-entering through the gate, moving past her towards the house.

"What?" she cried, turning to follow. "What is it?"

"We have much to do," said Brynn ap Hywll, who had slain Siggur Volganson long ago. "I cost us three days, not going up before tonight. They may be coming back."

She never asked who *they* might be. Or how he knew. But with the words she felt a seizure, a roiling spasm within herself. She stopped, clutching at her waist, and bent over to throw up what was in her stomach. Shaking, she wiped at her mouth, forced herself to straighten. She followed her father into the house. His voice could be heard, roaring an alarm like some half-beast come down from the trees, rousing everyone from sleep.

Everyone, but not *enough* of them. Too many of his men were north and east. Days away. Even as she re-entered, tasting bile, that thought was in her head. Then another one: swift, blessedly so, for it gave her a pulse-beat of time to anticipate.

"Rhiannon!" her father said, wheeling to look at her. "Get the stablehands to saddle your horses. You and your mother—"

"Must ride out to alert the labourers. I know. Then we'll begin preparing to deal with any wounded. What else?"

She stared at him as calmly as she could, which was not easy. She had just been physically sick, her heart was pounding, there was sweat cold on her skin.

"No," he said. "That is not it. You and your mother—"

"Will ride to the farm workers, then begin preparations here. As Rhiannon said."

Brynn turned and confronted his wife's steady gaze. A man stood behind her holding a torch.

Enid wore a blue night robe. Her hair was down, almost to her waist. No one ever saw it that way. Rhiannon, seeing the look exchanged between her parents, felt unsettled by the intimacy of it. The hallway was filled with people, and light. She felt herself flush, as if caught in the act of reading or hearing words meant for another. It occurred to her, even in that moment, to wonder if she would ever exchange such a glance with anyone before she died.

"Enid," she heard her father say. "Erlings come for the women. You make us . . . weaker."

"Not this time. They are coming for you, husband. Erling's Bane. Volgan's slayer. The rest of us are ordinary fare. If anyone leaves, we should all leave. Including you."

Brynn drew himself up. "Abandon Brynnfell to Erlings? At this point in my life? Are you seriously—?"

"No," said his wife, "I am not. That is why we stay. How many are coming? How much time do we have?"

For a long moment he looked as if he were going to hold his ground, but then, "More than last time, I think. Say eighty of them. Time, I'm not sure. They'll come from Llywerth again, through the hills."

"We need more men."

"I know. Castle's too far. I'll send, but they won't get back in time."

"What do we have here? Forty?"

"A little less than that, if you mean trained to weapons."

There were two lines on her mother's forehead. Rhiannon knew them, they came when she was thinking. Enid said, "We'll get as many of the farm workers as we can, Rhiannon and I, and their women and children for shelter. We can't leave them out there."

"Not the women. Send them north to Cwynerth with the young ones. They'll be safer away. As you said— Brynnfell is what they want. And me."

"And the sword," his wife said quietly.

Rhiannon blinked. She hadn't thought of that.

"Likely so," her father was saying, nodding his head. "I'll send riders to Prydllen and Cwynerth. There should be a dozen men at each, for the harvest."

"Will they come?"

"Against Erlings? They'll come. In time, I don't know."

"And we defend the farm?"

He was shaking his head. "Not enough men. Too difficult. No. They won't expect us to have a warning. If we're quick enough, we can meet them west, at a place we choose. Better ground than here."

"And if you are wrong?"

Brynn smiled, for the first time that night. "I'm not wrong."

Rhiannon, listening, realized that her mother, too, had not asked about the warning, how Brynn knew what he seemed to know. She wouldn't ask, unless perhaps at night when the two of them were alone. Some things were not for the light. Jad ruled the heavens and earth and all the seas, but the Cyngael lived at the edge of the world where the sun went down. They had always needed access to knowledge that went beneath, not to be spoken.

They weren't speaking of it.

Her mother was looking at her. Frowning again, doing so, that expression everyone had been giving her since the end of spring.

"Let's go," Rhiannon said, ignoring it.

"Enid," her father said, as the two women turned away. They both looked back at him. His face was grim. "Bring every lad over twelve summers. With anything at all that might do for a weapon."

That was too young, surely. Her mother would refuse, Rhiannon thought.

She was wrong.

॰๑॰

Brand Leofson, commanding five Jormsvik ships as they made their way west, knew where he was going. He'd rowed his first dragon-ships in the final years of the

Volgan's raids, though never with Siggur's men. Had lost his eye in one of those, had been recovering at home when the last of the Volgan's journeys had ended in disaster in Llywerth. Hadn't been there.

Depending on his mood, in the intervening years, and on how much he'd been drinking, he either felt fortunate to have missed that catastrophe, or cursed not to have been one of those—their names were known—who'd been with Siggur in the glory years, at the end.

You could say, if your mind worked that way, that his failure to be in Llywerth was a reason he was taking five undermanned ships west now. The past, what we have done or not done, slips and flows, like a stream to a carved-out channel, into the things we do years after. It is never safe, or wise, to say that anything is over.

They were at risk, he knew it, and so would the other captains, all the more experienced men here. They still had all their ships but they'd lost sixty men. If the weather turned, it would get bad at sea. So far, it hadn't. On the second night the wind switched to southerly, which pushed them closer than he liked to the rocky coast of Cadyr. But they were Erlings, mariners, knew how to stay clear of a lee shore, and when they reached the western end of the Cyngael coastline and turned north, that wind held with them.

Your danger could become your gift. Ingavin's storms could drown you at sea—or terrify your foe on land, adding fire and the flash of lightning to your own war cries. And the god, too, Brand was always telling himself, his private thought, had only one eye, after his nights on the tree where the world began.

Salt in the air, sail full on each ship now, stars fading above them as the sun rose, Brand thought of the Volgan and his sword—for the first time in years, if truth be told. He felt a bone-deep stirring within. Ivarr Ragnarson had been malformed, evil and devious, had deserved to die. But he'd had a clever-enough thought or two in his head, that one, and Brand wouldn't be the one to deny it.

To have turned home with sixty dead and nothing to show for their loss would have been a disaster. To come back and report the Volgan's slayer slain and the sword found and reclaimed . . .

That would be something different. It could make up for the deaths, and more. For not having been one of that company, twenty-five years ago.

IT HAD OCCURRED TO BERN, rowing west, that there was something unsettling about what he was and how the world saw them all. They were Erlings, riders of the waves, laughing at wind and rain, knifing through roiling seas. Yet he himself was one of them, and he had no idea what to do in rough weather, could only follow directions as best he could and pray the seas did not, in fact, roil.

More: they were Jormsvikings, feared through the world as the deadliest fighters under sun and stars and the two moons. But Bern had never fought a battle in his life, only one single combat on the beach below the walls. That wasn't a battle. It was nothing like a battle.

What, came the thought, as they turned north and wind took the sails, if all of the others were—more or less—like him? Ordinary men, no better or worse than others. What if it was *fear* that made men believe the Jormsvik mercenaries were deadly? They could be beaten, after all; they *had* just been beaten.

Aeldred's *fyrd* had used signal fires and archers. Brand, and Garr Hoddson, had called it cowardly, womanish, making mock of the Anglcyn king and his warriors, spitting contempt into the sea.

Bern thought that it would be better to consider learning to use bows themselves, if their enemies did.

Then he thought, even more privately, almost hiding the notion from himself, that he really wasn't sure raiding in this way was the life for him.

He could curse his father again, easily enough, for it was Thorkell's exile that had thrust Bern into servitude, and then off the isle without an inheritance. But—in sunlit truth—that channel of the thought-stream wasn't so easy any more. The farm, his inheritance, was only theirs because of raiding, wasn't it? His father's long-sung adventure with Siggur in Ferrieres, a cluster of men burning a royal sanctuary.

And no one had *made* Bern take Halldr Thinshank's horse to Jormsvik.

He thought of his mother, his sisters on the mainland, and then of the young woman at the woman's compound—he'd never learned her name—who'd been bitten by the *volur*'s snake, and saved his life because of it. Partly because of it.

Women, he thought, would probably see this differently.

He rowed when ordered, rested when the wind allowed, took food to Gyllir among the other horses standing tethered in the central aisle of the wide ship, shovelled horse dung overboard.

Felt a surge of excitement, despite everything, when they reached the harbour that Garr and Brand both knew, in Llywerth. No one in sight, all along the coast coming north, or here. They pulled the ships ashore in the hour before dawn and spoke their thanks to Ingavin on the beach.

They'd leave the boats here, men to guard them—he might be one of those, had no clear sense of how he'd feel about that. Then the others would head inland to find Brynnfell and kill a man and claim a sword again.

You couldn't deny it was matter for skald song, through a winter and beyond. In the northlands, that mattered. Perhaps everyone shared these doubts he was having, Bern thought. He didn't think so, actually, looking at his shipmates, but it would have been good to have someone to ask. He wondered where his father was. Thorkell had told him not to let them come this way.

He'd tried. You couldn't say he hadn't tried. He wasn't leading this raid, was he? And if your life steered you to the dragon-ships, well . . . it steered you there. Ingavin and Thünir chose their warriors. And maybe— maybe—he'd come out of this with a share of glory. His own. A name to be remembered.

Men lived and died pursuing that, didn't they? *Fair fame dies never*. Was Bern Thorkellson of Rabady Isle the one to say they were wrong? Was he that arrogant? Bern shook his head, drawing a glance from the man next to him on the beach.

Bern looked the other way, embarrassed. Saw, beyond the strand, the darkly outlined hills of the Cyngael, knew that the Anglcyn lands lay beyond, far beyond. And farther east, across the seas, where the sun would rise, was home.

No one, he thought, travelled as the Erlings did. No people were so far-faring, so brave. The world knew it. He drew a breath, pushed the dark thoughts away from him. Sunrise came. Brand Leofson picked his men for the raid.

Bern started east with the other chosen ones.

∾

They had been living for three days on nuts and berries, like peasants foraging in a dry season or during a too-long winter with the storeroom empty. Cafall led them to water, so there was that, for themselves and the horses.

It was oppressively dark in the forest, even in daytime. On occasion a square of sky could be seen through the trees, light spilling down, a reminder of a world beyond the wood. Sometimes at night they caught a glimpse of stars. Once they saw the blue moon, and paused in a glade without a word spoken, looking up. Then they went on. They were following the dog north and west towards Arberth—or they had to assume that was so. None of them could do more than hazard a guess at where they were, how far they'd come, how far yet there was to go. Five days, Alun had said the passage through the forest might be: that, too, had been a guess.

No one had ever done this.

They pushed themselves and the animals hard: an awareness of urgency and the equally strong feeling that it was better to keep moving than be still in one place for too long. They never again heard or sensed the beast-god that had come the first night, or the green creatures of the half-world that had followed.

They knew they were here, however. And when they slept, or tried to (one always awake, on watch), the memory of that unseen creature would come back. They were intruders here, alive only on sufferance. It was frightening, and wearying. One had to work to avoid startling shamefully at sounds in the wood—and all forests were full of sounds.

They knew they had been three nights here, but in another way this had become for them a time outside of time. Athelbert had a vision once, almost asleep in the saddle, of the three of them coming out to a world entirely changed. He didn't know, for he didn't speak of this, that Alun had had that same fear, meeting a faerie outside Esferth, before the *fyrd* had ridden south.

Through the first two days they'd talked, mostly to hear voices, human sounds. Athelbert had amused the others, or tried to, singing tavern songs, invariably bawdy. Thorkell, after extended urging, had offered one of the Erling saga-verses, but the younger men became aware he was doing it only to indulge them. By the fourth day they were riding in silence, following the grey dog in the gloom.

Near sundown, they came to another stream.

Cafall was doing this without urging. Each one of them was aware that they'd have been lost days ago without Alun's dog. They didn't speak of this, either. They dismounted, bone-tired, to let the horses drink. Dim, filtered twilight. Clink of harness, creak of saddle leather, crunch and snap of twigs and small branches by the stream, and they nearly died again.

The snake wasn't green. It was Alun who trod too close, Athelbert who saw it, whipping out his dagger, gripping it to throw. It was Thorkell Einarson who snapped a command: *"Hold! Alun, don't move!"*

The black snakes were poisonous, their bite tended to be lethal.

"I can kill it!" Athelbert rasped through clenched teeth. Alun had frozen where he was, in the act of approaching the water. One foot was incongruously lifted so that he was poised, like some ancient frieze of a runner in one of the villas left behind when the Rhodian legions retreated south. The snake remained coiled, its head moving. An easy-enough target for someone skilled with a blade.

"I swore an oath," Thorkell said urgently. "Our lives depend—"

In that same moment Alun ab Owyn murmured, very clearly, "Holy Jad defend my soul," and sprang into the air.

He landed in the water with a splash. The stream was shallow; he came down hard, knees and hands on stone, and cursed. The snake, affronted, disappeared with a slither and glide into underbrush.

The bear cub, which none of them had seen, looked up from the far side of the water where it had been drinking, backed away a few steps, and essayed a provisional growl in the direction of the man in the stream.

"Oh, no!" said Athelbert.

He wheeled. Cafall barked a high, furious warning and streaked past him. The mother bear had entered the clearing already, roaring, her head swinging heavily back and forth. She rose on her hind legs, huge against the black backdrop of trees, spittle and foam at her gaping mouth. They were between her and the cub. Of course they were.

The horses went wild—and they were untethered. Alun's plunged through the stream. Thorkell seized the reins of the other two and hung on. Alun scrambled to his feet, splashed over, and claimed his trembling horse on the far bank—it was blocked there by trees, had nowhere to go. Frantically, it tried to rear, nearly pulled him off the ground. The cub, equally frightened, backed farther away, but was much too close to him. Athelbert sprinted over to Thorkell and the horses, fumbling for his bow at the saddle.

"*Mount up!*" Thorkell shouted, fighting his way into his own saddle. Athelbert looked at him. "Do it!" the Erling screamed. "We are dead if we kill here. You *know* it!"

Athelbert swore savagely, hooked a leg into a swinging stirrup. The horse skittered sideways; he almost fell, but levered himself up. On the far bank, Alun ab Owyn, also a horseman, clambered on his mount. It wheeled and bucked, eyes white and staring.

The bear came forward, still roaring. It was enormous.

They had to move past it to get out. "I'll shoot to wound!" Athelbert cried.

"Are you mad? You'll make it wild!"

"What is it *now*?" the Anglcyn prince screamed back. "Jad's blood," he added very quickly, and with extreme, necessary skill, mastered his rearing mount and, leaning far over to one side, lashed it past the bear, which was almost on top of them.

Thorkell Einarson was an Erling. His people lived for longships, white foam, a moonlit sea, surf on stony strands. Not for horses. He was still struggling to control his spinning, terrified steed.

"Move!" Alun screamed from the far bank, not helpfully.

There wasn't enough time in the world, or room in the glade, to move. Or there wouldn't have been, if a lean, blur-fast, grey creature hadn't knifed over and sunk its teeth into the hind leg of the bear. The animal roared, in rage and pain, turned with shocking speed on the dog. Thorkell kicked his horse in that same moment, sawed at his reins, and moved, following Athelbert out. Alun joined them in that same instant of reprieve, splashing across the water, cutting out of the glade.

It was very hard to see. A bear was roaring behind them, a noise that shook the woods. And entangled with it back there was a wolfhound with unspeakable courage and something more than that.

They were out, though, all three of them. It was far too black and tangled to gallop. They moved as quickly as they could along the twisting, almost-path. A little distance farther they stopped, of one accord, turned to look back, staring—ready to move if anything remotely bear-like should appear.

"Why in the name of everything holy did we *keep* our weapons if you won't let us use them?" Athelbert was breathing in gasps.

So was Thorkell, gripping his reins too tightly in a big fist. He turned his head. "You think . . . you think . . . if we get out of this Ingavin-cursed forest they'll be dancing to greet us?"

"What?"

The big man wiped at his face, which was dripping with sweat. "Think it! I'm an Erling enemy, you're an Anglcyn enemy, that one is the prince of Cadyr, and we're heading for *Arberth*. Which of us do you think any men we meet will want to kill first?"

There was a silence. "Oh," said Athelbert. He cleared his throat. "Um. Indeed. Not dancing. Ah, you, I'd wager. You'd be first. What, er, shall we bet?"

They heard a sound along the path; both men turned.

"Dear Jad," said Alun ab Owyn quietly.

He slipped down off his horse, walked a few steps back along the way they had come, crunching twigs and leaves again. Then he knelt on the path. He was crying, although the other two couldn't see that. He hadn't cried since the beginning of summer.

Out of shadow and tree the dog limped towards them, head low, moving with effort. It stopped, a short distance from Alun, and lifted its head to look at him. There was blood everywhere, he saw, and in the near-black he thought an ear was ripped away. He closed his eyes a moment, swallowed hard.

"Come," he said.

A whisper, really. All he could manage. His heart was aching. This was his dog, and it wasn't. It was Brynn's wolfhound. A gift. He'd accepted it, been accepted after a fashion, never allowed himself a deeper bond, something shared. Companionship.

"Please come," he said again.

And the dog stepped forward, slowly, the left front paw favoured. The right ear was indeed missing, Alun saw, as it drew near and he put an arm around it, gently, and laid his face carefully against that of the creature which had come to him the night his brother's life and soul were lost.

THORKELL WAS AWARE that the dog had saved their lives. He wasn't about to get drunk on the thought. He and Siggur had saved each other at least half a dozen times, each way, years ago, and other companions had

guarded him or been saved by him. It happened if you
went into battle, or at sea when storms came. Once a
spear thrust he'd not seen had missed him only because
he'd stumbled over a fallen shipmate's body in a field.
The spear had gone behind him, and above. He'd
turned and cut through the spearman's leg from below.
That one, as it happened, he remembered. The blind
chance of it. He'd never been saved by a dog before, he
had to acknowledge that.

The animal was badly hurt, which might be a difficulty, since they had no hope of getting through the
wood without it. Ab Owyn was still on his knees,
cradling his dog. He'd known men who treated their
hounds like brothers, even sleeping with them; hadn't
thought the Cyngael prince was one such. On the other
hand, something extraordinary had happened here. He
owed his life to it. It wasn't quite the same as Siggur
covering his left side on a raid.

He looked away, feeling unexpectedly awkward
watching the man and dog. And doing so, he saw the
green figure among the trees. It wasn't far away. Out of
the corner of his eye he registered that Athelbert had
also seen it, was staring in the same direction.

The curious thing was that this time, he didn't feel
afraid. The Anglcyn didn't seem frightened either, sitting
his horse, looking into the trees at a green, softly glowing
figure. It was too far away for details of face or form to
be clear. The thing looked human, or near to being so,
but a mortal didn't shine, couldn't hover over water as
these things had done. Thorkell looked into the darkness
at that muted glow. After a moment it simply went away,
leaving the night behind.

He turned to Athelbert.

"I have no least idea what that is," the prince said
softly.

Thorkell shrugged. "Why should we have an idea," he said.

"Let's go," said Alun ab Owyn. They looked back at him. He was on his feet, a hand still touching the dog, as though reluctant to be parted now.

"Can he lead us?" Thorkell asked. The dog had at least one bad leg. There seemed to be blood, not as much as there might have been.

"He can," Alun said, and in the same moment the dog moved ahead of them. He turned back and waited for ab Owyn to mount up and then started forward, limping, not going quickly, but taking them through the spirit wood towards his home.

They rode through that night, dozing at times in the saddle, the horses following the dog. They stopped once more for water, cautiously. Alun bathed the dog by that pool, washing away blood. The animal's ear was gone. The wound seemed strangely clean to Thorkell, but how could you say what was strange and what was proper in this place? How could you dream of doing so?

They reached the end of the forest at sunrise.

It was too soon, all three of them knew it. They ought not to have been able to get through nearly so quickly. Athelbert, seeing meadow grass through the last of the oaks, cried aloud. He remembered his thoughts about time passing differently, everyone dead, the world changed.

It was a thought, but not an actual fear. He was aware (they all were, though they never spoke of it) that something out of the ordinary had happened. It felt like a blessing. He touched the sun disk around his neck.

Why should we have an idea? the Erling had said.

It was true. They lived in a world they could not possibly comprehend. The belief that they *did* understand

was illusion, vanity. Athelbert of the Anglcyn carried that
as a truth within himself from that time onward.

There is something—there is always something—about
morning, dawn's mild light, end of darkness and the night.
They rode out of the trees into Arberth and saw the
morning sky above green grass and Athelbert knew—he
knew—that this was their own world, and time, and that
they had come through the godwood alive in four nights.

"We should pray," he said.

A woman screamed.

IT REALLY SHOULD HAVE BEEN POSSIBLE, Meghan thought
indignantly, for a girl to crouch and relieve herself in the
bushes outside the shepherd hut without having a man
on a horse appear right beside to her.

Three men. Coming from the spirit wood.

She'd screamed at the voice, but now a colder fear came
as she realized that they'd ridden out of the forest. *No one*
went into the wood. Not even the older boys of their
village and farms, daring each other, drunk, would go
farther than the first trees, in daylight.

Three men, a dog with them, had just emerged on
horses from the woods. Which meant that they were
dead, spirits themselves. And had come for her.

Meghan stood up, adjusting her clothing. She would
have run, but they were on horses. They looked back at
her oddly, as if they hadn't seen a girl before. Which
might be true of ghosts, perhaps.

They *looked* ordinary enough. Or, if not ordinary, at
least . . . alive, human. Then—third shock of a morning—
Meghan realized that one of them was an Erling. The
riders from Brynnfell that had come and taken all the men
away with them had spoken of an Erling raid.

There was an Erling here, looking down at her from
his horse, because—of course—her scream had revealed

to them where she was, peeing in the bushes before seeing to the sheep.

She was alone. Bevin had gone with the others to Brynnfell yesterday at sunrise. Her brother would have laughed at her for screaming. Maybe. Maybe not, with men coming out of the wood, armed, one of them an Erling. The first man had spoken in a tongue she didn't know.

The dog's fur, she saw, was torn, streaked with blood.

They were still looking at her strangely, as though she were someone important. The Erlings had blood-eagled a girl named Elyn—another farm girl, only that—to the west after the Brynnfell fight. Meghan would have screamed again, thinking of that, but there was no point. No one near them, the farmhouses too far and the sheep wouldn't help her.

"Child," said one of them. "Child, we mean you no harm in all the god's sweet world."

He spoke Cyngael.

Meghan drew a breath. A Cadyri accent. They stole cattle and pigs, scorned Arberth in their songs, but they didn't kill farm girls. He dismounted, stood in front of her. Not a big man, but young, handsome, actually. Meghan, whose brother said she would get herself in trouble if she wasn't careful, decided she didn't really like it that he'd called her "child." She was fourteen, wasn't she? You could *have* a child at fourteen. That was what her brother meant, of course. He wasn't here. No one was.

The Cadyri said, "How far are we from Brynnfell? We must go to them. There is trouble coming."

Feeling extremely knowledgeable, and not as shy as she probably should have been, Meghan said, "We know all about it. Erlings. Riders came from Brynnfell and took our men with them."

The three men exchanged glances. Meghan felt even more important.

"How far is it?" It was the Erling, speaking Cyngael.

She looked dubiously at the one standing beside his horse.

"He's a friend," he said. "We must get there. How far?"

She thought about it. They had horses. "You can be there before dark," she said. "Up the swale and back down and pretty much west."

"Point us to the path," the Erling said.

"Cafall will know," said the Cyngael quietly. The third one hadn't spoken since his voice had made her scream. His eyes were closed. Meghan realized he was praying.

"Did you really come out of the forest?"

She had to ask. It was the wonder at the heart of this. It . . . made the world different. Bevin and the others would not believe her when she told them.

The one standing in front of her nodded. "How long ago did your menfolk leave?"

"Yesterday morning," she said. "You might almost catch them up, on horse."

The one who seemed to be praying opened his eyes. The one on the ground swung back into the saddle, pulled at his reins. They left without another word, the three of them, the dog, not looking back at her.

Meghan watched until they were out of sight. After, she had no idea what to do with herself. She wasn't used to being here alone—yesterday had been the first time, ever. The sun rose, as if declaring it was just another day. Meghan felt tingly, though, all strange. Eventually, she went back to the hut and built up the fire. She made and ate her morning pottage and then went to count the sheep. All morning, all day, she kept seeing them in her mind, those three riders, hearing what they'd said. Already it was beginning to feel too much like a dream, which she didn't like. She felt as if she needed to . . . root it in herself like a tree, make it real.

Meghan mer Gower told the story all her life, only not the part about how she'd been squatting to pee when they came out of the trees. Given what followed, who the three of them had turned out to be, even Bevin had to believe her, which was very satisfying.

Half a century later, it was Gweith, her grandson—having heard his grandmother's story all his days—who took thought one autumn morning after a fire had destroyed half the houses in the village.

After, he walked south, cap in hand, to the sanctuary at Ynant and spoke with the clerics there, asking their blessing for what he was of a mind to do. It was not the sort of thing you did without a blessing.

He received more than that. Fifteen clerics from Ynant, yellow-robed, most of them unhandy in the extreme, came walking with him back to the village.

The next morning they offered the dawn invocation and then, with all the villagers gathered to watch, in awe and wonder, the clerics began to help—after a fashion—as Gweith set about cutting down the first trees at the edge of the spirit wood. Some of the other young men joined them. They were more useful.

Gweith didn't die, nor did anyone else. No one was stricken with palsy or dropsy or fever in the days that followed. Neither were the clerics, though many of them did complain of blistered hands and muscle pains.

Men began taking axes to the wood.

At about that same time, in the way of such things, where an idea, a notion, reaches the world in many places at once, the same forest in the Anglcyn lands was entered into by men in search of urgently needed wood.

They brought their axes to the trees west of Esferth and farther south, beyond Retherly, towards where the young king had ordered a new shipyard and *burh* to be built. A growing kingdom needed lumber, there was no getting around it. At a certain point, in the name of Jad, you couldn't let old women's tales stop you from doing what had to be done.

None of the first woodcutters on that side of the wood died either, except for those suffering the usual accidents attendant upon sharp blades and falling trees and carelessness. It began, it continued. The world does not stay the way it was, ever.

Years after all of this, a great many years, actually, an Anglcyn charcoal burner at what had become the south-eastern edge of a considerably reduced forest came upon something curious. It was a hammer—an Erling battle hammer—lying in the grass by a small pond.

The odd thing was that the hammer's head, clearly ancient, gleamed as if newly forged, unrusted, and the wood of the shaft was smooth. When the charcoal burner picked it up he swore he heard a sound, something between a note of music and a cry.

Actions ripple, in so many ways, and for so long.

CHAPTER XV

Kendra would remember the days before and during the fair that year as the most disconnected she'd known. Intensity of joy, intensity of fear.

The *fyrd* had been home for two nights, after riding in loud triumph through the wide-open gates of Esferth amid shouts and cheering and music playing. The city was thronged with merchants. There could not have been a better time for Aeldred to achieve such a victory over the Erlings. Slain in numbers, driven away, no losses at all for the Anglcyn.

If you didn't count a prince, gone into the godwood.

Riding up the main street from the gates, a screaming, colourful crowd on either side, her father had waved, smiled gravely, let the people see a king calmly aware of achievement, and as calmly set on repeating it as often as necessary. Let his subjects know this, and let all who were here from abroad carry word back to their homes.

Kendra, with her mother and sister and brother (the one brother here), in front of the great hall, had looked at her father as he'd dismounted, and she'd known—right then—that he was dissembling.

Athelbert outweighed sixty Erlings killed, by so much.

There had been sea-raids for a hundred years, and they would not stop with this one. But the king of the Anglcyn had only two sons who'd survived infancy, and the older was gone now into a deadly place, and the younger (they all knew) had never wanted to be a king.

Truth be told, it was Judit, thought Kendra, beside her red-haired sister on the steps, who ought to have been a boy at birth, and now a man. Judit could have sat a throne, incisive and confident in the fierce brightness of her spirit. She could have wielded a sword (she *did* wield swords!), commanded the *fyrd*, drunk ale and wine and mead all night and walked steadily away from a trestle table at dawn when all those who had been with her lay snoring amid cups. Judit knew this, too, Kendra thought; she *knew* she could have done these things.

Instead, she was going off this winter, escorted by most of the court, to marry a thirteen-year-old boy and live among the people of Rheden to bind them close: for that is what young women in royal families were born to do.

Things went awry sometimes, Kendra thought, and there was no one to give her a good answer why Jad had made the world that way.

They'd feasted that night, heard music, watched jugglers and tumblers perform. The rituals of victory. Theirs were lives on display, to be seen.

More of the same at sunrise. At chapel to pray, then she and Judit (dutiful just now, more shaken than she'd want to admit by what Athelbert had done) had made a point of walking through the thronged, roped-off marketplace three separate times (to be seen), fingering fabrics and brooches. They'd made Gareth come with them the third time. He'd been quiet, extremely so. Judit bought a jewelled knife and a gelding from Al-Rassan.

Kendra bought some fabrics. She made her way through the duties of the day with difficulty, then after the evening rites she went looking for someone. She had questions that needed answering.

Ceinion of Llywerth had not been at the royal chapel for the sundown services. There were a small number of

Cyngael merchants here for the fair (they'd come along the same coastal path he had, or been granted passage through the Rheden Wall). She found the cleric with his own people at a chapel on the eastern side of Esferth, leading the rites there.

He had just finished when Aeldred's younger daughter arrived, with one of her women in attendance. They waited until the cleric was done talking with some of the merchants, and then Kendra had her woman withdraw and she sat down with the grey-haired cleric towards the front of the old chapel, near the disk. It needed polishing, she noticed. She'd tell someone tomorrow.

Ceinion's eyes, she thought, were curiously like her father's. Alert, and just as unsettling when you had something you wanted to hide. She wasn't here to hide. She wouldn't *be* here if she were hiding.

"Princess?" he said calmly, and waited.

"I am afraid," she said.

He nodded. His face was kind, smooth-shaven, less lined than was usual for a man his age. He was small and trimly formed, not a laden-table, wine-cup cleric like the other one here, from Ferrieres. Her father had told them some time ago, before the first visit, that this man was one of the most learned scholars in the world, that the Patriarch in Rhodias sought his views on clashes of doctrine. In some ways it was hard to credit—the Cyngael lived so cut off from the world.

"Many of my people are greatly afraid just now," he said. "You are generous to share it with us. Your father has been very good, sending a ship to Arberth, messengers to the Rheden Wall. We can only hope—"

"No," she said. "That isn't it." She looked at him. "I *knew* when Alun ab Owyn entered the wood with my brother and the Erling."

A silence. She had shaken him, she saw. He made the sign of the disk. That was all right; she'd have done the same.

"You . . . you see spirits?"

He was very direct. She shook her head. "Well, once I did. One of them. A few nights ago. That isn't what I . . . from the time you came across the river, the other morning? When we were lying on the grass?" She heard herself sounding like a child. This was *so* difficult.

He nodded.

"Well, from that time, I . . . I can't explain this well, but I *knew* . . . ab Owyn. The prince. I could . . . read things in him? Know where he was."

"Dear Jad," whispered the high cleric of the Cyngael. "What is it that is coming among us?"

"What do you mean?" she asked.

He was looking at her, but not with eyes that spoke denunciation or disbelief. "Strange things are happening," he said.

"Not just . . . to me?" She was extremely determined not to cry.

"Not just to you, child. To him. And . . . others."

"Others?"

He nodded. Hesitated, then moved a hand sideways, back and forth. He wasn't going to say. Clerics, she thought, were good at not telling what they didn't want to tell. But he'd already said something, and she'd needed to know it, so much. She wasn't alone, or going mad.

He swallowed, and now she did see a hint of fear, which frightened her, in turn. She knew what he was going to ask, before he spoke.

"Do you . . . see him now? Where they are?"

She shook her head. "Not since they went in. I've been having dreams, though. I thought maybe you could help me."

"Oh, child, I have so little help to give in this. I am . . . enmeshed in fears."

"You're the only person I can think of."

Her father's eyes, very nearly. "Ask me, then," he said.

It was quiet here. Everyone had gone, except the aged cleric of the chapel, straightening candles at a side-altar near the door, and her own woman in a far row, waiting. This chapel was one of the oldest in Esferth, the wood of the benches and flooring worn smooth with years. It was dark where the lamps didn't reach, softly lit where they did. A feeling of calm. Or there ought to have been, Kendra thought.

"What can you tell me," she asked, "about the Volgan's sword?"

The ambit of a woman's life could not be said to be very wide. But how wide might it be for the majority of men alive on the god's earth, struggling to feed themselves and their families, to be warm in winter (or sheltered from the sandstorms in the south), safe from war and disease, sea-raiders and creatures in the night?

The Book of the Sons of Jad, more and more widely used in chapels now, even here in the Cyngael lands, taught that the world belonged to the mortal children of the god, saying so in words that were incantation: eloquent and triumphant.

It was difficult for Meirion mer Ryce to believe this to be true.

If they were all the glorious children of a generous god, why did some of them end up blood-eagled, soaked in blood, ripped apart, though they had only been a girl walking back from pasture with brimming pails after milking the two cows on a morning at the end of spring?

It was *wrong,* thought Meirion, defiantly, remembering her sister, as she did every single time coming back from the milking in the mist before dawn. Elyn was not a person who ought to have died that way. It wasn't what life should have held for someone like her. Meiri knew she wasn't wise enough to understand such things, and she knew what the cleric in the village had been telling them over and again since summer began, but Cyngael women were not particularly submissive or deferential, and if Meirion had been asked by someone she trusted to describe what she really felt, she would have said she was enraged.

No one ever asked (no one was trusted so much), but the anger was there, each day, every night, listening for sounds that never came now from the empty pallet along the adjacent wall. And it was with her when she rose in darkness to dress and go past the bed where Elyn wasn't any more, to do the milking her sister used to do.

Her mother had wanted to take the pallet apart, make more space in the small hut. Meiri hadn't let her, though lately, as summer had turned towards harvest and autumn, a chill now some nights, she'd begun thinking she might do it herself one afternoon after work was done.

She'd choose a clear day, when flame and smoke could be seen a long way, and she'd burn the bedding on the sun-browned tor above the fields as a memorial. Not enough, no remotely adequate answer to loss and helpless fury, but what else was there?

Elyn hadn't been a noblewoman or a princess. There was no consecrated place in the vault of a sanctuary for her bones, no carved words above or image on stone, no harp songs. She wasn't Heledd or Arianrhod, lost and lamented. She'd been only a farmer's daughter in the wrong place one too-dark pre-dawn hour, raped and carved open by an Erling.

And what was there that a sister could make for her remembering? A song? Meiri didn't know music, or even how to write her own name. She was a girl, unmarried (no man to fight for her), living with her parents near the border between Llywerth and Arberth. What was she going to do? Take fierce and fell revenge? Intervene in some battle, strike a blow against Erlings?

In the event, she did do that. Sometimes, despite all the weight of likelihood, we can. It is a part of the mystery of the world and needs to be understood that way.

In an hour before sunrise at the end of that summer Meirion heard sounds, muffled in mist, to her right, as she made her way home along the worn, grassy path from the summer pasture.

The path ran parallel to the road from Llywerth, though to call it a road was somewhat to overstate. Roads weren't much a part of the Cyngael provinces. They cost a great deal in resources and labour, and if you made a road it was easier to be attacked along it. Better, times being what they were, to live with some difficulty of travel and not smooth the way for those who meant you ill.

The rough path south of her, running past their farm and the hamlet, was one of the main routes to and from the sea, however, cutting through a gap in the Dinfawr Hills to the west and continuing east below the woods along the north bank of the Aber.

That's why Elyn had died. People passed too near them all the time, going east and west. That's why Meirion stopped now and carefully, quietly, set down her neck yoke with the brimming pails on either side. She left it in the grass, stood a moment, listening.

Horse hooves, harness, creak of leather. Clink of iron. There was no good reason for armed horsemen to be on this path before sunrise. Her first thought was a cattle raid: Llywerth outlaws (or noblemen) crossing into Arberth. Her village tried to stay out of these affairs; they didn't have enough cattle (enough of anything) to be a target for raiders. Better to let them go by, both ways, know nothing or as little as possible if pursuit came after (either way) with questions asked.

She'd have gone quietly back along her own path, walking home with the morning milk, if she hadn't heard voices. She didn't understand the words—which was the point, of course. She would have, if these men had been from Llywerth. They weren't. They were speaking Erling, and Meiri's sister, fiercely loved, had been slain and defiled by one of them at the beginning of summer.

She didn't go home. Anger can channel fear sometimes, master it. Meiri knew this land as she knew the tangles of her own brown hair. She crouched down, leaving the milk behind in the path (a fox found it later in the day, drank its fill). In the greyness she moved towards the voices and the trail. After a bit she went on her belly among the grass and scrub and wriggled closer. She didn't know anything about how Erlings (or anyone else) arranged themselves on a march-and-ride, so it was good fortune more than anything else that no outriders were sweeping the scrub-land north of the trail. Much of what happens in a life turns on good fortune or bad, which unsettles as much as it does anything else.

What she saw, peering through brambles, was a company of Erlings, some horsed, more of them afoot, stopped to talk, barely visible in the darkness and not-yet-lifted fog. What she heard was "Brynnfell," twice, unmistakably, the name springing at her from snapped and snarled words that made no sense at all, over the hammering of her blood.

She knew what she needed to know. She started to wriggle backwards on knees and elbows. Heard something behind her. Froze where she was, not breathing. She didn't pray. Ought to have, of course, but was too bone-frightened.

The lone horseman continued moving, passing just behind where she lay. She heard him cut down beyond the bushes she'd been peering through and rejoin the company on the road. Any raiding party had outriders, especially in hostile country where you weren't sure of your way. A dog would have found her, but the Erlings had no dogs.

Meirion fought a desire to stay where she was, motionless, forever, or until they went away. She heard the riders dismount. The river was close here, just to the south. They might be stopping for water and food.

She wanted that.

Listening carefully, behind her as well now, she crawled backwards, regained her own path. Left the milk where it was and began to run. She knew where these raiders were going and what needed to be done. She wasn't certain if the men in the fields would listen to her. She was prepared to kill someone to make them do so.

She didn't have to. Sixteen farmers and farmhands, and ten-year-old Derwyn ap Hwyth, who never let himself be left behind, set off before the sun was fully up, running east to Brynnfell, taking the old track. That one stopped at their forest. It was a known and tamed wood, though, source of kindling and building logs, and there was a trail that would bring them out, eventually, near Brynn ap Hywll's farm.

Meirion's father, whose bad leg meant he couldn't keep up, took the one horse in the village and went north to Penavy. Found twelve men working by there. Said what needed to be said. They, too, went running, straight from the harvest fields, seizing whatever came to hand that was sharp and could be carried for a day and a night at speed.

Almost thirty men. Meirion's response. Not trained fighters, but hardy, knowing the land, and filled—each one of them—with anger bright and cold as a winter sun. This wasn't a vast invading fleet of dragon-prows from Erling lands. This was a raid, skulking through their land. They would fear the northmen, always, but they would not run from them.

It was crippled Ryce's daughter, his surviving daughter, who had come upon the raiders and carried—like a queen of legend—needful tidings back of where they were bound. A woman of the Cyngael, worthy of song. And they all knew, in the lands and villages around, what had been done to her sister.

They would reach Brynnfell half a day before the Erlings did.

The afternoon of the day she saw the raiders, Meirion—in a frenzy born of waiting—took Elyn's pallet apart. She began to carry the straw and bedding up the tor. Her mother and the other women saw what she was doing and set themselves to help, gathering wood, arranging it on the flat summit. All of them working, women walking up and down the hill. Late in the day, the sun westering and the last crescent of the blue moon rising (no moons at all tomorrow), they lit a bonfire there for Elyn. Only a girl. No one important at all, by any measure you might ever think to use.

Bern could not shake a premonition, death hovering like some dark bird, one of Ingavin's ravens, waiting.

Fog among encroaching hills. Sounds muffled, vision limited. Even when day broke and the mist lifted, that sense of oppression, of a waiting stillness in the land, lingered. He felt they were being watched. They probably were, though they saw no one. This was a strange land, Bern thought, different from any he'd known, and they were moving away from the sea. He had no illusions of being prophetic, of any kind of truesight or knowing. He told himself this was no more than apprehension. He'd never been in a battle, and they were heading towards one.

But it wasn't fear. It really wasn't. He had memories of fear. The night before his Jormsvik fight he'd lain beside a prostitute, hadn't slept at all, listened to her untroubled breathing. He'd been quite certain it was the last night he'd know. Fear had been within him then; there was something different now. He was wrapped in a sense of strangeness, something unknown. Fog in these hills and the nature of the lives men lived. His father entangled in it, much as he might want to deny that.

Denial would be a lie, simple as that. Thorkell had *told* him not to let them sail to the Cyngael lands. Brand had *killed* the last of the Volgans for his deception, yet here they were now, on the quest Ivarr had tried to deceive them into taking on.

Brand One-eye and the other leaders had seized upon Ivarr's idea: vengeance and the Volgan's sword. A way out of humiliation. So they were doing what he'd wanted them to do, even though they'd killed him for it and tossed him to the sea. It could make you feel things had gone awry.

Brand had spoken of it calmly enough, sailing west and then north with the wind to where they'd beached. How this was a bad time for them to suffer defeat. (Was there a *good* time, Bern had wondered.) How claiming the sword would be a triumph, hewn brilliantly out of failure and defeat. A talisman against ambitious men in the north who thought they could be king and impose their will upon the Jormsvikings.

Bern wasn't so sure. It seemed to him that these named reasons were covering something else. That Brand Leofson was wishing he'd thought of Ivarr's quest himself, that what the one-eyed man was seeing, in his mind, was glory.

That would be fair enough, ordinarily. What else, as the skalds sang to harp by hearth fire all winter, was there for the brave to seek? *Wealth dies with a man, his name lives ever.*

Ingavin's halls were for warriors. Ripe, pliant maidens with red lips and yellow hair did not offer mead (and themselves) to farmers and smiths at the golden tables of the gods.

But his father had told them not to come this way.

They weren't even certain where they were going in these hills and narrow valleys. Brand and Carsten had known the harbour from years before, but neither of them, nor Garr Hoddson, had ever been as far inland as Brynnfell. They'd started east, thirty riders, sixty on foot, fifty left to the ships to get them offshore if they were found. Scarcely enough for that, Bern had thought, but he was one of the youngest here, what did he know?

Carsten had urged a fast out-and-back raid with just the horsemen, since they were only going to kill one man and find one thing. Brand and Garr had disagreed. Ap Hywll's farm would be defended. They'd have to go more slowly, with men on foot, a larger force. Bern, on Gyllir, was one of the horsemen sweeping both sides of the path (just a track, really) as they went.

They saw no one. A good thing, you might have said, preserving their secrecy—but Bern couldn't shake the feeling that others were seeing *them*. They didn't belong here—somehow the land would know it—and the sea, their real haven, was farther away every moment.

On the second day, going through a range of hills in a drizzle of rain, one of the outriders had found a woodcutter and brought him back, hands tied behind him, running before the horse at sword-point.

The man was small, dark, raggedly clothed. His teeth were rotting. He didn't speak Erling; none of them spoke

Cyngael. They hadn't *expected* to be here, hadn't chosen any of those who did know the tongue. This was supposed to have been a raid on undefended Anglcyn *burhs*. That's what Ivarr had paid them for.

They tried talking to the woodcutter in Anglcyn, which should have been close enough. The man didn't know that language either. He'd soiled himself in terror, Bern saw.

Brand, impatient, edgy, angry now, had drawn his sword, seized the man's left arm and sliced his hand off at the wrist. The woodcutter, hair plastered with rain, drenched in his sweat and stink, had stared blankly at the stump of his wrist.

"Brynnfell!" Brand had roared in the falling rain. "Brynnfell! Where?"

The woodcutter had looked up at him a moment, vacant-eyed, then fainted dead away. Brand had sworn savagely, spat, looked around as if for someone to blame. Garr, scowling, put a sword through the Cyngael where he lay. They'd moved on. The rain continued to fall.

Bern's feeling of oppression had begun to grow then. They'd travelled through the evening, stopping only briefly at night. They heard animals moving, owls overhead and in the trees on the slopes around, saw nothing at all. Before morning they'd come out of the hills into more open lowlands though the mist was still there.

There would be farms here, but Brand thought Brynn's was another day away, at least. He was going by half-remembered stories. They made a stop before dawn, doled out provisions, drank at the river just south of them, moved on as the sun came up.

Bern thought of his father, mending a barn door on Rabady, a sunset hour. Glory, it occurred to him, might come at a heavy price. It might not be the thing for every man.

He leaned forward, patted Gyllir on the neck. They continued east, a forest appearing north of them, the river murmuring south, running beside their path and then turning away. Bern didn't like the secretive, green-grey closeness of this land. The sun went down, the last crescent of the blue moon was in front of them, and then overhead, and then behind. They stopped for another meal, continued through the night. They were mercenaries of Jormsvik, could do without sleep for a night or two to gain the advantages of surprise and fear. Speed was the essence of a raid: you landed, struck, left death and terror, took what you wanted and were gone. If you couldn't do that you didn't belong, you shouldn't be on the dragon-ships, you were as soft as those you came to kill.

You might as well be a farmer or a smith.

It was a brighter morning, at least. They seemed to have left the mists behind. They went on.

Late in the day, with a breeze and white clouds overhead, they were met by Brynn ap Hywll and a company of men at a place where they were moving up a slope and the Cyngael were waiting above them. Not soft, not surprised, or afraid.

Looking up, Bern saw his father there.

ALUN DIDN'T SEE IVARR RAGNARSON. The sun was behind the Erlings, forcing him to squint. Brynn had taken the higher ground, but the light might become a problem. The numbers were close, and they had twenty men in reserve, hidden on either side of the slope. The Erlings had horsemen, twenty-five or so, he guessed. They weren't the best riders in the world, but horses made a difference. And these were Jormsvikings they were about to face, with a company that was mostly farm labourers.

It was better than it might have been, but it wasn't good.

The Erlings had stopped at first sight of them. Alun's instinct would have been to charge while the horses were halted, use the downslope to effect, but Brynn had given orders to wait. Alun wasn't sure why.

He found out, soon enough. Ap Hywll called out, the big voice carrying down the slope, "Hear me! You have made a mistake. You will not get home. Your ships will be taken before you return to them. We had warning of your coming." He was speaking in Anglcyn.

"That is a lie!" A one-eyed man, easily as big as Brynn, moved his horse forward. Battles began this way in the tales, Alun thought. Challenge, counter-challenge. Speeches for the harpers. This wasn't a tale. He was still scanning the Erlings for the man he needed to kill.

Brynn had the same thought, it seemed. "You know it is true, or we wouldn't be here with more men than you have. Surrender Ivarr Ragnarson and give hostages and you'll sail alive from these shores."

"I shit upon that!" the big man shouted. And then, "Ragnarson's dead, anyhow."

Alun blinked. He looked at Thorkell Einarson, beside him. The red-bearded Erling was staring at the opposing forces. His own people.

"How so?" Brynn cried. "How is he dead?"

"By my blade at sea, for deceiving us."

Amazingly, Brynn ap Hywll threw his head back and laughed. The sound was startling, utterly unexpected. No one spoke, or moved. Brynn controlled himself. "Then what in Jad's name are you doing here?"

"Come to kill you," the other man said. His face had reddened at the laughter. "Are you ready to find your god?"

A silence. Late afternoon, late summer. Late in life, really, for both of the men speaking now.

"I've been ready a long time," said Brynn, gravely. "I don't need a hundred men to go with me. Tell me your name."

"Brand Leofson, of Jormsvik."

"You lead this company?"

"I do."

"They accept that?"

"What does that mean?"

"They will follow orders you give?"

"Kill any man who doesn't."

"Of course you will. Very well. You leave two ships to us, twenty hostages of our choosing, and all your weapons. The rest of you will be allowed to go. I will send a rider to Llywerth and another to Prince Owyn in Cadyr—they will let you leave. I cannot speak to what will happen when you sail past the Anglcyn coast."

"Two ships!" The Erling's voice was incredulous. "We *never* leave hostages, you shit-smeared fool! We never leave our ships!"

"Then the ships will be taken when you die in these lands. You will never leave, any of you. Decide. I am not of a mind to talk." His voice was cold now.

One of the Erlings came forward on foot, stood by the stirrup of the one-eyed man. They whispered together. Alun looked at Thorkell again. Saw that the other man was gazing over at Brynn.

"How do we know you aren't lying about Llywerth and Cadyr? How would they know about us?" It was the second Erling, standing by the one named Leofson.

A horseman twitched his reins and moved forward to sit his mount beside Brynn. "You know because I tell you it is true. We rode through the spirit wood, three of us, to bring warning of your coming here."

"Through the spirit—! *That* will be a lie! Who are . . . ?"

The Erling fell silent. He'd sorted the answer to his own question. It was the accent, Alun realized. The flawless, courtly Anglcyn tones.

"My name is Athelbert, son of Aeldred," said the young man beside Brynn, who had ridden with them through the godwood to serve a cause that wasn't his own. "Our *fyrd* killed sixty of you. I will be unspeakably happy to add to that number here. My father has sent a ship from Drengest, right behind yours, with a warning for Cadyr. They will have had it days ago, while you were coming here. Ap Hywll speaks truth. If we do not send to stop them, the Cyngael will take your ships or drive them offshore, and you will have nowhere to go. You are dead men, where you stand. Jormsvik will never be the same. They will mock your names forever. You cannot possibly imagine the pleasure it gives me to say these words."

A murmuring among the Erling host below them. Alun heard anger but no fear. He hadn't expected to. He saw some of them begin to draw blades and axes. With a hard, fierce sense of need, he unsheathed his sword. It had come, it had finally come.

"Wait," said Thorkell quietly beside him.

"They're drawing weapons!" Alun rasped.

"I see it. Wait. They will win this fight."

"They will not!"

"Trust me. They will. Ap Hywll knows it too. Numbers are close, but they have horsemen and fighters. Brynn has his thirty men but the rest are farmers with scythes and sticks. *Think!*"

His voice carried towards the front. Later, Alun decided he had meant it to do so. Brynn turned his head slightly.

"They know they cannot leave these shores alive," he said, softly.

"I think they do," Thorkell Einarson said, still quietly, speaking Cyngael. "It won't matter. They cannot give you hostages or ships and go back to Jormsvik. They will die first."

"So we fight. Kill enough of them so that tomorrow or the next—"

"And what will your wives and mothers say, and the fathers of these two princes?" Thorkell never raised his voice.

Brynn turned around. Alun saw his eyes in the late-afternoon light. "They will say that the Erlings, accursed of Jad and the world, slew yet more good men before their time. They will say what they have always said."

"There is a way out."

Brynn stared at him. "I am listening," he said. Alun felt the breeze blowing, making their banners snap.

"We challenge him," Thorkell said. "He wins, they are allowed to leave. He loses, they yield the two ships and hostages."

"You just said—"

"They cannot *surrender* ships. They can lose a fight. Honour requires they deal fairly then. They will. This is Jormsvik."

"That difference matters enough?"

Thorkell nodded. "Always has."

"Good," said Brynn, after a moment, smiling. "Good. I fight him. If he will do it."

Looking back, Alun remembered that four people said *No* at the same moment, and he was one of them.

But the voice that continued, when the others stopped in surprise, was a woman's. "No!" she said again.

Alun turned, they all did. On the side slope, quite close in fact, on horseback, were the lady wife and the daughter of Brynn ap Hywll. He saw Rhiannon, saw her looking at him, and his heart thumped, a barrage of memories and images falling like arrows from the bright sky.

It was the mother who had spoken. Brynn was gazing at her. She shifted her mount to come forward among them.

"I told you to stay at home," he said, mildly enough.

"I know you did, my lord. Chastise me after. But hear me first. The challenge is proper. I heard what he said. But it is not yours this time."

"It has to be mine. Enid, they came to kill me."

"And must not be allowed the pleasure. My dear, you are the summit and glory of all men living."

"I like the sound of that," said Brynn ap Hywll.

"I imagine you do," said the lady Enid. "You are vain. It is a sin. You are also, I grieve to tell you, old and short-winded, and fat."

"I am not fat! I am—"

"You are, and your left knee is aching as we speak, and your back is stiff each day by this hour."

"He's old too! That one-eyed captain carries his years—"

"He's a raider, my lord." It was Thorkell. "I know the name. He is still a fighting man, my lord. What she says is truth."

"Are you here to shame me, wife? Are you saying I cannot defeat—?"

"My love. Three princes and their sons stood aside for you twenty-five years ago."

"I see no reason why—"

"Do not leave me," said Enid. "Not this way."

Alun heard birdsong. The doings of men here, the wrack and storm of them, hardly mattering at all. It was a summer's day. The birds would be here when this was over, one way or another. Brynn was gazing at his wife. She dismounted, without assistance, and knelt on the grass before her husband. Brynn cleared his throat.

It was Athelbert who broke the stillness. He twitched his reins and moved towards the Erlings, down the slope a little way. "Hear me. We are told that you cannot surrender the ships. You must understand you are going to die, if so. A challenge is now offered you. Choose a man, we do the same. If you are victorious, you will be permitted to sail from here."

"And if we lose?"

They were going to accept. Alun knew it, before they'd even heard the terms. It was in the quickened voice of the one-eyed captain. These were mercenaries, bought to fight, not *berserkirs* lusting after death. He was feeling something strange, a circling of time.

Three princes and their sons. His father had been one of those sons, twenty-five years ago. Alun's age, very nearly. Brynn had been, too. What was unfolding here felt as if it were part of a skein spun back to that strand in Llywerth.

Athelbert was speaking again. "You forfeit two ships, your weapons, including those on the ships, and ten hostages as surety, to be released in the spring. Not a surrender. A challenge lost."

"How do we get home without weapons? If we meet anyone at all—"

"Then you had best win, hadn't you? And hope you don't encounter my father's ships. Accept now, or fight us here."

"Accepted," said Brand Leofson, even faster than Alun had thought he would.

Alun's heart was beating hard now. It had come. He was thinking of Dai, of course. Ragnarson was dead, but there was an Erling raider below them with a sword. The skein was spun. He drew a steadying breath. His turn to twitch reins, move his horse forward towards the destiny that had been shaped for him at the end of spring.

"I'll do it," said Thorkell Einarson.

Alun pulled up his horse, looked quickly back.

"I know you will," said Brynn, very softly. "I suppose that's why Jad led you here."

Alun opened his mouth to protest, found he had no words. Reached for them, urgently. Thorkell was looking at him, an unexpected expression in his eyes.

"Think of your father," he said. And then, turning away, "Prince Athelbert, have I leave to use the sword you gave me in the wood?"

Athelbert nodded, did not speak. Alun wondered if he looked as young as the Anglcyn did just now. He *felt* that way, a child again, allowed passage among the men, like the ten-year-old who had joined them with the farmers from the west.

Thorkell swung down from his horse.

"Not a hammer?" Brynn asked, brisk now.

"Not in single combat. This is a good blade."

"Will you suffer a Cyngael helm?"

"If it doesn't split because of cheap workmanship."

Brynn ap Hywll didn't return the smile. "It's my own." He took it off, handed it across.

"I am honoured," said the other man. He put it on. "Armour?"

Thorkell looked down the slope. "We're both in leather. Leave it be." He turned to the woman, still kneeling on the grass. "I thank you for my life, my lady. I have not lived a life deserving of gifts."

"After this, you will have," said Brynn, gruffly. His wife looked at the red-bearded Erling, made no reply. Brynn added, "You see his eye? How to use that? Kill him for me."

Thorkell looked at him. Shook his head ruefully. "The world does strange things to a man if he lives long enough."

"I suppose," said Brynn. "Because you are fighting for us? For me?"

Thorkell nodded. "I loved him. Nothing was ever the same, after he died."

Alun looked at Athelbert, who was looking back at him. Neither said a word. The birds were singing, all around them.

"Who fights for you?" shouted the big Erling down the slope. He had dismounted and come up alone, halfway to where they were. He'd put on his helmet.

"I do," said Thorkell. He started down. A murmur rose from below, when they saw it was an Erling.

Alun saw that Enid was wiping at tears with the back of one hand. Rhiannon had come up beside her mother. He still didn't have his own heart's beating under anything like control. *Think of your father*.

How had he known to say that?

BERN WATCHED HIS FATHER coming down. He had been staring in disbelief from the moment they saw the Cyngael. Thorkell was easy to see, he always had been, half a head taller than most men, with the red banner of his beard.

So the son had known, without hearing a word spoken but watching the telltale gestures of the men above them, that it had been Thorkell who had spoken of single combat when battle had been upon them. So many of the stories told and sung—all the way back to Siferth and Ingeld in the snow—were of single combat. Glory and death: what brighter way to find either of them?

He'd heard others beside him, calculating swiftly, trying to decide if there were Cyngael hidden behind the slopes either side, and if so, how many. Bern had no sense of such things, could only register what he'd heard: they could win this fight, it was judged, but would take losses, especially if there were arrows among those in reserve.

And they wouldn't leave these lands. They had understood that from the moment the Anglcyn prince— impossibly here among them—said what he did.

Bern had had those premonitions of disaster, on the longship coming here and all the way through the black hills east. It seemed he might have more claim to foresight than he'd ever thought. Not the best time to discover that.

Then the Anglcyn prince came forward a second time and offered the challenge. It would be easy to hate that voice, that man, Bern thought. Terse muttering beside him, experienced men: if they gave up their weapons they might as well be naked, one said, heading back through a hostile land, then trying to get home, rowing into the wind, desperately vulnerable to anyone they met, with Aeldred's ships waiting for them. Without weapons, they couldn't winter over, either.

It was a challenge that offered the illusion of survival if they lost; not more than that. But they were dead if they did battle here, win or lose.

"Brand, you can slice the fat man apart," he heard Garr Hoddson rasp. "Do it, we get home. *And* you'll have killed Brynn ap Hywll. Why we came!"

Brynn ap Hywll. Bern looked up at the Volgan's slayer. Erling's Bane. He was an old man. Brand *could* do it, he thought, remembering the speed of Leofson's blade, looking at the hard, scarred tautness of him. He would save them, as a leader should. There was a window opening, Bern thought.

Brand shouted, *"Accepted!"* and drew his sword.

Then he cried, "Who fights for you?" And the window closed.

Bern heard his father say, "I do," and saw him start down towards where Brand was waiting.

The setting sun made a firebrand of Thorkell's beard and hair. They were so far, Bern thought, looking up at

him, from the barn and field on Rabady. But the light—the
light now was the same as on evenings he remembered.

NEITHER MAN WAS YOUNG. Both had done this before.
Combat could start a battle or avert it, and there was
fame for the winning, even if this was a skirmish, a raid,
not a war.

They approached each other, both eyeing the ground,
in no obvious haste to begin. Brand Leofson smiled thinly.
"We're on a slope. Want to move to flatter ground?"

The other man—Brand had a vague sense he ought
to know him—shrugged. "Same for both. Might as well
be here."

The two swords were the same length, though Brand's
was heavier than the other's Anglcyn blade. They were
both big men, of a height, pretty much. Brand judged he
had several years' advantage. Still, he was disconcerted to
be facing another Erling. It was unexpected. Just about
everything on this Ingavin-cursed raid had been.

"What did they do? Promise to free you if you won?"

The other was still looking around at the grass,
gauging it. He shrugged a second time, indifferently.
"I imagine they might do that, but it didn't come up.
I suggested this, actually."

"Hungry for death?"

The other man met his gaze for the first time.

He was still higher up, looking down. Brand didn't
like it, resolved to do something about that as soon as
they started.

"It comes for us. No need to be hungry, is there?"

One of those, it seemed. Not the sort of man Brand
liked. Good. Made this even easier. He took a few
more moments to do what the other was doing; noted
a fallen branch to his left, a depression in the ground
behind it.

He looked at the other man again. "You suggested it? Did me a service, then. This has been the worst voyage."

"I know. I was with Aeldred when they butchered you. It's because of Ragnarson. Ill luck in the man. You really killed him?"

"On my ship."

"Should have turned home, then. Didn't someone tell you to? A good leader cuts losses before they grow."

Brand blinked, then swore. "Who in Thünir's name are you to tell me what a leader does? I'm a Jormsvik captain. Who are you?"

"Thorkell Einarson."

Only that, and Brand knew. Of course he knew. Strangeness piled on strangeness. Red Thorkell. This one was in the songs; had rowed with Siggur, his companion, one of those on the Ferrieres raid when they'd found the sword. The sword Brand had come to regain.

Well, *that* wasn't about to happen.

A weaker man, he told himself, would have been disturbed by this revelation. Brand wasn't. He refused to make too much of it. All that history just meant the other man was older than he'd guessed. Good, again.

"Will they honour the terms?" he asked, not commenting on the name or showing any reaction. It was on his mind, though: how could it *not* be?

"The Cyngael? They're angry. Have been since the raid here. You kill anyone on the way?"

"No one. Oh. Well, one. Woodcutter."

The red-beard shrugged again. "One isn't so much."

Brand spat, cleared his throat. "We didn't know how to get here. I told you, a terrible raid. Worst since a time in Karch." That was deliberately told. Let this one know Brand Leofson had been about, too.

Something occurred to him. "You were the Volgan's oarmate. What are you doing fighting for the pig who killed him?"

"A good question. Not the place to answer it."

Brand snorted. "You think we'll find a better place?"

"No."

Einarson had courteously moved down and to one side, so they stood level on the slope, facing each other. He lifted his blade, pointing to the sky in salute. The conversation, evidently, was over. An arrogant bastard. A pleasure to kill him.

"I'm going to slice you apart," Brand said—Hoddson's words a moment ago, he liked the ring of them. He returned the salute.

Einarson seemed unruffled. Brand needed more from him. He was trying to work himself into anger, the fury that had him fighting his best.

"You aren't good enough," Thorkell Einarson said.

That would help. "Oh? Want to see, old man?"

"I suppose I'm about to. You've charged your companions with what you want done with your body? Have you a request of me?"

Courtesy again, Erling ritual. He was doing everything properly, and Brand was beginning to hate him. It was useful. He shook his head. "I am ready for what comes. Ingavin watch now and watch over me. Who guards your soul, Einarson? The Jaddite god?"

"Another good question." The red-haired man hesitated for the first time, then smiled, a curious expression. "No. Habits die hard, after all." With that same odd look on his face he said, exactly as Brand had done, "I am ready for what comes. Ingavin watch now and watch over me."

And whatever all that meant, Brand didn't know, nor did he care. Someone had to start. You could kill a man at the start. They were only wearing leather. He feinted a thrust and cut low on his backhand. If you took someone in the leg he was finished. A favourite attack, done with power. Blocked. It began.

WHAT HE KNEW of fighting he knew from his father. A handful of lessons as he'd grown through boyhood, offered irregularly, without notice or warning. At least twice when Thorkell had been suffering the after-effects of stumbling at dawn out of a tavern. He'd grab swords, helms, gloves, order his son to follow him outside. Something in the way of a father's duty, was the sense of it. There were things Bern needed to know. Thorkell told them, or showed them, briskly, not lingering to amplify, then had Bern take the weapons and armour back in while he carried on himself with whatever else needed tending to on a given day. A son's footwork as important—not necessarily more so—as a milk goat's bad foot.

You noted your opponent's weapon, looked to see if he had more than one, studied the ground, the sun, kept your own blade clean, had at least one knife on you always, because there were times when weapons could clash and shatter. If you were very strong you could use a hammer or an axe, but they were better in battle, not individual combat, and Bern was unlikely to grow big enough for them. He'd do better to be aware of that, work at being quick. You kept your feet moving, always, his father had said.

Nothing ever in the tone, Bern remembered, beyond simple observation. And observation, simple or otherwise, was the underlying note to all the terse words spoken. Bern had killed a Jormsvik captain with these injunctions in his head: judging the other man to be hot-tempered, overconfident, too full of himself for

caution, riding a less-sure horse than Gyllir. Bern was a
rider, Gyllir his advantage. You watched the other, his
father had said, learned what you could, either before or
while you fought.

Bern watched. The late-day light was uncannily clear
after the mist of the mornings through which they'd come
to this ending. The two men circling each other, engaging,
breaking to circle again, were etched by brilliant light.
Nothing shrouded now. You could see every movement,
every gesture and flex.

His father was years removed from fighting days, had
the bad shoulder (his mother used to rub liniment into it
at night) and a hip that nothing really helped in wet
weather. Brand was harder, still a raider, quicker than such
a big man ought to be, but had the bad, covered eye.

He also, Bern realized, after the two men had exchanged
half a dozen clashes and withdrawals, did something when
he tried a certain attack. Bern was watching; saw it. His
father had taught him how. His father was fighting for his
life. Bern felt unsteady, light-headed. Couldn't do anything
about that.

"JAD'S BLOOD! He's too old to keep parrying. He needs
to win quickly!"

Brynn was at Alun's side, swearing and exclaiming in
a steady, ferocious undertone, his own body twisting with
the two men fighting below. Alun didn't see either man
faltering yet, or any obvious opportunities to end it
quickly. Thorkell was mostly retreating, trying to keep
from being forced below the other man on the slope. The
Jormsvik leader was very fast, and Alun was putting real
effort into resisting a deeply private, shaming awareness
of relief: he wasn't at all sure he could have matched this
man. In fact—

"Hah! Again! See it? *See*? Because of the eye!"

"What?" Alun glanced quickly at Brynn.

"Turns his head left before he cuts on the backhand. To follow his line. He gives it away! Holy god of the sun, Thorkell *has* to see that!"

Alun hadn't noticed it. He narrowed his gaze to concentrate, watch for what Brynn had said, but in that same moment he began to feel something strange: a pulsing, a presence, inexplicable, even painful, inside his head. He tried to thrust it away, attend to the fight, the details of it. *Green* kept impinging, though, the colour green; and it wasn't the grass or the leaves.

RHIANNON, WATCHING TWO MEN FIGHT, was dealing with something so new to her she couldn't identify it at first. It took her some moments to understand that what she was contending with was rage. A fury white as waves in storm, black as a piled-up thundercloud, no shading to it, no nuance at all. Anger, consuming her. Her hands were clenched. She could kill. It was in her: she wanted to kill someone right now.

"We should not have come," her mother said, softly. "We make them weaker."

Not what she wanted to hear. "He'd have taken the fight himself if you hadn't been here."

"They'd have stopped him," Enid said.

"They'd have tried. You're the only one who could. You know it."

Her mother looked at her, seemed about to say something, but did not. They watched the men below. It was eerily clear and bright just now.

The men below. What, Rhiannon mer Brynn thought savagely, was a woman? What was her life? Even here in the Cyngael lands, celebrated—or notorious—for their womenfolk, what, really, could they ever hope to be or do at a time like this? A time that *mattered*.

Easy enough, she thought bitterly, as swords clashed. They could watch, and wring their delicate hands, her mother and herself, but only if they first disobeyed clear and specific instructions to stay away and hide. Hide, hide! Or they could be targets for an attack, be violated, killed, or taken and sold as slaves, then mourned and exalted in song. Song, Rhiannon thought savagely. She could kill a singer, too.

Women were children till they first bled, then married to make children, and—if Jad was kind—their children would be boys who could farm and defend their land or go off to fight one day. There was a ten-year-old boy here with a small scythe. *A ten-year-old*.

She stood by her mother, aware that Enid was still trembling (uncharacteristically) because she'd been so sure Brynn would fight and die here. There might be some pattern or purpose at work, that her mother had saved a red-bearded Erling's life in the farmyard that night, claiming him, and now that man had taken Brynn's fight upon himself.

There might be a pattern. Rhiannon didn't care. Not right now. She wanted them all dead, these Erlings, here simply because they *could* come, in their longships with their swords and axes, because they exulted in killing and blood and death in battle so their gods would grant them yellow-haired maidens for eternity.

Rhiannon wished she had the powers of the Cyngael goddesses of old, the ones they were forbidden even to name since they'd embraced Jad here in the west. She wished she could invoke stone and oak, kill the raiders herself, leave bodies hacked in pieces on this grass. Let those yellow-haired maidens put them back together. If they wanted to.

She'd blood-eagle them. See if the so-fierce raiders of the sea came back here after *that*. Her mood of the long summer was entirely gone, swept like fog before wind: that wistful, aching, sleepless sense that things had gone awry. They had, they had. But there was a lesson to be learned: love and longing were not what life in the northlands was about. She knew it now. She was seeing it. The world was too hard. You needed to become harder yourself.

She stood beside her mother, her face expressionless, showing no least hint of what was raging within her. You could look at Rhiannon, limned in that brilliant light, and see her as a dark-haired maiden of sorrows. She would kill you, if she could, for thinking that.

ANOTHER YOUNG WOMAN, in Esferth far to the east, would have entirely understood these thoughts, sharing many, though with a different fire in her, and one she'd lived with all her life, no sudden discovery.

The bitterness of a woman's lot, the helplessness with which you watched brothers and other men ride out to glory with iron at their sides, was nothing new for her. Judit, daughter of Aeldred, wanted battle and lordship and hardship as much as any Erling raider cresting waves in a dragon-ship, coming ashore in surf.

Instead, she was readying herself for her wedding this winter to a boy in Rheden. She was working, this day, with her mother and her ladies, embroidering. There were skills a highborn lady was expected to bring to her marriage house.

By contrast to both of these, King Aeldred's younger daughter saw the world in a very different way, although this, too, had been suffering change, moment by moment, through these last, late days of summer.

Right now, with a pulsing pain behind her eyes and images impinging, erratic and uncontrollable like sparks from a fire, Kendra knew only that she needed to find the Cyngael cleric again, to tell him something important.

He wasn't at the royal chapel or the smaller one where he'd been before. She was in real distress. The sunlight, late in the day, forced her to screen her eyes. It occurred to her to wonder if this was what happened to her father when his fever took him, but she wasn't warm or faint. Only hurting, and with a terrifying, impossible awareness of fighting in the west, and a sword in her mind, flashing and going, and coming again, over and over.

It was her brother who found Ceinion for her. Gareth, summoned by a messenger, had taken one frightened look at Kendra sitting on a bench in the small chapel (unable to go back into the light, just yet) and had gone running, shouting for others to join him in the search. He came back (she wasn't sure how much time had passed) and led her by the elbow through the streets to the bright (too bright), airy room her father had had made for the clerics who were transcribing manuscripts for him. She'd kept her eyes closed, let Gareth guide her.

The king was there, among the working scribes, and Ceinion was with him, blessedly. Kendra walked in, one hand held by her brother, the other to her eyes, and she stopped, desperately unsure of how to proceed with her father here.

"Father. My lord high cleric." She managed that much, then stopped.

Ceinion looked at her, stood quickly. Could be seen to make a decision of his own. "Prince Gareth, of a kindness will you have a servant bring the brown leather purse from my rooms? Your sister needs a remedy I can offer her."

"I'll get it myself," said Gareth, and hurried out the door. Ceinion spoke a quiet word. The three scribes stood up at their desks, bowed to the king, and went out past Kendra.

Her father was still here.

"My lady," said Ceinion, "is this more of that matter of which we spoke before?"

She hesitated, in pain, in something more than pain. They burned witches, for heresy. She looked at her father. And heard Ceinion of Llywerth say, gravely, changing the way of things one more time, "There is no transgression here. Your royal father also knows the world of which you speak."

Kendra's mouth fell open. Aeldred had also stood, looking from one to the other of them. He was pale, but thoughtful, calm. Kendra felt as if she were going to fall down.

"Child," said her father, "it is all right. Tell me what you are seeing from the half-world now."

She didn't fall. She was spared that shame. They helped her to a high stool where a cleric had been working. The manuscript in front of her on the tilted surface of the desk had a gloriously coloured initial capital, half a page in height: the letter "G" with a griffin arched along its curve. The word it began, Kendra saw, was *Glory*.

She said, as clearly, as carefully as she could, "They are through the spirit wood. Or the Cyngael prince, Alun ab Owyn, is. He's the one I can . . . see. There are blades drawn, there is fighting."

"Where?"

"I don't know."

"Athelbert?"

She shook her head. The movement hurt. "I don't . . . see him, but I never did. Only the Cyngael, and I don't know *why*."

"Why should we understand?" her father said after a moment, gentle as rain. He looked at Ceinion, and then back at her. "Child, forgive me. This comes to you from me, I believe. You have the gift or curse I carry, to see that which most of us are spared. Kendra, there is no sin or failing in you."

"Nor in *you*, then, my lord," said Ceinion firmly, "if that is true, and I believe it is. Nor need you punish yourself for it. There are purposes we do not understand, as you say. Good, and the will of the god, are served in different guises."

She saw her father look at the grey-haired cleric, in his pale yellow robe of the god. The brightness of the robe hurt her eyes.

"They are fighting?" her father said, turning back to her.

"Someone is. I see swords and . . . and another sword."

"Close your eyes," said Ceinion. "You are loved here and will be guarded. Do not hide from what you are being given. I do not believe there is evil in it. Trust to Jad."

"To Jad? But how? How can I—"

"Trust. Do not hide."

His voice held the music of the Cyngael. Kendra closed her eyes. Dizziness, disorientation, unrelenting pain. *Do not hide.* She was trying not to. She saw the sword again, the one she'd asked the cleric about before, small, silver, shining in darkness, though there were no moons.

She saw green again, *green*, didn't understand, and then she remembered something, though she still did not understand. *Green* was wrapped around this, as a forest wrapped a glade. She cried out then, real pain, grief, in a bright room in Esferth. And on a slope in Arberth above where two men were fighting to the death, someone heard her cry, in his mind, and saw what she saw, what she gave him, and knew more than she knew.

She *heard* him say her name, in fear, and wonder, then another name. And then, with exquisite courtesy, given what she'd just done to him and what he had understood from it, he paused long enough to offer clearly to her, mind to mind, across river and valley and forest, what she surely needed to be told, so far away.

Who can know, who can ever know for certain, how the instruments are chosen?

Kendra opened her eyes. Looked at her father's hand which was holding hers the way he hadn't done since she was small, and she gazed up at him, crying, first time that day, and said, "Athelbert is there. He came alive through the wood."

"Oh, Jad," said her father. "Oh, my children."

If you wanted to defeat a man like this you had a narrow path to tread (and you kept your feet moving). Brand Leofson wasn't going to fall to some reckless thrust or slash and he was too big to overpower. You needed enough time to mark him, discover inclinations, the way he responded to what you tried, how he initiated his own attacks, what he said. (Some men talked too much.) But the time passing cut both ways as it slashed by: the Jormsviking was fast, and younger than you were. You'd be lying to yourself, fatally, if you thought you could linger to sort things out, or wear him down.

You had to do your watching quickly, draw conclusions, if there were any to be drawn, set him up for whatever it was you found. Such as, for example, a habit—clearly never pointed out to him—of turning his head to the left before he slashed on the backhand, to let the good right eye follow his blade. And he liked to slash low, sea-raider's attack: a man with a wounded leg was out of a fight, you could move right past him.

So you knew two things, quite soon in fact, and if you wanted to defeat a man like this you had an idea what needed to be done. You were also, a quarter-century past your own best years, still more than good enough to do it.

And no lying to the self in that. Thorkell Einarson hadn't been prone to that vice for a long time. There was a hard expression on his face as he retreated again and read the backhand cut one more time. He blocked it, didn't let it seem too easy. Circled right around again, below and then back to level, denying the other man the upslope he wanted. Not hard, not *really* hard yet. Knew what he was doing still. Could be worn down, would grow tired, but not too soon if Leofson kept signalling half his blows like that. There was a sequence you could use when you knew the other man had committed to a backhand slash.

The light was really very bright, an element in this combat, the westering sun shining along their slope, striking the two of them, the trees, the grass, the watchers above and below. No clouds west, dark ones piled up east— and those, underlit, made the late-day sky seem even more intense. He'd known evenings like this among the Cyngael, perhaps more valued because of the rain and mist that usually wrapped these hills and silent valleys.

A land some men could grow accustomed to, but he didn't think he was the sort, unless in Llywerth by the sea. He needed the sea, always had; salt in the blood didn't leave you. He parried a downward blow (heavy, that one) then feinted a first low, forehand blow to see what Leofson would do. Overreacted—he would worry more on that side because of his eye. Hard on the hip, though, slashing that way. Ap Hywll's wife had named her husband's ailments. It might have been amusing, somewhere else. Thorkell's could have done the same with his. He briefly wondered where Frigga was now, how the two girls were faring, the grandsons he hadn't seen. Bern was here. His son was here.

It had been, thought Thorkell Einarson, a long-enough life.

Not without its share of rewards. Jad—or Ingavin and Thünir, whatever was waiting for him—hadn't been unkind to him. He wouldn't say it. You made your own fortune, and your own mistakes.

If you wanted to defeat a man like this . . . He smiled then, and began. It was time.

The raider facing him would remember that smile. Thorkell feinted again, as before, to draw the too-wide response. Followed, quickly, with a downward blow that Brand blocked, jarringly.

Then he let himself seem to hesitate, as if tired, unsure, his right leg still forward, exposed.

(*"Watch!"* said ap Hywll sharply, higher up the slope.)

(Bern, below them, caught his breath.)

Brand Leofson went for the deception, signalling his backhand again with a turned head. And once he'd committed himself—

Thorkell's blade moved high, to his own backhand.

Too soon.

Before Leofson had fully shifted his weight. A terrible mistake. Right side and chest wide open to a man still balanced. A fighting man with time (*It was time*) to change from a sweeping backhand slash to a short, straight-ahead thrust with a heavy sword. Heavy enough to pierce leather and flesh to the beating, offered heart.

Watching, Bern sank to his knees, a roaring in his ears. A sound like the surf on stones, so far inland.

Leofson pulled free his blade, not easily. It had gone a long way in. He had an odd expression on his face, as though he wasn't sure what had just happened. Thorkell Einarson was still standing, and smiling at him. "Watch the backhand," the red-haired man said to him, very low, no one else in the world to hear it. "You're giving it away, every time."

Brand lowered his bloodied sword, brow furrowing. You weren't supposed to . . . you didn't *say* things like that.

Thorkell swayed another moment, as if held up by the light, in the light. Then he turned his head. Not towards ap Hywll, for whom he'd taken this fight, or the two young princes with whom he'd gone through a wood and out of time, but to the Erlings on the slope below them, led here to what would have been their dying.

Or to one of them, really, at the end.

And he had enough strength left, before he toppled like a tree cut down, to speak, not very clearly, a single word.

"Champieres," he seemed to say, though it could have been something else. Then he fell into the green grass, face to the far sky, and whichever god or gods might be looking down, or might not be.

A long-enough life. Not without gifts. Taken, and given. All mistakes his own. Ingavin knew.

CHAPTER XVI

Kendra had been keeping her eyes closed. The light entering the room was still too bright, making the pain in her head worse, and when she looked around, the sense of disorientation—of being in two different places—only grew. With eyes closed, the inner sight, vision, whatever it was, didn't have to *fight* against anything.

Except her, and all she'd thought she knew about the world. But now she made herself look up, and open her eyes. Her father and Ceinion with her, no one else. Gareth had come with the herbs, and had gone back out. She'd heard her father giving him another task to do.

They were really just sending him from the room, that he not be burdened, as they were, with the awareness that King Aeldred's younger daughter seemed to be having the sort of visions that had you condemned for trafficking with the half-world. The world the clerics said—by turns— either did not exist at all, or must be absolutely shunned by all who followed the rites and paths of holy Jad.

Well and good to say, but what did you do when you saw what you did see, within? Kendra said, her voice thin and difficult, "Someone has died. I think . . . I think it is over."

"Athelbert?" Her father had to ask that, couldn't help himself.

"I don't think so. There is distress but not . . . not fear or pain right now. In him."

"In Alun? Ab Owyn?" That was Ceinion. She had to close her eyes again. It really was difficult, seeing and . . . seeing.

"Yes. I think . . . I don't think either of them was fighting."

"Single combat, then," her father said. Shrewdest man in the world. All her life. A gift for her and Judit, a burden at times for his sons. She had no certain idea he was right, but he almost always was.

"If two men fought, someone has lost. There is . . . Alun is heavy with sorrow."

"Dearest Jad. It will be Brynn, then," said Ceinion. She heard him sit heavily at one of the other stools. Made herself look, squinting, in pain.

"I don't think so," she said. "This is not so . . . sharp a grief?"

They looked at her. The most frightening thing of all, in some ways, was that these two men believed every impossible thing she was telling them.

Then she had to close her eyes once more, for the images were in her again, imposed, pushing *through* her towards the other one, so far away. Same as before, stronger now: green, green, green, and something shining in the dark.

"I need this to stop," Kendra whispered, but knew it wasn't going to. Not yet.

෧෨

Brynn was the first one down the hill, but not the first to reach the two of them, one standing with a red sword, the other lying in the grass. Brand Leofson, still caught in strangeness, not sure yet what had happened, saw—another mystery—his young shipmate come up to them and kneel on the grass beside the dead man.

Brand heard a sound from above, saw ap Hywll coming down.

"You will honour the fight?" he asked.

Heard Brynn ap Hywll say, bitter and blunt, "He let you win."

"He did not!" Brand said, not as forcefully as he wanted to.

The young one, Bern, looked up. "Why do you say that?" he asked, speaking to the Cyngael, not to his own leader, the hero who had saved them all.

Brynn was swearing, a stream of profanity, as he looked down at the dead man. "We were deceived," he said, in Anglcyn. "He took the fight on himself, intending to lose."

"He did *not!*" Leofson said again. Brynn's voice had been loud enough for others to hear.

"Don't be a fool! You know it," snapped the Cyngael. Men were coming over now, from below and above. "You show your backhand every time, he set you up for that."

Bern was still kneeling, for some reason, beside the dead man. "I saw that," he said, looking again at ap Hywll.

Brand swallowed hard. *Watch the backhand. You're giving it away* . . . What kind of a fool . . . ?

He stared at the boy beside the fallen man. The late light fell on both of them.

"Why are you there?" he said. But he wasn't a stupid man, and he knew his answer before it came.

"My father," said Bern.

No more than that, but much came all too clear. Brynn ap Hywll gazed down at the two of them, the living one and the dead, and began to swear again, with a ferocity that was unsettling.

Brand One-eye, hearing him, and with duties here, said, again, loudly, "You will honour the fight?"

Within, he was badly shaken. *What kind of a fool did something like this?* Now he knew.

Brynn ignored him, insultingly. The force of his fury slowed. He was looking at Bern. "You understand that he prepared *all* of this?" Still speaking Anglcyn, the shared tongue.

Bern nodded. "I . . . think I do."

"He did." It was a new voice. "He came through the godwood with us to do this, I think. Or make it possible."

Bern looked over. Aeldred's son, the Anglcyn prince. There was a smaller young man, Cyngael, beside him. "He . . . almost told us that," Prince Athelbert went on. "I said I was in the wood because of my father, and Alun was for his brother, and . . . Thorkell said he was a fit with us and would explain later how. He never did."

"Yes, he did," said Brynn ap Hywll. "Just now."

Leofson cleared his throat. This was all blowing much too far in a bad direction. You had to be careful when the rocks got close. "I killed this man in fair combat," he said. "He was old, he grew tired. If you want to try to—"

"Be silent," said ap Hywll, not loudly, but with no respect in his voice, *none* of what should come to a man who'd just saved his entire company. "We will honour your fight, because I would be shamed not to, but the world will know what happened here. Would you really have gone home and claimed glory for this?"

And to that, Brand Leofson had no reply.

"Leave now," Brynn continued bluntly. "Siawn, we do this properly. There is a dead man to be honoured. Send two riders to the coast to bring word to those of Cadyr who might be looking for the ships. Here's my ring, for them. No one is to attack. Tell them why. And take an Erling, their best rider, to explain to the ones left there."

He looked at Brand again, the way one looked at a low-ranking member of his household. "Which of your men can handle a horse?"

"I can," said the one kneeling beside the dead man, looking up. "I've the best horse. I'll go." He hadn't stood up yet.

"Are you certain? We will bury your father with all proper rites. If you wish to stay for . . ."

"No. Give him to us," Brand said, assertive for the first time. "He entrusted his soul to Ingavin, before we fought. This is truth."

Brynn's mood seemed to change again. Sorrow in his face, anger spent. The Cyngael, it was said, were never far from sadness. Rain and mist, dark valleys, music in their voices.

Ap Hywll nodded his head. "That seems fitting, I have to say. Very well. Take him with you. You will do him honour?"

"We will do him honour," Brand said, with dignity. "He was the Volgan's shipmate once."

HER OWN ANGER, Rhiannon realized, had also gone. It was more than a little unsettling: how one could be consumed, defined by rage, the desire—the *need*—to kill, and then have it simply disappear, drift away, leaving such a different feeling behind. She hadn't cried earlier; she was weeping now for a treacherous Erling servant of her mother's. She shouldn't be doing this, she thought. She shouldn't.

Her mother put an arm about her shoulders. Enid was calm again, thoughtful, holding her child.

It is over, Rhiannon told herself. *At least it is over now.*

IN THE SAGAS, Bern thought, when the hero died, to the monster's claws and teeth or the assembled might of deceitful foes, he always lay alive for some last moments so those who loved him could come and say that, and hear the last words he would speak, and carry them away.

Siferth had died that way, years after killing Ingeld on the ice, and so had Hargest in his brother's arms, speaking the words at the heart of all the sagas:

Cattle die kinsmen die.
  Every man born must die.
Fierce hearth fires end in ash.
  Fame once won endures ever.

It made for good verse. It might even be true. But not all of us are granted final words with those we are losing, not all of us are equal to the task of the last, memorable thing to say, or allowed it even if we are.

You were *supposed* to have that moment, Bern thought bitterly. In the Jaddite songs, too, there were such exchanges. The king speaking to his servant words to be remembered, to echo down the ages. The dying high cleric telling a wavering acolyte that which confirms him in faith and mission and changes his life—and the lives of others, after.

It wasn't right that there was nothing here but this . . . kneeling beside a death among so many strangers, enemies, in a distant land far from the sea. It wasn't right that your own last encounter had been so harsh. His father had saved him there, too, carrying him out of Esferth to his horse, sending him away, with instructions not to come to Brynnfell.

If they'd listened, if they'd gone home, this wouldn't have . . .

It wasn't his fault. Not his doing. He'd taken heed. A good son. Ivarr Ragnarson was *dead* because Bern had exposed him, as his father had wanted. He'd done what he'd been told. He'd . . . he'd honoured his father's words.

His father had killed two men, been exiled, cost his family home and freedom, the shape and pattern of their lives.

Had given one life back, here, bought with his own.

They were speaking above him of needing an Erling to ride to the ships with the Cyngael. Bern looked up, hoping they couldn't see how blurred and unmoored he felt, and said he'd go.

He heard Brand say, quietly, that Thorkell had chosen Ingavin for his soul at the end. He wasn't surprised. How could that be a surprise? But it did give him a thought. He slipped the hammer from about his neck and lifted his father's head, still warm in the late-day sunlight, and he gave Thorkell back his gift to carry up to the god's halls, where mead was surely (surely) being poured for him now, with Siggur Volganson there to lead the cries of welcome after waiting for so long.

He stood up carefully. Looked down at his father. It had been dark in the river the last time, nothing clearly to be discerned. It was bright here now. Some grey in the hair and beard, but really very little for a man of his years. Red Thorkell, still, at the end.

He looked over, met the gaze of Brynn ap Hywll. Hadn't expected what he saw there. They'd come to kill this man. Neither of them spoke. It crossed Bern's mind to say that he was sorry, but an Erling didn't say that to a Cyngael. He just nodded his head. The other man did the same. Bern turned away and went down the slope, to get Gyllir and ride. It was over.

In the great stories there were last words from the dying, and for them from those left behind. In life, it seemed, you galloped away, and the dead were borne after you towards a burning by the sea.

IT IS OVER, Bern thought, riding away, and Rhiannon mer Brynn had told herself the same thing, a little higher up the hill. Both were wrong, though young enough to be forgiven for it.

It does not end. A story finishes—or does for some, not for others—and there are other tales, intersecting, parallel, or sharing nothing but the time. There is always something more.

Alun ab Owyn, so pale that it was noted by all who looked at him, walked over towards Brynn. He was breathing carefully, holding himself very still.

"Lad. What is it?" Brynn's gaze narrowed.

"I need . . . I must ask something of you."

"After coming through that wood for us? Jad's blood, there is nothing you could ask that—"

"Don't say it. This is large."

The older man stared at him. "Let us walk away, then, and you will ask me, and I will say if I can do what you need."

They walked away, and Alun asked. Only the dog, Cafall, whom both of them had called theirs, was near to them, following. There was a breeze from the north, sliding the clouds away. A clear night coming, late-summer stars soon, no moons.

"It is very large," Brynn agreed, when Alun had done. He, too, was pale now. "And this is from . . ."

"This is from the half-world. The one that we . . . both know."

"Are you certain you understand . . . ?"

"No. No, I'm not. But I think . . . I have been caused to see something. And I am being . . . besought to do this."

"From when you were in the godwood?"

"Before. It began here."

Brynn looked at him. He wished Ceinion were with them. He wished he were a wiser, better, holier man. The sun was low. The Erlings, he saw, glancing down the slope, had taken the body of the dead man. Siawn had detailed men to go with them, escorts. Brynn didn't think there would be trouble. Something had changed with Einarson's death. He was still trying to sort that through, if he'd have done the same thing to save his own son, or daughters.

He thought so, but didn't know. He honestly didn't know.

Owyn's son was waiting, staring at him, his mouth pinched, clearly in great distress. He was the musician, Brynn remembered. Had sung for them the night the Erlings came. His brother had died here. This one had come through the spirit wood to warn them, and sent a faerie ahead to Brynn. Three nights she had waited above the yard for him to come to her. Failing that, the farm would have burned tonight. And Enid, Rhiannon . . .

He nodded his head. "I'll take you to Siggur Volganson's sword, where I buried it. Jad defend us both from whatever may befall."

It does not end. There is always more.

SHE IS WATCHING. Of course she is watching. How could she not have followed here? She is trying, from a distance, away from all the iron, to understand movements, gestures. She is not skilled at this (how could she be?). She sees him walk away with the other one, with whom she'd spoken on the slope, who is afraid of her, of what she is.

They do not see her. She is in the trees, muted, trying to understand, but distracted by the aura of other presences gathering as sundown nears: the Ride is close by, of course, and *spruaugh*, many of them, whom she has always disliked. One of those, she thinks, will have flitted to tell the queen already: about what she's done, what she is doing now.

There was one dead man, taken up by the others now. Only one. She has seen this before, years ago and years ago. It is . . . a game men play at war, though something more than that, perhaps. They die so swiftly.

She sees the two of them turn and go to their horses
and start back east, alone. She follows. Of course she
follows, among the trees. But just then, watching the two
of them, she feels—inexplicably strange, at first, then not
so—something she has never felt before, in all the years
since wakening. And then she realizes what it is. She is
feeling sorrow, seeing him take horse and ride. A gift.
Never before.

She enters the small wood above Brynnfell with the
two of them and the grey dog. The Ride is waiting by the
pool. She feels the queen's summons and goes to her, as
she must.

IT GREW DARKER as they rode, both carrying torches
now. The first stars out, clouds chased south by the wind.
Cafall loped beside the horses. No one else was with
them. Alun looked at the sky.

"No moons tonight?"

Brynn simply shook his head. The big man had been
silent on the ride. Alun was aware that this particular
journey would be laden with memory for him, like a
weight. *This is very large,* he had said. It was.

No moons. That, Alun thought, but did not say—for
Brynn was carrying enough—was the other reason time
had altered for the three of them in the spirit wood,
coming here.

Allowed to come here. He was remembering
Thorkell's hammer, laid upon the grass where they'd
heard the creature roaring. An offering, and perhaps
not the only thing offered. He, too, had ended up lying
on grass.

This was a different wood. The insistent images,
painfully imposed, coming from an Anglcyn princess in
Esferth, were green and shining still, as they entered
among the trees carrying their flames.

He'd chased Ivarr Ragnarson here, and his Erling horse had entered the pool and been frozen there, and he'd seen faeries, heard their music, seen Dai with the queen.

Never found Ivarr. That one was dead, it seemed. Not by Alun's hand. Not *his* revenge. Something else, a larger thing, to be done now. He was afraid.

The images in his mind had stopped. They were gone, as if the girl had been worn out sending them—or wasn't needed any more, now that he was here. He was supposed to know, by now, why he was in this wood. He was almost certain he did. That sense of something *pushing* into awareness was replaced by something else, more difficult to name.

He dismounted when Brynn did, and he followed him through the darkness; a twisting path through high summer trees (a small wood, this, but an old one, surely so, with faeries here). They were cautious with the torches. A forest could burn.

He saw the pool. His heart was beating fast. He glanced at Brynn, who had stopped, saw that the other man's face was rigid with strain. Brynn looked around, aligning himself. The sky was clear above the pool, they could see stars. The water was still, a mirror. No wind here. No sound in the leaves.

Brynn turned to him. "Hold this," he said, handing Alun his torch.

He set off around the edge of the pool, towards the south. Long-striding, almost hurrying, now that they were here. He would be tangled in memories, Alun thought. He followed, carrying light. Again Brynn stopped, again took his bearings. Then he turned his back on the water and walked over to a tree, a large ash. He touched it and went past. Three more trees, then he turned to his left.

There was a boulder, moss-covered (green), massive. Here, too, Brynn rested his hand a moment. He looked back at Alun. It was too hard to read his thoughts by torchlight. Alun could guess, though.

"Why didn't you destroy it?" he asked softly, his first words in the wood.

"I don't know," the other man said. "I felt as if it should stay with us. Lie here. It was . . . very beautiful."

He stayed that way a moment, then he turned his back on Alun, drew a breath, put a shoulder to that huge rock, and pushed, an enormously strong man. Nothing happened. Brynn straightened, wiped at his face with one hand.

"I can—" Alun began.

"No," said the other. "I did it myself, then."

Twenty-five years ago. A young man in his glory, a life ahead of him, the greatest deed of his days already done. What he'd be remembered for. He'd taken that fight for his own, over those whose rank should have made it theirs. Today, he had let a man take another combat, for him.

This was a proud man. Alun stood with the torches, Cafall beside him, and watched as Brynn turned back to the rock, spat on both his hands, and put them and his shoulder to it again, driving with body and legs, churning, grunting with exertion, then crying aloud Jad's name, the god, even here.

And the boulder rolled with that cry, just enough to reveal, by the light of Alun's torches, a hollow beneath where it had been, and something wrapped in cloth, lying there.

Brynn straightened, wiped at his dripping face again with one sleeve then the other. He swore, though softly, without force. Alun remained where he was, waiting. His heart was still pounding. The other man knelt, claimed the cloth, and what lay inside it. He stood up and carried it back before him the few steps out of those trees, past the ash to the grassy space by the starlit pool.

He cried aloud, raised a quick, warding hand. Alun, following, looked past him. They were here. Waiting. Not the faeries. The green, hovering figures he'd seen with the others in the spirit wood.

They were here, and they were the reason he was here. He knew what these were now, finally, and what they needed from him.

Besought. He was being pleaded with. To intervene. A mortal who could see the half-world, who had been in the Ride's pool here, had lain with a faerie in the northern reaches of the spirit wood. They would know this. When he'd entered the wood again with Thorkell and then Athelbert, they had come for him.

His heart was twisted, entangled, holding a weight that felt like centuries. He didn't know how the girl in Esferth was part of this (didn't know she'd been in the wood that same night) but she had given him the images they needed him to see. She had . . . a different kind of access to this.

And had brought him here, a second time.

"They will not harm us," he said quietly to Brynn.

"You know what these are?"

"Yes," said Alun. "I do now."

Brynn didn't ask the next question. Either he didn't want to know or, more probably, he was leaving this, in courtesy, to Alun.

Alun said, "If you will give me the sword, I think you should take Cafall and go. You do not need to stay with me."

"Yes I do," said the other man.

Hugely proud, all his days. A man had died, taking his fight this afternoon. Brynn unwrapped the cloth from around what it had held for so many years and Alun, coming nearer with both torches, saw the Volgan's small, jewel-hilted sword, taken from the raid on Champieres, and carried as a talisman until the day he died in Llywerth, by the sea.

The man who'd killed him held it out towards Alun. Alun handed him a torch, took the sword, gave Brynn the other flame. He unsheathed the blade, to look upon it. It was silver, Siggur Volganson's sword. Not iron. He'd known it would be, from the girl.

There came a sound from the green shapes gathered there—twenty of them, or nearly so, he judged. A keening noise, wind in leaves but higher. Sorrow was in him. The way of the Cyngael.

"You are . . . certain you wish to stay?"

Brynn nodded. "You don't want to be alone here."

He didn't. It was true. But still. "I don't think I have . . . permission to do this. I don't expect to live. Your wife asked you—"

"I know what she said. I will not leave you alone. Do what you must. We will bear witness, Cafall and I."

Alun looked beyond him. One of the green shapes had come nearer. They were almost human, as if twisted by time and circumstance a little away. He knew what they were, now. What they had been.

Brynn stepped away, back towards the encircling trees, carrying the torches. The dog was silent when it might have growled. It had done so in the spirit wood, Alun remembered. Something had changed. He set the scabbard down.

"You wish this, truly?" he said. Not to the other man this time. Brynn was behind him now. He was holding a silver sword and speaking to the green creatures that had come. They were in a clearing by the faerie queen's pool under stars on a night when neither moon would rise. Souls walked on such nights, so the old tales told.

No reply, or none spoken aloud. He had no idea if they could speak any tongue he might know. But the figure before him came nearer yet (slowly, so as not to startle him or cause fear, was the thought that came) and it knelt upon the dark grass before him.

He heard Brynn make a sound (the beginning of a prayer) and then stop himself. The other man had just realized, Alun thought, what was about to happen, though he wouldn't know why. Alun knew why.

He had not asked for this. He'd only ridden north from home one bright morning at the end of spring with his brother and favourite cousin and their friends on a cattle raid, as young men of the Cyngael had done since all songs began. He had ridden into a different, older story, it seemed.

Much older. These green things, and he still didn't know what they were called, had been human once. Like Brynn, like Alun himself, like Dai.

Entirely like Dai. These, he understood, heart aching, were the souls of the faerie queen's mortal lovers after she tired of them and sent them from her side. This is what became of them, after who could know how many years. And he was here (in a tale he had never known he was in) to set them free with silver, under stars.

His eyes were dry, his hand steady, holding the small sword. He touched the point and still-sharp edges. Not a warrior's blade this one, a slender, ceremonial sword. This was a ceremony, as much as anything else.

He drew a breath. There was no reason to wait, or linger. He'd been brought here for this. He stepped forward.

"Let there be light for you," he said. And thrust the Volgan's blade into the kneeling, shimmering creature, below what would have been its collarbone, long ago.

He was ready this time for the sound that came, and so did not flinch or startle when he heard that cry of release, or the deeper sound that came from the others gathered here. No wind, the water utterly still. Stars would be reflected in it.

There was nothing kneeling before him now, where the blade (too smoothly, almost no resistance) had gone. Alun understood. It was a soul, not a mortal body. It had died long ago. He was stabbing hearth smoke and memory.

He told himself that, again and again, as he besought light *(besought)* for each of them, one by one, as they came and knelt and he did what they had drawn him here to do for them. He became aware of how grateful he was that Brynn had stayed, after all, that he wasn't here alone to do this in the dark, wrapped in sorrow, hearing that aching joy in each of them at their release, the sound they made.

His hand was steady, each time, over and again. He owed them that, having been chosen for this. Exchanges in spirit woods, he was thinking. A hammer laid down in one forest that a sword might be lifted from under a boulder in another. Thorkell's life for his and Athelbert's, and so many others on that slope today (mortals, all).

He had no idea how much time had passed or if, indeed, it had.

He looked down upon the last of these kneeling souls taken once, and discarded, by the faerie queen. He offered his prayer for it and plunged the sword and heard the cry, and saw this last one flicker and drift from sight as the others had done. Nothing green left glimmering in the glade. And so this, Alun thought, was the last exchange, final balancing, an ending.

He, too, was young. To be forgiven this error, as the others were.

He heard music. Looked up. Behind him, Brynn began, quietly, to pray.

Light upon the water, pale, as if moonlight were falling. And then the light (which was not moonlight) took shape, attained form, and Alun saw, for a second time, faeries coming across the surface of the pool, to the sound of flutes and bells and instruments he did not know. He saw the queen (again), borne in her open litter, very tall, slim, clothed in what would be silk or something finer, silver-hued (like his sword). Faeries, passing by.

Or not, in fact, passing. Not this time. The music stopped. He heard Brynn behind him, ceaselessly speaking the invocation of light, the first, the simplest prayer. The dog was silent, still. Alun looked at the queen, and then made himself look beside her.

Dai was there, as he had been before (so little time would have passed for them, he thought). He was riding a white mare with ribbons in her mane, and the queen was reaching out and holding him by the hand.

Silence upon the water. Brynn's murmuring the only sound in the glade. Alun looked at that shining company, and at his brother (his brother's taken soul). Without having intended to, he knelt then on the grass. His turn to kneel. They were so far inside the half-world; only with mercy would they ever come out, and faeries were never known for mercy, in the tales.

They did make bargains, though, with mortals they favoured, and there *can* be a final balancing, though we might not expect it or know when it has come.

Kneeling, looking upon that tall, pale, exquisite queen in her silvered light upon water, he saw her gesture, a movement of one hand, and he saw who came forward, obedient, dutiful, from among those in her train, to her side. No sound. Brynn, he realized, had fallen silent.

Grave, unsmiling, achingly beautiful, the faerie queen gestured again, twice, looking straight at Alun, and so he understood—finally—that there could be indulgence, mercy, a blessing, even, entangled with all sorrows (the cup from which we drink). She reached out one arm and laid it like a barrier before the small, slim figure of the one who had come forward. The one he knew, had spoken to, had lain with in a forest, on the grass.

Will you come back into the wood?

Will you sorrow if I do not? he had asked.

Her hair was changing hues, as he watched, golden to dark violet, to silver, like the queen's. He knew these changes, knew this about her. From behind the barrier of that arm, that banning, she looked at him, and then she turned her head away and gazed at the figure on the other side of the queen, and Alun followed her glance, and began, now, to weep.

Final balancing. The queen of the faeries released his brother's hand. And with those fingers, a gesture smooth as water falling, she motioned for Dai to go forward, if he wished.

If he wished. He was still wrapped (like a raiment) in his mortal shape, not green and twisted away from it as the others had been. He was too new, still her favoured one, riding the white mare at her side, holding her hand amid their music, upon water, in the night woods, within the faerie mounds.

If he wished. How did one leave this? Go from that shining? Alun wanted (so much) to call to him, but tears were pouring down his face and his throat was blocked with grief, so he could only watch as his brother (his brother's soul) turned to look at the queen in her litter beside him. He was too far away for Alun to see what expression was on his face: sorrow, anger, fear, yearning, puzzlement? Release?

It is, as has long been said, the nature of the Cyngael that in the midst of brightest, shining joy, they carry an awareness of sorrows to come, an ending that waits, the curving of the arc. It is their way, the source of music in their voices, and—perhaps—what allows them to leave the shining behind, in due time, when others cannot do so. Gifts are treasured, known not to be forever.

Dai twitched the reins of his mare and moved forward, alone, across the water. Alun heard Brynn again, praying behind him. He looked, for one brief moment (that could be made to last a lifetime if held clearly enough in memory) upon the faerie that had come to him, his own gift, a shining left behind, and saw her raise a hand to him from behind the arm of the queen. Final balancing.

Dai reached the water's edge, dismounted. Walked across the grass. Not hovering as the others had, not yet, still clothed in the form his brother had known. Alun made himself stand still. He held the Volgan's sword.

Dai stopped in front of him. He did not smile, or speak (no words spoken, across that divide). Nor did he kneel, Owyn of Cadyr's older, slain son. Not before a younger brother. One could even smile at that perhaps, later. Dai spread his feet a little, as if to steady himself. Alun was remembering the morning they had ridden north from home, coming here. Other memories followed, in waves. How could they not, here? He looked into his brother's eyes and saw that they had changed (were still changing). It seemed to him there were stars to be seen there, a strangeness so great.

"Let there be light for you," he murmured, scarcely able to speak.

"Let it be done with love," said Brynn behind him, soft as a benison, words that seemed to be from some ancient liturgy Alun didn't know.

"How not?" he said. To Brynn, to Dai, to the bright queen and all her faeries (and the one he was losing now), to the dark night and the stars. He drew back the sword a last time and drove it into his brother's chest, to accept

the queen's gift of his soul, the balancing, and set it free
to find its harbour, after all.

When he looked up again, Dai was gone (was gone)
and the faeries had disappeared, all that shining. It was
dark upon the water and in the glade. He drew a ragged
breath, felt himself shivering. There was a sound. The
dog, come up to nuzzle him at the hip. Alun put a trembling hand down, touched its fur between the ears.
Another sound. He turned towards it wordlessly, and he
let Brynn ap Hywll gather him in his arms as a father
would, with his own father so far away.

They stood so for a long time before they moved.
Brynn claimed the scabbard, wrapped the sword in its
cloth again, as before, and they walked over and he laid
it in the hollow where it had been. Then he looked up. It
was dark. The torches had burned out.

"Will you help me, lad?" he asked. "This accursed
boulder has grown. It is heavier than it used to be, I
swear."

"I've heard they do that," said Alun quietly. He knew
what the other man was doing. A different kind of gift.
Together, shoulders to the great rock, they rolled it back
and covered the Volgan's sword again. Then they left the
wood, Cafall beside them, and came out under stars,
above Brynnfell. Lanterns were burning down there, to
guide them back.

There was another torch, as well, nearer to them.

SHE HAD WAITED by the gate the last time, when her
father went up. This time Rhiannon slipped out of the
yard amidst the chaos of returning. Her mother was
arranging for a meal to be served to all those who had
come to their aid, invited, and unexpectedly from the
farms west, where someone—a girl, it seemed—had seen
the Erlings passing and run a warning home.

You honoured such people. Rhiannon knew she was needed, ought to be with her mother, but she also knew that her father and Alun ab Owyn were in the wood again. Brynn had told his wife where he was going, though not why. Rhiannon was unable to attend to whatever duties were hers until they came out from the trees.

Standing on the slope above their farmyard, she listened to the bustling sounds below and thought about what it was a woman could do, and could not. Waiting, she thought, was so much a part of their lives. Her mother, giving swift, incisive orders down below, might call that nonsense, but Rhiannon didn't think it was. There was no anger in her any more, or any real feeling of defiance, though she knew she shouldn't be up here.

Needful as night she had said in the hall at the end of spring, entirely aware of the effect it would have. She'd been younger then, Rhiannon thought. Here she was, after nightfall, and she couldn't have said what it was she needed. An ending, she'd decided, to whatever had begun that other night.

She heard a noise. The two men came out from the trees and stood there, the grey dog beside Alun. She saw them both look down upon the farmhouse and the lights. Then her father turned to her.

"Jad be thanked," Rhiannon said.

"Truly," he replied.

He came over and brushed her forehead with his lips, as was his habit. He hesitated, looked over his shoulder. Alun ab Owyn had stayed where he was, just clear of the last trees. "I need to drink and drink," Brynn said. "Both at once. I'll see you below." He went over and took both horses' reins and led them down.

She was unexpectedly calm. The springtime seemed so long ago. The wind had died down, the smoke from her torch rose up nearly straight.

"Did you—?"

"I have so much—"

They both stopped. Rhiannon laughed a little. He did not. She waited. He cleared his throat. "I have so much need of your forgiveness," he said.

"After what you did?" she said. "Coming here again?"

He shook his head. "What I said to you—"

This, she could address. "You said some things in grief and loss, on the night your brother died."

He shook his head. "It was . . . more than that."

She had stood by the gate, seen her father go up. The two of them had just come out of the wood. She knew something of this. She said, "Then it was more. And you are the more to be forgiven."

"You are gracious too. I have no right . . ."

"None of us has a right to grace," Rhiannon said. "It comes sometimes. That night . . . I asked you to come to me. To sing."

"I know. I remember. Of course."

"Will you sing for me tonight?"

He hesitated. "I . . . I am not certain that I . . ."

"For all of us," she amended carefully. "In the hall. We are honouring those who came to help us."

He rubbed at his chin. He was very tired, she saw. "That would be better," he said quietly.

That would be better. Some paths, some doorways, some people were not to be yours, though the slightest difference in the rippling of time might have made them so. A tossed pebble landing a little sooner, a little later. She looked at him, standing this near, the two of them alone in darkness, and she knew she would never entirely move beyond what had happened to her that night at the end of spring, but it was all right. It would have to be all right. You could live with this, with much worse.

"Will you come down, my lord?" she said.

"I will follow you, my lady, if I may. I am not . . . entirely ready. I will do better after some moments alone."

"I can understand that," Rhiannon said. She could. He'd been in the half-world, would have a long way back to travel. She turned away from him and started down.

Just outside the gate to the yard, a shadow moved away from the fence.

"My lady," said the shadow. "Your mother said you would be up that slope and unlikely to welcome someone following. I thought I would risk coming this far." Her torchlight fell upon Athelbert as he bowed.

He had come through the spirit wood to bring them a warning. They were not even allies of his people. He was the king's heir of the Anglcyn. He had come out to wait for her.

Rhiannon had a vision then of her life to come, the burdens and the opportunities of it, and it was not unacceptable to her. There would be joys and sorrows, as there always were, the taste of the latter present in the wine of such happiness as mortals were allowed. She could do much for her people, she thought, and life was not without its duties.

"My mother," she said, looking up at him by the light of his lifted torch, "is generally right, but not always so."

"It is," said Athelbert, smiling, "a terrible thing when a parent is always right. You'd have to meet my father to see what I mean."

They walked into the yard together. Rhiannon closed and latched the gate behind her, the way they had all been taught to do, against what might be out there in the night.

HE WASN'T ALONE. He had said that he needed to be, but it was a dissembling.

Sitting on the grass above Brynnfell, not far from where he'd first walked up to the faerie (he could see the

sapling to his left), Alun set about shaping and sending a
thought, again and again in his mind.

It is over. It begins. It is over. It begins.

He had no idea what the boundary markers of this
might be, if she could sense anything from him, the way
he'd been so painfully open to the images she'd sent. But
he stayed there, his dog beside him, and he shaped those
words, wondering.

Then wonder ceased and a greater wonder began, for
he felt her presence again, and caught (soundlessly, within)
a note of laughter. *It is over. If you are very fortunate, and
I am feeling generous, it begins.*

Alun laughed aloud in the darkness. He would never
be entirely alone again, he realized. It might not have
been a blessing, but it was, because of what she was, and
he knew it from the beginning, that same night, looking
down upon the farm.

He stood up, and so did the dog. There were lights
below, food and wine, companionship against the night,
people waiting for him, with their needs. He could make
music for them.

Come back to me, he heard.

Joy. The other taste in sorrow's cup.

CHAPTER XVII

Nine nights after leaving Brynnfell, as they rowed into the wind back east, skirting close to Ferrieres to be as far from Aeldred's ships as they could, Bern realized that his father *had* spoken a last word to him.

It was a bright night, both moons in the sky, a little more light than was entirely safe for them. He remained thinking for some time longer, hands to his oar in the night. He rocked his body back and forth, pulling through the sea, tasting salt spray and memories. Then he lifted his voice and called out to Brand.

They were treating him differently now. Brand came directly over. He listened as Thorkell Einarson's son shared a thought which seemed to Leofson to come, under the two moons, as guidance from a spirit (burned with all proper rites on a strand in Llywerth) benevolently mindful of their fate.

At dawn they lashed the ships together on choppy seas and took counsel. They were Jormsvik mercenaries, feared through the north, and they'd had humiliations beyond endurance on this journey. Here was a chance to come home with honour, not trammelled in shame. There were reasons to roll these dice. It was past the end of raiding season; they'd be entirely unexpected. They could still land nearly a hundred men, and Carloman of Ferrieres had his hands full (Garr Hoddson pointed out) farther east with the Karchites, who were being pushed towards him by the horsemen of Waleska.

And most of them had heard—and each now believed he understood—the last cry of Thorkell Einarson, who'd lost a single combat deliberately, to save their lives. Brand One-eye had stopped even trying to proclaim it otherwise.

There was no dissent.

They put the ships ashore in a shallow cove west of the Brienne River mouth. They knew roughly where Champieres was, though not with certainty. Since the Volgan's raid, no one had been back to that hidden valley where kings of Ferrieres were laid to rest, chanted over by holy men. In the early years, they'd known it would be guarded after what had happened. And later, it was as though Champieres had become sacred to the Erlings too, in Siggur's memory.

Well, there were limits to that, weren't there? A new generation had its needs.

They did, in the event, know enough to find it: beyond the river, an east-west valley, entered from the east. It wasn't hugely difficult for trained, experienced men.

What followed, three nights later, was what tended to follow when the Erlings came. They sacked the royal sanctuary of the Sleepless Ones, set it afire, killed three dozen clerics and guards (not enough fighting men any more, Garr had been right about the Karchites). They lost only eight of their own. Carried—loading the horses, burdened like beasts themselves—sacks of silver and gold artifacts, coins, candlesticks, censers and sun disks, royal gems, jewel-hilted blades (none silver, not this time), ivory caskets, coffers of sandalwood and ebony, spices and manuscripts (men paid for those), and a score of slaves, whipped towards the ships, to serve them in Jormsvik or be sold in a market town.

A raid as gloriously triumphant as anyone could remember.

An echo, even, of what the Volgan had done. Enough looted to leave each one of them wealthy, even after the share given over to the treasury when they came home.

A hearth fire story, too. You could hear the skalds already! The dying hero's last word, Volgan's friend, understood only by his son one night at sea, sending them to Champieres, where the father had been twenty-five years and more ago. In the name of Ingavin, it made a saga by itself!

There were storm winds in their faces for two days and nights as they continued home. Lightning cracked the sky. Waves high as masts roared over the decks, drenching them, sweeping some of the horses screaming overboard. They were Erlings, though, lords of the sea roads, however wild they might become. This was their element. Ingavin and Thünir sent storms as a trial for men, a test of worthiness. They wiped streaming water from eyes and beards and fought through rain and gale, defying them, as no other men alive dared do.

They came into Jormsvik harbour on a bright, cold afternoon, singing at their oars. They'd lost one ship, Hoddson's, and thirty-two men. To be lamented and honoured, each one of them, but the sea and the gods claim their due, and where was glory, after all, when the task was easily done?

It was a very good winter in Jormsvik.

IT WAS JUDGED the same way in Esferth and Raedhill and elsewhere in the Anglcyn lands. King Aeldred and his wife and court travelled north to Rheden to celebrate the marriage of their daughter Judit to Prince Calum there. The red-haired princess was fiercely beautiful, even more fiercely strong-willed, and clearly terrified her younger husband. That, her siblings agreed privately, had been predictable. Why should the prince be different from anyone else?

Not remotely overlooked in the ceremonies and entertainments of that fortnight was the moment in the Midwinter Rites when Withgar of Rheden knelt before King Aeldred, kissed his ring, and accepted a disk of Jad from him, while clerics chanted praise of the living sun.

You paid a price to join your line to a greater one, and Rheden was not unaware that Esferth was increasingly secure from the Erlings. It wasn't difficult to guess in which direction Aeldred's eyes might turn. Better to marry, turn risk to advantage. They were all one people in the end, weren't they? Not like the dark, little, cattle-thieving Cyngael on the other side of the Wall.

As it happened, some time before leaving Esferth for the north, the Anglcyn king had put his mind (and his clerics) to work on the formal terms of another marriage, west, with those same Cyngael. Withgar of Rheden hadn't been told about these plans, as yet, but there'd been no reason to inform him. Many a marriage negotiation had broken down.

This one, however, seemed unlikely to do so. His daughter Kendra, normally the gentle, compliant one of his four children (and best loved, as it happened), had spoken with her father and the Cyngael cleric in privacy shortly after certain events that had taken place at summer's end by a farm called Brynnfell in Arberth. Events they knew altogether too much about because of her and the young prince of Cadyr, Owyn's surviving son and heir, the man she intended to wed. She told her father as much.

Aeldred, notoriously said to anticipate almost all possible events and plan for them, was not remotely ready for this. Nor could he furnish any immediate reply to his daughter's firm indication that she would follow her mother straight to the sanctuary at Retherly if the union—so clearly a suitable one—were not approved.

"It is marginally acceptable, I grant you. But do you even know he wants this? Or that Prince Owyn will approve?" Aeldred asked.

"He wants this," Kendra replied placidly. "And you've been thinking about a union west for a long time."

This, of course, happened to be true. His children knew too much.

The king looked to Ceinion for help. The cleric's manner had greatly changed over the course of a few days, with word of events at Brynnfell. He bore a genial, amused manner through the days and evenings. It was difficult to provoke an enjoyable argument on doctrine with him.

He smiled at Aeldred. "My delight, my lord, is extreme. You know I hoped for such a union. Owyn will be honoured, after I finish speaking with him, which I will do."

So much for help from that quarter.

"It doesn't matter," Kendra said, with alarming complacency. "Alun will deal with it."

Both men blinked, looking closely at her. This, Aeldred thought, was his shy, dutiful daughter.

She closed her eyes. They thought it was self-consciousness, under the doubled scrutiny.

She looked at them again. "I was right," she said. "He'll be coming here, with my brother. They'll be taking the coastal road. They are on the way to Cadyr now, to speak with his father." She smiled gently at the two of them. "We've agreed not to do this too much, before the wedding, so don't worry. He says to tell Ceinion he's making music again."

There wasn't a great deal one could do about this, though prayer was clearly indicated. Kendra was diligent about attendance at chapel, morning and evening. The marriage *did* make sense. There had been some brief discussion, the king remembered, about Athelbert and Brynn ap Hywll's daughter. Well, that wouldn't need to be continued, now. You didn't marry *two* children to achieve the same result.

Ceinion of Llywerth offered his own two wedding gifts to the king. The first was his long-sought promise to spend part of each year with Aeldred at his court. The second was quite different. It emerged after a conversation between the high cleric of the Cyngael and the extremely devout queen of the Anglcyn. In the wake of this frank and illuminating exchange, and after two all-night vigils in her chapel, Queen Elswith arrived at her husband's bedchamber one night and was admitted.

The queen placidly informed her royal spouse that—upon reflection and religious counsel—his soul was not *so* very gravely in danger as to require her to withdraw to a sanctuary immediately after Judit was married, after all. She was content to wait until Kendra, in turn, was wed to this prince in the west. Perhaps in late spring? Aeldred and Osbert, in her view, would be incapable of properly dealing with this second celebration without guidance. Further, it now struck the queen as reasonable to spend *some* of her time at court even after she retired to the sanctuary. These matters could be addressed in a . . . balanced fashion, as the teachings of faith suggested for all things. On the subject of balance, the king's earthly state was, certainly, part of her charge.

His diet, for example, with the winter feasting season approaching (Judit's wedding in Rheden ahead of them), was excessive. He was gaining weight, at risk of gout, and worse. He would need her with him, at intervals, to observe and assess his needs.

The king, who had not suffered another of his fevers since a certain conversation with Ceinion on the ride back from chasing the Erlings to the coast (and would not endure one again, ever), happily proposed she begin such assessing right where they were. The queen declared the suggestion indecent at their age but allowed herself to be overmastered, in this.

YOU'RE TAKING *a long time.*

You know why. I had to go to my father first, couldn't rush away. I'm almost with you. Three more days. There are emissaries with us. We'll present the marriage proposal to your father. I'll ask Ceinion to help. I think he will.

Doesn't matter. My father's going to consent.

How do you know? This is a very—

I spoke with him.

And he just said yes?

Right now I think he'll say yes to anything I ask of him.

A small silence in the shared channel of two minds.

So will I, you know.

Oh, good.

She'd done her first harvest-time sacrifice, two lambs and a kid. Anrid had added the goat to the ceremony, naming it as Fulla's offering, mostly to be seen to be doing things the old *volur* had not done. Changes, setting her own imprint upon rituals, as a seal marked a letter. She'd worn the accursed snake about her neck. It was growing heavier. It had crossed her mind that if the ship from the south came back in spring, it would be prudent to arrange for another serpent. Or perhaps they'd have one on board, perhaps arrangements had already been made.

Frigga, when consulted, thought this might be so.

The harvest turned out to be a good one, and the winter was mild on Rabady. The new governor and *volur* were both toasted in the taverns, and the women's compound saw its share of after-harvest gifts. Anrid claimed only a dark blue cloak for herself, let the others divide the rest—they needed to be kept happy. And a little bit afraid.

The serpent helped with that. The wound on her leg had become a small pair of scars. She let the others see them now and again, as if by chance. Serpents were a power of earth, and Anrid had been given some of that power.

It was mild enough through winter that some of the younger men took their boats across to Vinmark for the adventure of it. In a hard winter the straits might freeze, though not safely so, and Rabady could be entirely cut off. This year they did learn things, although in winter there wasn't much to know. A blood feud in Halek, six men dead after a woman had been stolen. It appeared the woman had consented, so she was killed as well when reclaimed by her family. People were too close to each other when the snow came. In spring the roads and sea opened again and pent-up violence could be sent away. It had always been like that. They were shaped by the cold season; preparing for winter, needing it to end, preparing again.

One day, with spring not yet arrived, a small boat was rowed across to the isle. Three mariners aboard, heavily armed, spears and round shields. They came ashore with a chest and a key, spoke courteously enough to the men sent down to meet them. They were looking for a woman. From the town they were sent through the walls and across the ditch to trudge snow-clad fields to the women's compound. A half-dozen boys, glad of the diversion, escorted them.

The chest was for Frigga. It revealed, when opened in Anrid's chamber (only the two of them there for the turning of the key), silver enough to buy any property on the isle, with a good deal left over. There was a note.

Anrid was the one who could read.

Frigga's son Bern sent his respects to his mother and hoped she remained in health. He was alive himself, and well. He was sorry to have to tell her that her husband (her first husband) had died, in Cyngael lands, at summer's end. His passing was honourable, he had saved other men with his death. He had been given rites and burning there, done properly. The silver was to make a new beginning for her. In a hard way to explain, the note said, it was really from Thorkell. Bern would send word again when he could, but would probably not risk coming back to Rabady.

Anrid had expected the other woman to weep. She did not—or not when Anrid was near. The chest and silver were hidden (there were places to hide things here). Frigga had already made her new beginning. Her son could not have known that. She wasn't at all certain she wished to leave the compound and the women, go back to a house in or near the town, and she wouldn't go to her daughters in Vinmark, even with wealth of her own. That wasn't a life, growing old in a strange place.

It was a great deal of money, you couldn't just leave it in the ground. She'd think on it, she told Anrid. Anrid had memorized the note (a quick mind) before they put it back in the chest.

Probably not, was what he had said.

She took thought, and invited the governor to visit her.

Another new thing, Sturla's coming here, but the two of them were at ease with each other now. She'd gone into town to speak with him as well, formally garbed, surrounded by (always) several of the women.

Iord, the old *volur,* had believed in the mystery that came with being unseen, removed. Anrid (and Frigga, when they talked) thought power also came from people knowing you were there, bearing you in mind. She always had the serpent when she went to the town, or met with Ulfarson at the compound, as now. He'd deny it, of course, but he was afraid of her, which was useful.

They discussed adding buildings to the compound when the last snow melted and the men could work again. This had been mentioned before. Anrid wanted room for more women, and a brewhouse. She had thoughts of a place for childbirth. People gave generously at such times (if the child was a boy, and lived). It would be good to become known as the place to come when a birth drew near. The governor would want a share, but that, too, she'd anticipated.

He wasn't difficult to deal with, Sturla. As he was leaving, after ale and easy talk (about the feud, over on the mainland), she mentioned, casually, something she'd learned from the three men with the chest, about events a year ago, when Halldr Thinshank's horse had gone missing.

It made a great deal of sense, what she told the governor: everyone had known there was no love lost between the old *volur* and Thinshank. Ulfarson had nodded owlishly (he had a tendency to look that way after ale) and asked, shrewdly, why the boy hadn't come home by now, if this was so.

The boy, she told him, had gone to Jormsvik. Choosing the world of fighting men to put behind him the dark woman-magic that had brought him shame. How did she know? The chest was from him. He'd written to his mother here. He was greatly honoured, it seemed, on the mainland now. His prowess reflected well on Rabady. His father, Thorkell Einarson, the exile, was dead (it was good to let a man have tidings he could share in a tavern), and even more of a hero. The boy was wealthy from raiding, had sent his mother silver, to buy any home on the isle she wished.

Ulfarson leaned forward. Not a stupid man, though narrow in the paths of his thought. Which house? he asked, as she had expected he would.

Anrid, smiling, said they could probably guess which house Thorkell Einarson's widow would want, though buying it might be difficult, given that it was owned by Halldr's widow who hated her.

It might be possible, she said, as if struck by a thought, for someone else to buy the house and land first, turn a profit for himself selling to Frigga when she came looking. Sturla Ulfarson stroked his pale moustache. She could *see* him thinking this through. It was an entirely proper thing, she added gravely, if the two leaders of the isle helped each other in these various ways.

Construction of her three new buildings, Sturla Ulfarson said, when he rose to leave, would commence as soon as the snows were gone and the ground soft enough. She invoked Fulla's blessing upon him when he left.

When the weather began to change, the days to grow longer, first green-gold leaves returning, Anrid set the younger women to watch at night, farther from the compound than was customary, and in a different direction. There was no spirit-guidance, no half-world sight involved. She was simply . . . skilled at thinking. She'd had to become that way. It could be seen as magic or power, she knew, mistaken for a gift of prescience.

She had another long conversation with Frigga, doing most of the talking, and this time the other woman had wept, and then agreed.

Anrid, who was very young, after all, began having restless nights around that time. A different kind of disturbance than before, when she hadn't been able to sleep. This time it was her dreams, and what she did in them.

HE WAS DOING what his father had done long ago. Bern kept telling himself that through the winter, waiting for spring. And if this was so, it was important not to be soft about it. The north was no place for that. Being soft could destroy you, even if you left raiding for a different life, as Thorkell had done.

He would leave with honour. Everyone in Jormsvik knew by now all that had happened on what had come to be called Ragnarson's Raid. They knew what Red Thorkell had done to keep them from going to Arberth, and what Bern had done, and how the two of them (the skalds were singing it) had shaped destiny together, after, leading five ships to Champieres.

Two of the most experienced captains had spoken with Bern on separate occasions, urging him to stay. No coercion—Jormsvik was a company of free and willing men. They'd pointed out that he'd entered among them by killing a powerful man, which boded well for his future, as did his lineage and the way he had begun on his first raid. They hadn't known his lineage when he'd entered; they did now.

Bern had expressed gratitude, awareness of honour. Kept private the thought that he really didn't agree with this vision of his prospects. He'd been fortunate, had received aid beyond measure from Thorkell, and even though the idea of the attack in Ferrieres had been his by way of his father, he'd discovered no battle frenzy in himself, no joy in the flames, or when he'd spitted a Jaddite cleric on his blade.

You didn't have to *tell* people that, but you did need to be honest with yourself, he thought. His father had left the sea road, eventually. Bern was doing it earlier, that was all, and would ask Ingavin and Thünir not to pull him back, as Thorkell had been pulled back.

He set about balancing accounts through the winter.

When you changed your life you were supposed to leave the old one behind cleanly. Ingavin observed such things, cunning and wise, watching with his one eye.

Bern had wealth now. A fortune beyond his deserts: the Champieres raid was being talked about, word spreading, even on the snowbound paths of winter. It would be in Hlegest by now, Brand had told him in a tavern one night, icicles hanging like spears on the eaves outside. Kjarten Vidurson (rot his scarred face) would know that Jormsvik was still no fortress to set himself against, though he was likely going to try, sooner or later, that one.

Bern had begun making his reckoning that same night. Had left the tavern for the rooms (the three rooms) in which he'd kept Thira since returning. He'd offered her a sum of money that would set her up back home with property and the choosing (or rejecting) of any man in her village. Women could own land, of course, they just needed a husband to deal with it. And keep it.

She'd surprised him, but women were—Bern thought— harder than men to anticipate. He was *good*, he'd discovered, at understanding men, but he'd not have expected, for example, that Thira would burst into tears, and swear at him, and throw a boot, and *then* say, snapping the words like a ship's captain to an oarsman out of rhythm, that she'd left home of her own choice for her own reasons and no man-boy like Bern Thorkellson was going to make her go back.

She'd accepted the silver and the three rooms, though.

Not long after, she bought herself a tavern. Hrati's, in fact. (Hrati was old, tired of the life, said he was ready for the table by the fire and an upstairs room. She gave him that. He didn't, as it happened, last long. Started drinking too much, became quarrelsome. They buried him the next winter. Thira changed the name of the tavern. Bern was long gone by then.)

He'd had to wait until spring, when challengers began coming again. In the meantime, he paid three of the newer, younger ones to carry a chest to Rabady as soon as the weather made that possible. These were Jormsvikings, they weren't going to cheat him, and mercenaries could take a paying task from a companion as easily as from anyone else.

More balancing in that chest. His mother would surely be locked into a grim life, a second husband dead (and she only a second wife in Thinshank's house), no rights to speak of, no sure home. Bern had left her to that, taking Gyllir into the sea.

Silver didn't make redress for everything, but if you didn't let yourself get soft you could say it went a long-enough way in the world.

He couldn't safely return to Rabady: he'd almost certainly be known (even changed in his appearance), taken as a horse thief, and more. The horse had been named and marked for a funeral burning, after all.

The horse, in fact, he sold to Brand Leofson, a good price, too. Gyllir was magnificent, a warrior's ride. Had been wasted on the isle with Halldr Thinshank, bought by him merely because he *could* buy such a creature. The pride and show of it. Leofson wanted the stallion, and wasn't about to bargain with Bern, not after all that had happened. Bern hadn't hesitated or let himself regret it. You couldn't allow yourself to be soft about your animals, either.

You could get irritated, mind you, and swear at them, and at yourself for not choosing more carefully. He'd picked a placid bay from the stables for his new mount, discovering too late its awkward trot and a disinclination to sustain a gallop. A landowner's horse, good for walking sedately to town and tavern and back. He wasn't going to *need* more, he kept telling himself, but he was accustomed to Gyllir. Was that softness? Remembering a horse you'd had? Maybe you didn't talk or boast about what you'd done, where you'd been, but surely you could remember it? What else was your life, except what you recalled?

And perhaps what you wanted next.

He waited, as he had to, for spring to unlock the roads and the challengers to begin arriving at the gates. He was letting Brand advise him. Leofson had been taking a protective attitude towards Bern since they'd returned, as if killing Thorkell (being allowed by Thorkell to kill him) gave him responsibilities to the son. Bern didn't feel he needed it, but he didn't really mind, and he knew it wouldn't last long. It was useful, too: Brand would take care of Bern's money, send it where he needed it, as he needed it.

Once he'd figured out where that was.

They watched the first few men arrive before the walls and issue their challenges and Brand shook his head. They were farmhands, stableboys, with outsized dreams and no possible claim to being Jormsvik men. It would be unjust to his fellows to claim their challenges and ride away and let them in. They drew the runepieces inside the walls and the challenges were randomly taken. Two of the boys were killed (one by accident, it appeared to those watching, and Elkin confirmed that when he came back in), two were disarmed and allowed to go, with the usual promise that if they returned and tried again they'd be cut apart.

The fifth challenger was big-boned, older than the others. He had a serviceable sword and a battered helmet with the nose-guard intact. Brand and Bern looked at each other. Bern signalled to those on duty at the gate that he was taking this one by choice. It had come. You waited for things, and then they were upon you. He and Leofson embraced. He did the same with a number of the others, who knew what was happening. Shipmates, drinking companions. It had only been a year, but warriors could die any time, and forming bonds here didn't take long, he'd discovered. Bonds could be cut, though, Bern thought. Sometimes they *needed* to be.

Thira, hard little one, only waved to him from behind the counter of her new tavern when he went to bid her farewell before going out. Her life was the opposite of his, he thought. You took care *not* to form any links. Men sailed from you and died, different men climbed your stairs every night. She'd saved his life, though. He lingered in the doorway watching her a moment. He was remembering the fourth stair, the one missing on the way up to her room. Important, he reminded himself, not to be soft.

He took his new horse from the stable, and the gear he'd carry north, and his sword and helm (roads were dangerous, always, for a lone man). They opened the gates for him and he went out to the challenger. He saw relief and wonder in the man's blue eyes when Bern lifted an open hand in the gesture of yielding. He motioned to the gates behind him. "Ingavin be mindful of you," he said to the stranger. "Honour yourself and those you are joining."

Then he rode away along the path he'd taken coming here. He heard a clashing sound behind him: spears and swords being banged on shields. His companions on the walls. He looked back and lifted a hand. His father wouldn't have, he thought.

No one troubled him going north. He didn't avoid the villages or inns this time. He passed the place where he'd ambushed a single traveller himself because he'd needed a sword for the challenge. Hadn't killed the man, or didn't think he had.

It wasn't as if he'd lingered to be sure.

Eventually, after what felt like a long, slow journey, he caught his first glimpse of Rabady in the distance on his left as the road dropped near to the coast. (Inland, the mountains rose, and then the endless pines beyond, and no roads ran.)

He came to the fishing village they all knew on Rabady, the one they usually went to and from. He might even be known here, but he didn't think so. He'd grown his beard and hair, was bigger now across shoulders and chest. He waited for twilight to fall and the night to deepen and even begin its wheeling towards dawn before he offered the prayer all seamen spoke before going upon the water.

He prepared to push the small boat out into the strait. The fisherman, roused from sleep in his hut, came to help; Bern's payment for borrowing it had been generous, far more than a day's lost catch. He left the horse with the man to mind. He wouldn't be cheated here. He'd said he was from Jormsvik, and he looked it.

It was black on the water as he rowed towards the isle. He looked at the stars and the sea and the trees ahead of him. Spring. Full circle of a year, and here he was again. He dipped a hand in the water. Bitterly, killingly cold. He remembered. He'd thought he was going to die here. He missed Gyllir then, thinking back. Shook his head. You couldn't be this way in the north. It could kill you.

He was stronger now, steady and easy at the oars. It wasn't a difficult pull, in any case. He'd done it as a boy, summers he remembered.

He beached the small craft on the same strand from which he'd left. He didn't think that was an indulgence, or weak. It felt proper. An acknowledging. He gave thanks to Ingavin, touching the hammer about his neck. He'd bought it in autumn, nothing elaborate, much like the one that had burned with his father in Llywerth.

He moved inland, cautiously. He really didn't want to meet anyone. People here had known him all his life; there was a better-than-decent chance he'd be recognized. That was why he'd come at night, most of the way towards dawn, why he hadn't been sure he would come at all. He was here for three reasons, last of the balancings before he changed his life. All three could be done in a night, if the gods were good to him.

He wanted to bid farewell to his mother. She was in the women's compound now, those who'd brought the chest had told him. A surprise, a good decision for her, though with his silver she could change that.

After, in the same place, he intended to find the old *volur*. He wouldn't need long with her but he'd probably have to leave quickly, after. Though he also wanted to speak, if possible, perhaps only for a moment, depending how events unfolded, to a girl with a snakebite scar on her leg. He might not actually be able to do so. It was unlikely he could linger after killing the *volur*, and he wasn't sure he could find a girl he wouldn't recognize. The women kept watch at night, even in the cold. He remembered that.

Remembered these fields, too. He'd ridden Gyllir the last time, had a long walk now. He kept close to the woods, screened by them, though it was unlikely any lovers would be out this early in spring. The ground was cold. You'd need to be wild with desire to come out here with a girl, and not find a barn or shed with straw.

He had two farewells to make, he told himself, and someone to kill, then he could leave with his past squared away, as much as that was ever really possible. He was going to Erlond, he'd decided, where his people had settled in the Anglcyn lands. It was far enough away, there was land to be claimed, room to settle and thrive. He'd had a winter to think about possibilities. This one made the most sense.

He heard a twig snap. Not his own footfall.

He froze, drew his sword. He had no desire to kill yet, but—

"The peace of Fulla be upon you, Bern Thorkellson."

When all you have to remember, through the circle of an eventful year, is a voice in the dark, and the voice is that of someone saving your life, you remember it.

He stayed where he was. She came forward from the trees. Carried no torch. He swallowed.

"How is the snakebite?" he said.

"Only a scar now. My thanks for asking."

"She is . . . still sending you out on cold nights?"

"Iord? No. Iord is dead."

His heart thumped. He still couldn't see her, but the voice was embedded in him. He hadn't realized until this moment how much so.

"How? What . . . ?"

"I had her killed. For both of us."

Matter-of-fact, no hint of emotion in her voice. One less task for him tonight, it seemed. He struggled for words. "How did you . . . ?"

"Do that? One of the young women in the compound told the new governor how the *volur* had used magic to force an innocent young man to steal a horse from someone she'd always hated."

He was still holding his sword. It seemed silly to be doing that. He sheathed it. Was thinking hard. He was *good* at thinking. "And the young man?"

"Went to Jormsvik after the spell left him. Wanting to win glory, efface his shame. And did so."

He was fighting an entirely unexpected urge to smile. "And the young woman?"

She hesitated for the first time. "She became the *volur* of Rabady Isle."

The desire to smile seemed to have gone, as suddenly as it had come. He couldn't quite have put into words why this was so. He cleared his throat. Said, "A great and glorious destiny for her, then."

After another pause, a stillness in the dark, he heard her say, just a shape, still, an outline in the night, "It isn't, in truth, the destiny she would choose, had she . . . another path."

Bern found it necessary to draw a breath before he could speak again. His heart was pounding, they way it had at Champieres. "Indeed. Would she . . . have any willingness to leave the isle, make a different life?"

The other voice grew softer, not as assured. *Like mine,* he thought.

"She might do that. If someone wished her to. It . . . it could also be here. That different life. Here on the isle."

He shook his head. Tried to make himself breathe normally. He knew a little more of the world than she did, it appeared. In this matter, at least. "I don't think so. Once she's been *volur* it would be too hard to live an . . . ordinary life here. There's too much power in what she's been. This is too small a place. Whoever became *volur* after wouldn't even want her here."

"The next *volur* might give permission, a release from power," she said. "It has happened."

He didn't know about that, had to assume she did. "Why would she do that?"

She waited a moment. Then said, "Think about it."

He did, and it came to him. He felt a prickling at his neck. That sometimes meant the half-world, spirits, were nearby. Sometimes it meant something else. "Oh," said Bern. "I see."

She realized, with a kind of thrill, that he really did. She wasn't used to men being so quick. She said, still carefully, "Your mother asked me to welcome you home, to say that she is waiting, at the compound, if you wish to see her now. And to tell you that the door on the barn needs fixing again."

He was silent, absorbing all of this. "I know how to do that," Bern said. "How do you know it is broken?"

"We've been to the farmhouse together," the girl said. "Your father's. It . . . can be bought again. If you want."

He looked at her. Only a shape. You were not to be soft. It was *dangerous* in these lands. But you were allowed, surely, to feel wonder, weren't you? A man went through the world carrying only his name. Some left that after them when they died, lingering, like a burning on a hill or by the sea. Most men did not, could not. There were other ways to live through the days the gods allowed you. In his mind, he spoke his father's name.

"I've never even seen you," he said to the girl.

"I know. There are lights in the compound," she said. "She's waiting. Will you come?"

They walked that way, the two of them. It wasn't very far. He saw the marker stone in the field, a greyness beyond. Dawn, he realized, would be breaking soon, over Vinmark and the water, upon the isle.

A GREYER, WINDIER DAWN would also come, a little later, farther west.

He still liked to keep a window open at night, despite what wisdom held to be the folly of doing so. Ceinion of Llywerth sometimes thought that if something was offered too readily as wisdom, it *needed* to be challenged.

That wasn't why he opened the window, however. There was no deep thinking here. He was simply too accustomed to the taste of the night air after so many years moving from place to place. On the other hand, he thought, awake and alone in a comfortable room in Esferth, the year gone by had made one change in him.

He was entirely happy to be lying on this goose-feather bed and not outside on the ground in a windy night. Others would deny it, some of them fiercely (with their own reasons for doing so), but he knew he'd aged between the last spring and this one. He might be awake, sleep eluding, but he was comfortable in this bed and guardedly (always guardedly) pleased with the unfolding of events in Jad's northlands.

He had wintered here, as promised, would be going home to his people, now that spring was upon them again. He would not travel alone. The Anglcyn king and queen would be sailing west to Cadyr (showing their new fleet to the world), bringing their younger daughter to the Cyngael.

He had wanted this—something like this—so much and for so long. Alun ab Owyn, to whom she would be wed in what could only be named joy, was the heir to his province, and a hero now in Arberth, and Ceinion could deal with his own Llywerth, easily. There was so much that might come of this.

The god had been good to them, beyond any deserving. That was the heart of all teachings, wasn't it? You aspired to live a good and pious life, but Jad's mercy could be extended, as wings over you, for reasons no man could understand.

In the same way, he thought, as the night outside began to turn (a ruffle of wind entering the room) towards morning and whatever it might bring—in the selfsame way no man could ever hope to understand why losses came, heart's grief, what was taken away.

Waiting for sunrise, lying alone as he had these long years, he remembered love and remembered her dying, and could see, in the eye of his mind, the grave overlooking the western sea behind his chapel and his home. You lived in the world, you tasted sorrow and joy, and it was the way of the Cyngael to be aware of both.

Another breeze, entering the room. Dawn wind. He would be going home soon. He would sit with her, and look out upon the sea. Morning was coming, the god's return. Almost time to rise and go to prayer. The bed was very soft. Almost time, but the darkness not quite lifted, light still to come, he could linger a little with memory. It was necessary, it was allowed.

END IT with the ending of a night.

I know not, I,
    What the men together say,
How lovers, lovers die
    And youth passes away.

Cannot understand
    Love that mortal bears
For native, native land
    —All lands are theirs.

Why at grave they grieve
    For one voice and face,
And not, and not receive
    Another in its place.

I, above the cone
    Of the circling night
Flying, never have known
    More or lesser light.

Sorrow it is they call
    This cup: whence my lip,
Woe's me, never in all
    My endless days must sip.

—C. S. LEWIS

ACKNOWLEDGMENTS

Laura, as always: calmly confident from the days when I was first charting the sea lanes of this journey, and remaining so when I cast off and shoals (and monsters) appeared that hadn't been on the charts.

Charts can take one only so far in a novel, but in a work of this sort, drawing upon very specific periods and motifs of the past, it is folly to embark without them, and I have had the benefit of some exceptional cartographers (if I may be indulged in a continuing metaphor). There are too many to be named here, but some must surely be noted.

On the Vikings, I owe much to the elegant and stylish synthesis of Gwyn Jones, and to the work of Peter Sawyer, R. I. Page, Jenny Jochens, and Thomas A. Dubois. I have drawn upon many different commentaries on and translations of the Sagas, but my admiration for the epic renderings of Lee M. Hollander is very great.

Histories of the North are caught up in agendas today (as is so much of the past), and clear thinking and personal notes became a necessary aid. I am grateful to Paul Bibire for answers, suggestions, and steering me to sources. Kristen Pederson provided a score of articles and essays, principally on the role of women in the Viking world, and offered glosses on many of them. Max Vinner of the Viking Ship Museum at Roskilde kindly answered my questions.

For the Anglo-Saxons, I found Richard Abels invaluable on Alfred the Great. Peter Hunter Blair, Stephen Pollington (on leechcraft and warcraft), Michael Swanton's version of the *Chronicles,* and the splendidly detailed work of Anne Hagen on Anglo-Saxon food and drink were variously and considerably of use. So were works written or edited by Richard Fletcher, Ronald Hutton, James Campbell, Simon Keynes, and Michael Lapidge, and the verse translations of Michael Alexander.

With respect to the Welsh, and the Celtic spirit more generally, I must mention Wendy Davies, John Davies, Alwyn and Brinley Rees, Charles Thomas, John T. Koch, Peter Beresford Ellis (on the role of women), the verse translations and notes of Joseph P. Clancy, and the classic, unruffled overview of Nora Chadwick. I am deeply grateful to Jeffrey Huntsman for permission to use his translation of the epigraph, and for generously sending me alternative variants and commentary. The poem that concludes the book is from *The Pilgrim's Regress,* copyright C.S. Lewis Pte. Ltd., 1933, and is used here with their kind permission.

On a more personal level, I owe gratitude to Darren Nash, Tim Binding, Laura Anne Gilman, Jennifer Heddle, and Barbara Berson—a panoply of editors—for enthusiam en route and when I was done. Catherine Marjoribanks brings more wit and sensitivity to the role of copy editor than an author has a right to expect. My brother Rex is still the first and perhaps the most acute of my readers. Linda McKnight, Anthea Morton-Saner, and Nicole Winstanley remain friends as much as agents, greatly valued in both regards.

For many years, when asked where my website was, I would paraphrase Cato the Elder, the Roman statesman. "I would rather people asked," I'd reply, "where Kay's website is, than *why* Kay has a website." Cato, famously, said that about the absence of statues honouring him in Rome. A while ago the markedly intelligent and insistent Deborah Meghnagi persuaded me that it was time for a statue online (as it were), and I gave her permission to devise and launch brightweavings.com. I am deeply grateful for all she's done (and continues to do) with that site, and I remain impressed and touched by the generous and witty community evolving there.